"YOU DID THAT?" The boy turned to Te

He spoke Prexci of such an ancient d

to make out the words. He slid into the

from there.

Once he had, he focused and refocused his sight, not believing what he saw.

Above the filthy creature's head spiraled a collection of structures that nearly gave Terian an erection. A fascinated awe fell over him as he stared at those rotating and glimmering shapes.

The boy spoke again. "You did that? You shot him?"

"Yes," Terian told him, clicking out. "I did."

For a moment, the boy looked only at the wasted human.

He turned to Four.

"Yes. I will go with you."

Without fully turning his head, Terian spoke to the other two. "What the *fuck* is this precious bundle of joy?"

The woman turned sheet white. "You said you knew. You said he entrusted you!"

The old man gave another of those sick, grating chuckles.

"I told you: He likely killed your precious Teacher with his own hands."

"You wouldn't be far off with that, old man." Terian raised the gun. "But you still haven't answered my question."

The woman lifted her hands to Terian in pleading supplication, her eyes darting nervously between him and the boy. "You must understand. It was for his own protection. For all of our protection! We feed him well—"

Terian gave a harsh laugh. "Yes. This is practically the Ritz. But I'm not here to spank you for your housekeeping skills, *Fraulein.*"

Even so, he realized in some surprise he was angry. Beyond angry. He was furious. His hand shook as he pointed the gun at the two "monks." That they would keep any seer in such a place, much less a seer like this, with structures like he had… it was inconceivable.

That Galaith could have been a part of such a travesty…

"Unchain him." Terian motioned the gun towards the boy. "Now."

The nun's face drained further of blood. "Sir?"

"You heard him. He's coming with me."

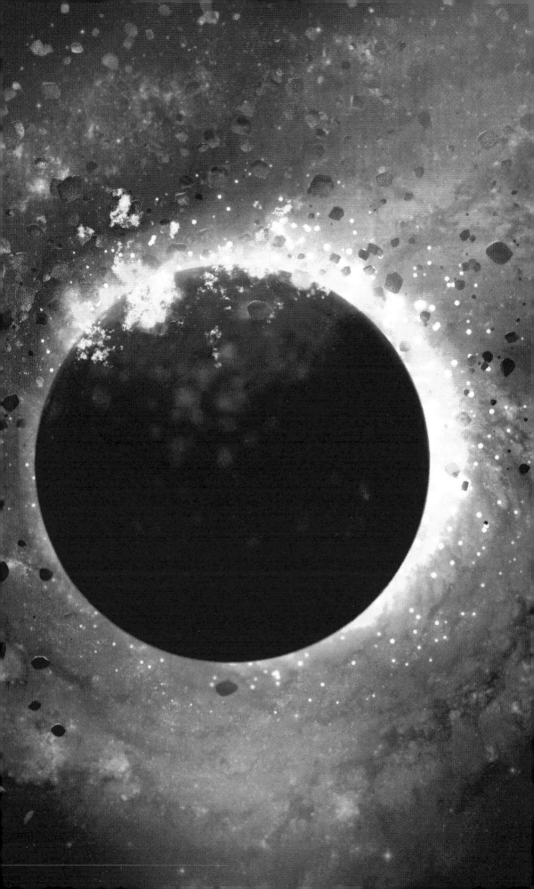

MATED SEERS

BRIDGE AND SWORD: BOOK TWO

JC ANDRIJESKI

WHITE SUN PRESS

Mated Seers (Bridge and Sword: Book Two)

Copyright 2022 by JC Andrijeski

Published by White Sun Press

First Edition

ISBN: 9798829376154

Cover Art & Design by Camila Marques

2022

Link with me at: https://www.jcandrijeski.com

Or at: https://www.patreon.com/jcandrijeski

Mailing List: https://www.jcandrijeski.com/sign-up

White Sun Press

Printed in the United States of America 2022

Dedicated to
The man dancing in the stars
(you know who you are)

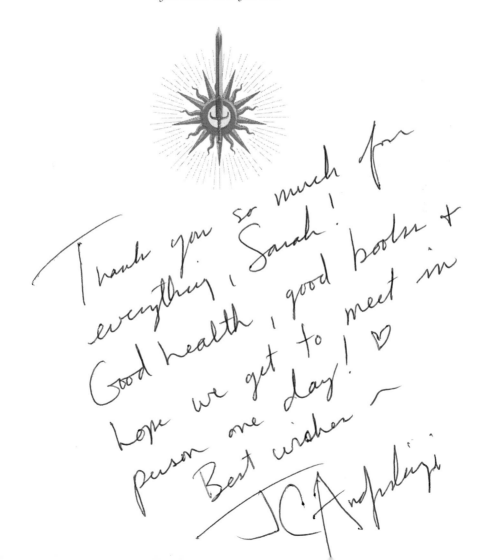

Thank you so much for everything, Sarah! Good health, good books & hope we get to meet in person one day! ♡ Best wishes ~

JC Andrijeski

"The time is still not ripe. But through the blood sacrifice, it should ripen. So long as it is possible to murder the brother instead of oneself, the time is not ripe. Frightful things must happen until men grow ripe. But anything else will not ripen humanity. Hence all that takes place in these days must also be, so that the renewal can come. Since the source of blood that follows the shrouding of the sun is also the source of new life."

~ Carl Jung, *The Red Book*

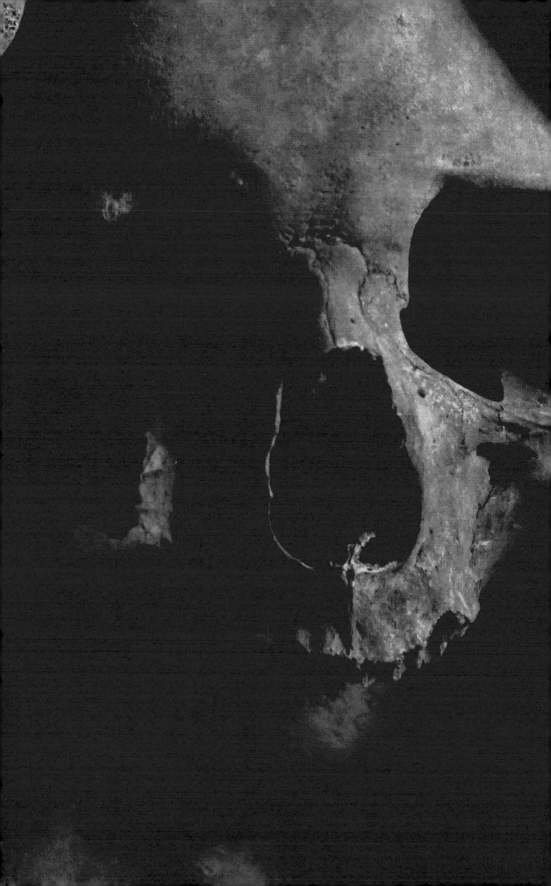

CHAPTER I
DEATH

I try to view death objectively.

Everything dies.

Humans die. That has always been the case.

Trees burn. Countries go to war with one another for reasons more terrible than the wars themselves. The world is insane, in a way.

All of us are insane.

But this time, it's not abstract.

This time, I had a direct hand in what's unfolding.

"HOLD HIM!" CHANDRE CAUGHT ANOTHER INFILTRATOR BY THE NECK.

Her braids whipped behind her like a dark tail as she slammed the smaller, Tibetan-looking female into a wall, knocking down wall hangings and flecks of blue paint. She shoved the barrel of a gun into the hollow of the woman's throat, aiming upwards, throwing the image of her intent into the other's mind so there'd be no mistake.

She still held the squirming seer, when Chandre's eyes jerked to mine.

"Stay back! I mean it, Bridge!"

I held a gun myself. You wouldn't know it by the way they were all treating me. I had six babysitters, all of them sure they were doing God's work, protecting me from harm.

Being leader wasn't all it was cracked up to be.

I trained my gun on the other seer in the room, a male, as Maygar, Dorje, Brevin, Nardik, and Cass came in behind me.

I knew Chandre didn't want me there at all. All of them, even Cass, would rather if I'd stayed on the plane. I pushed my increasingly long mane of dark hair out of my face, wishing I'd tied it back with one of the leather thongs Cass used.

It still had burgundy at the ends, from when I'd dyed it in Seattle.

I spoke Prexci, the language all seers knew.

"Where is it?" I aimed the gun at the male infiltrator's chest. I switched to his mind. *We know you're holding it for him. You can come with us. We can protect you.*

The seer laughed. A young male, he had high cheekbones and violet eyes he probably wore contacts over when working with humans.

He spat in my direction, not bothering with words to respond to my offer.

He wore fatigues, the uniform of Russian infantry.

I took a step nearer, wiping my face.

"Where is it?" I raised the gun, pointing it at his face.

Maygar crossed the room behind me. Walking to where I stood, he grabbed the collar of the seer I had in my sights. He proceeded to drag him across the room.

"Maygar, wait!" I said in English. "Don't hurt him!"

The muscular seer with the sword and sun tattoo on his arm acted like he didn't hear me.

I clicked at him in irritation as he pulled a hunting knife from the sheath on his thigh, showing it to the other seer before he set it against his neck. He growled something in Russian.

I saw the violet eyes lose their confidence as he spoke.

Then I heard a word I recognized, and the violet eyes shifted to me, just before they widened in fear.

"Bridge?" he whispered in Prexci.

"Where is it?" Maygar said in English. *Or she'll create a new orifice in that pretty face of yours. Without even breaking a sweat.*

I lowered my gun, biting back my irritation.

The seer began jabbering at him again, in Russian.

Maygar listened for a moment, then looked at me.

"The other room," he said, in accented English. He motioned with his head. "There's a box in there. He says it's all paper. No organics." He shook the seer, asked him something else in Russian.

The seer nodded emphatically. He pointed again to the other door.

"Paper only," Maygar confirmed.

Fighting an impulse to snap at Maygar, I walked to the door.

When I entered the small bedroom on the other side, I passed Cass, who gave me a half-smile that stretched the scar on her face.

It still hurt me a little, each and every time I saw it.

But Cass had changed so much since that day in the diner, I might not have recognized her back then—and not because of the scar.

The scar was barely a part of that.

Now she clutched a gun in both hands, looking like something in a guns and ammo magazine with her shocking black and scarlet-dyed hair. A thin T-shirt stretched across her chest with a picture of one of her favorite graphic novel characters. Words across the front read *Spacegirl Don't Need a Reason.*

Unlike my adopted brother, Jon, Cass had embraced living with the seers in a way I couldn't possibly have imagined a year ago.

Of course, being tortured for months by a psychotic seer could do that to a person.

Somehow, she never blamed me.

I wished I could say the same.

Touching her shoulder as I passed, I entered the bedroom. A flapping rag covered the one, broken window.

Terian, the aforementioned psychotic seer, had been cleaning up, ever since he managed to come into power in the human world.

Thanks to me, the craziest, possibly smartest, definitely most blood-thirsty seer I'd yet encountered was now President of the United States.

He'd figured out a way to spread his consciousness across numerous physical bodies, and placed one of those bodies in the White House—all because I'd killed the previous president, a genetically-evolved human who happened to be the head of the Rooks' international network of seers.

Yay, me.

I walked to the wooden crate. It lay on a bed with broken springs that sagged nearly to the floor. The whole room smelled of mold, cat piss, and rotted wood.

"Wait!"

I turned. Chandre glared at me with her dark red eyes.

"Don't touch it, Bridge! *D'gaos!* You're like a child wandering in a wild animal park covered in blood."

I backed away from the box, even as Cass laughed at Chandre's visual.

"I scanned it," I said, feeling a little put out. "No bombs, Chandre. No Barrier traps. I was just going to look inside."

"Well, don't. You may not value your life, but I value mine. Your husband would kill me—literally—if he knew we'd even let you in here."

"No," I said, warning her. "Don't bring up Revik again."

"Does he even know you are here?" she asked sourly.

"No." I glanced at Cass, then more pointedly at Maygar. "…And I see absolutely no reason why he needs to find out."

Smiling, Maygar slung his rifle over his shoulder, walking back towards the main room. He blew me a kiss with thick fingers. "You can lie to your husband all you want, Bridge," he said, winking. "I don't mind."

I watched him go, biting my tongue.

"Well, then." Chandre said, causing me to turn. She folded her muscular arms. "As Dehgoies is the only person you let order you around, I think someone else should get the honor, in his absence. I figure, why not me?"

Cass laughed again from the doorway, giving me an apologetic grin when I swiveled my gaze to hers. Reaching into her vest, Chandre pulled out a stone-like, olive green device, about the size of a fist. She laid it on the crate, where it promptly began to vibrate.

Tendrils erupted from the smooth surface, making me flinch.

I still hadn't gotten used to the types and prevalence of organic machines.

According to the World Court, they were supposed to be illegal, but seers relied on them heavily, especially for military-type ops.

Fascinated and repulsed, I watched the legs softly probe the sides of the wooden box before sliding down the slats of the crate and into the papers stacked and crammed inside.

"I don't let him order me around," I muttered.

"Well, you pretend to listen to him at least."

Chandre gave Cass a wink when the human laughed again.

Touching her earpiece to read some signal off the organic, Chandre straightened, training her gaze narrowly on the insect-like creature climbing on the crate. The three of us watched its pale tentacles slide through layers of paper.

"Can it disarm anything that might be in there?" I asked.

"Let's hope so, Bridge," Chandre said. "I don't want to be picking bits of you out of my hair, with your human-like reflexes."

I grimaced, refolded my arms tighter.

Insulting my seer prowess by calling me human didn't seem weird to her, apparently. Not even with Cass—who literally *was human*—standing right next to her.

The pseudo-organism let out a pale tone, just before the serpentine legs retracted, leaving it smooth, and lifeless-looking.

"It's clean," Chandre announced.

"Grab it," I said to Maygar, who appeared in the doorway, watching over my shoulder. "Put it with the others. And check the walls with the sonar. There could be more."

I watched Cass follow Maygar as seers dispersed around me, doing as I asked.

No one argued anymore when I told them to do things.

Even Maygar and Chandre obeyed direct orders, although they might give me a hard time as they did it. I wasn't sure if that fact unnerved me more than eased my mind.

I was "the Bridge," after all.

I had to get used to a lot of things.

More than half of those in both the human and seer worlds believed me to be a reincarnated mythological being whose presence on earth heralded the end the world.

But I didn't like thinking about that.

I had a new name. There'd been this whole ceremony.

I had to wear a blue robe. Afterwards, I was "Dehgoies Alyani," at least on paper.

The name made me nervous. Seers put family names first, like in a lot of Asian countries. It made sense to take Revik's, I guess, at least temporarily, but it felt pretty strange. After all, the one and only time Revik and I talked specifically about our marriage, he'd asked me for a divorce.

Since it wasn't really a seer tradition for females to take on the names of their husbands, I tried to let it go. But it wasn't easy.

The Alyani part was less of a big deal. I'd asked Vash for a seer name I could still shorten to Allie. Alyani was as good as anything.

Anyway, I couldn't remain Alyson May Taylor—for a lot of reasons.

Not the least of which being that Allie Taylor was wanted for alleged terrorist acts in like twenty countries. Then again, I wondered if we were really fooling anyone, with Terian alive.

I still didn't have a clan tattoo.

Apparently that had more serious ramifications, in terms of familial duties and so on, so Vash gave me permission to wait. Regardless of what Revik thought about our "marriage" these days, I definitely got the impression he didn't like his adoptive family much. I didn't want to use them as a fallback for something I couldn't reverse, not without talking to him about it first.

All of the clans had petitioned for my inclusion in their lineage, now that I'd been formally ID'd as the Bridge by the Council of Seven, so I had options.

Which also meant, no matter what I did, someone would be pissed off.

When I told Vash that, he smiled and said, "Welcome to leadership."

He wasn't wrong. Still, he didn't have to be so blatantly happy about the fact that it was no longer his problem.

In Seertown itself, my new identity was completely wasted.

Everyone but Cass and Jon called me "Bridge."

I had to deal with human and seer religious types coming to Seertown to pay homage, some from as far away as South America. A big festival took place just three weeks earlier, where I'd been asked to bless babies, and lots of religious-types named their female babies "Alyson."

I'd also blessed at least one "Revik," which I couldn't help finding cute.

I was pretty sure at least a few people filmed me on the dais that day, even though any kind of imaging device was technically illegal within the compound walls.

My face still showed up in the human news, too—my real face, not an avatar—which meant I was still officially classified as a terrorist.

So, yeah… I probably could have kept my old name.

In any case, the last thing I needed was more people giving me shit about Revik.

CHAPTER 2
WAR

June 12th, 1944
Journals of Roderick Biermann (aka Galaith), later known as US President Daniel Caine
Berlin, Germany

I think we may finally have enough force to exert an influence for good.

Young Dehgoies is a blessing. Already, I find myself wanting to give him more responsibility, to see how far that talent for strategy and organization might stretch.

He will be my architect of this new world. Across this racial divide, he feels like a true collaborator. A visionary.

I so wish to trust him. With all of my being, I wish to trust that he will help me with this, my greatest burden.

The boy is the key to peace.

Not peace in the short term. Ending these wars is just the start, a prerequisite for all that must follow. Nor do I mean the kind of peace that implies capitulation among those who should never be forced to lie down or beg.

I mean real peace. The kind that lasts.

As for Feigran, he has a role to play as well. His ambition is limitless, it seems, but he is more than that. There is something in his soul, some key to the next step, the ultimate outcome of the Displacement, that I still cannot fathom.

They still have no idea who they really are.

A STREAK OF FIRE ILLUMINATES THE DARKENED SPACE OF THE BARRIER.

I know in reality a missile just exploded, sending up a plume of flame. Trees fall under the blast, birds fly up in a cloud, screeching in fear.

I watch the cloudy, indistinct lights of humans blown back.

I know they are real people. I know they are being ripped apart down there, limbs torn from torsos, shrapnel embedding in soft flesh and skin.

Some separate from their bodies totally, ejected at once into the Barrier's dark sky.

At first, when only a few died out here, I tried to help them.

Now, there are too many.

Still, I try to reassure those who pass near to me in the Barrier's waves.

I tell them simple things.

No, you cannot return to your body. You cannot force your way back into broken flesh. Yes, the vessel really is broken. See it? That's it, there. That was your body. Yeah, I know it looks bad. No, I'm not God, or an angel. No, I don't know how to contact your wife...

Getting them to listen is difficult.

Most run from me.

Their fear causes them to resonate with other lights, other beings, to disappear—*poof*—into some other, more confused Barrier space. They are unused to the Barrier's dark clouds and shifting appearance. They don't know that, in principle at least, they can travel as I do here, if only they would just relax.

They can't relax.

Some, a very few, do listen.

Other seers try to help, but it is a discouraging process. There are too many of them. And for humans, all of this is too new.

Trying to help in outside, before they are dead, is even more futile.

I've learned that quickly in the last few weeks.

It's difficult as hell to talk to humans about psychic stuff, even Jon and Cass. There are simply no words for some of what is everyday for me now. Even as they listen, I can feel the chasm between their imaginations and reality. Like all beings, humans explain the world in terms of what they already know.

The problem is, they don't know anything.

This war, for example.

To an American human, this is happening because China attacked the U.S.A., and killed its president. To them, this war is about revenge, national security, the safety of the nation, and sending a message to other tyrants and terrorists.

To someone like me, and all the seers with whom I work, this war is simply the invention of a mad seer's mind. A mad seer I put in power, in a country capable of making war on all the rest simply by shouting emotion-laden slogans.

The other seers tell me it's not my fault.

No part of me believes that, though.

Sir? You have seen enough?

I turn my head, my consciousness still split. I focus on his face, watching it flash back and forth to his physical one, positive to negative...

...and I lose it.

My mind snaps back.

I leave the Barrier. My consciousness resumes its march in real time, and...

...SOUND EXPLODED AROUND ME.

Whirring helicopter blades slammed overhead, thudding and rotating in a deafening heartbeat, long metal wings blocking and unblocking the sun. Hair whipped my face.

I locked eyes with the pilot, a tall, Chinese-looking seer named Tenzi.

We are too close, he sent, apologetic.

I cursed, angry at how easily I'd been pulled out.

I needed to get better at being in both places at once.

For a while, working with Yerin and Maygar daily, I seemed to be improving. Lately, I'd plateaued, hitting a wall I couldn't seem to make my way over. I could hold both places simultaneously if no one bothered me, and if nothing startled me.

Which meant if I stayed away from the world and all people, I was fine.

Sometimes, like now, I could hold the split for a few seconds of distraction.

Sometimes, I flat-out couldn't do it at all.

It was especially irritating to note in juxtaposition to my aforementioned husband, Dehgoies Revik, who could split his consciousness four or five ways, his attention focused on each to greater or lesser degrees, seemingly for as long as he wanted.

Most esteemed Bridge, Tenzi sent politely. *We cannot stay.*

I gestured dismissively with my hand, seer-fashion.

Let's go a little further in, I sent.

No, Esteemed Bridge.

I glanced over, eyebrows raised.

I hadn't gotten a flat-out no in a while.

Tenzi's thoughts remained stubborn. *Sir, we must go back.* He surprised me by smiling. *You promised, Esteemed One. Vash said to remind you. He said to tell you "no do-overs." If you persist in arguing, I have license to rule your judgment irrational, and bring you back of my own authority.*

I laughed in spite of myself. "Esteemed One, my ass," I yelled over the heartbeat of blades.

Still, he'd managed to make me laugh, no mean feat these days, and while he might be overdoing the politeness thing, he had a mind of his own.

Gazing down through the open door, I watched the fires burn, this time with my physical eyes. I focused on the line of smoke through the trees.

A loud whistle broke into my thoughts.

Tenzi swerved the joystick-like cyclic sideways, alternating his feet on the anti-torque pedals. Lurching sideways and feeling my stomach drop as we lost altitude, I grabbed the opening of the helicopter door, catching a glimpse of something sliding by above as the helicopter went down. Whatever it had been, it was loud, and moving fast.

They are shooting at us, sir, Tenzi sent.

I caught that. I grinned at him, and he surprised me, grinning back. "Okay. Take us back," I said aloud. "You win."

He was already turning us around, accelerating as we rose above the canopy and headed for the snow-covered mountains to the southwest.

I continued to grip the door as I looked back. Leaning into the harness I wore, I watched flashes from small arms fire light up the dark mass beneath the treetops.

Then we banked, accelerating faster for the border to India.

Infiltrators back at Seertown held a shield around us to hide us in the Barrier, mainly from seers working for either the Chinese or the Americans. Still, those same seers had eyes. If they managed to pick us up via drone image-capture, or heck, with binoculars, they might be able to ID me from facial-rec alone.

From the lack of Barrier imprint, they would already know we were being shielded.

That really could only mean one of three things: we were seers ourselves, we were important, or we were rich.

Any one of those things could cause them to take a closer look.

I remembered Maygar's grumpy warning the last time I went out. He'd tried guilt that time, and it came closest to working. If I was to be captured now, he reminded me, it would affect more than just Tenzi and myself.

I'd come anyway.

Sitting back on the ripped vinyl seat, I closed my eyes, taking in breaths of cold air. I had plenty to do back at the compound. I now had crates of Galaith's papers to go through. I'd have more in a few days, assuming the team I sent to Bavaria found anything.

I could have given some to Vash's seers to sort through, or even the Adhipan, now that they were starting to trickle into town, but that would mean telling more of them what I'd been up to than I really wanted.

So far, only a handful of the Seven's Guard knew what those trips were about.

I couldn't afford to tell even Jon and Cass the whole story. They were human, and vulnerable to being read by any seer for information. I'd let Cass come along, and gave her the same story I gave Vash—that I was looking for artifacts from the Rooks' pyramid now that it was destroyed.

Which, essentially, was the truth.

I gazed out over the sea of ice and snow, lost in my own thoughts as we slid through passes in the high mountains. We rounded a sheer rock outcrop, and a green and brown valley appeared at my feet.

Familiar tile rooftops began to break up the long valley floor.

Houses, shrines, and larger structures soon appeared with more frequency, along with white-painted cairns and colorful flags flapping in the cold wind.

I saw the stone house of the Old City high on the crest of the hill with its sprawling gardens and white statuary, and knew we were home.

Seertown market and commons, including Vash's more modest-looking compound, stretched down the hillside below, where buildings had a much more lived-in look. Laundry hung from balconies, even at the compound itself, and most of the houses had peeling, brightly-colored paint: pink and white, orange and red, sky blue and sea green.

Monkeys stood on balconies and slate roofs, looking over the bustle of humans and seers in the town below.

Tenzi brought us to the center of the white cross marking the helipad above Vash's house.

We landed with scarcely a bump.

Hanging up the sound-muffling headphones on their hook inside the cockpit, I climbed out of the battered seat as the rotating blades powered down with a descending whine. Ducking low, holding my hair ineffec-tively off my face, I walked out of their range, smiling at the four people waiting for me on the other side.

I grinned at Jon first.

"Miss me?" I asked.

"No," Chandre said pointedly, but she smiled.

"He's coming back, you know," Jon shouted over the blades. "Would be nice if you were alive when he got here."

"Who?" I said, giving Jon a quizzical look.

Cass laughed, her long, black and red hair whipping around her deli-cate face.

I grinned at her. I saw her look down the hill from where the helipad sat, taking in the view of Seertown with its colorful prayer flags and bamboo-walled houses.

"I assume he means your husband," Yerin answered for Jon, drawing my eyes.

The narrow-faced seer stood perfectly still on the platform, despite the robes whipping around his elongated form. His dark eyes held a thread of humor.

"And I must say," Yerin added. "He is likely right that Dehgoies Revik would not approve of these excursions of yours, if my last conversation with him was any indication. He expressed concern that you were not better protected, even in Seertown. He fears you are too visible, given the number of people who already—"

"Where's Maygar?" I asked, cutting him off.

They exchanged looks.

Every last one of them knew Revik and I had agreed to not talk during the period he was away. Even so, no one seemed to get that I didn't want to hear about them talking to him either.

Looking around, partly to distract myself from their meaningful silence, it occurred to me that Maygar really was missing. Still my official bodyguard, he never failed to be present on the landing pad to lecture me on the pure stupidity of letting myself be seen beyond the compound walls.

I would have loved, one day, to tell Revik just how alike the two of them really were.

"Really," I said. "Where is he? Is he sick?"

"He's gone to Cairo, Bridge," Chandre said.

"Cairo?" I turned on her in surprise. "Why?"

"Who knows?" Chandre shrugged. "Good riddance."

"Maybe Revik missed him." Cass gave me a slanting smile.

There was a silence, filled with nothing but powering down helicopter. Then I choked out an involuntary laugh. Jon and Chandre laughed with me, and even Yerin, who rarely understood our humor, smiled at the joke.

Revik would be about as happy to see Maygar as he would to be dipped in an unwashed septic tank. Naked.

CHAPTER 3
FEIGRAN

Feigran floats. Feigran dreams.

Discordances live inside rolling waves, musings previously held in check behind one or more locked doors. He builds mansions with his mind. He builds and builds…

The Pyramid is gone.

He struggles to feel. He struggles…

Wisps of mind twist into and around themselves like dead flowers through cloudy wraiths of light. They belong to him, these clouds, yet their exact relation to himself eludes him. Freed from the constraints of meat and bone bodies, freed from the Pyramid, the crowd descends on what remains.

They bring… unease.

Some in this crowd frighten him.

He sees shadows. He sees them, and wonders…

The walls are gone. The part of his mind stuck inside a pale, twisted body inside a drifting metal cone finds this sad.

His father is gone. Galaith is gone.

Feigran sleeps. Hurtling through the dark beauty of night and its endless carpet of stars, he slumbers. Dangers lurk just out of reach, in a different darkness, one so deep he cannot bring himself to imagine its folds. Pain lurks there, and worse. It is not the womb-like darkness where he dreams, but the dark of silence, death.

The end of being.

Voices whisper, reminding him, causing him to doubt, to wonder at...

But he is good.

He, who has suffered misery and redemption, contained more light and intelligence and imagination than a thousand of the ordinary... he is good.

God watches his footsteps.

He has seen it, how God singles him out.

Deep in the basement of a house in the Bavarian mountains, a man dug through piles of documents, cursing.

Papers circled him in a thick, teetering ring. A fire burned in the grate and he fed handfuls in periodically of those he'd already deemed useless or that simply annoyed him by their monotonous, bureaucratic prose.

He watched the edges turn black, then curl and crinkle up before bursting into flame.

He held them until the fire nearly burnt him.

Like most humans, Galaith marked every moment of his life worth saving, so sorting the dross from the few things of value proved a complex and time-consuming task. Really, Galaith himself should have been a Nazi, given his obsession with narcissistic self-documentation.

As it was, Terian could only wade through, and hope his tedious searching would yield fruit.

This particular Terian body/personality configuration had once been a number in a much longer lineup. However, since Galaith killed most of his bodies, Terian renumbered what remained.

This body was now Terian-3.

Scandinavian in appearance, he stood a hair above six-four.

When pretending to be human, his ident cards described him as being in his late twenties. But he wasn't human. He was a seer, with a sight ranking well above average, and a body approximately one hundred and twenty years old.

The original Terian-3 body hadn't survived.

None of the first ten had. Those earlier prototypes had all been destroyed when his mentor and friend of over one hundred years, a being sometimes known as Galaith, sometimes as Daniel Caine or Roderick Biermann or even Hraban Novotny, decided to eliminate the body politic that was Terian.

Terian had colleagues working to correct that problem now.

Even if everything went exceedingly well, however, it would take time. It could take a lot of time. The reality was, without the Pyramid, it may not be possible at all. Unless he found some way to rebuild the network, he might be forced to live in this fragmented, uncoordinated manner until his very last body died of natural—or unnatural—causes.

It had been many years since the different parts of himself were forced to live in so few bodies. Truth be told, he had grown unskilled at negotiating compromises between the more crystalized elements of his own personality. Before, while they'd been inhabiting separate bodies, he kept the different parts compliant through the strict hierarchy of the Pyramid.

Now, with two or three of those personalities living crammed inside a single physical form, they bled into one another, argued, fought for their own wants and needs, even attacked one another outright.

And yet, they'd also never been so separate.

With the Pyramid, Terian had been able to coordinate all of his bodies as a single unit; the Pyramid itself gave them an overarching structure.

Now they operated as truly separate entities, forced to coordinate as any individuals would.

This particular Terian found the intricacies of their power struggles tedious.

How ordinary seers or even humans dealt with the competing wants and voices of their own minds lived entirely beyond his ability to comprehend. It amazed him that more didn't stick a gun in their mouths to silence the cacophony.

One voice in particular—appearing in his mind as a sobbing, despondent boy in constant need of reassurance—made Terian want to gouge out his own eyes whenever it slid to the forefront of his consciousness.

Yet, this new world had its compensations.

Galaith was dead.

Terian was Head of the Rooks' network now.

For now at least, he lived as a king without a kingdom, but he would remedy that. The beings previously swelling Galaith's ranks scattered across the globe like so many bees without a hive, but Terian would draw them home.

In the meantime, there were other things he must do.

All that remained of the historical records of the Rooks lived in these boxes, and those like them scattered across Europe and Asia.

Unfortunately, Alyson caught on to that fact faster than he would have credited her, especially given that her mate still hadn't resurfaced.

Terian pulled himself to his feet, stretching his back as he fumbled in his shirt pocket for a *hiri* stick—a sweet-smelling, faint-high-inducing wrap of dark weed.

Hiri had been cultivated by Sarks for millennia before being mass-produced in more diluted forms by humans. Of course, Terian smoked the expensive kind—the undiluted kind, handmade by actual seers, using the old methods.

Lighting the end, he sucked at it for a few seconds, letting the resin calm him as he stared around at the mess on the floor.

He had been so sure he'd find something here.

This was the building where they trained Dehgoies, years ago.

Galaith's mountain home served many purposes back then. Training grounds, interrogation center, vacation spot. Galaith entertained Third Reich bigwigs with extravagant parties up here, staged to pay off the Gestapo and bigwigs in the SS.

Mostly, Galaith needed them to look the other way as he exported seers through Asia. The mountain retreat had also been a place of negotiation when the Allies passed through these mountains, and later, the site of that final treaty between the Rooks and the antiquated Council of Seven.

The thing was, Terian knew they'd learned things about Dehgoies during his training. In every seer training, such insights were the foundation for all that came after, no matter who the seer, no matter what their eventual role.

Yet, in Dehgoies' case, Terian couldn't for the life of him remember what any of those things were. It was a fairly telling detail, that absence.

The first rule of infiltration was to start with what one had.

Right now, what Terian had was that giant hole in his memory.

The training would have begun with an extremely thorough scan. That scan would have debilitated the trainee for days, if not weeks.

Copious records would have been kept.

Those records might have been destroyed following the advent of electronic storage—if it were anyone other than Galaith. The mere fact that Terian couldn't remember told him they'd indeed found something in Dehgoies' past worth keeping, which meant originals.

Unfortunately, after six days of looking in every nook and cranny and storage box in the place, even ripping up floorboards and doing sonar readings of the basement foundations, he still had nothing.

Well… practically nothing.

He found a yellowed receipt that indicated the three of them had, at one point, ordered several cases of single-malt Scotch.

Terian's eyes drifted to the fireplace.

Pushing aside a stack of worn papers, he stepped up to the mantle. A funnel-shaped edifice of river stones and blackened elm, the fireplace wore the face of an old-fashioned clock embedded in the chipped mortar.

He scanned it with his *aleimi*, but felt nothing.

Inert matter yielded little in a scan anyway, unless it contained an energetic imprint of some kind, and he didn't get that kind of ping.

He began feeling over the river stones.

He came upon a loose one, rubbed smooth by countless washings, robin's egg blue in color. He jiggled it a little, working it out of its indentation in the mortar.

Once he could get a real grip, he tugged it the rest of the way out with his fingers.

As he did, the stone next to it came loose as well. Then the next.

Terian stacked them on the mantle, removing stones and mortar until he found himself looking at a hole about seven inches in height and a foot wide that stretched far back into the mortar and stone. He felt around inside with his hand.

Seconds later, he pulled out a leather notebook a few inches thick, tied together with a frayed leather thong.

Terian unwound the cord from around the cover.

He moved closer to the fire, thumbing the book open carefully.

The neat, square lettering filling each page didn't come from Galaith.

Terian knew his old boss's sprawling, calligraphy-style handwriting on sight.

Yet, the style of these characters, he knew also.

The block letters with their quirks in spelling and punctuation, the odd letter in cursive, unmistakably belonged to Dehgoies Revik.

Terian flipped through more pages and found more of the same even pen strokes.

He glimpsed illustrations, what looked like mathematical formulae. Dehgoies had always been spatial in his thinking. Back in the day, he'd draw diagrams on bar napkins to illustrate points, even when drunk. Galaith called him his "multi-dimensionist" due to his fascination for stretching dimensional rules between the Barrier and the physical.

It was a no-brainer, really, to set Dehgoies to the task of making the network secure to outside infiltration.

Feeling a shiver of excitement, Terian flipped through page after page, turning each with care, until he found it.

Staring down at the meticulously-drawn blueprints for the original Pyramid, Terian felt another shiver go down his spine. He'd always suspected Dehgoies had created it. He'd known, somehow, in some part of his mind, even back then.

Still, to have it here, in his hands.

Dehgoies's first sketches, drawn by his own hand.

From what Terian could tell, studying the meticulous lines, the final hadn't deviated much from these initial drawings, at least at its core. He traced the details lovingly with a finger, marveling again at his old partner's genius. The Pyramid had been Revi's creation, after all—not Galaith's. And it had worked flawlessly.

Until a few months ago.

Forcing back the whiny, irritating part of himself that wanted to make the memory maudlin, Terian read the text on the page before the first drawing. He hoped the book contained at least some clue as to the step-by-step building of the Pyramid's structure.

But the words were about something entirely different.

The boy unnerves me.

Terian frowned. Dehgoies's block script continued on the line below.

It is weeks now, and I still cannot reach him. Honestly, I do not understand why we cannot simply kill him, and risk whatever result, but Galaith says that is impossible. It is something to do with the stasis, with what that doctor, the seer female with the face of a reptile, did to him. Despite who and what he is, I find everything about him disquieting. He looks at me as if he would kill me. I hope Galaith knows what he is doing, letting him live.

Frowning, Terian flipped forward in the book, looking for an earlier passage that might give him a clue as to who or what Dehgoies was referring. Stopping at random, he read aloud, hearing Dehgoies' cadences even in his own voice.

They wiped my mind almost entirely, perhaps not long after I came to live in the Pamir. From what Galaith and I have been able to piece together, I was maybe eight or nine solar years when the memories just stop.

And yet, there is no way to be sure. These games of the Seven add layer upon layer. There is no way of knowing where false begins and truth ends.

I remember my parents' deaths. But as to whatever brought me to that dismal prison in Sikkim, I have no memory whatsoever. I have vague memories of the first world war, but I must have been too young to fight. Everything is blurred through this period, only starting up again when I began training under Vash.

Terian flipped forward a few more pages.

For now, Galaith wants the other one in the dark about this. He didn't seem too happy about being sent away. He's an odd one, Terian. I don't know if he's simply crazy, or the smartest seer I have ever met. Galaith tells me it is a mixture of the two.

Terian reread the last line, frowning harder.

He flipped forward then back in the crinkled pages. The dates spanned from Dehgoies' initial training all the way to entries written in the 1950s, long after he'd been a fully functioning member of the Rooks' network of seers.

So who brought the journal back here?

Throwing a few more split logs on the fire, Terian sat cross-legged in front of the blaze.

Turning the crinkled pages all the way back to the front of the book, he settled himself in to read.

CHAPTER 4
LEADER

"Bridge! Hey, Bridge!" The seer in the doorway waved excitedly to his friend. "Over there! She's over there. Do you see her? She's right there!"

His voice rose over the babble of words in the poolroom, pulling me out of my head long enough to stare numbly at where he stood.

We sat in one of the out-of-the-way bars in Seertown, on an edge of hillside overlooking a section of valley with a human monastery and a school. The bottom floor was an internet café and a store that sold everything from toilet paper to chocolate-covered biscuits and T-shirts with sayings written in Prexci for the tourists.

A lot of them also had Vash's—and now, regrettably, my—face on them.

The upper floor was pretty sparse, which meant mostly locals and expats came here, not tourists so much. I'd taken to hanging out here with Jon and Cass when we just wanted to sit somewhere and drink a beer. There was no alcohol in Vash's compound, and most of the other bars were usually crowded enough that I'd be mobbed the second I walked in the door.

Someone had long ago painted the walls of the upstairs bar lemon yellow.

Mercifully, the color had since faded, and now sported water damage down part of the back wall, to the right of the antique-looking bar. The bar itself looked vaguely European, and may once have been expensive. Bottles covered the warped mantle just below an elaborately etched mirror worn through to metal at the edges.

Dips in the floor made the pool tables a little squirrel-y to play on, but locals staked out the two tables anyway. Posters of the Dalai Lama and a painting of the sun and sword covered the two main walls.

A picture of me stood on the bar itself, but it was small enough that it didn't bother me.

Tin lamps swung in lazy circles overhead every time someone slammed the door to the espresso bar below.

"Bridge! Hey, Miss Bridge! Esteemed Holy One!"

Before I could stop myself, I faced the male by the door.

My looking in his direction only made him beam wider—and anyway, it was already too late. Every seer and human in the place now stared at me. Those who hadn't noticed me in my hoodie and jeans did a double-take, surprise visible in their expressions.

Glancing at Jon and Cass, who sat with me at the bar, I sighed inwardly, even as Jon laughed.

"He's subtle," Cass said, sipping her beer. "Like a ninja, really."

Jon grinned, leaning towards me. "Do you think he wants your autograph, Al? Or maybe just to touch you? Get some of that Bridge mojo?"

"Yeah," Cass said. "I hear 'end of the world' is very in this year."

"Maybe you could just sneeze on him?" Jon suggested.

"Or fart," Cass added. "Given all the momo you ate this morning, that might knock him out cold."

I snorted, in spite of myself. "You're a friggin' riot, both of you."

I took a drink of the beer I'd been nursing for over an hour. Glancing at the beaming seer heading rapidly in our direction, I moved my glass around in a slow circle, then made up my mind and slid off the stool.

I was about to stand up when the Seven's security detail headed the guy off, escorting him back out the door firmly, one hand on his shoulder.

The seer looked confused but compliant.

At least Maygar wasn't there. He would have thrown the guy into a wall by now.

"Well," I said. "I guess that's my cue."

"No, stay." Cass put a hand on my arm. "You never just hang anymore. You have time to be the Great Leader later."

I glanced at Jon, who nodded in agreement.

Chandre stood up, on Cass's other side. She steadied herself by placing a hand on Cass's shoulder.

"Yes!" she said, and I nearly laughed again, realizing she was actually tipsy. "Stay, Bridge! It is a holiday today!"

"Yeah, yeah," I said, fighting not to roll my eyes. "I know."

It was the day before they celebrated Syrimne's birthday. I had to get used to the fact that the guy I'd grown up believing was the greatest mass murderer of all time was, in the world of the seers, a kind of folk hero.

"So?" Cass gave me a not-so-subtle smile, raising an eyebrow along with her fruity-looking drink.

With her red lipstick and the low-cut T-shirt, she almost looked like herself, or how I remembered her in San Francisco. She was still a little on the thin side, though.

"Revik's coming back soon, right?" she said.

"He's been delayed again," I told her.

I didn't want to talk about that, either.

"What's with all the delays?" Jon muttered.

"Beats me," I said. But I'd wondered, too.

"Maybe he's worried about hurting his new bride," Chan said, grinning, hanging over Cass's shoulder. "You being human-raised and all."

I gave her a hard look. "What's that supposed to mean?"

"Nothing." Her voice grew mock-serious. "It's just he's probably learning meditative techniques to keep himself calm. You know... so he doesn't permanently damage you when he finally gets your clothes off."

I gave her an incredulous look. "Jesus. What is *with* you?"

Chan leaned further over Cass's shoulder, laughing. "You sure you ready for him, Bridge? We seers like some violence in our sex. If he's been faithful, he's going to be hungry. Hungry seers are dangerous." She laughed again. "...Even the males."

She took a drink of her beer, squeezing Cass's shoulder.

Cass shrugged at me with a mock apologetic look.

"I can't take her anywhere," she said.

"What the hell have you two been feeding Chan?" I complained.

I glanced at Jon, who just smiled, waving me off. "Don't look at me."

Chandre rested her chin on Cass's shoulder, still grinning. "You ever been with a seer yet, Bridge? Not just Dehgoies. Any of us?"

Feeling my face redden, I gave her a bare glance. "Piss off, Chan."

The seer laughed. "You're in for a surprise. He's going to have to be careful when he pops your cherry... you being the Bridge and all."

"Chan, Jesus. Put a sock in it, all right?" I turned on her, even as an unwelcome flush of pain heated my light. The last thing I needed was to talk about Revik and sex in the same goddamned sentence right then.

I was about to say more on that subject.

Seeing her stroking Cass's arm brought me up short.

It hit me that I'd been totally blind to all the affection going on there.

I swiveled my head, cocking an eyebrow at Cass.

Rolling her eyes up subtly, she gave me an impatient look before she shrugged, the equivalent of, "Well, duh." Her face, still delicate on the parts untouched by the thick scar, quirked in a small smile.

I saw Chandre look between us, then grip Cass's shoulder more tightly with her fingers. I couldn't fail to miss the possessiveness in the gesture, or the affectionate look Cass gave the dark-skinned seer when she glanced up.

"Huh," I said, mostly to myself.

"Not trying to offend you, Bridge," Chandre said. "Just teasing. It's a tradition you know, to give crap to newlyweds."

"Well, lay off the—" I began, but someone else yelled from the door.

"Bridge! Look, it is the Bridge! I told you! There she is!"

I sighed internally.

"Hey, Bridge!" Another excited voice. "That's her, see! Wave to her! She is raised human, wave! Yes... like this..."

I tried not to notice the enthusiastic hand-waving coming from the direction of the red-painted door. When I smiled, nodding back with a short wave, more excited murmurings erupted from that end of the room.

I glanced around subtly, but my guard seemed to have disappeared.

"I'll get rid of him, Bridge," Chandre said, businesslike. "They should not be here, bothering you."

"Yeah, yeah." I waved her off. "Just what I need... a drunk infiltrator with a gun. It's okay. You guys stay here, I need to find Yerin anyway.

Supposedly the rest of the Adhipan are getting here today. I should be at the compound to greet them. Do the leader thing."

Jon glanced up. "Want me to come?"

I snorted. "So you can check out all the cute seer boys from China? No. I don't think so."

I was totally kidding, but Jon colored a little anyway.

He was the last one on earth to go out on the open prowl like that. Seeming to realize I was teasing him then, he raised his eyebrows a few times in quick succession.

"Is it my fault I'm ridiculously good-looking?"

"No," I said. "It's not. But someone has to bear that burden." Rolling my eyes then, I called his bluff. "I wish you *would* hit on someone. Jeez Louise, Jon. You're thirty-two years old. You've been propositioned by half of the unattached male seers in Seertown and you still spend all your time hanging out with those monks, reading books covered in chicken-scratches and staring at blank walls."

"I'm learning." He flushed a little. "I'm not really in the mood to be chatted up by a bunch of horny seers. Give me some credit, sis."

"I give you credit. I give you loads of credit. What about that Garend guy? He seemed cool. And he's cute."

"Seers are too promiscuous." He glanced at Chan, then, seeming to remember, back at me. "...No offense. I just mean the unattached ones. I don't really want to be the curiosity of the week. They're only interested because I keep saying no, anyway."

"No," Chan said, shaking her finger at him, seer-fashion. "They are interested because you are indecently cute, and horny as hell under all your fake human monk airy-fairy bullshit." She took another swig of beer. "You are being stupid, worm. Why turn down perfectly good sex? It is a waste."

I laughed. "See? I don't even have to lecture you anymore. You've got Chan here." I made a face. "Only I hope I don't sound so... crass."

"You don't." He swallowed a mouthful of seltzer. "...Usually."

When I started to say something more, Jon cut me off.

"Just leave it, Al. I don't need a talking to, okay? I'm good."

"Okay, okay." I held up my hands. "It's typical projection, anyway. Since I'm not getting any, I figure I might as well meddle with your love life, right?"

He shook his head, granting me a short laugh. "Sure."

Patting him on the shoulder, I slid off my barstool, just in time to find four seers barring my way. Startled, I came to a stop, then smiled, putting on the leader face.

They were harmless.

Besides, Vash gave me this whole talk about morale, about how my presence here gave them all hope. According to him, the arrival of the Bridge helped some of them make sense of all the atrocities they'd been forced to endure at the hands of humans.

I got his logic—sort of—but I still felt like I was acting in a play and didn't know the script.

I took a cautious step, still smiling, and they moved to let me pass, touching my clothing reverentially as I aimed my feet for the door. Only two of them spoke; the others seemed only to want to stand next to me. I felt their light whisper around mine, even as they made respectful gestures with their hands.

Their heads remained bowed as they followed me to the door.

Once I reached the exit, I stiffened, seeing the crowd waiting outside through the rectangular window in the plank door. So much for traveling incognito. It must have something to do with the holiday for Syrimne.

Pasting the smile wider on my face, I braced myself, opening the door.

Just then, someone grabbed my arms from behind.

I let out a yell as my feet left the ground. Whoever it was didn't hit me, though; they forced me to the floor. Before I could take a breath, he'd covered me with his body.

I heard the shots a second later—just before the sound of breaking glass.

Screaming broke out on the street below.

Craning my head back, I saw my friends already off their stools and crouched by the long bar. Chandre, all business now, every trace of alcohol gone from her expression, was gesturing to someone else in the room, holding Cass's wrist as she clicked her fingers sharply.

Jon already had a gun in his good hand.

More shots were fired.

Screaming echoed up from the street, but it was getting quieter, so the crowd must have scattered. Someone was shooting a rifle from the poolroom window only a half-dozen feet from where I lay, but it wasn't at me; it was at someone outside.

Two others ran past me, darting through the open door swinging on its hinges and clattering down the rickety wooden staircase on the other side.

Seconds later, those same feet pounded on the street.

The man lying on me was half-crushing me; all I could think was that I wanted him off.

Instantly, the pressure on me lessened—which told me one thing at least.

He was a seer.

I could still feel his heart beating through my back.

Glancing up, I met his gaze, startled by the nearness of his gray eyes.

"Thanks," I said.

Returning my appraisal, he smiled. "Of course, Esteemed Bridge."

A FEW HOURS LATER, I SLID THROUGH AN OPENING IN THE CLOTH DRAPE hanging over the door, entering a wide room with a bamboo ceiling.

A wall-sized painting of the blue sun and sword met me, along with a wooden altar covered in candles and brass depictions of various gods and goddesses making up the seer pantheon. A number of gold tapestries decorated with intricately embroidered blue, gold and white thread hung on either side. Beyond the altar, a window opened out on the Himalayas, which still looked like something from a painting to me.

I saw Vash first, seated cross-legged beside the stone fireplace on the other side of the altar. He smiled when he saw me.

His smooth-faced, monk-like students didn't.

Cass and Jon had beaten me there, as had Chandre. All three sat against the far wall next to a row of young infiltrator types, many of whom I recognized as Maygar's friends. Unlike Vash's students, they wore street clothes and most were heavily tattooed.

I saw the seer who wrestled me to the floor of the poolroom, as well. He watched me cross the room. Curiosity shone in his gray eyes.

I'd asked who he was, of course, before I got there.

I'd been surprised at the answer, and not only because I'd actually heard of him.

His name was Balidor, and I'd first heard his name from Revik, on the ship we boarded in Vancouver.

Balidor was the senior infiltrator of the Adhipan—a mysterious and elite cadre of infiltrators loyal to the Seven. The Adhipan were legendary, a type of holy warrior monk that operated and trained in secret, and were extremely exclusive in membership. Most Adhipan seers were hand-chosen as children for recruitment, based on their potential sight rank, along with various traits of light and temperament known only to them.

They normally operated in secret, out of a stronghold somewhere in the Pamir. Apparently for years they functioned more along the lines of myth, but lately, according to Yerin, they'd become more visibly active in the human and seer worlds.

Revik talked them up quite a bit to me, during our training sessions.

He mentioned this man in particular, making him out as a kind of seer superhero.

His name was Balidor only. No clan name. Everyone in the Adhipan gave up their clan affiliation when they joined.

Their clan became the Adhipan.

According to Dorje and Yerin, Balidor had only just come to Seertown, but his people had been protecting me secretly for weeks. Now he crouched before Vash on one knee, a hand raised in mid-gesture.

I had interrupted something.

Not at all, Most Esteemed Bridge, Balidor sent politely, rising from his knee. He gestured for me to approach, his smile disarming. *We were waiting for you. I simply wished to pay my respects.*

I nodded. "I understand. I can wait until you're finished."

"There is no need," he said, stepping back.

Hearing him speak English, I realized that was the language I had used. Most seers in Asia didn't know English. Stumped, I only nodded again.

Balidor resembled a human in young middle-age, which told me he likely topped the four hundred year mark. Still, there was no way to know for certain. Chandre looked like she was in her early twenties to me, and I found out from Maygar she was over two hundred years old, nearly twice Revik's age, although he looked closer to thirty.

According to Maygar, Chandre looked young for her age.

I'd been thinking all this as I approached, and was surprised when Balidor smiled.

That she does, he sent.

He smiled a nod towards Chandre, who gave me a "thanks a lot" sideways eye roll.

Still, I could tell it didn't bother her. She wasn't into guys, anyway.

Chandre snorted. I saw a faint smile touch Balidor's lips, just before his eyes followed Chandre's to Cass.

He didn't miss much, this Balidor.

"So," I said, clearing my throat. I used Prexci, the seer language. Like I mentioned, most seers didn't know English. My Prexci was still pretty bad, though—my accent, according to Maygar, "comical." I could understand most of what was said, especially with Vash's help in the background, but I needed practice speaking it.

"Can we begin?" I asked.

Balidor bowed, moving back, so that he joined the ring of cross-legged seers.

They all looked up at me expectantly.

When I nodded to Balidor, their eyes all swiveled to him. He bowed to me a second time in thanks. I had to fight not to give him the "just get on on with it" hand gesture.

Seers were big on formality.

Smiling faintly, Balidor turned to the rest of the group.

"We caught one of the shooters." He glanced at me. "Female. She wasn't local. From preliminary scans, it is clear she once ran with the Rooks. She had the Barrier signature of having being detached from the Pyramid. We have not yet determined where her loyalties lie now, but we got the sense of some organization there, perhaps a splinter group, something that formed after Galaith' death. The other, a male, is still being tracked. They tell me we should have him by nightfall. Wellington…"

He glanced at me, then elaborated for the others.

"…The Terian-being who is impersonating the human President of the United States, Ethan Wellington… has a significant number of seers protecting him, seemingly more every day. We have identified twenty-six in his direct employ, not including those seers working for the Secret Service, or any of the other branches of law enforcement tasked with his protection. None of that includes the humans in his personal employ, either. He moves between several constructs within the White House, and those in other governmental buildings. Several of these have been fortified from constructs that existed when Daniel Caine... the being we now know as Galaith... held the Presidential seat."

He flashed images as he spoke.

Having been American most of my life, I recognized a lot of the locations.

Those I didn't know were likely either specific to Wellington, or close enough to military or security concerns that un-doctored images didn't make it to the news feeds.

"Since the dispersion of the Rooks' main network..." Balidor continued.

He paused while a brief flash showed the Pyramid crumbling, breaking apart on its moorings. The image touched every seer in the collected group, and I felt every one of them pause to acknowledge me silently.

Again, I inwardly sighed.

"...He seems to have made it a priority to gain absolute control of key pieces of the human infrastructure," Balidor said, giving me another faint smile. "Namely the military and corporate leadership, but also communications."

He looked at me, his mouth suddenly grim.

"...Including all news feeds deemed legitimate by the human public. So your interest in outing him as a seer is likely not feasible at this juncture, Esteemed Bridge. Such a strategy also carries with it certain dangers."

I blinked at him, then looked at Vash.

Clearly, my ideas were traveling a lot further than I had realized.

"For one," Balidor added. "We now have reason to believe the Wellington body is biologically 100% human. So a disclosure of that kind could backfire. It could also make him seem like a terrorist target, which would give them license to activate even more draconian civil rights curtailments domestically. At the very least, it would likely damage your credibility further with the humans."

"What else?" I asked, motioning him on.

"He is clearly attempting to isolate the United States as a geographic and political entity within a particular Barrier construct. He wants them cut off from the rest of the world."

Balidor flashed the image of a bubble of light solidifying over the land mass of the United States.

"He is fanning racial tensions internally, and not only between Sarks and humans. He is inciting ethnic prejudices as well, particularly against those humans whose ancestors come from Asia. He does this mainly through subtle phrasing in his speeches, and, of course, by manipulating the construct he uses to control them."

"To what effect?" One of the monks spoke up. "What purpose does this serve?"

I noticed the rest of the monks leaning forward as well, long fingers clasped on knees or folded together in laps as they awaited Balidor's response. Traditional seers were extremely curious about human-to-human interactions and conflicts. Things that had obvious meaning to someone raised human were unfathomable to the majority of seers.

Balidor, however, could not possibly belong to that camp of seer.

He'd been in at least two major human wars.

Dorje also told me Balidor had been the leader of the Adhipan when they helped to bring down Syrimne. He'd shown me a picture they had framed in one of the prayer cabins of the final hunting party.

In the center stood the human who claimed the killing shot, a defector from the Bavarian army with the unlikely name of Hraban Novotny, thereafter known only as "Galaith"... as in, you guessed it, Galaith.

Looking at the photo though, I understood why no one made the connection.

The photograph was grainy, and Galaith disappeared soon after, rumored to have been killed by angry seers.

When he emerged forty years later as Daniel Caine, another human, who would have connected the dots, especially since he hadn't aged?

In that same photograph, right behind Galaith, stood Balidor.

He'd been looking away from the camera, out over a burnt field, holding a German infantry rifle in the crook of his arm and frowning. He looked very much the same as he did now, only a lot dirtier.

I asked Dorje how Balidor failed to recognize Daniel Caine when he stepped up as president later. After an awkward silence, Dorje confessed to me, somewhat apologetically, that most seers barely noticed the differences between humans.

From the Barrier, they all looked the same.

According to Dorje, Balidor probably just figured Daniel Caine looked a bit like Hraban Novotny, and never gave it another thought. Most seers never really believed Galaith made the killing shot, anyway. The fact that Caine always tested human further removed any reason to look at him more closely.

Humans, after all, aged visibly in fifty years.

Now, in Vash's chambers, Balidor just shrugged at the monk's question. He glanced at me before turning to face the peaceful, nonviolent seers sitting around him in a half-circle.

"To heighten paranoia and aggression," he explained. "To help other humans, civilians, feel a willingness to make war against humans who have done them no personal wrong. To make those same humans feel afraid of those they would be fighting."

I saw the monks whisper to one another, looking dismayed.

I didn't want to be insensitive, but we couldn't treat this as an anthropological experiment, either.

"Okay." I cleared my throat. "Balidor? What are your thoughts? Can we influence from the Chinese side?"

Balidor clicked softly as he shook his head.

"We now suspect Terian has at least one operative high up in the Chinese government. We are having difficulty identifying who. It is a serious impediment, in terms of finding means of effective influence. The Chinese government is also suffering from a number of factional issues at this time. We suspect Terian is fanning those difficulties, and persuading them that war is the easiest solution to reunite the populace.

"The Chinese are less naïve about seers, however," Balidor added. "Therefore, it is not only Terian who is blocking our attempts to gain access. We must negotiate with factions who are attempting to discern from inside China what outside influences may be contributing to the unrest. They have a few thousand of their own highly-trained infiltrators, many of whom are genuinely loyal to the Chinese government. We have attempted to speak with a few of them, to persuade them that we mean their masters no harm, but they are highly suspicious of us.

"The most elite of these were raised in the Forbidden City since birth. Some of the older ones grew up and played alongside the royal family. It is a different kind of seer soldier the Chinese have cultivated. They are honored as sages, treated as family, and they have been incorporated into many aspects of Chinese religious and traditional beliefs, as well as Communist ideals around 'brotherhood.' These higher-echelon seers, known as *Lao Hu,* 'Tiger People,' are not likely to trust us, simply because of who we are."

I sat down, plopping cross-legged on the floor even though I knew it would upset the monks. With my current rank as "oldest soul," I was supposed to be above their eye level at all times.

Right now, that meant stacking up a bunch of cushions in the chair-less room, and I couldn't be bothered.

I saw a few of the seers tense, their faces conflicted as they tried to decide how they might adjust their seats so I remained above their eye level.

Vash waved to them that it was all right, smiling at me.

"Terian's tactic in inciting war in the United States seems pretty straightforward," Balidor continued. "Wellington has accused the Chinese of harboring seer terrorists, and of using money from illegal trade of seers to bolster its military and fund terrorism. He claims the traitor, Caine, was aiding them."

"Doesn't he also accuse them of *assassinating* Caine?" Jon asked.

Balidor looked at him. "Yes. Wellington presents this as an alliance gone wrong."

I sighed internally. "So what next? How do we get them to talk to us?"

"I've told you the difficulties, Bridge Alyson."

"Okay, but those are temporary problems, right?" Glancing around at their blank faces, I fought not to frown. "We're never going to stop this without the Chinese on board. We need them. We need their seers, especially. How do we convince them to play ball? Do we have anyone who has contacts there?"

The monks were staring at me curiously.

"Stop this, Esteemed Bridge?" Balidor asked politely. "Stop what?"

"The war. You know... I'm looking for solutions here."

The monks gaped at me. Then they all looked to Vash. The ancient seer studied my eyes. He smiled kindly, letting out a kind of clicking sigh.

"You cannot stop the Displacement, Alyson," he said, his voice gentle. "Our hope is to soften the worst of its effects, to slow it down. If possible, to influence the war's direction as well as reach those humans who might be aided in making the transition. I do not imply that any of this is futile. The longer we hold off hostilities, the more hope we have of preparing the ground, of finding ways to reach humans before it is too late."

He sighed again, and it felt sincere.

"But you cannot stop the Displacement, Alyson," he said. "Eventually, the humans must be put in severe discomfort. Otherwise, they will not change."

I stared back at him, then around at the circle of seers.

Besides Vash, only Balidor's face held something other than puzzlement.

It took me another moment to identify the look in his gray eyes as sympathy.

That night, I lay awake on my back, staring up at a bamboo ceiling.

I wanted to view this rationally—or superstitiously, maybe, the way they did.

I couldn't, though.

I'd read all the literature about these wars. Supposedly they'd kill all the trees, "blot out the sun," "make the oceans boil," "kill everything that crawls or flies or climbs." Children would be slaughtered, disease would run rampant, people wouldn't have enough food or water or clean air.

That wasn't a world I wanted to live in.

It wasn't a world I'd wish on anyone else, either.

Then there was Revik.

Some part of me hadn't given up on having a life with him, even apart from all this. I knew I couldn't just run off and play house like most people, but I thought we might have *some* of it. Providing, of course, he wanted any of that with me.

He was already three weeks overdue from when they'd first told me he'd be back.

If I went on what they'd *first* told me, it was more like a month.

So I lay there, and worried. I worried about the war, and I worried about Revik. I knew I pulled on him all through it, but for once, I just let the separation pain be there, without trying to cover it over, or pretend I was doing fine.

I wasn't doing fine. I hadn't been fine in a long time.

Beyond all the rest of it, the seer part and the world ending part and the pseudo-marriage part—I missed him. In those weeks we'd been together on the ship, he'd been my best friend. Despite all our problems, and everything that went down in the year or so we'd known one another, I still trusted him more than anyone apart from Jon and Cass.

I wanted to talk to him about this.

I wanted to talk to him about the war, about Terian, about what I should do.

I wanted to know if he thought war was inevitable, too.

I wondered if he'd say the same things the rest of them said, that it was a waste of time, trying to stop it.

Curling up on the thin mattress, I willed him home.

I knew he wouldn't feel it, not with a dozen infiltrators monitoring his light, making sure nothing got to him from outside.

A part of me thought he really did hear me under all of those shields though, and that he understood.

CHAPTER 5

CAVE

Terian walked the yard, using a bone-handled cane as a walking stick.

This personality configuration wore a body once called "Terian-11," before Galaith decimated his ranks. Now, to the other Terians, he was "Terian-4," or simply "Four."

Four was a two-hundred-year-old seer with an alias as a thirty-something human who operated an import-export business out of Beijing. He was unmarried, but had a local girlfriend, an actress named Bai-Ling.

Now, he was far from her, and from his home.

Four surveyed the faces turned towards his.

Unwashed, they seemed to consist only of giant, liquid eyes surrounded by bone-stretched skin. Metal collars of a dull silver ringed filthy necks above protruding collarbones and coarse-spun clothes. The loose-fitting garments looked closer to burlap sacks cut with holes for arms, necks and legs than the shirts and long pants they were meant to approximate.

Flies lazily circled and clustered in the yard, settling on eyes and untreated cuts scabbing on arms and legs. Most went unswatted by the owners of the flesh they craved.

The age range in this pen looked to be approximately twelve solar years to twenty. As a result, the seers were small, thin-boned, pale. Most had been separated from their parents at a young age, if they'd ever spent any time with parents at all.

Four sniffed, his nose and mouth scrunching involuntarily.

They could certainly wash the product more often. Feed it occasionally, to ensure it developed well enough to be of some value. He'd hose off the whole yard right now if he could, first with soapy water, then with clean—maybe a few times for good measure.

Still, he knew the realities of water in India and China well enough.

The problem of water had only become worse in recent years, and promised to be still worse in future. The Himalayas themselves had become a battleground as governments on all sides of the great mountains fought over the snow and water from its peaks.

This particular camp had not been run by Rooks, strictly speaking.

Even so, the monk he traced through Galaith's invoices had definitely been paid for through his private funds. While Three dug through paperwork in Bavaria, Four was tasked with hunting down every bank account accessed directly by Galaith, which meant diving into the endless rattrap of human aliases he'd built over the years, along with dead seers whose names he'd borrowed, seers who'd "willed" all their financial holdings to him, humans who had been "relatives," etc.

The Rooks, even now, with half of those accounts unclaimed or unaccounted for, had a greater GNP than the majority of first world human nations.

Despite that, Galaith paid this bill from his personal funds, from a secret account, not as part of regular operations expensing. Whatever these monks were doing for Galaith, he hadn't wanted it known by anyone who handled finances in the network.

The anomaly was intriguing enough that Terian sought to check it out himself.

He still wasn't sure what he'd found.

The seer in front of him, an overweight and severely aged nun, perhaps six hundred years old, looked nervous as she shot Terian over-the-shoulder glances. Galaith's record books and the monks and nuns themselves called this a "school," but Terian recognized a work camp when he saw one.

He should, since he'd run a number of them in his time with the Rooks, and overseen the science arm of a few others.

Terian had never been overly fond of the camps himself, but one of his personas had a talent for genetics. The seer camps provided an almost unparalleled playground for conducting experiments utilizing both physical and *aleimic* structures, as well as creating functioning cross-breeds that might fool human seer detection devices.

Terian followed the woman through a heavy wooden door at the other end of the yard. He watched her fumble with an iron key kept on a chain around her neck and inside her robes. He smiled at the quaint security system, then followed her into the foyer of an inside chamber, watching somewhat impatiently as she lit a torch from the one hanging on the wall.

"The electricity is not reliable up here," she explained apologetically, although Terian had been fairly certain his thoughts were shielded. "We have found that traditional methods are less likely to leave us groping in the dark."

Terian grunted a noncommittal response. He motioned for her to continue.

She began stepping carefully down the steep stone stairs.

"You are quite sure he told you the full extent of our protocols here?" She glanced back at him, her pale, soft face appearing ghoul-like against the pitch black beyond the torch's reach. "He had no other names on his list. In fact, he was quite adamant that—"

"Would you like to see the mark in my *aleimi* again, Sister?" Terian's voice was calm, the picture of polite. "I assure you, I was debriefed in full at the time of succession."

The woman picked up on the edge underlying his words.

"No," she said. "The access was clear enough, sir. My apologies."

Her unease remained, discernible in her voice.

Terian glanced at the rough-hewn stone walls, stained by smoke and accumulated mold.

They walked on in the dark, tunneling deeper into the mountain. The air grew increasingly stale the further down they traveled, reeking of stagnant water and decaying plant life. As they descended another flight, Terian found himself breathing tighter. He realized he was having what amounted to the beginnings of a panic attack.

Claustrophobia. That was new.

He scanned the space, trying to determine if it was his or something imposed by the Barrier field he'd just entered.

"How much further?" he asked her in Mandarin.

She glanced over her shoulder from a small chamber that served as a landing, her fleshy face contorted by the torch's flickering.

"I apologize for the state of our caves," she said. "The Teacher thought it better if it looked like this part of the structure wasn't in use, so we deliberately let it fall into disrepair."

She began walking again down the next set of steep steps, touching the shining wall with one age-spotted hand.

"Almost there now," she said, panting a little. "Not much longer, sir."

His interest further piqued, Terian followed her plodding steps.

A few more landings down, a few more turns and walks through arched stone corridors later, Four saw a flickering light up ahead. It illuminated a medieval-looking door either sheeted with, or made entirely out of iron.

A narrow slot stood at head-height, its iron sliding cover closed.

Just outside the door, seated in a wooden chair, a monk with a long gray beard and dark pits for eyes glowered at us. Terian studied the wrinkled face as the woman put the torch in a second iron bracket on the opposite side of the door. He found himself torn with an odd feeling that he almost recognized that sallow face.

The old seer stared back at him. The male's dark eyes blazed with a dull hatred that only served to irritate Terian.

"You should not be here," the old man said in heavily-accented English. "You should not have brought him," he told the woman. "He should not be here."

"He has the mark," she said.

"I know this one," the old man sneered. "If he has it, he stole it. He should not be here."

Terian lost patience. He pulled the gun from the inside of his coat, pointing it first at the old man, then at the woman. The woman gaped at the gun as if she'd never seen one before.

"Open the door," Terian said.

"You can kill me," the old man said. "I do not care."

"That may happen anyway," Terian said. "Your godawful stink is enough for murder. But for now, I will tell you this. You get in my way—even if you kill this body of mine—I will be back. And next time, I'll take out every living soul in this complex, not just yours, old man. I'll take out hers, and all the young pups upstairs. You wouldn't want that on your conscience now, would you? All those progeny above, when you're so short for this world?"

The old man chuckled.

The malice behind it made Terian stare at him again, trying to place the wasted face.

He knew this being. He could feel it.

"Bunch of diseased rats," the old man said, his voice filled with phlegm. "You'd be doing the world a favor." He stared at Terian's face. "Yes, I remember you. They said you would come. One day."

"'They' did, did they?" Terian smiled, but felt anger underlying it somehow. "How nice. Now open the fucking door."

"You know who I mean. The two that brought him back."

Terian shot the old man in the hand.

The woman screamed, flattening her back against the iron door. Terian pointed the gun at the old man's face, glancing at the woman.

"You're still not opening the door," he observed. "And you have a lot of body parts left."

The woman half-walked, half-stumbled into the old man, who bent over, gasping in pain, holding his bleeding hand against filthy robes, his long, wrinkled face pale. The woman fumbled across his clothing with clumsy, frantic hands.

Even now, the old man tried feebly to ward her off. She pushed his hands aside, her eyes white-rimmed with fear.

"It's too late, Merenje," she whispered. "He'll only shoot you for it now—and he'll still get the key."

"Let him!" the old man said.

But Terian had stopped breathing, hearing the man's name.

"Merenje?" He turned, looking at the man's face in the torchlight.

He'd heard the name before. He'd heard it over and over in fact.

From the lips of a drugged and beaten captive he'd housed deep in the Caucasus Mountains, he'd heard that name until he'd been irritated enough to silence the voice uttering it. Dehgoies Revik muttered about Merenje and "the cave" for hours at times, hallucinating from lack of water and food. He did it again while begging for the beatings to stop, when Terian pushed him past the point of knowing who he was with or where he was.

Terian glanced around the walls of dungeon-like space.

The cave. How many times had he wondered what that meant?

"What is your clan name?" Terian demanded, pointing the gun at the old man. "Where do you come from? Are you from here?"

The man laughed, a sound like he'd first filled his mouth with broken glass.

Terian saw the hard, black eyes shine in the light of the torch's fire, filled with a bitter meanness, like an attack dog that's been kicked too many times. It struck Terian that the man hadn't always been so old and feeble.

Then he realized something else.

"You're human."

Four lowered the gun. He stared at the emaciated form in front of him, realizing in a kind of shock that he wasn't looking at a seven hundred year old seer, but a human being who had seen ninety-plus years, possibly more.

The woman retrieved the key, and Terian motioned at her with the gun, still staring at the ancient human.

"Open the door," he said.

Turning her back to him, she hastily complied.

The lock made a squealing sound as if it hadn't been turned in months.

When the door swung wide, Terian had to fight to keep from gagging at the smell that flooded the hallway from the light-less hole. Bile rushed to his throat; he covered his mouth and nose with the hand holding the gun. He swore profusely, fighting the impulse to shoot the two people close enough to blame for this abomination.

"Not so pleasant is it?" the old man sneered. "Hiding the sins of the past? Not so neat and clean."

Terian raised the gun, pointing it at him, then thought better of it and stepped around him instead, snatching one of the torches from an iron bracket and entering the small chamber, the sleeve of his forearm firmly over his nose and mouth. He swung the torch in a wide arc, taking in the small space.

The ceiling rose higher than he would have expected, at least twice the height of the corridor outside, but the floor space stood only at about eight-by-eight feet.

Terian turned around twice in the small cell, then stopped, startled when he saw a gleam of eyes reflect light back from his torch. He'd missed the creature entirely in his first turn around the room.

Even now, it stood as still as a posed corpse.

Four lowered the torch, blinking as his eyes adjusted.

The boy stood with every muscle in his small frame relaxed. Yet his demeanor wasn't one of subjugation or defeat, like the boys above-ground. On the contrary, his expression was calm, even politely interested. His shoulders sloped down below his neck, his arms relaxed, all the way to his hands, open at his sides, with delicate fingers.

In appearance he was adolescent, perhaps fourteen or fifteen years old for a human, twenty to twenty-five for a seer.

He stood so motionless and his skin shone with such a dull gray sheen he appeared to be made of wax. His eyes followed Terian's every movement as if gliding on smooth rails, not once jerking or showing a reaction.

After a few seconds, Terian realized he, himself had tensed.

He felt as though he were being hunted, watched the way a giant cat might watch the motions of an antlered buck.

Behind the boy, a palate of rags and what might have been an ancient mattress stood near one wall of the cell, all the same dark gray with black streaks. The smell concentrated from there, and more so from a bucket that stood near enough to the "bed" that Terian wanted to shove it further away with the toe of his boot, if only to get the image of this creature sleeping next to its own excrement forever out of his mind.

"What is your name, cub?" Terian asked. He found himself fascinated by the black eyes, the utter lack of expression. "Can you speak?"

The boy's expression changed.

Terian saw a dense hatred concentrate in those pupils, so fathomless it actually caused him to flinch back. Hearing noise behind him, he turned. The woman stood in the doorway, as did the old man. The boy's look of murder aimed precisely at the man with the hole shot through his hand.

"You did that?" The boy turned to Terian.

He spoke Prexci of such an ancient dialect, Terian had to concentrate to make out the words. He slid into the Barrier, tried to look at the boy from there.

Once he had, he focused and refocused his sight, not believing what he saw.

Above the filthy creature's head spiraled a collection of structures that nearly gave Terian an erection. A fascinated awe fell over him as he stared at those rotating and glimmering shapes.

The boy spoke again. "You did that? You shot him?"

"Yes," Terian told him, clicking out. "I did."

For a moment, the boy looked only at the wasted human.

He turned to Four.

"Yes. I will go with you."

Without fully turning his head, Terian spoke to the other two. "What the *fuck* is this precious bundle of joy?"

The woman turned sheet white. "You said you knew. You said he entrusted you!"

The old man gave another of those sick, grating chuckles.

"I told you. He likely killed your precious Teacher with his own hands."

"You wouldn't be far off with that, old man." Terian raised the gun. "But you still haven't answered my question."

The woman lifted her hands to Terian in pleading supplication, her eyes darting nervously between him and the boy. "You must understand. It was for his own protection. For all of our protection! We feed him well—"

Terian gave a harsh laugh. "Yes. This is practically the Ritz. But I'm not here to spank you for your housekeeping skills, *Fraulein.*"

Even so, he realized in some surprise he was angry. Beyond angry. He was furious. His hand shook as he pointed the gun at the two "monks." That they would keep any seer in such a place, much less a seer like this, with structures like he had... it was inconceivable.

That Galaith could have been a part of such a travesty...

"Unchain him." Terian motioned the gun towards the boy. "Now."

The nun's face drained further of blood. "Sir?"

"You heard him. He's coming with me."

"Sir! You don't understand! His collar... the restraint wire on his sight is attached to the chain. It was a safeguard, so no one could ever leave with him!"

She trailed when Terian raised the gun to point at her face. Terian cocked his head, his expression unmoving.

The woman stared at the boy, then back at Terian.

"You can't possibly understand what you are doing!" she cried. "He cannot be allowed to leave this place!"

"The boy won't hurt me. Will you, lad?"

"No. I won't hurt." He paused. "…You."

Terian smiled. "See? We're going to be pals, me and this handsome devil."

The old man with the bleeding hand laughed, stopping only when he broke into a paroxysm of thick coughs. He spat a gob of phlegm in the direction of the boy. Wiping his mouth on his dirt-encrusted robe, he spoke.

"I'll unchain him." His voice had a note of finality to it. "I'll do it… I'll let the little bastard go. It's mine to do."

"Merenje, no!" the nun cried, but Terian swung the gun back on her, stopping her from going after him.

The old man stumbled across the room, still holding his bleeding hand to his robes.

The boy stood perfectly still as Merenje reached him. He didn't move as the old man fumbled with the metal collar around his neck. Terian hadn't seen it until then, since it blended so perfectly with the color of the grimy neck.

Now that he did see it, Terian realized the thing was an antique.

Instead of the light, thin organic hybrid metals used on the seers in the pens upstairs, the boy's collar weighted his neck with several inches of what appeared to be iron. The organic skin on the outside looked like it came from some kind of reptile.

The back end, instead of having a thumbnail release valve triggered with retinal or other scanner, consisted of an iron ring that connected to a thick chain bolted into the wall above the palate of rags where the boy slept. The chain didn't even give him the full range of the small cell. No wonder the bucket remained by the bed.

Feeling his anger return, Terian watched the old man grasp the chain, which was also coated in organic skin.

"Use the key." The old man's pitted eyes stared at the boy's. "Use the key now. I've triggered the lock."

"No!" the woman screamed.

But Terian already understood.

Chuckling, he entered the Barrier space, and found himself facing an elaborate structure that had Dehgoies' and Galaith's *aleimic* fingerprints all over it. A golden weaving of light, it configured into a sphere of delicate beauty around the boy, strangling his *aleimi* through the organic components of the collar.

Recalling the symbol he'd found in Dehgoies Revik's journal, the same one he'd used to fool the woman into thinking Galaith had sent him, Terian imprinted it on the Barrier structure. It fit perfectly into the missing piece woven into the restraint collar around the boy's neck and its organic tissue.

As he withdrew from the Barrier space, Four heard an audible click.

His vision cleared, leaving him back in the pitch-black dungeon.

The boy met his gaze, and smiled.

CHAPTER 6
DISTRACTION

I jerked awake, half in a panic.

It took me another few breaths to realize why.

I'd dreamed that he'd gone, that he'd left me again, before I even saw him.

I lay curled into a half-moon, wedged in a cushioned seat next to a window with no glass. When I first opened my eyes, I gazed up at a wooden ceiling supported by thick crossbeams. Galaith's journal lay open by my hand, where I'd let go of it when my fingers loosened in sleep.

I wondered how long I'd been lying there.

Monkeys screeched from tree branches that sagged and swayed under their weight. Meanwhile, seers play-fought in a stone and crab-grass courtyard a few hundred feet below my window.

I saw my adoptive brother Jon there, standing with lingering awkwardness among a crowd of seers, watching them fight, eyes serious as he studied their moves. He'd been a fourth-degree black belt in Choy Li Fut in San Francisco, but here I knew he still felt kind of lame. Even apart from his hand, seer fighting arts included a lot of work with sight capabilities he simply couldn't do.

I recognized the look on his face as he watched them scuffle, though; he wanted to fight. He wanted to be in the middle of it.

"Yes," a voice behind me said. A soft clicking sound punctuated the quiet, low enough to be a purr. "It's all right now. I need exercise..."

The voice grew even lower, until I couldn't make out words.

I held my breath.

I recognized his deep voice.

I probably would have even without the German accent.

Hearing it affected me more than I expected, but he wasn't talking to me. In fact, we hadn't exchanged a single word yet.

Cass met me at the helipad again that morning.

She and I had gone to Seertown market, wandering through the maze of booths where humans and seers hawked blankets, clothes, prayer beads, handheld mechanical prayer wheels, shoes, radios, and Tibetan momo, a stuffed dumpling to which I was fast becoming addicted. Cass bought a scarf and a pair of earrings. She and Jon were doing pretty well here, in terms of money. Both worked a few hours a day, teaching English to seers.

By the time I made it back here, to Vash's compound, most of the seers had finished their morning rituals of chai and meditation and socializing in the wide gardens below the complex.

Jon refused to meet me on the platform, convinced I'd turned suicidal in my sudden need to see the front lines "every damned day" as he put it. I think Jon was really angry because he'd expected it to stop as soon as Revik got back.

Which he had, the night before.

Admittedly, Revik was part of the reason I decided to go that morning.

They'd drugged him for the flight, which was standard in security transports, but he hadn't woken up when they expected. They timed that kind of thing to the minute, especially where infiltrators were involved, and I'd already been told that Revik had the opposite tendency, meaning he was more likely to wake up early from a dose than late.

In fact, they had to calibrate personalized doses for him, to make sure he slept at all.

I worried they'd given him too much, but the seers attending him said no.

They explained he'd suffered some kind of "hit" during the last leg of the flight—meaning, he'd been tagged in the Barrier by another seer, or seers.

Whoever had done it, they'd drained his light to a dangerous level.

When he still wasn't awake when I got back, I was a lot more worried.

They told me he was fine.

His vitals had stabilized and he was replenishing light normally again. I tried lying next to him, thinking I might be able to speed that process along, but with the separation pain being what it was, I only lasted about ten minutes before I retreated back to the window seat.

I'd already spent most of the night there, anyway, my head propped on a cushion to stare out the window while I waited for him to wake and told myself I wasn't worried.

I must have fallen asleep myself.

Revik had company now.

Vash must have come in while I dozed.

Listening to the tone of their voices, I found myself wishing I'd slept somewhere else. I didn't want to interrupt, though, not even to leave.

The old seer's voice grew audible. "…I am so sorry, my son."

I heard him say more, but I lost his words in the emotion I felt around them.

Revik answered him, but not in a language I knew.

Vash moved on the bed, making the springs creak. "Is it true what they tell me? That you remember more now?"

I swallowed, wishing more than ever I'd slept in the other room.

I didn't want to overhear anything he wasn't ready to tell me himself, but it was hard not to strain for his answer. Revik lost most of his memory when he left the Rooks. Now, reading Galaith's diaries, I had a better idea of what those years had looked like for him.

I also increasingly wondered if his memory loss had been such a bad thing.

He'd been married in that life. To someone else, I mean.

His marriage to Elise had been more what I'd call a "real" marriage, though. Thanks to Galaith, I'd even seen the tail end of their ceremony from the Barrier, and Revik looked damned good in a tux. From how happy he appeared in my one glimpse, he must have been fully on-board with the marriage thing, too, at least when it came to Elise.

In other words, his marriage to Elise hadn't consisted of a night where two near-strangers got immersed in each other's light and accidentally started the energetic bond that formed the first stage of seer marriage.

Nor had it likely been followed by months of anger, denial, epic misunderstandings, no sex, a request for divorce, and finally, infidelity.

No, that had been his marriage to me.

Through the window, I watched seers continue to scuffle as their dirt ring turned to clomping damp patches, then to mud. They seemed oblivious as they faced off against one another, sparred, clinched, repositioned, faced off again. Laughter rolled up when the smaller of the two swept the other's leg, landing him on his back.

I tried not to hear the emotion that clouded Vash's words.

"I should never have let you go. You were so determined that it be you."

Revik answered, his voice too low for me to make out words.

He lay wrapped in furs, propped up on pillows.

Feeling glimmers of his light, I realized again how long it had been since I'd seen him, and how short a time we'd had together then. At Gatwick Airport in London, right after everything had gone down, we'd only had about ten minutes alone to say goodbye before the infiltrators took him away.

That had mostly involved us kissing.

He'd asked me to wait for him, though. It was the closest he'd ever come to telling me anything, in terms of the two of us.

I got to India via plane and train, on a roundabout trip through Eastern Europe.

Revik, on the other hand, traveled most of the way by cargo ship, going all the way around the Cape of Good Hope at the southernmost tip of Africa and up the Suez before being transported by land to Cairo.

It took four months. They promised me it wouldn't be more than three. I found myself remembering the look on his face as they led him away.

I was still staring down at the sparring seers, not seeing them...

...when the door shut softly behind me.

I stopped breathing.

For a long moment, there was nothing.

I wondered if he was waiting for me. I steeled myself, trying to decide if I should speak.

"Allie?" His accent was stronger.

I took a breath. I had things I wanted to say to him, assuming he even wanted to talk to me yet. I felt pretty strongly the conversation needed to happen, and relatively soon.

I also knew whatever he might say in the next few minutes could derail me completely. I kept my *aleimi* wound tightly around my physical form as I slid off the window seat, letting my bare feet touch the floor.

Even so, seeing him awake, and sitting up, made me pause.

His black hair had been cut.

It was short, maybe shorter than I'd ever seen it.

He still looked thin, although the bruises on his face and neck were mostly gone. I saw scars, and not all of them were old. A faint, reddish ring remained visible around his neck. It was more than a fading bruise; it looked almost like a burn.

But it wasn't really the differences that threw me.

It was where he was the same.

His pale, nearly colorless eyes studied mine expressionlessly. His narrow face didn't move, never seemed to age even though his cheek-bones stood out more than they had before he'd been imprisoned by Terian. The lines of his jaw and the outline of his face appeared more angular, but his narrow mouth looked the same. He wore the soft gray T-shirt he'd been wearing when they first brought him in, and his arms looked smaller but the same as well, sinewy and somehow less young than his face.

I took a few steps in his direction and stopped. I folded my arms.

I knew it probably came off as somewhat aggressive to do that, but it felt more defensive—especially since I couldn't think of a single argument I'd won with him in the year plus I'd known him.

"Are you okay?" I hesitated. "Do you need anything?"

I saw him wipe his eyes with the heel of his hand, and swallowed, realizing it hadn't only been Vash who'd been crying. Damn it. I felt myself soften, more than I should have. Gently, he patted the furs next to where he lay, his eyes carefully on mine.

"Can we talk?" His voice was polite, like always.

I shook my head, exhaling in a kind of humorless laugh.

"No. Not yet. Not like that."

"You're angry," he said.

"No." I shook my head, surprised. "No, I'm not angry." I paused, thinking about his question, then my own words. "I just need a minute, I guess. And we should talk, yes, but I'd rather do it from here. If that's okay."

He nodded, leaning against the wall. He seemed to have expected this. Or maybe he was reading me. It was so hard to know with him.

"You want to talk," he said. "Is it about the divorce thing, Allie?"

His words hit like a blow.

I swallowed, looking away.

He was back on that—the divorce thing. I don't know why it should have surprised me. It was the last thing he'd asked me for, when we talked on the ship.

Still, it pretty much silenced me. I wasn't sure where to go from there at all.

I saw him realize his mistake.

Hesitating, he folded his arms, shifting his weight on the bed. His eyes narrowed up at mine.

"Then what?"

"Look." I bit my tongue.

I hesitated, trying to collect my thoughts, which had pretty much scattered as soon as we were face to face. I looked away, refolding my arms tighter. "I'm not assuming anything. I'm really not. But I don't want you to think things with us are just going to…"

I stopped, rethinking that approach.

"I don't know what you want… or what you think I…"

I stopped again, rethinking that approach, too.

"Look." I exhaled in a near sigh, raising my eyes. "We can talk about the divorce thing if you want. That's fine. And I'll do whatever you want in that area." I swallowed, meeting his gaze. "But I'm in love with you, Revik. You must know that."

I felt his shock.

It stopped me in my tracks.

I opened my mouth, about to stammer something to cover over what I'd said… when his *aleimi* sparked out.

"Alyson." Emotion filled his voice. "Alyson… gods. Come here…"

Seeing the look on his face, I couldn't breathe.

An intensity had risen to his eyes; they were nearly bright. When he leaned forward, reaching for me with his light, I sidestepped him, holding up a hand.

"Wait." My shoulders unclenched. I was relieved at his reaction, but also completely thrown. I forced my voice level. "I love you... so that's clear. I don't know if anything else is with us, though." Biting my lip, I refolded my arms. "I really don't think I can do this anymore. Not the way we were."

I glanced up, nervous at his silence.

He was still staring at me, clearly in some stage of disbelief.

"You need to tell me what you want," I added. "Don't soft-pedal it. I don't need that, I really don't. Just be clear. Please... try to be clear. Before we get all..." I flushed a little, motioning with my hands. "...you know. Friendly."

Waiting for understanding to reach his eyes, I refolded my arms once it had.

I kept my voice calm, matter-of-fact.

"Okay. So I guess I should ask this first. Do you still want a divorce?"

"No."

It came out at once, without doubt.

I relaxed a little more. "All right. So what does that mean? To you, I mean." I hesitated, watching his eyes. "...and if there's any seer custom or subtext involved that has to do with being raised seer, could you please explain it to me? I can pretty much guarantee I won't get it."

I took a breath as his wary look faded.

I watched him take a breath, too, even as he pulled his light back around his body. He stared at the foot of the bed, his thumb rubbing his bare arm as he thought. He cleared his throat then, glancing up. His jaw tightened as he studied my eyes.

"I want to make love, Allie."

I felt my face warm. "Okay. Well, I sort of knew that part. That's not exactly what I..."

He was already shaking his head.

"What?" I folded my arms tighter.

"I don't think we should," he said.

I flinched a little. "Oh. Okay."

He added, "Right now, Allie. Just right now. A few weeks. Possibly longer. We should give it some time."

I pulled my *aleimi* a little closer to my body. "Sure. That's fine."

"Allie." He waited for me to look over. "You don't understand."

"Okay." I nodded, fighting the tightening of my jaw. "Could you explain it to me then? Is this one of those custom things?"

He shook his head, clicking softly. "No." He took a breath. "I just want you to be sure."

"You want *me* to be sure?"

"Yes."

There was another silence. That time, I found myself fighting to keep my expression level. I pursed my lips.

"Okay," I said. "But isn't that kind of up to me?"

"I want you to have time with me. Without sex."

"Haven't we had that?" I said. "...Months of that, actually?"

"Yes." He folded his arms tighter. His jaw hardened, but he wasn't looking at me now. "You haven't had much time to know other seers. You were married to me before you had met any other males."

There was another silence. I folded my arms tighter, too.

"I know other males now—" I began.

"Allie." He gave me a warning look. "Don't."

A little bewildered, I watched his face as he looked away.

After a few seconds more where neither of us spoke, I sighed.

"Okay," I said. "So what does that mean? You want us to date for a while? Do you want me to see other people? What?"

Something glanced past his expression.

Feeling a harder pulse off him, I sighed.

"Revik, relax, okay? I'm not looking to date other guys. I'm trying to understand what you're saying."

He didn't look up. "I'm explaining something about seers. You may not know what you're getting yourself into. This isn't the same..."

He trailed, his mouth firming. He gestured vaguely.

"The same as what?" I asked.

"As having sex with a human," he said. "Or even..." I saw his throat move. "...or even with a seer you're not married to, Allie."

"Revik." I fought to control my impatience. "Will you please just spit it out? Please. Whatever it is. Say it."

His eyes flickered back to mine, holding a kind of dense focus. Within that, I saw an emotional reaction I couldn't interpret, intense enough to make me pause. My irritation faded as I continued to look at him.

He was uncomfortable with this conversation, I realized.

It was making him nervous as hell, not only in relation to his feelings, but in terms of how I might react. He was serious about what he was proposing, with the no sex thing. He truly felt it was the right thing for us, and he was worried I was going to disagree—or worse, be offended. He was even worried I might retaliate.

It occurred to me then, what I was doing.

I was arguing with him when he said he didn't want sex.

I felt my face grow hot.

"Sorry." I shook my head, avoiding his eyes. "Revik, I'm sorry. Of course it's fine." Shoving my hands in my pockets, I looked out the window at the sun peeking through the clouds. "Hey, are you feeling up to a walk? Maybe we should get you some food. We could talk on the way."

He shook his head.

His voice and face grew openly frustrated.

"Allie... gods. I wish I could just..."

I swallowed, waiting as he trailed again.

For a moment he sat there, holding his head in his hands. When he spoke next, calm returned to his voice.

"I'm not angry with your questions," he said. "I just don't know how to make you understand." Glancing up, he sighed at my expression, focusing back on the bed. "Sex will make us married—in a way we haven't been. It's why I hesitated before, on the ship."

He leaned his back against the wall, his eyes on mine.

"When we do it, it'll change things. Do you understand? It's likely to throw both of us off balance, at least for a while."

"Off balance." I watched his eyes, cautious. "Like how, off balance?"

He gestured vaguely with one hand. "Some of it will be temporary. The separation pain... that pain we feel around each other... it's going to get worse for a while. It could even get a lot worse. I don't know for how long."

"Okay." I swallowed, nodding. "That's one. What else?"

He looked uncomfortable. "If we complete the marriage process, our life spans will likely be interdependent." At what must have been a perplexed look from me, he explained, "When I die, you die. And vice versa."

"Oh." Thinking about this, I nodded. It made sense, given what I knew about seers. "Okay. What else?"

Exhaling in a sigh, he glanced out the window, clicking to himself.

"Trust you to be blasé about that." His voice sounded calmer though, like he'd relaxed a little. He looked back at me. "Okay, there's one more. I've never been married to a seer before, but from what I know, it's likely to make us irrational."

Seeing the quirk in my mouth, he cut me off.

"...More irrational, Allie. Until the bond is complete, the possessiveness will be worse. We'll need to be considerate of one another. Really considerate." He gauged my eyes. "I need to hear something from you around that."

I nodded, folding my arms. "Okay."

He took another breath. "I want an agreement," he said. "A formal one. About other people." He must have read some portion of my thoughts, because when I glanced at him again, his eyes held an open disbelief. "Agreement means the opposite of what you're thinking. It's a commitment. I'm not going to comment on the 'may not be into it' if I sell myself thing I just heard."

"But isn't marriage a commitment?" I asked. "For seers, I mean?"

"Yes. But you weren't raised seer." A shadow touched his eyes. "For us, there's more to it than the physical."

"Okay," I prompted, waving him on. "So. Explain that."

His eyes hardened. Briefly, his accent grew thicker. "So, if we're going to do this... this trial period... I would like to ask you for monogamy."

Perplexed, I bit my lip.

I hadn't been with anyone since Nick the bartender in San Francisco, which was longer ago than I cared to admit aloud to anyone, much less him. Besides, he had to know that. It's not like I could have kept it from him.

Was he really going to make me go there?

"That's not a problem, Revik," I said.

He stared at me. "I mean *seer* monogamy, Allie."

I fingered my hair out of my eyes, exhaling again. "Revik. Please. Out with it. You want to say something. Just say it."

He nodded. "All right." His jaw tightened. "I would like to ask you not to have physical *or* Barrier sex with humans or other seers. During this period." His fingers pulled at the animal skins. "Or anything approximating sex. If you have any... lovers... of this kind, I am asking you to sever it with them. Until things are settled with us. It is a formal request, Allie."

I finally got what was bothering him.

There'd been one night, months ago, when Terian still had Revik and I thought he was dead, when me and my seer bodyguard, Maygar, had done something in the Barrier that apparently fit Revik's definition of cheating.

Revik clearly hadn't let it go.

I wasn't sure if I should laugh, or point out the obvious irony.

As it turned out, I did both.

"You're going to lecture *me* on fidelity?" I asked. "Seriously?"

"I might." He didn't sound entirely like he was kidding. "Alyson, I regret what I did, but it wasn't to be with other people."

I nodded, not believing a word. "Okay."

His eyes narrowed. "I didn't want us to be married. I didn't want to be married at all. And I wanted sex with you. Badly, at times. To the point where I struggled just being around you. I had sex with other people to buy me time. To distract me."

Seeing me flinch, he folded his arms tighter.

"I'm not feeling that way now. If you are, for any reason, we should sever it... before we consummate... and try to be friends."

His skin darkened, just before he looked up.

"I would never hurt you, Allie. Never. I never want you to fear that, not from me. But this is a deal-breaker for me. I'm goddamned jealous enough, without—"

"Jealous?" I gave a short laugh, half in disbelief. "Jesus... Revik. I've never given you a single reason to be—"

"I'm in love with you," he said.

This last startled me into silence.

I opened my mouth to answer, then didn't.

My silence seemed to throw him, too.

When he looked away, I forced myself to breathe, then to think.

Before I let myself second-guess any of it, I moved. Walking the rest of the way over to him, I sat down on the end of the bed. I made sure I sat far enough away, and I didn't touch any part of his light.

"Revik." I focused on his hands, which were bruised at the knuckles, lying white on the caramel-colored skins. I laid a hand on his leg. "The monogamy thing, it's fine with me. You must know that, even if you're… you know, worried."

At his silence, I took a breath.

"It's more than fine. It's what I want, too."

I paused again, keeping my voice calm as I shrugged.

"Just, you know. If you need distracting again… tell me. Before you act on it. Warn me, at least."

He returned my gaze, studying my eyes.

I was about to get up when his light encircled mine.

Something like guilt lived there, which I avoided.

His light slid deeper, wrapping into me until pain started to whisper through the veins in my *aleimi*, vibrating my skin. I tensed as it got stronger. I had trouble keeping my eyes on his when he opened to me, really opened, bleeding more of himself through his voice.

"Allie," he said. "Once we do this, we can't reverse it. I don't think even Vash could."

"Revik, if you don't want to, it's fine—"

"I do." His pain intensified. "*Gaos*…I really fucking do, more than anything. This delay isn't for me. I want you to be really, really sure."

"And you're that sure?" I asked.

"I'm older than you," he said. "I've been with other seers."

I smiled, but didn't feel it. "Yeah. I know."

"Allie." His light slid deeper. I swallowed, having trouble holding his gaze. "Allie… I won't need any more distracting. I promise."

I nodded. When he didn't say anything else, I slid backwards a little on the bed, extricating myself from his light. I did it mostly to give myself space to think. Feeling his eyes on me still, I looked out the window.

The sun had come out for real.

Giant clouds clustered around the peaks I could still see, but the sky reflected a deep blue. I watched birds alight on the bamboo roof. One little brown bird played in a puddle on a curved stave, shivering so that drops splattered out in a mist before dunking its head. Another bird started chirping at it, vying for the same puddle.

Smiling, I glanced over, and found Revik watching me again.

When I didn't look away, he held out a hand.

Hesitating only a bare second, I slid nearer.

I knew now, at least, that nothing was going to happen.

It got some of the suspense out of the way.

Once I was close enough, he curled an arm around my waist, pulling me smoothly and tightly into his arms. It startled me.

Okay… a lot, but I didn't resist him.

I stiffened as he resettled against the wall, bringing my back to his chest.

He wrapped an arm around me crosswise, gripping my shoulder, then relaxed deliberately, merging into me.

For a long moment, I felt nothing off him but warmth, a kind of pulling affection.

Realizing I was reacting to him sexually anyway, just from the mere fact of him touching me, I fought to relax, to clear my mind. I tried watching the sky outside. I was acutely aware of his fingers caressing my shoulder, his leg shifting behind my back. He held me tighter, wrapping his other arm around my waist.

"Allie."

When I looked up, I felt myself flush.

His face was only a few inches from mine.

He cleared his throat, gesturing towards me vaguely again, just before I saw his skin darken. I saw the question there, and looked from one of his eyes to the other.

Finally, I rested my head on his shoulder.

"What?" I asked.

His voice turned gruff. "I'd like to kiss you. Can I?"

My cheeks warmed.

Somehow it hadn't occurred to me that we'd still be doing that under the scenario he'd just outlined. My eyes settled on his mouth, then drifted back up to his. I found myself remembering saying goodbye to him at the airport.

Still, I knew at least part of the reason I was hesitating.

It was the distraction thing, what he'd said about other women.

I hadn't missed the plural he'd thrown in there, either.

I had to assume he meant Kat, that seer prostitute in Seattle, the same one he'd kissed right in front of me, who called me "worm" and taunted me ceaselessly about Revik and my general cluelessness. He told me in Vancouver, in his usual, tactful way, that he hadn't "fucked" her while we were in Seattle.

Now I had to assume they'd done everything but.

Hell, for all I knew, there were others on the ship. He could have been shielding his activities from me before.

But I had to let that go. I had to.

Looking up at him again, I nodded. "Okay."

His eyes grew pained. "Allie, I didn't mean anything—"

I shook my head. "Don't," I said. "Please. Don't ruin it."

After another pause, he nodded.

He slid a hand into my hair, caressing it back from my cheek, then my neck. He continued stroking my skin, studying my face as his fingers traced bone and muscle. I was trying to decide if I should touch him back, or say something, when I felt a shiver from him, just before he lowered his head.

His mouth was careful, just like I remembered.

Despite the near-familiarity there, it shocked me, just like it had all the times before. My heart stopped in my chest. My mind blanked out. I couldn't connect it at first to my feelings, or even directly to the person I'd known before all this, the one I'd thought about kissing all the time, at least on the ship.

For a long moment, he kept things warm, even affectionate, not using his tongue.

He kissed my mouth and neck, pausing to caress my cheek with his.

Then he went back to my mouth.

I couldn't decide whether I could relax into this. Every part of me was starting to hurt as he lowered his head, kissing my throat. I felt flickers of his tongue, nearly flinched against his breath on my skin, biting my lip to keep from reacting too much.

His mouth found mine again.

That time, he parted my lips.

His tongue was warmer than his skin.

That shocked me too, but I fell into it without really turning on my brain.

After a few seconds, I felt my stress from our conversation begin to evaporate. All that remained were his lips and tongue, his fingers caressing my face. My hands were in his hair, clutching the shorter part at the back of his head. I realized I was probably holding him too tightly... when his arm snaked once more around my waist.

I found myself being pulled and pushed backwards to the bed, until he was half-lying on me.

He kissed me again. I lost track of how long that kiss lasted.

We were both breathing hard when it ended.

His skin was flushed. He held me tighter, not looking at me now, but seemingly out the window. My hand was inside the gray T-shirt, my arm wrapped around his back. I felt scar tissue around the muscle, broken by smooth skin.

I was still caressing his back when he caught my wrist, pulling my fingers off him.

"We should stop." His voice was gruff. "Now, Allie."

"Okay," I said.

He looked down at me.

Before I could get my head around letting go of him, he was kissing me again. Emotion slid through me that time, a kind of disbelief mixed with wanting... I realized it was his. A few moments later, he rested his head on my shoulder. Pain flickered through me, and I realized that was his, too.

"Allie," he said. "...I've missed you. So much."

I swallowed, fighting a sudden hardness in my throat. I tugged on his hair.

"I missed you, too," I whispered.

He was looking at me again, and I felt the conflict, even before I saw it in his eyes. Everything hurt. My fingers clenched in his shirt.

"Revik," I blurted. "Please. What's the real reason? You can tell me."

Pain hardened his features. "Allie... *gaos.*"

"Are you still unsure about us? Do you need more time?"

The look on his face brought the pain back in a thick wave, intense enough that I closed my eyes, gripping his arms.

"Revik... please. Just tell me."

"Allie." His accent was thick again. "I'm not lying to you. This thing connecting us... it's fucking strong. I don't want you to feel trapped with me."

"I don't feel trapped!" I said.

He shook his head, his voice deep as he looked away. "You're not used to these kinds of *aleimic* pulls," he said. "You might not be able to tell the difference."

"I can tell the difference! I promise you, I can."

His pain hit at me again, sliding deeper into my light.

"I promised myself," he said. "I promised myself I wouldn't take advantage of this. Not until I knew what you wanted." He met my gaze, his jaw hard. "I loved you before Seattle. I know you don't trust me because of what I did, but please... *please* believe me about this. I'm doing this for you. Please."

I felt tears come to my eyes.

It mortified me, but I couldn't seem to stop it.

I saw him looking down at me, his expression helpless.

"We can't," he said. "We can't here, even if..." I saw him look around, at the room, at the bed. His pain slid through me again, and I let out a gasp.

Excruciatingly, his light started to withdraw from mine.

Something in me fought back.

I didn't mean to do it exactly; something about having him finally so close just opened all the floodgates.

I'd been in pain for so long I couldn't remember what it was like not being in pain. I couldn't remember the last time anyone had touched me, much less him—which brought back all those times of nearly touching him but not, of looking for him in the Barrier when he was with Terian just so I could feel him, sometimes only for a few seconds.

Some nights it took hours to find him.

I'd still look forward to being able to sleep so I could look.

My light flared towards his.

Everything went silent. I felt naked...

I don't know how it felt from his side. His breath caught.

"Alyson. Gods... baby... don't..."

"I'm sorry." Pain crippled me. "I'm sorry."

"Don't be sorry... Allie."

His fingers wound tighter into my hair. He leaned into me, and I let out a low cry, wrapping my legs around his. He let out a gasp and I could barely see through my light—or maybe through his, which coiled into mine invasively as I lay under him.

I felt him losing control.

I felt him go deeper, pulling at me, and my fingers clenched in his hair. His face grew taut, nearly hard, as his hand wrapped around my thigh.

"Revik… please." I felt him flinch. "Please."

His hand slid up to my hip, gripping me painfully.

"Please," I murmured, kissing his throat. "Please, baby."

He was pushing me then, hard. Pushing on my light, pushing me closed, pushing me back, holding me away from him.

He climbed off me before I knew what was happening.

I could only lie there, in more pain than I'd ever been in my life.

I couldn't see. Time passed—what felt like a long span of time but could have been seconds, or hours. I lay there, holding my stomach with one arm. I lost track of where he was. I felt completely alone, and broken.

When I could focus again, I found myself staring at the ceiling.

My arm was still wrapped around my body.

Blood warmed my face. I fought to speak, to pull myself back, but he spoke before I could. He was lying next to me, I realized, doing something to my light, but clinically, as if from a great distance.

"Vash said you went out this morning." His light continued to calm mine, his voice soft. "Are you all right?"

I didn't move.

I felt like I had that morning in Seattle, waking up like I'd been cracked open and reassembled with a few pieces missing. Shifting away from him on the bed, I fought to extricate my light.

The pain came back up in another thick, black wave.

"Slow," he murmured. He held my arms, pulling me back against him. I felt him caressing my fingers, holding my hand as he pulled me closer. "Allie. Tell me about the trip this morning. The helicopter."

I tried to think.

"No problems," I said. "We didn't have any problems." My voice sounded bleak. "It was only recon. We didn't get close."

I felt that part of me pulling on him still.

I couldn't stop it, or stop touching him apparently, as I caressed his arms where he held me. Swallowing, I leveled my voice.

"We couldn't see much. The fires are worse. There hasn't been any rain on that side of the mountains. A lot of dead people." I shook my head. "Too many. They burned the trees. They burned the bodies. Hiding what they did."

Tears came to my eyes as I remembered.

I remembered the smoke, the smell as we flew over, the dark, poisoned clouds. He seemed about to say something else, but I pushed his concern aside gently.

"I'm all right," I said. "I'm all right. I don't know what happened."

His arms tightened. "Allie."

"I'm sorry. I really am. I didn't mean—"

"Allie!" He caught my hand in his, silencing me. "Can we get food?"

Turning my head, I met his gaze, saw a kind of pleading there.

"Food." I forced my mind to logistics. Folding my arms to keep from touching him, I avoided his eyes. "Food. Sure. Here? Do you want me to get you something from the kitchen? Or—"

"No." He voice was adamant. "In the village. Outside. Are you hungry?"

"Yeah, I could eat…"

He was already climbing over where I lay.

He regained his feet before I realized what he was doing. Watching him open the closet doors, I held my stomach with the same arm, tensing against the pain that flared as soon as he moved away. I tried to block it, to not think about whatever just happened—or what I might have said to him when I lost it.

Wearing boxers, he snatched up a duffle that lay inside the closet doors.

He dug through the bag for pants, pulling them on without looking at me. This whole scene was suddenly reminding me a little too much of the ship.

"Revik, whatever I did, I—"

"No." He looked over his shoulder at me. "Allie, can we not talk here? Please." He tugged a thick shirt over the gray tee. "Please."

"Yeah," I said. "Okay." I closed my eyes. I wished there was a hole big enough to swallow me. "Revik." I forced my eyes open again. "Maybe you should just go. Without me, I mean. We can talk later."

Without answering, he pulled on his second shoe and straightened, hopping on one foot to settle it before he shrugged on a longer coat. He grabbed my jacket off the chair before approaching me on the bed.

Before I could protest, he caught my hand, pulling me roughly to my feet.

"Come on," he said, gruff.

CHAPTER 7
I'LL FIND US A PLACE

W e didn't talk as we walked down the unpaved road from the compound.

I followed his eyes when he raised a hand in greeting to a group of seers clustered on the porch of a nearby house.

I didn't know any of them, but I saw them there, every day.

They knew Revik.

They catcalled him, in several languages. I only caught part of it. Probably the parts they meant for me to catch.

A man yelled, "I thought they banned you, Dag-o-ies?"

"Been years," another called out, seconding that. "You allowed back here then?"

"Oooh." A girl laughed, waving. "Check him out! Nice clothes, worm-bait! Your new girl give you those?"

"You married the Bridge, Dags?" an Asian-looking seer asked, raising a beer bottle. "Why you outside? Why not in for *Sakka-weh?*" He made thrusting movements with his hips and the others laughed. "You having performance issues? Need some help, brother?"

Revik gave them a wan smile, but I saw him glance at me.

"Piss off," he said.

"Awww. You're still one of us, right? So when you gonna sic your woman on the worms of this town, brother?" He thumbed the metal collar around his neck. "Set your people free?"

Revik made a dismissive gesture. "Sober up. I'll buy your freedom, Yan-le."

"Liar."

Revik flicked his fingers towards the others. "You have witnesses."

The male seer leaned back on the steps on his elbows. "Living with them's made you soft, brother. Maybe your woman can straighten you out." He grinned, winking at me. "If not, send her my way. The Esteemed Bridge can share my bed any time she wants…"

I felt a whisper of annoyance off Revik, but he just gave them another dismissive wave, not slowing his strides down the hill.

After we'd gone a few more steps, he glanced at me.

"It's a tradition, you know. To harass newlyweds. We'll get a lot of that."

I watched his face, not speaking.

His mind was somewhere else again.

I didn't know if I should be grateful, or worried. I knew he would tell me; I could feel it. Still, I wished I could read him better. He was closed up tight as a vault, which was getting harder not to take personally.

I was about to shove my hands in my pockets when he reached out, taking my hand before I could finish the motion.

"You're misunderstanding me, Allie. I just don't want to talk here."

"But what is 'here,' Revik? It clearly wasn't the room, or even the compound—"

"The construct, Allie. It ends at the border of the village."

Feeling a sort of light bulb go off, I glanced back up the hill.

A few minutes later, we reached the bottom, and turned onto the main street of Seertown, which was already full of midday shoppers and peddlers. We hadn't walked a full block when Revik pulled me through the crowd into a bricked side street—well, an alley, really, although in Seertown the difference was academic.

Before I could ask him anything, he caught me around the waist and half-carried me to the wall of a small store facing the main road.

I clasped his neck in surprise.

When he kissed me that time, his mouth wasn't careful—or particularly gentle.

He kissed me, hard, holding me against the wall as he fisted a hand in my hair, pulling on my light until I gasped. Sliding his body between my legs, he kissed me again, his arm clenched around my waist tightly enough that I barely had my weight on my toes.

I couldn't breathe until he paused.

I gripped his hair as he kissed me again, harder as I arched against him.

He made a low sound that I felt down to my feet... then abruptly pulled away, resting his forehead on mine.

Pain coiled around him, pulling on me, catching my breath.

"Allie... *gaos*." He kissed my face, pressing his cheek briefly to mine. "What are you trying to do to me? Don't you know every seer in the compound felt that?"

"Oh." My face grew hot. Understanding reached me. "Oh! Okay."

"The construct... it's completely open. I thought you knew."

I shook my head. "Sorry." I smiled, embarrassed. "Everyone probably figured it didn't matter, not for me anyway. They all know I haven't had sex with an actual person since..." I trailed, as something else occurred to me.

I tensed as the realization deepened.

Then I remembered who I was with. Glancing up, I tried to cut off the thought, but I already saw Revik looking at me.

About then, I probably turned bright red.

I felt conflict on him as he stared at me. When I tried to read him for the rest of it, he pushed me back. I knew he'd heard me, though.

Great. Just... perfect.

I felt my face burn hotter, and tried to decide if I should say something.

Wonderful. This was so completely how I'd wanted this morning to go—with my boyfriend-slash-husband picturing me masturbating in front of a bunch of single guys the entire period he'd been imprisoned and tortured.

I bit my lip when he still wouldn't look at me.

"Hey," I said, my voice low. "No one told me."

I saw his jaw harden. Once again, I was ready to climb into a hole.

Maybe one that popped out in, say, Portugal.

"Look, I'm really sorry."

His eyes swiveled in my direction. "Allie! Why do you think I would be angry at you for this?" His accent worsened. "It's nothing... it's none of my business. I'm just trying to think of a good reason why I shouldn't kick the living shit out of every seer in that compound for not telling you..."

Sliding my arms further around his neck, I tugged on his hair.

"Hey," I said. "Stop, okay?" I felt my face flush when he met my gaze, and forced myself to shrug. "So a few of them might have gotten their ya-yas off while I was sexual frustration girl. So what? Forget it."

He held me tighter. I felt pain on him again, mixed with what felt like affection.

More than affection—a dense emotion wound into my light, a confused mixture he seemed to be holding back, or muting maybe. I felt him remembering my face from earlier that morning, and it was odd seeing myself from his angle, lying on the bed, hair fanned on the covers as I caressed his face.

Without warning, liquid sexuality rode through him and into me.

My hand clenched the back of his neck as he lowered his voice.

"Allie... honey," he murmured. "I'm so sorry."

He kissed me again, but softer that time, almost gentle.

Even so, my mind glazed over when he fell into it, leaning without pressing into me. Seconds later, he drew back, releasing me with a reluctance I could now feel.

Avoiding my eyes, he took a full stride away from the wall.

His voice came out short, his accent stronger again.

"I am hungry," he said. "Can we eat?"

I stood by the wall, half bent over, fighting to control my light.

Embarrassed, I nodded, trying to pull myself back into that space where I'd been for more than a year—that shut off, commander-type space I'd cultivated when I didn't have any choice. I knew Revik could see past it, but at that particular moment, I didn't care.

I'd just gotten thrown into the deep end of what it was like to be around him full-time again. Only now, with us openly talking about sex, it would be about a hundred times worse. I knew it was a package deal, part of sharing light with another seer, but knowing that didn't make it any easier.

He walked with me to a place I'd been to before, high up on the hill on one of the tributary streets off the main market roads. We climbed the steps to the top-floor restaurant, which had a view of the entire valley under a plastic corrugated roof.

They also had some of the best Tibetan food in town.

Over lunch—or breakfast, maybe—we talked about India, the compound, what I'd been doing. I edited what I told him. I didn't mention getting shot at a few weeks earlier, for example, or much at all about my trips out of Seertown.

I saw him frown a few times anyway, as if reading between the lines of at least some of what I didn't say.

He didn't reference what had happened that morning until he walked me back.

Reaching the border between the town and the construct, he kissed me goodbye, saying only that he had business to do that afternoon.

When I got nervous, he kissed me again, pulling me to him.

"Allie," he said, soft. "I won't be gone long. I promise."

I glanced up. "It's not that. You're being weird. Even for you." I tugged on his hand. "I can't tell if you're mad at me... or what."

"Mad at you?" He kissed my cheek, clicking softly. "No. Maybe a little at myself." He fingered hair out of my eyes, and I felt a pulse of regret on him again. "I'm sorry, Allie. About this morning."

"Sorry?" I smiled. "What for? You were rational guy... as usual. I'm the one who lost it." I tugged on his shirt. "Maybe we just shouldn't be making out on beds for a while. Find a nice park bench. Or an alley."

"I think that would be a bad idea," he said cryptically.

Giving him a mock frown, I smacked his chest lightly. "So, what? I blew it? Honestly, Dags. It's fine. I'll be ready for it next time."

His eyes turned opaque.

I could feel there was something he wasn't telling me.

I was about to ask, when he cut me off.

"I'll find us a place," he said.

"A place?"

"Where we can talk. Privately. In the meantime, be careful, okay?" He kissed my face. I felt pain on him again, enough that my fingers clenched on the fabric of his coat. "Chandre's waiting for you at the compound.

The town isn't particularly safe, either." He kissed me again. "I'll find us something, Allie. I promise."

Safe? I wondered.

I didn't voice it aloud though, and he left me standing there, watching after him as he disappeared back into the crowds of Seertown market.

CHAPTER 8
CLAIM

"Hey… Bridge! Wait! Stop, okay?"

I hadn't made it through the courtyard when his voice halted my steps.

I turned, a little warily.

I'd noticed more than my usual quota of stares just in my short walk through the common rooms to get outside. Given what Revik said about us being overheard, I wasn't particularly thrilled with the prospect of hearing details of their reactions.

The man running up to me would probably tell me.

And keep telling me… even after I told him to stop.

Were the stares because they'd overheard Revik and I talking? Were they just curious because I was the Bridge, and until now hadn't been sexually involved with anyone? Or was I now the pathetic wife who couldn't seduce her own husband?

Maygar grunted a laugh, jogging up to my side.

"Hardly," he said, a little out of breath.

I gave him a sharp look. "Mind your own business, Maygar. You're on my shit list already, you know." At his raised eyebrow, I scowled. "What's with you taking off for Cairo? Didn't even have the decency to tell me…"

Trailing, I stopped, taking in his appearance.

One whole side of his broad, tanned face was covered in fresh bruises, as were his knuckles. Doing the math with the appearance of Revik's hands, I exhaled in exasperation.

"What happened? What did you say to him?"

"Nothing he didn't have coming." Maygar made a dismissive gesture, folding his arms. He gave me a quick once-over, a half-smile.

"Come on, Bridge. Spar with me."

I snorted a laugh. "You ran all the way over here to see if I'd let you take swings at my head?" I started to walk around him, heading for my cabin on the other side of the garden.

"If you want to annoy Revik," I said. "...there are easier ways."

Maygar stepped in my path.

"I doubt that," he said, smiling. His eyes were serious. "Come on, Bridge. I want to spar, and you're faster than these bozos." He gestured at a cluster of seers sitting on the benches near the sparring circle. "You're right that he won't like it... that's why I thought we could do it now. You're alone, right?"

He glanced back at the main compound, his voice casual.

"Where is he?"

My eyes flickered to his, sharp.

"I don't know," I said. "Maybe you should go look for him."

Again, I started to walk around him, but he stepped in my path.

"Hey, hey, Bridge." Maygar caught my arm, lightly. "Don't be so touchy. You know me. I didn't mean anything by it."

But I stopped dead.

I looked between his dark brown eyes, suspicious.

"Yeah," I said. "I do know you. Why are you being so nice to me? What's going on?"

"Nothing." He released my arm, holding up his hands in a peace gesture. "I want to spar is all. I figure I'm not going to see much of you for the next few weeks, so—"

"Really?" I stared at him. "And why is that?"

That time, Maygar really did look surprised.

Recovering, he gave another half-laugh, clicking to himself, but his voice sounded close to angry.

"That *dugra-te di aros* really doesn't tell you anything, does he?" His voice hardened. "Where is he, Bridge? Saying goodbye to all the unwillings he won't be able to afford, now that he has a wife to keep? Is that why he was saving his cock this morning?"

I felt my cheeks bloom bright red.

Son of a bitch heard us—of course he had.

If anyone would be listening in, it would be Maygar.

"You know, hitting you is sounding better and better," I said.

"Good!" he said, grinning. Slinging his arm around my shoulders, he led me towards the sparring circle. "I have money on me winning in three rounds. Point system. Twenty solid, minimum. Five spread to win. We'll have Yerin count. He's honest."

"Whatever," I muttered, elbowing him off me.

Yanking the sheepskin coat off my arms and tossing it on one of the stone benches, I saw a group of seers walking over from the common room inside the main compound.

All of them were male, of course, which was the case all over free Seertown. Female seers were five or six times more likely to be stolen at a young age. It meant that the majority of free, unowned females lived in the mountains and in underground communities.

It also meant the compound contained a roughly 90/10 split, male to female, which caused problems among the males... especially since over a third of those females were either married or liked other females, like Chandre.

I'd seen stats that showed murder of owners of girlfriends or wives as the single most frequent cause of non-military seer murder of humans.

"What do they want?" I grumbled, motioning towards the onlookers.

"Alyson." Maygar laughed. "They want to see the Bridge get her ass kicked!" He jumped up and down on the balls of his toes, smacking his hands together. "Come on. I feel a shut out coming on... easy twenty."

I watched Jon and Cass come out of the compound, too. They must have either asked or followed when they saw the place emptying out.

Jon was shaking his head at me already.

When I glanced at Cass, she held up her hands in a question.

I knew what she meant. I shrugged in response, letting her know I had no idea where he was. Then it struck me. Maygar might not be the only one annoyed at Revik. Hesitating on that thought for a split second, I shrugged it off.

This would be a quick spar, no big deal.

Revik didn't even need to know about it, if I didn't let myself get too bloodied up.

I swung my arms a few times, then stepped into the circle, waiting for Maygar.

He entered the other end of the ring, smiling.

I found Yerin among the faces. His expression appeared close to Jon's, meaning pinched and faintly worried, which was unusual for him. Yerin was generally the unflappable type, so I found myself giving him a second look.

You're judging this thing, right? I asked him. *Don't let him cheat, Yerin.*

"I won't cheat." Maygar grinned, falling into stance, his hands up in rough claws.

Half-smiling back, I shook my head and fell into stance on my side of the circle. Maygar acted like a big child half the time, but I couldn't hate him the way Revik did.

In an odd kind of way, we were friends.

I held up a hand, open palmed.

When the crowd quieted a little, I said the scripted words.

"Come, then."

Still smiling, Maygar circled, once.

He leapt in, a test as much as anything, and a total departure from his usual style, which I knew pretty well from training with him in the past. I stepped easily out of the way, shifting sideways and throwing a hook at his ribs.

I managed to surprise him. Sucking in a breath, he twisted around, threw a counter. I dodged that, too, aiming a kick at his sternum.

I connected, hard, pushing him back.

"You're a little wound up, Bridge." Maygar smiled, bouncing backwards on his toes. "Something bothering you, that you have all this aggression?"

"You're a pig, Maygar. Come a little closer, why don't you…?"

"Why aren't you grappling with your man right now?"

"Maybe I wasn't in the mood."

Nervous laughter erupted in the crowd of seers.

I caught Jon looking quizzically at Cass with my peripheral vision, and that's when Maygar's fist connected solidly with my jaw, just before he kicked my thigh with the flat of his foot. I staggered back, ducking in time to avoid another throw at my temple with his other hand.

"That's two," he said, smiling.

"You're forgetting I got you first," I said, smiling back. "Twice."

"No spread. Two and two," Yerin verified.

Maygar stepped sideways when I went in the next time.

I threw a few hard jabs, then a fast cross. One of the jabs connected, but not with enough force to drive him back. I was faster than him, but his arms were twice the size of mine, so it counted when he got me—an advantage he pressed.

I needed to hit him twice as often, and I couldn't be sloppy, or he'd stun me and make me into a piñata until I recovered.

He blocked a high and low kick, one after the other, then got more serious, throwing combinations of about ten, twelve, punches and kicks. He only got me a few times, but I found myself sinking into this mode, where my head fell silent, and I felt my limbs moving on their own. It felt good.

I was fighting well, and I liked this mindless space, where my body just reacted.

I circled back after a few more clinches, then darted in and got him with a feint to the knee followed by an immediate kick to the head, which connected.

Maygar staggered.

I slid around his returning kick and got him again in the sternum.

I was winning, which felt good, too.

I couldn't get cocky, though.

It would get tougher once we entered in sight skills.

If we made it to grappling, I'd be in for a serious fight.

Mulei was close to a lot of the human, Shaolin-based fighting arts, but only in the initial levels of fighting. Sparring in *mulei* had very definite rules. Straight hits and kicks in the first segment. No grappling or sweeps until it got called by the judge, usually in the last third of the fight, because that was when fights got dirty.

And no sight skills until eight hits had been reached by at least one opponent.

"That's seven," I told Maygar. "Five for you."

"Hmmm. That's not too bad, Bridge… but you're still going to lose."

I smiled, shaking my head. "You think so? Why is that?"

His eyes grew still, his voice soft.

"Because I want it more, Allie."

He never used my real name.

Him saying it now sent an odd shiver down my spine.

I was still staring at him when he leapt up, catching me off guard with a solid, full-force hit to my eye. He put his weight behind it, and it sent me backwards in a heap. I rolled, fought to get back up, but he got me three more times in quick succession...

...and then we were into sight skills.

Without waiting, he slammed into me with his *aleimi*.

He knocked me halfway out of my body before I turned, hitting him with a spinner in the lower half of his chest.

He'd have the advantage here, since he could split his consciousness without choking like I did. But I was getting better at accessing structures in my light. We couldn't just go all out and whale on each other anyway. There were rules here, too.

No hits to the structures above the head.

No breaking anything.

That left mostly shoves, misdirection and tapping to drain light.

Maygar went straight for a tap. Before I could shield, I felt him aim for the separation pain. Seeing it as an opening in my light, he fought to resonate with it.

Realizing too late that I was wide open from my morning with Revik, I jerked back in alarm. Unfortunately, panic opens your shields, so in my haste to get away from his probe...

I let him in.

He laughed in triumph.

We traded a few blows while I fought to keep him out of the Barrier and away from the tap. Then he circled back, putting some distance between us.

Still grinning, he slid into the line he'd created between us.

Before I could take a breath, he pulled roughly with the part of him that resonated.

When I opened involuntarily, he forced his way into me as far as he could go.

Pain blinded me.

My knees buckled. I fell before I realized what happened.

Gasping for breath, I slammed out instinctively when he came towards me, cracking him with my *aleimi*.

It broke his focus on the tap and the pain ebbed, briefly—but I didn't have much time.

Jumping up, I ran at him before he could re-establish the link.

While he was still halfway out of his body, I punched him in the stomach, then front kicked him before he could recover, hitting him in the upper chest.

He backed off, landing more of himself in his body.

He laughed aloud though, triumphant.

Was it good for you, Bridge?

What he'd done was within the rules, but it pissed me off, and he felt it.

What's wrong? That part a little tender, Bridge?

I guess if it's the only way you can hold your own, I retorted.

I told you, Bridge. I'm going to win.

Maybe I wasn't only talking about in the ring.

The humor on Maygar's face evaporated.

I heard snickers in the watching seers. Maygar's pulse of anger quieted them.

"Call it, Yerin." His eyes never left mine.

"Physical hits only for points." Yerin reminded us. "Legal play. Thirteen even."

"You ready to give up, Bridge?" he asked.

But I was remembering something Chandre told me about taps, about how every connection goes two ways. Without answering him, I split my *aleimi*, just long enough to find the thread.

The fact that he hit at such an obvious target actually made it easier.

In seconds, I pinpointed the tap.

Without waiting, I jumped out of my body.

Using several structures in my *aleimi* at once, I slid into his light...

...and yanked ruthlessly, draining him in one hard hit.

When my eyes clicked back into focus, he was down on one knee, panting. Pain rippled off him. He stared up at me, eyes glazed.

Smiling, I kicked him in the face.

Guess it's been a while for you, too, I sent.

I punched him again, and he fell to his back. I circled him once, getting in another hit and two more kicks before I backed off, letting him climb to his feet.

I gave him a taunting smile, but he didn't return it, or even look angry.

Instead, his eyes held a focus I'd never seen.

If I didn't know better, I'd think he was fighting for his life.

"Jesus," I said. "Just how much money do you have on this fight?"

Yerin cleared his throat.

"Open format. Grappling and sweeps." He looked at me, eyes worried. "I'm sorry, Alyson. I have to call it. You've got eighteen."

I blinked at Yerin, unclear why he was apologizing.

When I turned back...

Maygar punched me in the face. He moved so quietly I hadn't felt him. He swept my leg in the same heartbeat, knocking me flat.

I landed on my back, the wind knocked out of me.

I threw my hands behind my head to jump to my feet, but he leapt onto my middle, sitting astride me. He grabbed my arms where I'd reached back, pinning me.

"What if I claim you?" he said, panting.

Furious that I'd been so stupid, I struggled before meeting his gaze. A strange light had come to his eyes. I noticed his *aleimi* suddenly, snaking around me. He wasn't just pulling on the tap; he was doing the equivalent of feeling me up with his light.

Bucking my body, I struggled to get him off, but he held me there, fighting his way to my wrists despite my squirming, pinning me to the dirt.

"He's not even here to argue it," he growled.

Maygar looked down at my body.

I tried to head-butt him, but he moved out of the way.

His smile faded. Leaning closer, he held me down with his chest. He caressed my face with his, kissing my neck, then my cheek.

I froze, stopped breathing.

I would never have refused you, Allie.

I stared up at him in shock.

Kissing my face again, caressing it with his fingers, he raised his head, looking around at the rest of the crowd.

"He hasn't consummated," he said loudly. "I have the right." He scanned faces, looking for dissent. "There are witnesses. Many. You all heard her ask and saw him refuse her. Does anyone dispute that I have the right?"

I stared around at the others, trying to regain my breath, gripping his wrist in one hand, doing my best to dig my nails into his skin, to get him off.

Then his words really sank in.

I didn't understand, not really, no more than I understood half the seer rules and customs thrown my way, but it struck me that he'd planned this, that there was something happening here that had nothing to do with the reasons he'd given me for the fight.

Worse, he had accomplices.

I tried again to kick him off. Given that he weighed about a hundred pounds more than me, all of it muscle, my attempts were futile, and only seemed to reinforce my helplessness under him.

Normally, my strategy with sweeps went something like this, "Don't get knocked down."

I stared up at Yerin, panting. "Yerin! You're judging this. I surrender. He's won—"

Maygar punched me in the face, hard.

Shock silenced me, as much as the blow.

My head rolled on my neck.

"I don't accept," he growled. "We said play until twenty. Five point spread. That's only seventeen for me." His voice grew cold. "You have eighteen, Bridge. You can't surrender. I have six more hits before it's done."

When I could focus my eyes again, I stared up at him, bewildered, still dazed from the hit. Seers weren't exactly chivalrous when they fought. You could hit a downed or pinned opponent—in fact, it was pretty much expected. But I'd never had anyone refuse to let me tap out before hitting the point spread.

I realized suddenly, what he was doing.

He was keeping the coercion part of this legal somehow, doing it within the auspices of a fight. I stared up at him in disbelief, still fighting to process what my brain had already figured out.

"You wouldn't," I said to him.

Maygar stared back at me, all the humor in his face gone.

Holding my wrists in one hand, he caressed my face until I jerked away. His eyes shone dark and hard, a hunter's eyes, and I realized I was in trouble.

My commander's voice returned.

"Game over," I said. "And I'm not laughing. Get him the *fuck* off me!" I looked around at the watching seers. "Now! That's an order!"

The faces staring down at me paled, but none of the seers moved.

"What is this?" I demanded. "Gang rape? Are you a bunch of animals now?"

"He has the right, Alyson," Yerin said.

I swiveled my head, staring at Yerin in disbelief. "What is this?" I stared around at these people, many of whom I'd begun to think of as my friends.

I looked for Jon and Cass.

I saw them on the sidelines, being held by seers. Jon's eyes were glazed, not-home, the same with Cass, but I saw Cass's hand on her sidearm, as if she'd realized something was wrong right before they knocked her out.

They'd imprisoned my damned friends. Like common worms.

Fighting a rage that boiled up through my limbs, I struggled.

I looked for Chandre, but didn't see her. I didn't see Grent, Tenzi or Balidor, either. I looked back at Yerin, trying reason, knowing it was the only thing that would work on him.

"You can't subject me to a custom I know nothing about. You can't." I fought Maygar's hands. "Where's Vash? He's the keeper of custom, isn't he? I have the right of contest, don't I? At least *ask* him…"

I reached out with my light but Maygar blocked me, preventing my scan for Vash.

In desperation, I reached for Revik—

—and Maygar slammed me with his light.

He hit me hard enough that I nearly blacked out.

When I opened my eyes, blood trickled from my nose. I tasted it in my mouth. I sent another flare, trying to reach Revik again. Maygar blocked it, slamming my light again and I gasped, tasting more blood.

"He broke the rules…" I gasped. "Taps only, no damage."

"She's right." Yerin turned to Maygar, his voice worried. "Don't do that again. We'll shield her from him, if it's necessary."

I stared at the circle of faces. I realized none of them would help me.

"I'll be a good husband to you," Maygar said. ...*better than him.*

He shifted his weight. I felt his erection press against my belly, hard enough and deliberate enough that it couldn't be a mistake.

Letting out a yell, I fought him, still in disbelief as he unhooked his belt.

He slid his hand under my shirt, and I fought harder, shrieking.

I pleaded with him when I couldn't get him off, but he pinned me with his body, arm and legs. He was breathing harder. Sweat had formed on his forehead and upper lip. Pushing up my shirt, he caressed my skin, putting light into his fingers, pulling on mine. He kissed my breast, putting light into his tongue.

The same hand slid into my pants, between my legs.

Yelling out in disbelief, I screamed, trying harder to writhe away.

He pulled on my *aleimi* through the tap, holding me still, and my light responded without my willing it.

Pain coursed through me, nearly blinding.

His fingers were inside me then and I cried out, begging the others to stop him. I heard him groan, felt his other hand tighten on me as his weight grew heavy. He stopped what he was doing long enough to untie my pants, forcing them down over my hips, his hands suddenly urgent.

Panic exploded in my chest. Something in me ripped open.

I couldn't see.

My light flared around me. There was a folding sensation...

...and then the weight on me was gone.

I heard yells somewhere in the back of my mind.

I heard excited voices as I scrambled to my feet.

I couldn't see. Light blinded me, and yet I felt drained of light, too, almost drunk without it. I tied up my pants, fingers fumbling with the knots, my nose still bleeding. I saw blurred faces as they backed away from me.

Then I ran.

I dodged through bodies to get out of the sparring circle, out of the crowd, out of the courtyard. Once I broke free I sprinted as fast as I could, not into the compound where they might trap me again, but through the garden, jumping over benches and weaving to avoid trees, throwing myself down the hill at the garden's edge and half sliding, half running down the steep, weeded bank.

I heard someone call my name, but I only ran faster, until all I could hear was blood pumping in my ears and the sound of my feet through grass and gravel on the street below. I ran between buildings until I met another entrance to the trees, then I sprinted as hard as I could up the sloped dirt path leading into the forest.

I ran and ran, until I couldn't breathe, feeling air cut my throat as branches whipped past.

When I finally stopped, I didn't know where I was anymore.

CHAPTER 9
CUSTOM

Balidor heard a scream. It was a female's scream.

Hair rose on the back of his neck.

He glanced at his two companions, Laska and Grent. Laska unholstered her sidearm, nodding to Grent as he did the same.

Wordlessly, they took up a fan formation. Balidor followed them through the side entrance between buildings, his *aleimi* in hunting mode.

When they reached the courtyard, Balidor stopped short. Laska and Grent halted, too.

A crowd stood around the sparring ring in the corner of the weed-choked yard. Balidor recognized the Bridge's two humans. They were standing too still; he could see more than one seer holding them in restraint.

Staring between legs, he felt his chest clench.

Taking in the totality of the scene, he remembered that morning, the flare the Bridge sent out while she'd been with Dehgoies.

He swore in Chinese, recognizing the seer astride her now, a youngster named Maygar who'd been acting as her bodyguard for about a year. Balidor had gotten a bad feeling about him from the beginning, even apart from his past, his ridiculous pretensions to revolutionary status and his Rook mother.

He chambered a bullet, walking forward, cursing Dehgoies at each stride.

What the hell had he been thinking, letting her come back here alone?

He was about to shout out, to call a halt to whatever Maygar had put in motion, when he felt a pulse of what could only be terror, and realized it came from the Bridge. The intensity of it brought him to a halt.

The same sharp inhale spread to others as it hit the crowd.

A burst of light illuminated the Barrier space.

Then the punk, Maygar, lifted off her.

No—he *flew* off her.

He jerked like a rag doll through the air. Soaring about thirty feet across the courtyard, he slammed into a set of stone benches, his back and neck connecting solidly. He didn't make a sound apart from the thud of flesh.

Once he fell to the dirt, he didn't move.

There was an instant of dead silence.

Then the Bridge was on her feet.

Everyone backed away. She stared around as if half-blind, fumbling with her pants, pulling them up over her hips, wiping blood off her face... and her eyes were light, just light. It was the last glimpse Balidor got of her face before she bolted, running not for the street or for the compound but through the garden.

She was fleeing, he realized. Not just Maygar, but all of them.

Hesitating only a heartbeat, Balidor broke into a run after her.

He felt Laska and Grent do the same, only a little slower to react than he. They chased her through the garden, but she had more than a hundred paces on them, and leapt through the greenery as fast as a rabbit. When he saw her reach the edge of the plateau, he yelled her name, but she didn't turn, or even slow down.

Running at top speed as she approached the edge, she catapulted off the grassy border, windmilling her legs on tennis-shoed feet.

She vanished beyond the bank.

By the time he, Grent and Laska reached the edge of the same piece of lawn, she was disappearing into an alley between two apartment buildings, still running all out.

Cursing, indecisive, Balidor tried to decide what to do.

If he went after her now, she'd be sure to think he'd rape her, too.

According to traditional law, he even had the right.

Any marriage not consummated within six lunar cycles could be consummated by force through right of second claim. That is, providing that the female in question had been witnessed asking for sex and being refused by the husband.

It was an old, backwards law.

Balidor couldn't even remember the last time he'd heard of it being invoked, other than in jest. Severe separation pain was like a drug for unattached seers. Anyone nearby couldn't help but be affected. The elders made the rule during a period where those types of conflicts had been endemic to the political situation—meaning, a couple of thousand years ago.

For Maygar to pull that shit now was like a human evoking Biblical law as an excuse to stone someone to death.

He'd chosen his witnesses carefully—even Yerin, who was a carrier of the law to his core. Yerin would go along with it simply because it was still technically legal on the books.

"Barbarism," Balidor muttered.

Laska laid a hand on his shoulder.

He patted her fingers, feeling through the simple contact that the incident had shocked her, too. She was angry, both for personal reasons and on the Bridge's behalf. Like Balidor, she also worried they now had a serious problem on their hands. Given the number of people involved, the Bridge may never trust any of them again.

And then there was Dehgoies.

Everyone knew the story with Dehgoies and the Bridge.

Dehgoies' only crime lay in not explaining the facts of life to his wife at an earlier date, before her ignorance caused a near-aneurism in every unattached male in hearing distance.

He'd done everything technically right afterwards.

He removed her from the construct, offered apologies all around and accepted full blame. He'd even gone so far as to make it publicly known that he had every intention of dealing with the situation formally... and at the earliest possible opportunity.

He only erred in judgment, perhaps, by leaving her alone.

So in addition to being a pig for trying it—and he was a pig, there was no doubt about that—Maygar was an unmitigated fool.

If he wanted a wife that badly he could have gone to Europe or America, where most of the females lived. Mate poaching was a rare crime in the seer world for one simple reason: someone usually died.

It was one instance where a seer killing another seer would generally be overlooked.

Especially where coercion was involved.

Maygar would pay for his stupidity, Balidor thought grimly, and likely before the end of the day, assuming the Bridge hadn't killed him already.

He looked from Laska to Grent and sighed.

Nodding assent to Grent's unspoken question, he motioned them back towards the compound and the main street above.

They now had the unhappy job of finding Dehgoies and explaining to him what had happened.

That was assuming he hadn't already felt his wife's terror and was on his way up there to rip someone's head off with his bare hands.

I KEPT WALKING.

I didn't have a destination in mind.

I wasn't thinking at all yet really, but remained heavily shielded, walking in what I hoped was the opposite direction of Seertown. I wasn't ready to use the Barrier, not when I didn't know who might be looking for me.

I didn't call Revik.

Someone would tell him.

Hell, he probably knew, by now.

I sealed my light tight instead, giving myself the space to think. Reaching the top of a tree-lined ridge, I paused to catch my breath in the thin air. I was sweating. I didn't miss my coat yet, but I knew I would if I didn't find shelter by sunset.

Or earlier, if the weather changed, as it often did up here.

At the thought, I wiped my face, and realized there was still dried blood on it from when Maygar hit me with his light. I wiped it off as best I could.

For the first time, I felt my throat close.

I stood there for a moment, sniffling like a kid in the cold air, rubbing my face with my hand. Mostly, I think I was in disbelief.

I didn't know what to do. I had nowhere to go.

I should probably just call Revik, get it over with.

But I wasn't ready to face him yet, either.

I didn't want to explain how it happened, or think about why I'd ignored all the red flags around Maygar's weird behavior. I didn't want to deal with Revik's anger, or his sympathy, or his grief. I just wanted a quiet place to regroup.

A different voice rose in my mind.

You could come with me, Bridge.

I turned so fast my foot slipped on the edge of the cliff. I lost and regained my balance, but the close-call brought my heart pounding to my throat.

I'll leave you be, the voice added.

I thrust my hands out in front of me, ready to fight.

Just an offer, Bridge, the voice sent, softer. *No harm meant.*

"Get away from me!" I nearly shouted. "I mean it! Get back!"

Thinking it must be someone from the Guard, someone sent by Vash or Yerin or Balidor, I reached reflexively for my sidearm.

But I'd left for breakfast that morning without it.

Of course I had. Revik was with me.

What a complete and utter idiot I was.

"I'll do to you what I did to him," I said, my voice an open threat. "Come near me, and I'll throw you off the damned mountain! I swear I will!"

"Shh," they said aloud. "Won't hurt you, Bridge. Promise."

The physical voice sounded different than what I'd heard in my head.

It was deeper, rougher. It also spoke a kind of seer patois I'd only heard from the much older generation. I heard a hitch, like labored breaths. Or maybe laughter.

"Won't bite our precious leader," they said. "Or rape you, neither."

My heart pounded at her words, but my fear was gradually being replaced by confusion. The voice didn't sound like it belonged to anyone I knew.

It sounded old. It also sounded female.

"Aye. I'm old," the voice acknowledged. "Female, too."

"Who are you?" I asked.

"Don't worry. You're safe enough with me. Tough seer like you…"

For some reason, I wanted to laugh.

My mind went into overdrive, reminding me of seers who pretended to be friendly or harmless, only to turn on me. Hell, it could be one of Terian's. He'd done the same thing on that cruise ship, waited for me and Revik to be separated before he sent his people after both of us. He could have paid Maygar to jump me.

Now here I was, in the woods.

Half beat-up and weepy, just waiting to be picked off by one of his goons.

The old woman clicked audibly.

No grand conspiracies, Bridge. Just ordinary stupidity. He's his father's boy. Passionate. Not too bright, though.

"Maygar? Are you talking about Maygar?" Hearing her assent through the Barrier, I frowned. "Who's his father?"

"Knew him as a boy. Knew lots of seers as boys. Girls, too." I heard that wheezing laughter again. *Not you though, Bridge. Not you. Been a long time since you and I shared a meal together.*

Emotion clouded my mind, forcing me to wipe my eyes again.

I lowered my hands. "Just leave me alone, all right?"

"Pahhh. You are loved. More than you know."

Her words angered me for some reason.

"Great," I said. "I'll keep that in mind." Biting my lip, I went on in a more diplomatic voice. "Look, if you don't mind, I'd just really like some time to myself. I don't mean to be rude, but I…"

I trailed as the old woman pushed her way through thick-branched trees.

When she hit the sunlight in full view, I found my words drying up entirely.

She really hadn't been kidding about her age.

Before me stood the oldest-looking seer I'd ever seen.

Fine wrinkles accented the features of her oval face—so fine they reminded me of a baby turtle I once held in my palm, each wrinkle of its neck as thin as a thread. But her skin didn't look like an old human's, either. The near-perfection of the lines gave her dark, sun-beaten skin a smooth, almost alien quality.

She still managed to make Vash look young, despite her hair being as black as a raven's. Her pale eyes shone at me, strangely familiar.

The woman smiled, and the flash of her teeth surprised me. White and straight, they resembled the teeth of a twenty-year-old human.

She continued walking towards me until I raised my hands a second time.

"No," I cautioned. "Stay there. Please. Don't get too close."

She halted obediently. *Do you know me?*

"No," I said. "I've never seen you before."

Even so, I hesitated. A lot of the mountain seers didn't get down to Seertown much.

But this woman clearly knew who I was.

"Do you live around here?" I made a respectful gesture. "I could come to visit you another time, perhaps? Today, you've caught me on a bad day."

"But you'll be needing shelter, won't you?" she asked.

I blinked at the woman's pale, almost colorless eyes, fighting with the familiarity in them. She knew I'd been running from an attempted rape, she knew who I was, offered me shelter, asked if I knew her. Should I know her?

She studied me right back with those light-filled eyes.

"Biological, that's right," she said. "His mother's sister." She chuckled in that deep voice. "So he can't get rid of me. Though he's tried hard enough."

"Who?" I lowered my hands. "Who tried to get rid of you?" I was beginning to think she might be a bit senile. "A friend of yours?"

Your husband, the old seer sent. *I'm your aunt. By marriage.*

For an instant I doubted her.

Then I refocused on her face, understanding at once why I recognized her eyes.

They were Revik's eyes, only more slanted at the corners.

I still couldn't quite believe it. I'd been so sure he didn't have any biological family left. His adoptive family was related to him distantly in some way, but this woman looked like a bona fide relative.

"That's right," she said, nodding. "His mother's sister. Like I said."

Conscious suddenly of how I must look, I bowed stiffly.

Meeting family was a big deal among seers.

At one point, I was even taught the proper way to greet senior family members, but my mind was a complete blank. I bowed again, my hands at mid-chest. I figured that was at least less likely to cause overt offense.

"Apologies, Aunt. As I said—"

"A bad day, yes." She smiled, but I saw seriousness in her face. *A very bad day. For others, as well.*

Her eyes brightened as she glanced over the cliff.

Her stare carried a distance that made me strangely nostalgic.

"Got something to show you, Bridge," she said. "This isn't about your mate, or what happened back there. This is about you, and your new problem." Her pale eyes met mine. "You'll come with me? I'll call off the dogs."

I glanced over my shoulder, seeking what held her gaze.

A gold-feathered eagle drifted up and down in the currents just beyond the edge of the cliff where I stood.

I looked back towards her.

"Yeah," I said, trying a bit of the patois. "Sure. Just us girls. Sounds good."

At my stiff accent, the old woman laughed, and I smiled.

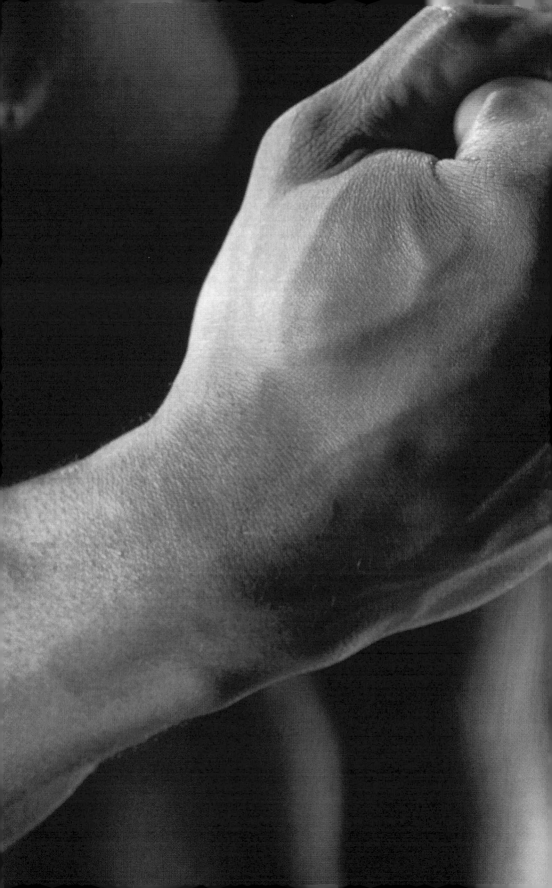

CHAPTER 10
CONSEQUENCE

J on heard the commotion before he realized what it meant.

Revik was back.

He glanced at Cass, who paled a little under her tan.

Then, wordlessly, both of them got up.

They'd been staying out of the way since the incident with Allie, although they'd talked quietly between them about what they should do.

They'd even wondered whether they should go looking for her, in the hopes she might want to talk to them more than any of the seers. Jon didn't particularly want to see any of those seers, either—definitely not the ones who turned him and Cass into wax dolls, then just stood there gawking while Maygar tried to rape Allie.

Unfortunately, despite the paralysis, Jon remembered all of it.

That included seeing his sister on the ground, screaming, while a seer three times her size shoved his hand down her pants.

Without really talking about it, he and Cass had been waiting for Revik to return.

No doubt lived in either of their minds about what his reaction would be, or how long it would take him to act on it.

Balidor had been polite to them both, and apologetic as he explained that they were having some difficulty locating Revik. Somehow, he'd managed to get himself clear over to some obscure corner of the settlement.

Jon knew full well that Revik would take it badly.

Cass and he hadn't talked much while they waited, but he knew Cass was nervous, too. They'd both seen a lot of different sides to Revik in that cave in the Caucasus Mountains, but none so scary as when Terian convinced him that he'd taken Allie captive and was hurting her. Terian managed to string him along with that fiction for about a month before Revik felt enough off Allie to know he was lying.

Well, that coupled with the fact that Terian was never able to produce a physical body.

Even so, when Jon opened the door leading to the courtyard, he couldn't quite believe his eyes. He stopped so fast, Cass ran into his back.

Before he could recover, Balidor turned, meeting his gaze.

"Jon! Cass! Get back inside!" he shouted in accented English.

Jon ignored him. He did grab Cass's arm though, stopping her right as she pushed past him into the sunlight. He needn't have bothered. Cass came to a dead stop as well, gripping Jon's hand as she stared into the courtyard.

Over thirty seers filled the small space.

Jon watched in shock as four of them grabbed a struggling Revik. They held him for only a few seconds before he twisted free, back-fisting a barrel-chested Adhipan seer named Garensche across the face.

He kicked another in the knee in the same fluid twist of his body, then climbed up the front of Garensche's body like an acrobat, using the height to kick another seer in the head, effectively knocking him out cold with the edge of his boot. Throwing himself up and driving his weight down in a punch, he knocked Garensche to the dirt, leaping off him sideways as he fell.

Garensche let out a surprised grunt, toppling to his back.

Jon barely tracked with his eyes as Revik then grabbed a mid-sized seer, using him as a shield before he threw his body at two others.

He was trying to get away, Jon realized.

He was fighting his way to the edge of the crowd.

Jon stepped forward to help him when someone grabbed his arm. Turning, Jon jerked free with an angry glare, but the seer holding him, whom Jon only vaguely recognized, looked pale and worried, and merely shook his head.

"Dangerous," he said in accented English.

Jon didn't recognize him from earlier that day, with Allie, so forced himself to relax, nodding. He turned back to the crowd.

He'd never actually seen Revik fight before.

He'd seen the aftermath, and he'd heard rumors about him in hand to hand. Revik had some kind of rep, but he was in penance so he couldn't fight recreationally, despite the occasional challenge from some up and comer.

Even knowing all that, Jon followed Revik with his eyes now, completely floored.

Revik lacked the flash of a lot of the young seers who screwed around in the sparring ring day after day, trying to one-up one another.

Back when it was his job, Jon would have classified Revik a purely economical fighter. Meaning, he was practical, through and through. He didn't waste a lot of movements. He rested between every beat, threw his whole weight behind every hit, no matter which part of his body he used.

And he was fast as hell.

At the moment, he seemed to be fighting about fifteen seers at the same time.

He aimed low with the vast majority of his kicks, downing opponents by going after weak points in joints and bone: shins, knees, ankles, ribs. For those he couldn't drive back or knock off balance that way, he misdirected through another punch or kick before he going for a blow to the head or jaw, trying to stun them.

In each case, his hits were calculated, aimed.

Temples, jaws, throats, solar plexus, kidney… a few upward hits to the nose.

He didn't fuck around, Jon noticed. Nothing showy at all.

He used them against one another, always keeping one mediocre fighter between him and the better fighters, using their momentum against them, their weight, getting in close to the stronger ones to offset their size, sliding between the limbs of the taller ones.

Jon watched him in a kind of admiring awe.

He understood why some of the more jaded fighters would want to take him on, even if they didn't expect to win. Revik fought like he'd trained for years against people twice his size, with every conceivable advantage over him. He fought like he was used to being outnumbered. He also fought like someone a lot smaller than he was, a lot weaker, and a lot slower. In fact, he fought as if he expected to lose.

Which, paradoxically, gave him an enormous advantage.

Even so, the odds were against him now, too.

Several of Balidor's men were closing on him already as Balidor shouted instructions from one side.

"No, goddamn it! Don't hurt him! Just get him down! Drug him if you have to, but don't let him leave!"

"Jesus," Jon muttered. He glanced at Cass. "Look at his face."

He hadn't noticed Dorje on her other side until the seer spoke.

"Yes." The Tibetan-looking seer sounded grim. Seeing Jon looking at him, he asked, "Is it true that the two of you were there? Today. For the claim."

Cass gave Dorje a hard look. "Sort of." Her voice turned openly caustic as she folded her arms, pushing up her breasts. "Are they going to punish Revik if he hurts Maygar?" She muttered, "What if I do it for him?"

Dorje looked at her, his face white and serious. "They tell me Dehgoies was looking for a place to make the request of her when Maygar did this."

"I don't know what that means," Cass said, dismissive. "I want to know why they're trying to stop him. Why not let him go?"

Dorje looked from Cass's face to Jon's, his eyes wide. "They are trying to protect his soul! To tell him they had to show him what Maygar did. If Dehgoies doesn't kill anyone today, it will be a miracle."

Cass made an angry noise, looking back at the scene in the courtyard.

Jon found himself thinking about Dorje's words, in spite of himself.

He forgot them entirely seconds later, when he saw Yerin push past on Dorje's other side, walking purposefully out into the courtyard.

Christ. Was Yerin really that dumb? If they really did show Revik what happened, he would absolutely see Yerin as an accomplice.

Jon reached out to catch the seer's arm, but Yerin avoided Jon's hand, and his eyes.

"Yerin!" Jon said, sharp. "Don't! Let him cool down!"

Yerin raised his voice, aiming it at Revik.

"You are in danger of breaking penance!" Yerin said. "You are prohibited from fighting except in the line of duty!"

"Asshole," Cass muttered, folding her arms tighter.

"Idiot, you mean," Jon retorted. "He's going to get his head ripped off."

"Maybe not," Cass said.

She motioned towards the courtyard and Jon followed her hand.

He watched as four of Balidor's men managed to catch hold of Revik by the arms and throat. Using their collective weight, they forced him to his knees, then flat forward onto his chest. Landing hard in the dirt, Revik made a low sound, then lay on his stomach, his arms behind his back, his legs pinned, gasping, the wind likely knocked out of him.

Cass tensed, gripping Jon's fingers.

"Dehgoies!" Balidor knelt beside his head. "Dehgoies! Calm yourself! Please, my friend! Try to disengage!"

Revik fought them, muscles straining in his arms and chest.

To Jon, he still looked thin from his captivity with Terian.

The muscles in his arms looked ready to burst out of his skin. He struggled harder, fighting to free himself, then to twist to his side to use his legs. He got off a single punch at one of his captors before they caught hold of his arm again, trapping it behind his back.

Jon winced as they clicked binders over his wrists.

"Hey!" Jon yelled out before he knew he intended to. His voice came out angry. "What the hell? How is it *he's* the bad guy in this?"

Balidor looked over at him, his face openly startled.

"He is not the bad guy, Jon," he said. "This is for his own protection."

"Bullshit!" Cass said, loudly. "This is *bullshit!*"

Balidor hesitated, but didn't answer.

Revik was looking around at all of them now. He stared at each of the seers. His eyes paused on faces Jon recognized from the crowd watching Maygar and Allie that afternoon. The look in his eyes remained borderline frightening. His expression didn't improve as his gaze made its way through the watching crowd.

"Let me go," he said, thickly.

"Dehgoies!" Yerin walked closer. "Calm yourself!"

"Gods, I'll kill you if you don't let me go…" His voice choked.

Jon gripped Cass's hand tighter.

Emotion rose in him, catching him off guard. He stared at the man on the ground, feeling helpless in a way he hadn't since Terian.

It hadn't occurred to him until then that Revik wasn't just angry. He was grief-stricken, desperate, nearly devastated. Knowing him, he also felt guilty. But the main emotion Jon saw was fear. He was out of his mind with fear.

"Brother—" Balidor began.

"Let me go! I haven't broken any laws!"

"Dehgoies!" Yerin squatted in front of him.

When Revik didn't look over, the other seer slapped him, making Jon and Cass flinch. Yerin hit him again, hard enough to force Revik's eyes to his. Revik's face changed. Jon saw the hunter cloak kick back in. He stopped struggling against the seers holding him and narrowed his eyes up at Yerin's face.

"Brother, please!" Yerin pleaded. "Calm yourself!"

There was a silence. Then Revik nodded.

"All right." His voice grew quiet. "I'm listening."

He relaxed his body almost completely.

"No!" Balidor shouted to the others. "Don't fall for it! Hold him!"

Revik lunged against their hands, and for a moment the four seers had to work to restrain him. Yerin stumbled backwards as Jon looked at Cass, who squeezed his hand in both of hers.

She looked furious, but she was crying too.

It was too close to home, seeing Revik on the ground in cuffs again.

Yerin repositioned himself in front of Revik once they had control of him again. "Dehgoies!" He raised his voice. "We are trying to help you! You need to disengage! Right now! You're not rational—"

"Yerin, for the gods' sake," Balidor said.

Yerin stubbornly continued to focus only on Revik.

"We won't hurt your mate!" he said. "We are looking for her. Right now. We have every available member of the Adhipan out already."

At this, Revik looked like someone had stabbed him in the chest.

"No!" Pain reached his voice, worsening as he struggled with the bindings. "No! Call off your hunt! I won't hurt him... I vow that I won't! Please! Please, gods... uncuff me. Let me find her!"

"Let him go!" Cass yelled, angry. "Jesus... you *fuckers!*"

Revik's voice rose. "Balidor, please! You have no right to hold me, I haven't done anything—"

"Dehgoies!" Balidor caught his shoulder. "We won't hurt your mate! No claims will be attempted. I promise you! And it is not only with my people. Vash has forbidden it. He has removed any right of second claim."

Revik didn't stop struggling, and it occurred to Jon he really would kill himself if they didn't let him go. He took a step closer as Revik threw himself against the seers holding him down. He managed to crack one in the face with the back of his head. Blood exploded over his shirt as the seer's nose was broken.

"Jesus. Stop it!" Jon yelled, as incensed as Cass.

Someone grabbed his arm.

Turning, he glared at Dorje when he saw the seer holding him.

"Do not get close!" Dorje said. "Yerin is right! He is not sane right now!"

Jon glared at the seer. "Why won't they just let him go so he can find her?"

Dorje's skin whitened. "Because he might kill every seer who witnessed the claim today! Not just Maygar, *all* of them!"

Cass snapped, "And that would be *bad*, because...?"

The seer with the broken nose turned to Balidor. "Sir. We have to drug him. We can't wait any longer."

"No!" Balidor held up a hand. "Not yet. Give him a minute!"

Jon was about to yell out again, when out of nowhere, calm began to seep over his mind. It wasn't a mental straightjacket, like earlier with Maygar's friends, but it definitely originated from somewhere outside of himself.

Balidor was manipulating the construct.

He and his seers were trying to reach Revik through his light. They were trying to reassure him... and likely, to refute the images in his mind of Adhipan males raping Allie in the woods.

Yerin didn't move from where he squatted in front of him.

"I am sorry, brother," he said, his voice emotional now. "You are right. You have broken no laws. But you are in danger of breaking penance." When Revik's eyes narrowed, Yerin lowered his voice. "We are only tracking her. No one is allowed to approach. No one. That is a vow. It will not be broken. She is safe, Dehgoies."

Revik laughed.

Jon felt his throat close at what he heard there.

"We are not your enemy, brother," Yerin said.

"You're wrong about that," Revik growled.

Yerin's dark eyes looked pained. "I am sorry you feel that way, brother."

"Fuck you," Revik's voice sounded clearer. "Fuck all of you. I'm taking her out of here! Tonight."

Yerin gestured negative. "You cannot leave with her. That request has been formally denied. She is the Bridge. Your rights do not extend to—"

"My *rights?* Watch me, Yerin. I'll see if I can help her learn a little more telekinesis while I'm at it. Then we'll talk about 'rights.'"

"We *can* refuse you in this, Dehgoies." Yerin's tone gentled. "And you're wrong. I felt tied by the law, but do not think I do not care."

He raised a hand to Revik's face, but Revik jerked violently away.

Yerin withdrew his fingers with pained eyes.

"I understand, brother. We all do. But you mated with the Bridge. You cannot simply *leave* with her. The Council has given permission for the two of you to conduct the preliminaries of your marriage wherever you like. There will be supervision of the construct, of course, but—"

"No. No way—"

"We are working on the security protocols now," Yerin continued, as if he hadn't spoken. His voice turned politely formal. "If you do not accept these terms, we will be forced to separate you from your mate until you see reason."

He clicked his fingers in Revik's face, forcing his pale eyes back to his.

"Compromise, Dehgoies," he urged. "It is the rational choice."

For a long moment, Revik just lay there, in the dirt, breathing hard, as if fighting to control himself. Jon glanced at Cass, who looked even angrier. She stared at Yerin like he was the Antichrist.

When Revik spoke next, his voice was hard. He looked at Balidor. "Maygar. Is he alive?"

Balidor glanced at Yerin, then gestured affirmative. "So far, yes."

"Is he awake?"

Balidor sighed, clicking softly. Unlike with Yerin, the sympathy Jon saw in his eyes seemed to have real understanding behind it.

"What difference does it make, brother?" he asked.

Revik's jaw hardened, changing the shape of his face.

"Because I want the fucker conscious while I beat him to death with my bare hands," he said.

There was a silence.

Then Balidor burst out with a laugh.

After the barest pause, Revik laughed too.

For a few seconds anyway, his laughter sounded almost real.

In the midst of those twenty or so seers, they continued to chuckle, Revik still half-crushed under four of the largest of them, his chest mashed into the dirt. When Jon gave Cass an incredulous look, she just rolled her eyes, refolding her arms and giving him the look that he recognized as her "Men!" look.

But as their laughter died down, Revik's eyes brightened.

Feeling the change, Balidor patted him reassuringly on the shoulder, clicking to him softly.

"She is all right, brother," he said. "You are blessed with a tough mate. A warrior." He chuckled, patting him again. "You should have seen that little shit fly." Waiting for Revik to glance over, he made an arc with his hand in the air.

"…Kaboom! Like swatting a bug."

Revik didn't answer. Jon saw his eyes close, just before he nodded.

Yerin spoke up from Revik's other side, seemingly oblivious to the fact that Balidor had finally reached him.

"There will be a hearing on the validity of Maygar's second claim," Yerin informed them. "He broke several laws I was not aware of at the time, setting the stage for his attempt. He will be punished for that." He made a "more or less" gesture with one hand. "…If he lives. But you cannot claim his life, Dehgoies. You are in penance, and…" Trailing, Yerin shrugged. "Well. From all appearances, he was within his rights. Technically."

"Technically." Revik stared at him.

"For the love of the gods, Yerin," Balidor said.

"She should have known the law," Yerin said. "If you had educated her, brother, she might have known to avoid that situation—"

Revik lunged, managing to catch the Adhipan infiltrators off-guard.

He head-butted Yerin in the face with all of his weight, knocking him flat to the ground.

The four seers holding Revik got control of him again and dragged him up to his feet.

Jon jumped a little when they slammed him down on a stone bench.

At a nod from Balidor, another seer forced the needle of a syringe into Revik's neck as he struggled to free himself. As soon as the stopper was all the way down, the four seers dragged him backwards towards the door, but not before Revik got in a few body kicks on the downed Yerin.

Balidor's eyes still looked angry as he pulled Yerin out of the way.

Releasing his arm, Balidor gave him a disgusted look before glancing around at the onlookers.

"Someone get a medic for brother Yerin. Now."

Jon and Cass moved aside as they dragged Revik towards the compound's main structure. Jon already saw a difference in the way Revik was moving from the drug.

Whatever they had given him, it was fast-acting.

Even so, he gave Jon and Cass a brief, searching look as they dragged him past, right before they steered him through to the basement door.

In that one look, his eyes were already starting to glaze, but Jon found himself thinking he understood, now, what Dorje meant.

It was probably better for everyone if Revik sat this one out for a while.

CHAPTER II
RECRUITED

Revik woke up alone, in a dim space. He had a headache that felt like it would rip his skull in half. He could barely get his eyes open.

They'd drugged him.

He blinked, fighting to focus.

They had him chained to the wall of one of the brick and mortar monk cells.

The posture felt familiar, in more ways than one.

With a little experimentation he found they'd left him enough slack to rest his hands on a table they'd dragged between him and the door. He could lie down, write, draw, even partially undress, awkwardly, if he felt so inclined. He might even have enough slack to throw the table at one of them, if he were feeling really industrious.

They'd shackled his ankles, set a bucket discreetly in one corner. They left him water, paper, pens that were useless against the semi-organic binders, a few of his books they must have pulled from Allie's room.

They hadn't restrained his sight, at least, so he spent the next however-long amount of time in the Barrier. He didn't stop looking for her even when he got up to relieve himself in the bucket they'd left.

He couldn't find her.

Which meant either someone had her, or she didn't want to be found.

He knew he should probably be more worried about the former, but he strongly felt the latter to be the truth.

He couldn't get Maygar's words to him in Cairo out of his head… or the images he'd picked up from the other seers as they explained what that *jurekil'a dule'ten* dirtblood pup bastard had done to her.

She might be furious with him. Knowing her, she might think he'd be angry with her, too. She might be embarrassed.

Whatever her reasons, he was getting increasingly frantic when he still couldn't feel her about an hour later. He tried pinging her, calling to her, resonating with her light, apologizing.

He got no response. Nothing.

He didn't come out of the Barrier at all until the door to his cell opened.

Clicking out, he focused abruptly on his visitor.

It was a different face than the one he'd been expecting.

Balidor stood looking at him critically, hands on his hips.

"Are you all right, brother?" he asked.

Revik had thought it would be Vash. Even so, he relaxed after scanning the older seer. He didn't feel any dire news on him. He had no complaint with the Adhipan leader himself. He'd tried to stop them, at least.

"Fine," Revik said. There was no embarrassment in his voice when he added, "I'm hungry. And I pissed in there." He nodded towards the rusted bucket. "So you might not want to get too close."

Balidor entered further into the room. He motioned for the guard behind him to deal with the bucket in the corner.

"Good," he said. "I am hungry, too. I'll request dinner for both of us."

When Revik raised an eyebrow, Balidor merely looked around the small cell.

"This is unfortunate… this space," he added, so that Revik wouldn't misunderstand. "I hope you know that the restraints were a sign of respect. I knew you could get out, if I left your hands, or perhaps even just your feet, free. I didn't want you getting in trouble for what happened today."

He stood over the chair across from Revik, shrugging with one hand.

"They will excuse you when you are obviously out of control. But I knew that regaining rationality might not deter you. It would not me."

He hesitated again when Revik didn't speak.

"I wanted to update you on our search," he added. "And to tell you there's been a development. Several, actually."

"Where's my *wife*, Balidor?"

He held up his hands, a peace gesture. "She's fine, brother."

Apparently giving up on being invited, he pulled the chair out and sat, resting his arms on the water-damaged wood.

"We found her about an hour ago. She's perfectly safe. She's with Tarsi."

"Tarsi?" Revik's tension faded only a little. "How did she find Tarsi?"

Balidor gave a knowing kind of shrug.

"I think it was the other way around. Tarsi claims she heard the girl 'miles off.' Called us all dogs. She gave Vash a real tongue-lashing, actually. Told him he'd raised a robot for a son, that he should have taken that ancient law off the books six hundred years ago. Vash tells me he'd never before felt her so angry."

Revik grunted. He rested his chained hands in his lap. "Is she all right? Allie."

"She's fine."

Revik shifted in his seat. After a pause, he gave the Adhipan leader an uncomfortable look. "Does she want to see me?" he asked.

"I don't know," Balidor replied apologetically. "No one spoke to her, only Tarsi. Tarsi herself claimed she had important business with the Bridge and that no one was to come looking for her or to talk to her until she gave permission." Pausing, he added, "Including you, my brother. I am sorry."

At Revik's silence, Balidor shrugged, holding out his hands.

"What could we do? It is Tarsi. We sent a guard..."

Revik gave him a sharp look.

"...Chandre," Balidor finished, holding up a hand. "She wasn't there for the claim, so the Bridge isn't as likely to send her away. In addition to the more obvious reasons."

"Where was she? Earlier today?"

Balidor gave him a puzzled look. His eyes cleared.

"Chandre. Yes, she mentioned to me that you'd assigned her guard duty to the Bridge while you were away. Maygar must have foreseen this. He drugged her. She was out for more than six hours."

Revik only nodded, but felt his muscles grow taut again.

The door opened behind Balidor.

In walked two seers Revik vaguely recognized, carrying covered trays. It occurred to him that they must be Adhipan, too.

He felt a twinge of nerves and glanced again at Balidor.

The man sitting before him was probably the best infiltrator the seers had ever had, on either side. If he were up to something, Revik would never know. Even with who Allie was, using the top of the food chain to guard and feed a house prisoner involved in a domestic dispute ventured past extreme.

It occurred to him to wonder if, with Allie gone, and the information he had on the Rooks pretty well used up—

Balidor slapped the table smartly with his palm.

"No!" he said. "Absolutely not."

Revik gave him a wary look. "No disrespect meant, brother," he said.

"I'm not offended. But you're completely wrong about my intentions." He smiled. "And, if you don't mind my saying it... a little paranoid." His smile widened. "Maybe a lot paranoid. But you come by it honestly."

He waited for the two seers to finish arranging trays of food.

They removed the wooden covers and exited the cell silently.

"Not everyone here wishes you harm," Balidor added, picking up chopsticks as the door closed behind them. "Not all of us are equally ignorant, either. I know what you did for us, by infiltrating the Rooks. I know your mate got the succession order from you... after you sacrificed thirty years of your life and much else of yourself to get it."

He paused, chopsticks hovering over his plate. "Do not think we are all your enemies, Revik. Quite the contrary. Some of us admire you a great deal."

Doing a quick hand-blessing over his meal, he filled his chopsticks with greens, taking a drink of thick, milky tea.

He added, "I do wonder why you haven't allowed Vash to enlighten the rest of our community as to the role you played in the events of the last year...?"

"No." Revik made the same hand-gesture over his food, copying the other out of habit, even though he hadn't done it in years. He pulled apart a piece of curried chicken with his fingers. "Respectfully, no. I'd prefer it if that remained between us. I'm sure Vash had his reasons for telling you—"

"He didn't," Balidor said. "...Tell me. I trained you for that assignment."

He smiled at Revik's surprise.

"Don't worry," Balidor added. "I have not told anyone, not even my own people. Before, it was a security issue. More recently, Vash cautioned me that you did not want it widely spread."

Watching Revik eat, he made his voice casual.

"I do wonder, though. Would it not improve your situation here, if it were known that you joined the Rooks, not as a traitor, but as a warrior for your people? It would legitimize your courtship and marriage to the Bridge, if nothing else."

"No." Revik shook his head, clicking softly.

He finished chewing, then swallowed.

"...It would not improve my situation to tell them. Or," he amended. "I suppose it depends on your definition of 'improve.' From my perspective, I see no improvement if those who have enjoyed condemning me for the past forty years suddenly wished me to come to their houses for dinner."

At Balidor's open laugh, Revik shrugged.

"I figure I owe Alyson a certain level of civility. But, since none of them pretends to like me anyway, I can hardly do her social damage if I drive social climbers and opportunists off our property with a gun."

"Indeed." Balidor laughed again. "And good. It makes my job easier."

Revik paused, chopsticks full of greens halfway to his mouth.

He finished the motion, chewing and swallowing.

"Which job is that?" he asked.

"Recruiting you, my young friend. I would like you to join the Adhipan."

Revik froze again in mid-bite.

He stared at Balidor, replaying his words, still not believing them. The Adhipan almost never recruited adult seers. Revik would have been overjoyed if he'd been offered such a thing, even a year ago—much less ten years ago.

Now it seemed a little suspicious, given who his wife was.

Balidor took a bite of his own, chewing and swallowing before he continued.

"You won't remember this, of course," he said. "But you made a deal with me, all those years ago, that you would join us once your stint with the Rooks was completed. I plan to hold you to that promise, whether you remember it or not. It would be much easier to keep your involvement a secret if everyone thought you unreliable. Or, at the very least, capable of corruption."

"Everyone is capable of corruption," Revik said.

He was still staring at Balidor, wary.

Raising an eyebrow, Balidor smiled, shrugging with one hand.

"Perhaps," he conceded. "But I have talked it over with Vash, and he agrees with my assessment of you. Now that you are finished with your assignment in safeguarding the Bridge, I would like you with us. Assuming you would not be adverse."

Balidor's eyes grew more serious.

"And on that note, I have an immediate opening. A job for which I would like you to accompany my team." He paused, taking another mouthful of greens. Chewing, he washed it down with tea.

"...Today, I mean. It will not obligate you."

Revik stared at him.

Then he gave a short laugh, letting the chains fall loudly to the table.

"A job, huh? How interesting."

"I know this likely seems calculated, my friend. I assure you, it is not."

"Really?" Revik leaned against the wall. "So this isn't at all meant to distract me, brother? Or as a conveniently legal means of getting me off the compound?"

"It is not designed that way, no." Balidor smiled. "Although it did perhaps occur to me that you could use some distraction right now. Tarsi says she will have your wife for at least a week. All I ask is a few days. I thought the timing rather opportune."

Revik grunted. "For you, perhaps."

Balidor did not laugh. "Actually, no. Not for either of us, I'm afraid. This is not a pleasant excursion on which I am inviting you. And I did not mean to make light of your situation. I assure you, the timing is coincidence only. I find myself short of people at a critical time, and this is an area in which you have demonstrated your expertise already."

He leaned over the table, his elbows on either side of his plate.

Seeing that Revik was thinking about his offer, he added,

"I will leave some of my people in the woods, to back up Chandre, if you like." He hesitated. "All females, if you prefer. I have more working for me than I generally make public."

Revik glanced at him, then nodded. "Thanks."

"You will do it, then?"

Revik hesitated.

Glancing out the one window in the cell, he fought back a reaction in his light. The thought of leaving her here, even if he couldn't see her, physically hurt. After that morning, it would be worse, even without what Maygar had done.

But the leader of the Adhipan was making a personal request of him. Revik had already been told he wouldn't be allowed to see her, even if he stayed.

Hell, he didn't even know if she wanted to see him.

They might keep him locked up if he remained here.

Logic tried to assert itself, but pain coursed through his *aleimi*, making it hard to think. He felt Balidor withdraw, giving him space.

Eventually, though, reason brought him back to the same conclusion.

Glancing at Balidor, he shifted his weight, nodding.

"All right."

"Good. It is settled, then." Balidor put down the napkin. "I must leave you bound until the plane lifts off. But after that, providing you promise not to hijack my vehicle, or physically attack any of my people, you will be a free man."

He rose to his feet, and Revik stared up at him, still holding chopsticks.

The Adhipan leader smiled at him.

"Can you be ready in a half-hour? I will have one of my people pack you a bag."

"Where are we going?" Revik said.

"Sikkim," Balidor said.

Two hours later, Revik found himself approaching a small dirt airstrip in a beat-up American sedan. After a ninety-plus minute drive down the mountains and through the human town of Dharamsala, the car he shared with two of Balidor's Adhipan left the main road, just south of the human airport.

It bumped along a frontage path to a secondary field.

That field was hidden just past a long stretch of banana trees.

Entering a fenced-in segment through automatic gates, the driver sped them out to the airstrip as two more seers locked the gates behind them.

The sedan came to a stop in front of an ancient and beat up looking Ilyushin Il-14 Russian military transport plane.

Glancing at the two seers, Revik returned their polite bows.

He got out of the car when they opened the door for him, his hands still bound in front of him. When the older of the two seers pointed him towards the plane's open door, Revik walked to the metal staircase and began to climb.

He paused only once, to glance over the scarred wings of the plane. He frowned at the ancient prop engines. His eyes paused on dark scoring on the metal plating from bullets.

He entered the oval door.

Ducking his head under the rim, he waited for his eyes to adjust to the absent glare and looked for Balidor. The Adhipan leader was alone on the plane so far, so Revik walked down the aisle and slumped into a seat across from him.

"You couldn't have found a new plane?" he grumbled.

Balidor glanced at him, a faint smile playing at his lips.

"We find these older models are less likely to raise questions." He raised an eyebrow. "You aren't afraid of flying, are you, brother?"

Revik propped his cuffed hands on the seat in front of him. "Afraid? No. Cautious when it comes to flying in things I shot at eighty years ago? Yes."

Balidor laughed, even as he glanced back at the others now boarding. "We have made a few repairs since then."

Revik's eyes followed his as seven more seers entered through the same rear-wing door. They scattered themselves over the thirty-odd seats inside the plane's cabin.

Two were the males who had driven him from Seertown. They'd been friendly enough on the way down, talking to him about the work they'd been doing tracking Terian bodies and the status of the human war.

Even so, the collective demeanor of the group put his nerves on edge.

They didn't laugh or joke, or even act like they were on the job.

They all looked grim, even emotional. A pall hung over the squad, even with them shielded up tighter than any group of seers Revik had ever encountered.

All were male but one, and, from what Revik could tell, all were older than him, the next youngest being at least two hundred years old.

The one female walked up the aisle to sit with Grent, the only seer on the plane with whom Revik had spoken more than a few words before today. Catching Revik's eye, Grent gave him a welcoming wave. Then he glanced up at the female and his face changed, sliding from grief into a smile as she leaned over to kiss him on the face, caressing his cheek with her hand and kissing him again.

Revik noticed the telltale then, woven into a structure of *aleimi* over each of their heads.

Mates. Interesting.

Revik found his mind drifting towards Allie, and shifted his focus back to Balidor.

"So what is this?" he asked. "Where are we going?"

Balidor's humor faded at once. "To investigate a mass killing. A bomb of some kind. Likely several, actually. The damage is pretty phenomenal. Hundreds were killed."

Revik nodded. He didn't get it, though.

That didn't explain the mood of the group.

"Seers?" he asked, glancing around at the others.

"Brother," Balidor said gently. "…They were children."

There was a silence.

Revik felt a knot form in his chest. Instead of loosening, it worsened with time, like someone had grabbed one of his lungs and squeezed it with their bare hand.

"Seer children," Revik said. It wasn't really a question.

"Yes. At least five hundred. Maybe as many as seven."

Revik felt light-headed.

"Seven hundred." His voice sounded far away. "Verified?"

Balidor nodded. "We have feed images. Underground, of course. None of the human stations are carrying it, at least not yet. We got the intel from an operative in Darjeeling. Some of the survivors fled there. We received amateur footage from the team who picked them up."

"Source?" Revik asked.

Balidor flipped his hand sideways. "Unknown. None of the ID'd Terian bodies were anywhere near the area. They're all accounted for. The ones we know of, that is."

Balidor hesitated.

"There are plenty of other possible culprits," he added. "At this point, we suspect retaliation. A number of slave camps run by the Rooks had similar incidents when we first started liberating them, right after the Pyramid went down. Killing the inventory, as it were. In this case, before it could be identified through the trade routes and brought over to our side." Balidor's lips thinned.

"My seers may have caused this. Inadvertently, of course. We had just started investigating that area for rumors of a school."

"Christ," Revik said in English.

Wiping his face with one hand, he looked out the window as the prop engines geared up.

A seer at the back of the plane swung the door shut with a sucking sound. Revik watched him lock it with the bar. He was buckling himself into the seat then, as the plane began rolling down the dirt runway.

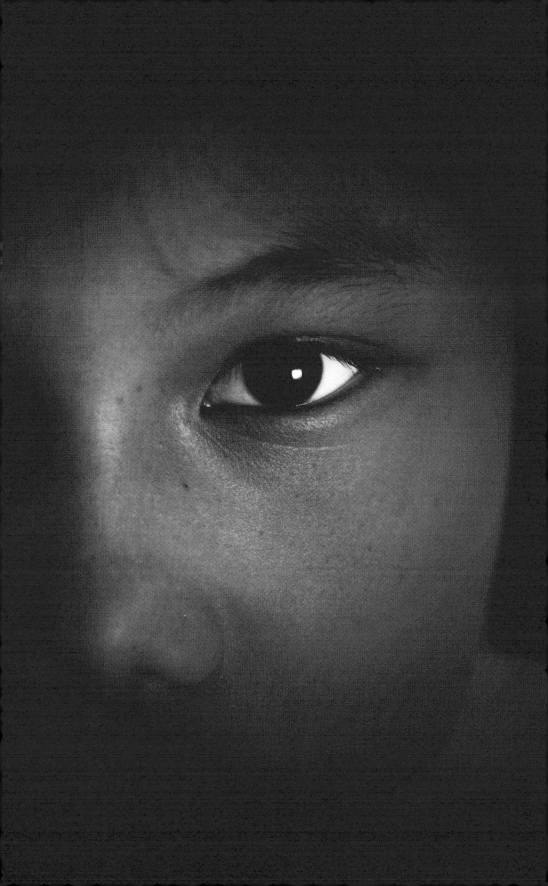

CHAPTER 12
CHILDREN

Tarsi walked alongside me on a steep, wooded path. She didn't stray far, but let me absorb the recording on her portable reader on my own.

Looking at the images of the miniature broken bodies, shown in full color and in every sickening detail of non-avatar flesh, it struck me with a fresh wave of nausea that these were the first seer children I'd ever seen.

These days, pregnant seers were usually sent away as soon as they learned of their condition. Seer children were born in secret, and sent to schools set up as monasteries, far outside of any official settlements. Those not run by the Rooks lay deep in the mountains to discourage slave traders, and were heavily guarded by specially trained squads under the Adhipan called Lokapaala, which translated roughly as "Guardians of the World."

It all seemed a bit overdone to me until Vash explained that each healthy child, once sight trained and "made docile," fetched anywhere from 100-500K Euros on the black market. Higher, if they fit one of the rare categories of coloring or sight rank, or if they displayed any one or combination of a few dozen preferential traits.

With seer traders, prevailing wisdom was the younger the better.

Girls were prized more than boys, for reproductive capability and perceived "relative docility," which was frankly laughable to me, given the female seers I'd met so far. Sex was almost always a factor, too, for those high-end purchases.

The majority of customers were still men.

I closed my eyes, breathing in cold air.

I couldn't help but wonder how many were left. In total, I mean. Had that been a third of the seer children currently alive? A fifth? A tenth? Half?

The complex where the massacre occurred had been located in the mountains of Sikkim, a kingdom in the far Northeast of India. It called itself a "school," but the recording I saw showed sensory deprivation cells, collars, restraints, iron bars and evidence of extremely crowded living conditions.

At least 1,100 kids had been interned there, ranging from 5-25 years.

That meant some had been babies.

I'd learned a few things about seers and their children since I'd first arrived in India. For one thing, seers didn't reproduce as easily as human beings. Children were a big deal, even before the trade wars following World War II.

There were a number of reasons for this.

A disproportionately high number of adult seers were sterile. Seers didn't reproduce until they were older, too—a few hundred years old, at least.

Now that life spans for all seers had generally decreased, seer children were considered a matter of community interest. Most diplomatic battles fought by the Seven involved the safety of their children in some way.

Maygar told me once that children were even buried in adult-sized coffins.

I handed the screen back to Tarsi. "Do I need to go back?"

"No." Folding up the organic monitor, she stuffed it into a bag that hung sideways across her body. She shrugged with one hand, seer-fashion.

Not yet. The Adhipan will go there.

Nodding, I looked out over the trees, trying not to worry about how long we'd been walking, or how dark it was getting. We'd been trekking through these mountain trails for hours. The sun was sinking between the mountains before us, and Tarsi still showed no sign that we might be getting close to our destination.

She wasn't doing anything to my light that I could notice.

I wasn't blocked from scanning for Vash or Balidor or anyone else.

I considered checking in with Revik. I didn't, though.

I had no idea what to say to him yet, and I still wasn't ready to deal with whatever emotional reaction he might have to the Maygar thing.

Tarsi told me she'd instructed all of them to leave me alone.

Even Revik, she said.

A number of feelings arose around that, not all of them relief.

A few times we stopped, breathing hard as we shared views of valleys filled with lush green and the occasional outlying farm.

I tried to engage her in questions, but only got vague or no answers. At one point, she lay a finger to her lips and gestured around us. I took that to mean that she wanted to wait until we were in some kind of construct.

After that, I left her alone.

A stillness lived in the Himalayas, even in their lowest foothills.

Spring had wound its way into the woods, and greenery erupted under my feet, turning the soil beneath a dark brown. A cry sounded overhead and I looked up, watching another gold-feathered eagle wheel in looping circles against the blue sky, its shadow flickering between cracks in the dark curtain of evergreens.

I decided to just be here, forget everything else.

Time passed easily from that space.

We reached our destination as the first stars grew faintly visible in the east.

Due to the angle and its position half-immersed in rock, I didn't even see the door at first. I just stood there, breathing hard, thinking we were resting on a grassy knoll before the next steep cliff, when I noticed light flickering between cracks in the rock face.

I stared at that flame-like light for close to a minute before my eyes drew the correct lines out of the natural fissures.

By then, my breath plumed out in clouds from the cold air, but my T-shirt stuck to my back with sweat from the last two hours of hiking, most of it straight uphill. Pine needles and mud caked my boots. Winded from the thinned oxygen, I trudged without stopping for the last mile, marveling that the ancient seer seemed to weather the climb better than me.

Patches of snow still dotted the ground, and cracking fingers of ice framed the water in a stone basin outside the wooden door. Recent snowmelt trickled down one side of the path in a ribbon-like stream. I continued to suck in breaths as we stood there, knowing my face was bright red from exertion.

"Your house?" I asked.

She gestured in affirmative.

Then I smelled it. Wood smoke wafted from a larger crack past the dugout's entrance. I stared at it, then looked at her.

"Someone's here?"

She made the affirmative gesture again. "Had the girl come to light it, so we'd not be so cold."

"The girl," I repeated.

Instead of words, she sent a flicker of imagery, as casual as a blown kiss.

"The girl" appeared to be around thirty, which meant she was likely closer to three hundred; she was clearly a seer from her wide, opaque-blue eyes. She lived with her mate on a farm in a nearby valley, and brought food to the woman, staples mostly, but also cooked meals when Tarsi was away (flying? traveling?).

I definitely got the impression these journeys didn't involve the old seer actually leaving her cave.

Clicking out of the Barrier, I studied Tarsi's face, shoving my hands in my front pants pockets. My fingers grew numb as soon as we stood still long enough for me to notice, and the pants didn't help much.

What I really wanted was a shower. Or maybe a good hour in a sauna.

The old woman clicked to herself softly, walking to the wooden door.

I followed, and saw a sliver of moon rising over the valley, already above the horizon. I remembered, somehow, that it was waning. In a few days, I'd be faced with yet another new moon.

So much drama, Tarsi teased. *He knows where you are.*

"Is he all right?" I realized how that sounded. *...With where I am, I mean.*

Of course not. She smiled. *But he knows you are safe.*

Not exactly reassured, I followed her through the door.

I stopped in the narrow foyer, watching her speak to "the girl," who stirred something over the stone fireplace. The fireplace itself reminded me of a pioneer dwelling I'd visited outside San Francisco as a kid. Tarsi poked at the fire with a metal rod, then nodded to the other female, speaking a language I couldn't understand.

The younger seer didn't look up when I first walked in, but she smiled at me now, her wide, brown face wrinkling into lines of sun, wind, and good humor. She had the faraway look of one who spent a lot of time staring at snow.

I raised a hand, smiling back, then just stood there, taking in the small space.

Rugs and blankets covered the stone floor. A kitchen nook was hung with dried plants beside a colorful cabinet without doors, filled with jars of different-colored spices and more plants, along with ceramic plates and bowls. The furniture was all wood, including a small table and two chairs made of what looked like driftwood near the fireplace.

On the mantle stood a row of candles in iron holders and a number of figurines that looked to be carved from volcanic stone.

There was only one bed, but a pallet had been set up on the floor beside it, dressed in thick furs. I assumed that was for me.

The girl clicked to the old woman in that oddly-accented Prexci.

"I bring…" (something I didn't get) "…grandmother?" the girl asked. "…for you and your…" (I lost it again). "She want now?"

Tarsi cuffed the back of the dark head affectionately. "Yes," was all I understood in the hand gestures that followed, but I saw the girl smile with perfect white teeth. She stood then, bowing to me with a palm tilted before her face, a seer gesture of respect.

I did it back, half-wanting to correct her and not knowing how.

Of course, I'd forgotten she was a seer.

Ah, but it is much deserved, Bridge Alyson! Grandmother is too kind, allowing me to serve you both while you are here!

"Serve," I muttered. I tried to return her warm smile, but mine felt strained.

I didn't want to seem ungrateful.

Thank you for your kind words, I sent.

She smiled, but I saw a thread of puzzlement in her opaque, indigo-colored eyes. The old woman shooed her towards me. I watched warily as the girl approached—more so when she gestured at my shirt, indicating that she would help me take it off.

I glanced at Tarsi.

"What's this?" I said. "Can we not do this?"

"No shower here, Bridge. No sauna, either."

I followed her pointing finger to a large wooden basin that reminded me of an old wine barrel, cut in half lengthwise. The water in it was steaming, and it occurred to me that the faint smell of flowers I'd noticed in the room came from there. It stood near to the fireplace, which made me hesitate.

"You're not going to eat me, are you?" I joked.

The old woman smiled, but her eyes sharpened a bit, looking even more like Revik's.

"Get in the water, Bridge. I can't have you getting sick." She smiled, and that time I felt humor behind it. *You'll be happy to have had it, soon enough,* she added, startling me again with her more cultured internal voice. *It's easy to get lost while hunting. You may not get a chance again for several days. The girl will not abuse you. She would not even think of such a thing, Esteemed Bridge.*

I glanced at the girl.

"Abuse" hadn't really occurred to me, either.

I more didn't like the idea of being naked in a strange place, even if it was in front of an old woman and a female seer whose kind eyes clearly didn't scream "infiltrator."

I glanced again at the tub. I watched steam curl off the water, rubbing my arms against the chill that seeped in from my wet shirt. I decided I was too far in to start having second thoughts about these people.

Ignoring the girl's offer of help, I yanked my shirt over my head.

Untying my pants and sliding those off with my underwear, I only hesitated another second before grabbing the wooden sides of the tub. I climbed in carefully, conscious of the two women watching me, wincing as the hot water sloshed over my skin. Once standing in the knee-high water, I lowered myself the rest of the way in, until it rose to within a few centimeters of the brim.

Sighing, I dunked my head all the way under and stretched out, eyes closed.

The old woman offered me a clay cup of something steaming and her arm brushed mine. Unlike the coarseness of her fingers, the skin of her forearm felt rubbed to the softness of lambskin. I took the cup from her, and sniffed the brown liquid.

It smelled like a nutty kind of coffee. I smiled in pleased surprise.

Tarsi sent, *Better now, Bridge?*

Nodding, I sipped the hot drink. It tasted even better than it smelled. I watched her pour herself a mug of the same.

"You really told them to leave me alone?" I snorted a little. "How long do you suppose that'll work?"

I told them at least a week, she sent, no trace of humor in her thoughts. *I'll extend it, if that ends up being not long enough. They won't come here.*

I felt the smile and blood leave my face.

I hadn't even thought of Revik consciously yet, but a dull ache started in my fingers.

Nausea slid through my chest when I tried to swallow.

"A week?" I sat up in the tub. "There's a war going on. Someone just went serial killer on a bunch of kids. I may be a crappy leader, but I'm still their leader." I clutched the mug tighter. "If this is about Maygar—"

"Not about rape," she said, her voice warning. "The conversation is long, Alyson the Bridge. Longer than one night. I need you here."

"Do I have a choice?" I asked, glancing at the girl.

"Always have a choice," Tarsi said with a shrug. *But I would think you could control your desire for my nephew long enough to do something of real importance. I would think this would matter to you more.*

I blinked at her, then looked at the girl. My jaw tightened.

Tarsi clicked softly. *No offense meant, Bridge. Just putting things in perspective. I understand your situation. But this matters more.*

A presence enveloped me—warm, immersing me in a dense softness that made my breath catch, that seemed to penetrate my heart.

For a moment, all I saw were her clear eyes.

If it could wait, she added. *I would. But it can't wait, Alyson.*

"I don't like being ordered around," I said. *I don't like it,* I repeated.

The old seer chuckled.

The presence lifted even as I realized it was hers.

He'll wait for you. Don't worry. Tarsi sat in one of the chairs beside the fireplace, smiling at me in a friendly way. The girl tucked a blanket around her feet and legs. *If it helps, you are calm compared to him right now.*

"It doesn't," I said, wiping my face with water. Because it was easier not having to think of the words in Prexci, I sent,

You know I'm not trained, right? Bridge or not, I can't actually do anything. I'm not even a Level 1 infiltrator yet.

Her eyes sharpened. *I know what you can do, Bridge.*

I found myself remembering earlier that day, what I'd done to Maygar.

Yeah, so maybe it was unconvincing, me saying I couldn't do much. Today, at least. But the reality was, I couldn't control the telekinesis either, or even evoke it at will. The Maygar thing had been dumb luck brought on by sheer, mind-numbing panic. If I'd managed to keep myself in denial for the duration of his attack, I probably would have just lied there, helpless, while he did whatever he wanted.

For the first time, it occurred to me that I may have killed him.

Ironically, even in the middle of all that, I'd hesitated before calling Revik.

I'd been worried he would overreact.

Tarsi clasped her hands in her lap. Her mind felt incredibly still to me, but her eyes held emotion when she turned.

This business with the children. She met my gaze, refolding her gnarled hands. *It's a bad business, Bridge.*

"Well, yes," I said. "It's horrible."

She clicked softly, shaking her head as if I'd missed her point.

Events are accelerating, she sent. *Too many players are involved now to see them all clearly.* She clicked again, softer. *The Broken One. I fear he is dabbling in things he cannot control. He is not the only one. These things have lives of their own.*

She gave me a meaningful look.

Unintended consequences.

"You mean the war with China and the United States?" I trailed when she gestured another negative with her hand. "What do you mean?"

You are missing things, Alyson. There is still much you do not know about the Displacement, and the forces behind it. Yet you know more than you realize. That book you found. The diary. Have you read it all yet?

"No." I lowered my mug halfway into the water, frowning. "And

how did you know about that? My own people don't know I found that."
When she didn't answer, I tried to think. *This is about those kids? You think
Terian has something to do with what happened in Sikkim? Because I would
have thought he'd be more into eliminating humans. Not killing a bunch of seer
kids.*

No, she said, shaking a finger. *I do not believe it was Terian who did the
killing.*

The old woman's eyes grew very sad.

In the firelight, she looked formidable to me, an aging warrior on a
driftwood throne.

No, she sent, as if lost in thought. *No, we all did that.*

I splashed water with my fingers, frowning. "Well, I didn't. Not that I
know of, anyway. I've never even authorized any ops in Sikkim."

The woman gestured absently in the negative.

I waited for her to go on, fighting irritation.

With another sigh, she met my gaze, her eyes reflecting orange from
the fire.

*I told Vash we would aid the Adhipan, you and I. Look at forces behind the
Barrier that might have led to this terrible thing.* Those pale eyes unnerved
me, being too much like Revik's, yet too different, too. *It will give me an
opportunity to assess what you can do, Bridge. Perhaps I can help you.*

Help me with what? I sent, again a little sharply.

Again, she acted like I hadn't spoken.

If I cannot get you ready in the next few months... She clicked softly,
shaking her head. *Well, that would be unfortunate.*

"Unfortunate, how?" I asked.

If this is what I think it is, I give us only weeks. Months at most.

"Weeks?" I stared at her, a little alarmed. "Weeks before what?"

Before the Displacement begins for real, she answered, taking a sip of the
dark brown drink. *...and the humans begin to die.*

CHAPTER 13
FOUND

...and they say Death will live among them in the guise of a child, for like air tears a cloud, or smoke kills flame, or a river wears down its own fire-blackened stones... Death breaks inside itself and cannot be mended.

—Seer proverb, Anonymous

"Sir, you won't believe what we've found. We've scarcely been able to... wait. I should get Ithren, sir..."

Already, Terian-3 was bored.

Leaning back in his chair, the tall, Scandinavian-looking seer laid the folds of his furred cloak over one knee.

Sequestered in Bhutan, he'd been prevented from crossing over to Four and the boy by the arrival of the Adhipan. Seertown being much closer in India than Three's base in Berlin, they beat him here. Then they managed to cut him off.

Three loathed Bhutan.

Really the entire Asian continent could be swallowed up by some kind of sea monster, leaving only the raw materials and a few pretty views and he would be quite content. He sat in an abandoned communications terminal inside a former military outpost outside Kurjey

Lhakhang, Bumthang, in what looked to be an out-of-service public queue from one Communist regime or another.

So far, no one had found the modified box; but then, Galaith, despite his other faults, always supplied him with the very best toys.

"Sir?" The voice resurfaced. "Apologies. You caught us at a bit of a bad time, and…"

At Three's stare, the seer trailed.

His VR shadow was a bipedal reptile with striped horns that protruded from a domed, iridescent-scaled head. Enhancements gave his voice a growling, hissing quality, causing the lizard's nostrils to flare as his voice rose with emotion.

The seer had obviously programmed it himself.

Terian took a drag of his *hiri* stick. "Go on," he said.

"We found another one, sir," the lizard told him. "Totally unknown."

Terian choked on the smoke.

He'd occupied himself with a secondary chore while he waited for the word from Washington D.C. Namely, he'd tasked the remainder of the Rooks' genetics team with comparing Alyson's bio-stats against all existing human and seer records.

He thought it an interesting idea that he might be able to ID other intermediary beings from their biological fingerprint alone. Once he had the idea, he simply could not resist trying it out; he ordered the scans to amuse himself, but also to be thorough.

He hadn't really expected a hit.

Little Allie's bio-samples disintegrated upon separation from her *aleimi* with a speed that made it nearly impossible to tag her DNA with total accuracy, anyway.

"Alive?" Terian queried.

"No." The man's face fell. "Not as such, sir."

Three inhaled smoke, chewing the end of the *hiri* to get at the resin. He felt his shoulders relax. "I am not interested in dead glow-eyes, Remsn. Find me one I can fuck. Otherwise, it is of academic note."

A second voice rose. "This one might interest you, sir."

A second, nondescript shadow appeared. This one had wire-like hair and wore a yellow smock, to mark him as a doctor.

Terian decided he liked the lizard suit better.

"We think it likely the record of Syrimne. There are several factors that—"

"Wait." Terian raised a hand. "What makes you think that?"

"The dates match," said the lizard. "We found him initially in colonial records of the French. But the same being appears in German records when we cross-referenced."

"Show me."

Both shadows faded.

Blood data floated, lines linking characteristics between the two subjects. Terian recognized Alyson's before shifting his attention to the other, obviously older record. From phrasing it was likely from a primary source, and handwritten.

After staring at it for a few seconds, Terian exhaled.

"There is some mild variation," he commented. "And it is not a DNA record as such, but the old style of seer blood-printing, which is less accurate—"

"Yes, sir," the doctor agreed. "Of course you are right. But all of the secondaries match. They even tracked the rate at which the blood lost its structural integrity, and it matches our rate of genetic decomposition. Factors indicate the possibility of at least two discernible Elaerian blood types. Given how closely tied these creatures are to their sight, it could also have something to do with their *aleimic* signature, or their specific connections to beings within the Barrier."

Ithren sounded apologetic.

"We still do not fully understand Barrier-mutable physiological factors, sir. We have a team working on mapping rules around…"

Seeing, or perhaps sensing the impatience emanating off Terian, the researcher quickly changed course.

"…In any case, the second specimen is clearly Elaerian. An exact match exists in all other relevant data: heart rate, reflexes, glandular make-up, brain activity, respiratory functioning, *aleimic* signature described. There is no doubt this is *not* a Sark. It is even more obviously not human."

Terian remained fixed on the dates. "Could the age be incorrect?"

"We pulled the records from a colonial school organized according to age groups. At the very least, he appeared this age physically, sir."

Terian quirked an eyebrow, smiling in spite of himself.

"A school? What was his claimed race?"

"Human, sir."

"Human?" Terian blinked. "Really?"

"Yes, sir. He claimed to be the son of a diplomat from Serbia. A blood illness, along with rumors of mixed ethnicity were meant to account for some of his secondary traits."

"And you believe this age to be correct?"

"It matches, sir," the lizard piped in. "Three of his classmates went on to take prominent roles in the German military in World War I. His guardian was a confirmed member of the resistance under Syrimne later."

"All right." Terian tapped his fingers. "What else?"

"Intelligence tests, emotional assessment, disciplinary reports—his intelligence scores were off the charts. Empathic didn't even register. Relational he was weaker, but still better than most Sarks."

The avatar gave Terian a grim look.

"…They thought he cheated, sir. Apparently he made a point of sabotaging every test they tried to perform on him, either rigging outcomes or refusing outright to participate. They have a lot of notes scribbled by the results…"

Trailing, the seer gestured vaguely. "The issue of his race was never raised. Of course, humans were ignorant about seers at the time—"

"What was the name again?"

"Nenzi, sir." The avatar turned, scanning other records. "That was likely his seer name, or a nickname, perhaps. At the school he's listed as Ewald Gottschalk. Could have been a joke though, sir, that name."

At Terian's blank look, Ithren shrugged.

"'God's servant in the Law,' is roughly how it translates. We were able to trace back a clan name, from the guardian. Humans knew him as the boy's uncle, and we've got him ID'd as a seer, as well. Sark, of course, so unlikely to be a true blood relative, but it has to be presumed he knew something was odd with his charge."

"Name?"

"Clan Argstaad, sir." He cleared his throat meaningfully. "Menlim, as given."

"You mentioned disciplinary reports." Terian scrolled through electronic records. "Were these all about faked tests?"

"No, sir. Most related to behavioral issues, but he was also written up for a number of... well, odder things. One of the teachers built a case for suspected child abuse, openly naming the boy's guardian in several reports. According to her, young Ewald refused to undress for physical examinations, fell asleep repeatedly in class due to sleep deprivation, passed out at least twice from lack of food, came to school visibly injured. Emotionally, he showed symptoms of trauma. He also displayed as nearly obsessive-compulsive in terms of certain rituals, and acted as though he thought he was constantly being watched—"

"Did they pursue it?"

"No." Ithren shrugged. "Given the political situation at the time, it is hardly surprising. One of the reports also has Nenzi cutting the throat of a classmate in a schoolyard fight, so he didn't make a particularly believable victim."

Seeing Terian's eyebrows rise, Ithren added,

"The classmate survived. And extenuating circumstances were present... but Nenzi wasn't popular. They actually had a petition at one point to drive him out of the school."

Terian lips twitched in a smile. "I'm beginning to like this kid. Did the petition succeed?"

"No, but only due to timing. His uncle pulled him, claiming his nephew 'Ewald' suffered from some sort of illness. We found no reports of him visiting medical facilities, however. In fact, there are never any reports of him visiting the human meds, except when his teacher forced the issue, and then the guardian nearly had her arrested."

"Any adult records?" Terian said.

"Two." Ithren's image receded, replaced by a VR record that had once been hand-written. "A double homicide in which he was the primary suspect. The records are incomplete, and the murders may have related to the war. There was a fire at the relevant police station prior to his transfer to military tribunal."

Terian skimmed details. "Was he prosecuted?"

"No, sir, but again, only due to timing. The second record I referenced is that of his death."

The image morphed again, replacing the first record with another, also hand-written, beside a death certificate in German.

"...which is listed as occurring one week prior to the first scheduled hearing before the military tribunal assigned the case."

"Death? But that would be before the war ended, surely?"

"Well before, sir. We believe his death must have been staged. Perhaps even with the complicity of the German military."

A news broadcast began playing in the background, describing an explosion in one of the military shipyards.

"It makes sense," Ithren said. "If his handlers were trying to keep him inconspicuous, they didn't do a particularly effective job. And the incident was used as a political weapon for a number of months after. The Germans claimed it was sabotage by the French."

The geneticist's tone shifted, as if he were reading details aloud.

"Nenzi was known to be a member of the Brotherhood, which was only a political organization at the time, handing out leaflets, giving speeches, holding protests, that kind of thing. He had a reputation as a fighter... even made money as a street boxer. He appeared to be around eighteen, in human years, by that time. It's impossible to know his true age. We now believe, from Alyson's records, that Elaerian are able to adapt to the chronological cycles of the dominant species around which they were raised, as a function of camouflage. If he were raised mainly around humans—"

"This was all prior to the ban. Are there any images of him?"

"No, sir. That's another odd thing. Images of his classmates exist, but his were destroyed. All of them, even in the official records."

Terian thought for a moment. "Who witnessed his death?"

"His guardian, a few neighbors, people he worked with. We looked into all the names. All Brotherhood, sir. No one thought to question it at the time."

"Any of them alive now?" Terian said.

Ithren shook his head, clicking softly. "Not on record. We'd have to do more digging to be sure. A lot of people changed identities following the war."

"Do it," Terian said. "What about the guardian?"

Ithren glanced at the lizard, as if for help.

The lizard cleared his throat. "Menlim was relatively unknown in Germany back then, sir. Locally, he was known only as a Bavarian scholar who adopted an orphan boy out of pity. Locals believed him to be human."

Resmn scrolled through images of the war.

"...A few months after his nephew's death, he and his Brotherhood went underground. That was right before they began attacking the French forces openly, sir. And, pardon my saying it, but you know what happened after that."

A map materialized, showing mountains Terian hadn't seen with his eyes in thirty years, but that formed a portion of the modern history curriculum of every school-aged child since the end of World War I.

He recognized the most picturesque of the peaks, had a sudden memory of walking up there once, with Dehgoies. It had been the other's idea, of course. Dehgoies never got the Himalayas out of his system; as long as Terian knew him, he always seemed to be looking for a mountain tall enough that he might stretch his legs.

"There, sir." Ithren pointed to infrared images of caves dotting the cliffs. "They likely hid him there, where Menlim and Syrimne both were reputed to live during the war. The Allied powers only found those headquarters after the Treaty of Versailles. Menlim had them protected with some kind of Barrier trick..."

But Terian was staring at the map.

His jaw loosened as the pieces clicked into place.

"Menlim of *Bavaria?* Do you mean to tell me this Elaerian child was adopted by *the* Menlim, the one behind the Brotherhood's military strategy?"

"Yes, sir." Remsn sounded relieved that Terian had finally caught on. "Most thought Menlim *was* Syrimne, sir. He was infamous in the Pamir, one of the few known experts in military tactics for seers at that time. He's one of the only seers who *could* have trained Syrimne to do those things, sir."

Terian leaned back in his chair.

There was something here, something important yet, and not only in regard to the puzzle around the boy from Sikkim.

He couldn't make the pieces fit, no matter how he assembled them.

"I want every record, every scrap and word you dug up on this person. Not just the summaries. I want originals."

"Yes, sir." Ithren said.

"Now." Terian steepled his fingers. "I will wait."

CHAPTER 14

FOUR

Terian-4 tensed. He half-fell to a fighting stance without knowing at first why he'd done it.

He watched the boy's face.

Focused. Attentive. His body frozen.

When nothing happened, he forced himself to relax.

It wasn't the first time he'd felt something off the boy's light that nearly gave him a heart attack. Unfortunately, he still had no idea what affected him so viscerally.

The interior of the cave where they'd stopped contained high, rough walls, forming an open space roughly the size of a small cottage. Drafty, but a blessing in that it kept off the elements, the cave stayed relatively warm and bright with a well-fed fire.

Not a lot of heat escaped out the low-ceilinged tunnel that led outside.

Still, it had been hell coaxing the boy in there the first time.

They had to build two fires and illuminate every crack in every wall before the kid would so much as venture past the threshold.

Four studied the boy's youth-rounded face now.

The deep black eyes shone with intelligence.

More than intelligence—at times he saw a depth of understanding there that shocked him, particularly given the boy's long isolation in that underground cell. He appeared to comprehend the problems raised by outside forces to a surprising degree, even when relatively sophisticated and modern elements were involved, such as satellites tracking them and the problems raised by modern scanning methods and drones.

He reasoned. He quickly grasped multiple variables and drew conclusions.

He adapted to his environment. He had adjusted to being outside of that dungeon faster than anyone could have reasonably expected.

But Four still couldn't reach him.

Not really. Not enough.

They were being followed. Four knew now by whom. It would certainly be easier if he could make the boy understand the specific problems associated with that as well.

So far, Terian's efforts to communicate had met with no discernible success.

Still, Four was alive. Moreover, the chemically-heated food he'd insisted his sherpas pack seemed to be a big hit.

He watched the boy stick small, corpse-white fingers into a bag full of something meant to approximate beef stroganoff. He seemed oblivious to temperature, responding only to the smell as he crammed chunks of seared meat and brown sauce into his dirty mouth. Terian witnessed the process in fascination. He wondered if his new charge would ever sleep long enough for a successful attempt to collar him.

He kept the thought very carefully in the back of his mind.

Even so, the black opal eyes darted up.

They met Terian's, and Four felt the hairs on his arms and the back of his neck rise. A curl of electrically-charged *aleimi* slid around his skin.

"No wire," the boy said.

English. That was new.

Up until that point, he'd spoken a form of bastardized Prexci, mixed with what Terian identified as Khaskura Bhasha, an older form of Nepali. Terian also caught a few muttered words in Mandarin and Hindi.

But the English was a first.

"Spracken zi deutsch?" he ventured.

"No wire," the boy said in German.

"I understand," Terian said in Russian, holding up his hands. "No wires."

"No wires," the boy repeated in Czech, or maybe Polish. "Try and... boom!" He grinned, his mouth filled with meat. "Boom!" he said again, throwing his hands up on spidery, stick-like arms.

He spilled some of the meat sauce on the rocks and pressed his foot in it, squishing the sauce between his toes. Frowning, he stopped, rubbing his foot deeper into the loose dirt. Four couldn't help but marvel that the boy still retained his revulsion reflex, considering how he'd been living.

Four bowed politely.

"Boom, yes," he said. "We understand one another, friend. No wires. Of course not. It was merely a passing thought."

The boy gave him a sharp look, and Terian realized he'd reverted to talking to him as though he were a much younger child. He would need to be careful if he wanted to avoid offense. Adolescent seers were prone to hyper-sensitivity when it came to being treated with respect.

Somehow that struck him as darkly funny, too.

The boy's focus returned to the bag.

He dug his hand into the metallic wrapping, bringing another fistful of meat and noodles to his lips and sucking the juice greedily off his knuckles. Terian's eyes fell to the boy's narrow ribcage, the bones poking through the skin of his small chest. He would clean him up first. Make sure he knew food was no longer a luxury.

Nor a bed, blankets, clothing, electronics, a roof, baths, cars, servants.

Hell, he'd get the kid a pony if he wanted one.

He might wait until he'd fattened him up a bit, though, so the kid didn't eat it.

The boy laughed, throwing a handful of the stroganoff in Terian's direction.

Terian sidestepped it neatly, keeping the smile on his face.

If there was one area he excelled in, it was in providing material comfort. He'd make sure the kid had all the comfort he could ever hope for, more than he'd dreamed of in that foul-smelling cave. Then they would talk.

The boy laughed again, dripping more meat juice onto his lips and into his mouth. His eyes narrowed at Terian, and the intelligence shone there again.

"Talk. Yes." He grinned, his teeth shockingly white under all the dirt and now juice running down his face, neck and fingers. "I like you, Sark. You get me things, and we talk."

He flung the remains of the bag at Terian.

That time, he managed to hit him, splattering his coat and pants with brown sauce.

Terian merely bowed as the young seer laughed again. He smiled politely.

"Of course, my dear friend. Whatever pleases you."

Still, in looking at the gleam in those fire-blackened eyes, he found himself glad, not the first time, that he still had a few bodies to spare.

"Bye-bye, Terry," the boy said. The smile remained on his face, but the black eyes once more turned sharp, hawk-like. "Bye-bye."

Four smiled stiffly, trying not to react to the familiarity he heard in that voice.

Or the fact that it suddenly sounded much older, and less randomly crazy.

Bowing lower still, Four removed himself from the boy's presence and into the adjoining opening in the cave, where the sherpas crouched in a corner, muttering amongst themselves and avoiding his eyes.

Terian squatted against the rock wall, and began wiping his trousers with a damp rag. Smearing and rubbing off the worst of the juice, he resigned himself to the fact that he'd likely attract mountain cats for days.

Pouring water on the same rag and then his pants, he cleaned his hands thoroughly before extracting the leather-bound diary from the inside pocket of his coat. Three sent the original to Four in Beijing for safekeeping, not knowing Four would end up in the middle of a shooting war within a week, and with the book on his person.

If he had to do it again, he would have brought a copy.

Settling his weight in a flat spot by the cave wall, Four flipped it open.

There had to be a key in here, somewhere.

Some clue to getting the creature to cooperate. Something the boy cared about.

Between the two Terians, they (or he) had read the damned book cover to cover five times. If the formula for enticing sanity from the child was written in code behind Revi's neat print, it eluded him.

No, the answers for that wouldn't likely come from Revi'.

Dehgoies had been the cage builder, the one who figured out how to keep the boy hidden and alive. The real answers would have resided with Galaith. Galaith would have researched the boy incessantly. He would have studied his every move, for years on end, looking for a way in, searching for every potential access point.

Ultimately, Galaith hadn't succeeded in time, but he would have been in process with this, somehow.

Unfortunately, Terian found nothing in any of Galaith's records even referencing the boy. Nothing in the organic-based computer library. Nothing in the originals he'd appropriated before Alyson could find them, or the Barrier fragments he'd managed to track following the Pyramid's demise.

Which meant if anything still existed, it remained lost.

Or Alyson had it.

In any case, the boy's presence explained a few things—notably why Galaith had been so ridiculously cautious in approaching Alyson while there was still some chance Dehgoies might kill her.

Galaith couldn't possibly have intended to pass up a breeding attempt on two full-blooded Elaerian. Whatever the boy's age, given the odds of ever coming across a biological pair again, it was inconceivable he wouldn't have considered it.

It occurred to Terian, of course, that whatever sanity once existed in the boy had long ago ceased to be. It wasn't like Galaith or Revi' to waste resources; if they'd resorted to chaining a seer of that talent in an underground dungeon like a rabid dog, it was likely because they'd exhausted every other means of securing his cooperation.

Sighing, Terian tucked the book back into his jacket.

All of his answers only seemed to breed more questions.

Where had they found the wretched creature? How had they managed to keep his existence a secret all this time, with nothing but a doddering human and a dimwitted nun to guard him? How was it the boy didn't appear to have aged?

Terian asked the Barrier, hoping faintly for some kind of inspiration.

None came.

A SOUND ROUSED FOUR FROM SLEEP.

He stiffened, looking around. Something was wrong.

The first thing he noticed was the quiet.

He lay by the embers of a dying fire; the only sounds came from outside the cave, along with the occasional soft pop from the red coals. He clutched at the gun he'd placed carefully under the sheepskin jacket he'd been using as a pillow, realizing he didn't hear any breathing besides his own.

The two sherpas no longer slept across the fire from him.

His first thought was that they'd skulked out, leaving in the middle of the night to escape him and the boy. Yet all of their bedding and packs mysteriously remained.

The second thing he noticed was that the boy stood over him, completely naked.

Four swore in Chinese, flipping reflexively to his back. He raised the gun, pointing it at the boy's face, feeling his heart leap to his throat.

The boy only stood there, unsmiling.

Glancing around the cave, Terian realized he recognized the coppery smell in his mouth. His eyes drifted down to the boy's small hands and arms.

They were no longer white, but red to the elbows. The deep scarlet liquid steaming on his skin contrasted sharply with his extreme pallor.

Four lowered the gun slowly. When the boy continued to look at him, he shoved the weapon back under the sheepskin jacket, but within easy reach.

"The humans?" Terian asked him.

The boy gestured fluidly.

Terian nodded, keeping his voice level. "But why? They were our guides."

I didn't want them here.

"But we needed them," Terian said. "It is fine to kill, but you do not kill what you need alive. Do you understand?"

"We do not need them," the boy said in Hindi.

"We do. To get through the mountains." Seeing indifference on the boy's face, he explained, *This part of me... it is only a merchant. I do not know these lands. This will be harder for us now. It will be harder for me to protect you.*

The boy frowned. *I don't need you to protect me. I can protect us!*

Terian didn't miss the "we" or the "us."

He watched the boy's face cautiously.

The kid showed no signs of moving away.

"It's fine," Terian said, conceding, *You are very good at protecting us, yes.* He looked at the boy's hanging arms. "Please go wash yourself." He glanced out the cave door, towards the steady sound he heard in the dark beyond the opening. "In the creek. Go wash your arms. And chest," he added, gesturing at the boy's bare body. "You shouldn't sleep like that."

He paused, looking around the dim cave.

"Where are the bodies?"

The boy pointed by the door.

Terian squinted in the firelight and shadows, just making them out. "Do you need my help, putting them outside?"

The boy jerked a finger sideways in "no."

"All right." Terian lay back on the pallet. "Go, then. Come back when you're done."

The boy walked obediently to the door of the cave.

Terian watched after him, sighing at the apparent success of his little experiment, and wondering at his own nerve in ordering the little butcher around.

A few minutes later, Terian heard the scuffle and breathing associated with dragging a body out the door.

Not a very long time after that, the boy returned.

His pale arms were white once more, nearly shining in the firelight. His hair and eyelashes dripped with water. Terian hoped he'd put the bodies out far enough, so they wouldn't stink up the confined space before morning, but he didn't intend to go out there and check. Relaxing into the skins, he studied the round face, wondering what now.

He still wasn't wholly convinced he wasn't next.

As he thought it, Terian got a flicker of feeling and intent off the boy, enough to garner his motives. The revelation bewildered him.

He studied the dark eyes, looking for confirmation.

Finding it, he hesitated only a few heartbeats, then grabbed hold of the skins half-wrapped around his body. He flipped them back.

Smiling, he patted the pallet below.

"Come, then," he said, oddly touched. He motioned him closer with his hand. "It's all right. You can come. I don't mind."

The boy knelt down by the fire, then turned his back, curling up in the hollow of Terian's body. Four wrapped the skins around both of him, and held the boy carefully, resting his head on the sheepskin jacket.

Even through the blankets and skins, he was amazed at the thinness of the small body, the pointed protuberances he felt at odd intervals against his chest.

"What should I call you?" Terian asked in Mandarin.

The boy shivered, burrowing closer to Terian's chest.

His hands curled together in front of him.

Briefly, Terian didn't think he would answer.

"Nenzi," the boy said then. "My name is Nenzi."

Four watched the boy's lips move in a silent prayer as his eyes closed, just before he relaxed into his body's warmth.

So he was religious then. That was good information to have.

It was also a little frightening, given what he'd just done.

He looked like an overgrown puppy, nothing like the creature Terian had witnessed at the school in Sikkim, or the one he'd seen eating a few hours earlier, who had called him by name, a vague cruelty behind his eyes.

Reaching up carefully, Terian stroked the boy's hair back from his face.

He would need to talk to Three about this.

The boy tensed at his first touch, but merged his light into Four's when he didn't stop petting him. He laid his dark head on Terian's lower arm.

Feeling the boy's breaths grow slower and more regular against his chest, smelling the sherpas' blood and the remains of stroganoff in the damp hair, Four smiled a little when he heard a soft snore, and continued stroking the small head.

CHAPTER 15
WELLINGTON

Director of U.S. Homeland Security Gregory Palmer stared around at the room's other twelve occupants, fighting to keep his temper in check.

"So," he said. "Explain this to me again. Pretend I'm an idiot. Pretend I'm a reporter from FeedNeedTV." He waited for the chuckles to subside. "We're 'taking a break' from the war?" Despite his attempts to sound humorous, his words carried an edge. "What the hell does that even mean?"

The Secretary of State gave a snort of restrained laughter.

"Is this some code for negotiations?" Palmer said. "Or—'"

"No." A different voice rose from a print couch.

A woman with a hard, dried face sat in near-perfect stillness, wearing justice's robes. Her thick white hair fit her head like a helmet. Her voice turned acidic, somehow making her appear even more reptilian:

"Did you neglect to read the brief?" she asked. "It's nothing like that, Palmer. This isn't about China at all."

The rest of the Cabinet stood and sat in various postures around the Oval Office, not speaking, or even looking at Palmer or the old woman directly.

No one ever wanted to tackle that old broad, he'd noticed.

He took a long drink from the bourbon on ice he clutched in his ex-athlete's hands, eyes darting around the beige-colored room. He wanted someone to argue with besides the old woman, but no one else would meet his gaze.

The reptile tilted her head, bird-like.

Palmer guessed he was the insect.

"Is Wellington serious about this?" he asked. "Are we really putting the entire operation on hold? For a handful of dead Sark brats?"

Something cold darkened the old woman's eyes.

A younger woman in a fitted navy suit folded her arms, watching the Justice hesitantly, as if trying to decide whether to speak. Palmer wished she would. He wondered again what the old fossil was even doing there. Since when had the Chief Justice of the Supreme Court sat in on military decisions?

And why was Jarvesch, the damned Secretary of Defense, catering to her?

Jarvesch, woman or not, was usually a bigger hawk than any of them.

She never held back when Wellington was in the room.

Yet here she was, looking at that old broad like a kid approaching a hall monitor, needing to go to the bathroom.

"Where is Wellington?" Palmer barked. "If he's going to sell us this load of crap plan, I want to hear it from him."

"Calm down, Greg," Jarvesch, began, but Palmer had been waiting for someone to argue with him. Someone else, that is.

He turned on the brunette in the navy suit.

"Does he think he'll actually win popularity points with a move like this?" He plunked his drained glass on a tray with a loud clink. "In case he hasn't noticed, no one's all that crazy about Sarks these days. Not after they exploded that damned ship, killing a couple thousand of *our* people. This is going to look weak. If not downright traitorous after the fiasco with Caine. We have to distance ourselves from that mess, now more than ever!"

"These are children, Palmer," the Chief Justice said quietly. "Innocents. And there are complications—"

"What about you, Jarvesch?" Palmer turned his back on the fossil on the couch. "Do you think it's 'complicated' too? Or do you have your nose so far up Wellington's ass that you've forgotten to use your military sense? Fucking women in charge, I swear. As if we don't have enough fits of undue emotionality around here."

Jarvesch's eyes narrowed.

"Palmer!" Chief of Staff Rogers rose to his feet. "That's the Secretary of Defense!"

"Yeah." Palmer snorted. "We all know *your* interest in this, Earl."

Rogers' face turned dark red, but Jarvesch waved him off, unperturbed.

"It's two days, Greg," she told Palmer. "And it makes sense, whether you like it or not. We need Europe's support if we're serious about China. They're a lot bigger on seer rights than we are." Frowning, she added, "You're absolutely right. We need the credibility after Caine went off the deep end. But we don't only need it at home."

She cocked her head at the shorter man, straightening her suit jacket.

"Besides, from my perspective, Greg, you're the only one here who appears to be suffering from a fit of 'undue emotionality.' Would you like a Xanex? I'm sure we can have one of the porters fetch one for you."

The Secretary of State suppressed another tense giggle.

Palmer ignored it.

"Really? Does it make sense to you, *Andrea?*" he said. "Because from where I stand, Wellington would have done better to work the terrorist attacks into the justification. If he really wanted European support, he could have claimed the damned Chinese destroyed their *own* stock. To prevent us from getting it alive."

His face reddened in anger at Jarvesch's smile.

"Hell, it's probably true! We still have no idea who killed them. Much less why!"

Jarvesch rolled her eyes. "Inter-seer rivalries don't interest us, Greg. We need to marginalize the fringe element. It's the trade we're after, and the illegal seer tech we know is still going on in Asia. You know all of this. You agreed with our strategy at the start."

"*Our* strategy?"

"Wellington's," she said impatiently. "We *all* agreed. Because it made sense. He has to be the rational one here. What might have been seen as 'impulsive' or 'manly' before Caine will only make them wonder if Wellington's unhinged, too. We need to maintain the moral high ground. Now more than ever."

When Palmer shook his head, she raised her voice.

"…Which means we do not fucking ignore the *butchering of children*, no matter what race they are. We do the right thing when atrocities happen, Greg. At least in front of the public."

Her voice rose louder when he scowled at her.

"This was an *atrocity*, Palmer. Get your head on straight about that, before you talk to any goddamn reporters! Whatever the feeds want to speculate, this wasn't a terrorist training ground. Our intel is clear. This was a bunch of kids being sold on the auction block by Chinese fascists to the highest bidder. You'd better stay on message about that, or we'll look like jackasses when the truth comes out. And you know it will."

"Kids?" he spat. "Little glow-eye rats!"

"They were *children.*"

"Enough!" the Chief Justice broke in.

Every eye turned to her.

Even Palmer fell silent. His lip curled at the woman's wrinkled face, the coldness of her eyes beneath those reptilian lids. When that gaze sharpened on his, he looked away.

Jaw hard, he walked to the drink cart parked in the middle of the room.

He began refilling his glass with square cubes.

"Where is he, anyway?" he muttered. "Speaking to his fans?"

"Something like that," another voice said.

EVERYONE IN THE ROOM TURNED, THIS TIME TOWARDS THE DOOR LEADING TO the garden.

Andrea Jarvesch couldn't help but shake her head at the human's theatrical entrance.

Wellington smiled from the east French door that led to the Rose Garden.

Smiling at their caught expressions, he shut the door behind him, making extra noise on purpose as he turned. He wore a slightly rumpled blue suit with a red silk tie. His dark skin shone under the warm lights of the Oval Office lamps. His handsome features stood out below amber-colored eyes as he chuckled.

"Aww." He looked at Jarvesch, then around at the other faces in turn. He paused on the Chief Justice. "You all look so sad. Did you miss me?"

"No," the old woman said.

The room erupted in laughter, louder from the tension being broken.

It wasn't until Palmer looked away that Andrea, the old justice and Wellington focused their eyes on him.

They gave one another brief glances.

Every government needs a little controversy, Ethan thought, clearly so that the two seers would hear him. *He's loud enough to be useful. Dim enough to not be a threat.*

I'm a little tired of his dimness myself, Jarvesch sent. *Can't we find one who's good-looking at least? If I could bring myself to fuck him, I'd have him under control in no time.*

Ethan's humor invaded the Barrier space.

He gave the barest shrug, hands clasped at the small of his back. *His lack of grace makes him easier to dismiss. Would you like a more articulate opponent, Sister?*

Jarvesch smiled sweetly. *Technically, you are not my brother, worm.*

How much longer for the delay? Xarethe barely masked her impatience that he managed to argue with himself, even in the midst of a crisis. *Four has secured the boy, has he not? Palmer is an idiot, but in this case, he is partly right. We must show the Chinese we are serious. We cannot afford to back down from a direct engagement. Humans can smell that kind of weakness.*

He has the boy, Ethan sent. *He is near the front lines, but there is a complication.*

When isn't there? Xarethe retorted.

Ethan smiled around at the room, pausing on Palmer, then on the others of his cabinet. His smile grew broader.

"I apologize," he said aloud.

Human or not, Jarvesch noted in somewhat self-serving admiration that he had the gift of sounding like he meant it.

"...a slight emergency has arisen," Wellington continued, after just the right amount of pause. "One that must be attended to prior to our debrief. I wonder if I could trouble you to wait for me outside? You're welcome to order anything you like from the kitchen, of course. I won't be long. I just need to have a word with our friend, Jarvesch, here."

Great, Jarvesch sent, folding her arms. *They already think I'm sleeping with you.*

No, sister, Wellington thought back humorously. *They know full well you're sleeping with Rogers. It was sweet of him to defend you just now, by the way.*

She rolled her eyes, giving Rogers a brief glance.

"Now?" Palmer's voice rose. "Is this a joke?"

"Only for a moment, gentlemen, I assure you." Wellington raised an arm, palm open, to indicate ushering them out. "Please. Wait in the foyer. Thank you."

Rogers complied first, setting his drink on the table before giving Jarvesch a nod on his way out the door. After a few more exchanged looks, the others began to rise, or to aim for the door if they were already on their feet.

The Chief Justice rose, too.

"Madam," Ethan said, with one of his charming smiles. "I'd like you to stay, as well."

Palmer glared around at all of them before downing half of his drink and leaving the remainder on the brass cart. He continued to mutter as he followed the others out the door.

The Chief Justice didn't move, but her mind focused on Wellington.

What is the issue now? Speaking directly into Ethan's mind, she ignored the humans as they continued to file out the door. *Are the children fighting? Or did he manage to lose the boy altogether?*

Smiling faintly, Ethan waited until the last person exited.

He shut the double doors himself after ushering out the porter.

He turned around to face them.

"He killed their guides," Ethan explained, glancing at Jarvesch.

Jarvesch chuckled.

The Chief Justice frowned, in the Barrier and outside.

"Four is concerned they are wandering too close to the front," Ethan added. "He has requested help. I thought we could stop the fighting long enough to get a chopper in there. Call it military aide, whatever. The problem is, now the Adhipan have arrived."

Is he in danger from the boy? the Chief Justice asked. *Four. Has the boy hurt him?*

"No." Ethan shook his head, loosening his tie. "The boy seems to have accepted him. That persona at least. He has even shown signs of affection. But he can't be controlled."

What about Three? Can he help? Jarvesch asked.

Ethan glanced at her. "We've already sent him. He's been ID'd by the Adhipan, though. They appear to be tracking him." Looking back to Xarethe, he added, "Dehgoies is with them."

Before the others could react, he waved them off.

"But that's not what I wanted to talk to you about. I think I can get Four and the boy out safe. It's the boy I'm worried about. He needs a mother. A friend, at least. Someone he'll actually listen to. He's positively starved for affection, which we might be able to use. Four seems to be bonding with him... better than I'd hoped, really... but to call the kid a loose cannon would be an understatement. If we can't figure out a way to control him, he will be useless to us. Assuming he doesn't kill us all."

Ethan turned to Xarethe. His amber eyes reflected light.

"Any ideas on how to expedite the process, Madam?" He gave the senior seer a polite bow. "In the American vernacular, I believe I'm 'tapped out.' The contributions of Dehgoies Revik's diary, helpful as they were, seem to be at an end. Given that the focus needs to remain on getting the boy out safe, it may be a few weeks yet, before I can steal back what Alyson took."

Silence fell while the old woman thought.

She stared out through the tall windows behind the desk.

While they waited, Andrea listened to the faint whisper of minds from the humans milling in the foyer. She shared what she heard with Ethan.

...do you have the press order yet?

...the latest word from SCARB is that there are still skirmishes occurring among seer factions in Sikkim. SCARB has it contained, but they're keeping an eye on...

Do we have the latest casualty report from Pakistan? What about...

Xarethe turned. She looked between the two Terians.

Her fingers drummed on one arm of the silk-upholstered couch.

"Yes," she said, somewhat cryptically. "Yes, I believe you've hit on exactly the solution, Ethan dear. Exactly what we need."

Wellington gave her a puzzled smile.

Then he grew quiet.

Xarethe had begun to send him images, packed information, a strategy.

He stood there, silent, as he absorbed what the ancient shared through the Barrier space. As a human, he of necessity absorbed such information more slowly, even with help from the two seers in the room.

Once he'd digested everything she sent, he nodded, rubbing his chin.

"I understand," he ventured. "But it won't be easy. Not anymore."

The old woman chuckled.

"I don't know, Terry. I think you may find it is easier than it has ever been. You may be astonished at how easy it is. Even if you can't use the boy." She looked to Jarvesch. "Find a way to make it happen. And do it quickly. We need him operational, and fast. All of our plans depend on securing his cooperation in the short term."

"I understand." Ethan bowed.

Jarvesch folded her arms. "So how do we get Four out?"

"Send Raven," Xarethe said.

Ethan's mouth pursed. "Raven? But then she'll know about the boy."

Jarvesch shook her head. "No outsiders."

Xarethe overruled both Terians. "She'll be on the same page with this. Believe me. You can trust her. Just make sure you pay her well."

Ethan and Jarvesch exchanged tense looks.

No doubt, Raven would be loyal to Xarethe.

That loyalty may or may not translate to any or all parts of him.

Ethan inclined his head towards the door.

"We'd better bring them back in."

Jarvesch rolled her eyes, putting her game face back on.

"Fine. Do it."

She downed the last of her drink as Ethan crossed the room and unlatched the double doors.

"Friends, please." He smiled, opening wide his arm, this time to usher them back inside. Winking at Jarvesch, he clapped Palmer on the back as he passed. "I think it is now official." He met Xarethe's lizard-like gaze. "We have a plan."

Waiting for the rest of them to file in, he closed the doors, still smiling.

"Apologies for the secrecy. Good news is, our direction is now clear. And it won't involve us stopping the war for more than a day. Which should suit even you, Greg."

At the surprised murmurs in the group, Ethan cleared his throat.

"We'll need to hammer out our press strategy. But first, a drink!"

Palmer grunted as, one by one, the rest of the cabinet found or refilled their glasses. More than one gave the Chief Justice a wary look as they passed, but each looked away before the old woman caught them staring.

Within seconds, Ethan had them gathered in a rough circle around the two facing couches in front of the room's fireplace. At his cue, they lifted and clinked glasses solemnly. Even Jarvesch managed a real-looking smile, raising her glass to tap it collegially against Palmer's.

"To the end of war," Ethan said.

"To winning!" Palmer said, and they all laughed.

"To winning," Ethan conceded, raising his glass again with a smile. "May it be swift, and relatively painless. To our side, at least."

Raising their glasses alongside his, they murmured assent and drank.

CHAPTER 16
VISITOR

I perched on a boulder in front of Tarsi's house.

I'd woken up early.

Too early, given the day I'd had before.

Moonlight had only just begun to fade through cracks in the cave walls when I gave up trying to sleep and dragged myself outside.

Now I sat wrapped in one of the cowskins that made up my bedding, watching stars fade, watching my breath plume out in clouds, distorting my view. An owl hooted in the darkness as it winged by silently, but otherwise, it was unnervingly quiet.

I still sat there when daylight birds began to sing.

It was about that time that I realized I was being watched.

Rising to my feet, I scanned the trees.

Using my eyes, then my light, I felt a whisper of another seer, but tightly shielded. I only hesitated an instant before calling out, still clutching the cowskin to my chest.

"Whoever you are, you've got about five seconds before I get my gun."

A shadow stepped out from behind a tree.

For an instant, my heart flared. I thought it might actually be him.

Then I saw the height of the silhouette.

Immediately, my light retracted back around my body, coiling there as if unsure where to go. Flickers of pain rose. Disappointment firmed my mouth.

"Chandre." I recognized her braids, even with her face in shadow. "What are you doing skulking around?" Anger leaked into my voice. "Did Yerin send you?"

"No." She cleared her throat. "Balidor."

I nodded, but my posture didn't relax. "And?" My hand remained a fist, balled inside the skins. "What do you want?"

The infiltrator hesitated, then stepped forward into the clearing.

She walked towards me as if I were a stray dog whose temperament she still hadn't assessed.

"You all right, Bridge?" she asked, soft.

My hands tightened more. She must have felt something, because she stopped again, about ten feet from where I stood.

"I'm alone," she said. "For now. They're sending more. Females only. Balidor's rules."

"Yeah? So why are you telling me? If they're 'Balidor's rules?'"

There was a silence.

I flinched then, confused by a pulse that enveloped my light. It came from Chandre, and it felt like pain—different than what I got from Revik, but with an emotional punch that startled me. I remembered that I hadn't seen her among the faces in the courtyard that day.

When she didn't meet my gaze, I forced myself to relax, to breathe.

"Well, I'm glad they sent you," I said, gruff.

I tugged the blanket tighter around me and sat on the boulder.

"Are you hungry? There's also this coffee-like drink Tarsi makes. It's not bad, if—"

"No." She took another step towards me, then stopped.

I felt her struggling. Realizing she was looking for a way to talk to me about that whole mess with Maygar, I headed her off.

"Jon and Cass," I prodded. "Are they all right?"

She gestured affirmative. "They're fine, Bridge."

"And… Revik?" I felt my mouth harden. "Where's he?"

Chandre's eyes flickered to mine. Emotion stood out plainly in her face.

After a few seconds where I could only stare, I looked away.

"He cannot come here, Allie," she said, soft.

I nodded, pulling the cowskin closer. "Yeah. Okay." I forced a sigh. "Is he all right? He didn't... you know... *do* anything?"

Chandre shook her head, clicking absently.

"No. They brought him back to the compound before they told him." She gave a low snort, folding her muscular arms.

For the first time she sounded like the Chandre I knew.

"You shield good, Bridge. He didn't know. Not until Balidor's people told him. Put up a hell of a fight once he understood. Took five of them to bring him down..."

Feeling something off me, she hesitated.

Her voice grew a little less flippant.

"They had to put him away for a while. Calm him down."

My jaw hardened to granite. "Did they hurt him?"

She clicked softly, shaking her head. "No, Bridge. Few bruises maybe. He clocked Yerin good. Broke a few of his ribs before they could get him off."

I stared at the ground, thinking about whether I wanted to ask the next.

"And Maygar?" I looked up, meeting her dark red eyes. "Did I kill him?"

"No." She gestured negative, shifting her weight. "Your husband didn't, either. Not yet. He's still alive."

My shoulders relaxed.

I wanted to ask more about Revik. I didn't know what to ask though, or even how. Nodding again, I tugged the skins back around me.

I didn't move when Chandre walked closer, but I must have tensed enough that she saw it. She paused before she would have sat down next to me.

She sank to the ground in front of me instead, crossing her legs.

"Bridge." She took a breath. "He asked me to watch you."

I nodded, forcing myself to look at her. "I figured that. He said something about finding you when I got to the compound. I just forgot."

"Did he tell you why?" Chandre asked.

"No." My voice turned curt. "And at this point, I don't really need a primer in seer legalese. Maygar spelled it out pretty clearly. Apparently I was open game, because I'd asked for sex, and didn't get it." I folded my arms tighter under the cowskin. "That's right, isn't it? Or did I miss some nuance in that little cultural tidbit?"

She winced. "It is a stupid law. No one does that anymore. No one, Allie. It is why Dehgoies didn't tell you. It didn't make any sense to bring it up."

"Yeah." I nodded, looking out over the valley. "No sense at all. Look, Chan, I appreciate you coming here. But I really don't need you to defend him. If he's worried about me being mad, he can damned well ask me himself."

"Allie." Chandre's voice turned pleading. "Please. It was my fault. I promised him. I *promised* I would not let anything happen. He was adamant that I meet you at the gate. I was stupid, letting that bastard and his friends get the jump on me. I should have had a back up in place. Someone else to look out for you, in the event I couldn't."

I stared at her.

Chandre never got emotional, not that I'd ever seen. I tried to decide if it was for Revik's sake, or for mine. Knowing her, it could be either.

I shook my head slowly, feeling my hands unclench.

"I'm not mad," I said. Thinking, then, I amended my words. "Well, okay. I *am* mad. But mostly, I feel like an idiot. I knew something was wrong. I knew Maygar was up to something, but I let him goad me into a fight anyway."

Still thinking, I clenched my jaw. "I'm not feeling a lot of love for the men at the compound who were there. You can tell Vash I'm not going back there to live. I don't care how many locks they put on my door."

Chandre nodded, her eyes and mouth pinched.

Biting my lip, I hesitated, then said it anyway.

"I also feel pretty shaky about my standing as 'leader' when I'm subject to some legal loophole that says I can be gang-raped whenever my husband's not in the mood."

"No." Chandre gestured vehemently in the negative. "It is only because you haven't consummated. Once you have, no one can touch you, Allie."

"Great." I snorted. "So I'll be *privately* owned then. What a relief that will be." Kicking at the dirt with my toe, I frowned. "Don't take this the wrong way, but I was hoping you were him. It's not as fun to yell at you about this."

She didn't smile.

Instead she nodded, looking dejected.

For a moment we just sat there. I watched a scattering of birds chase one another from one cluster of trees to the next.

Then I sighed, realizing I had to let this go.

The last thing I needed was to encourage the aggressively protective impulse in Revik. Punishing my friends wouldn't make me feel any better, either. Chandre didn't make the rules any more than I did.

I dug a hand into my pocket.

After a moment's pause where I located it tucked in a section of creased cloth, I pulled out the ring I'd been carrying with me since I got it back from Jon.

I held it out to Chandre, feeling my face warm.

"Hey," I said. "Do me a favor, okay?"

Chandre's dark red eyes showed a whisper of surprise.

The eagerness there made me feel guilty again, but I ignored it, holding out my hand more insistently. She put her palm under my closed fingers and I dropped the ring.

I waited for her to look at it.

"Could you give him that for me?" I subdued my voice. "It's a present. He can do whatever he wants with it. Adjust it for his finger size, toss it into the woods, put it in a drawer. Whatever."

"Which finger should I tell him he can wear it?" she asked, examining the ring. "If he asks, Bridge? Any?"

I shrugged. "I have no idea what that means. Are there seer finger-codes I should be aware of?" I quirked an eyebrow. "You know, like this one means, 'you're my love bunny,' but that one means, 'I'm going to stab you in your sleep one night'?"

She gave me a wan smile, but it was still tentative. Still very un-Chandre.

"Is this a marriage present?" she asked.

I ran my fingers through my hair, uncomfortable with the question. "Sort of." I tugged at the chain around my neck, pulling it out of my shirt. Fingering the silver ring that hung on it, I showed it to her with a sigh.

"He gave me this," I explained. "I know it's not like a human marriage, where rings are exchanged, I wear a white dress, he wears a tux, and people throw rice at us. I'm not even sure what he meant by giving his ring to me. But I wanted to give him something, too. Something that mattered to me."

I motioned towards the ring in her hand, feeling my face warm a little more.

"That was my father's. He was human, and he meant a hell of a lot to me. You can tell him that, too. He'll understand."

Studying my eyes, she gestured in affirmative.

I noticed she used the formal version, as if I'd asked her to lead an army into battle.

She put the ring carefully in a front pocket.

"I know what to do. Do not worry, Bridge." She smiled wider, looking almost like her old self. "You are a tolerant mate," she said. "Very tolerant. Dehgoies is a lucky man."

I wasn't sure if I liked that much.

"I'm a doormat, you mean," I muttered, kicking the ground.

She clicked at me, but softly.

"No. No, I would not say that. Not at all, Bridge."

Touching my arm with a pulse of warmth, she surprised me by kissing me affectionately on the cheek. I was still recovering from that as she rose to her feet.

Without looking back, she walked into the woods.

She disappeared through the shadowed opening where I'd first seen her.

Seemingly the instant she was gone, Tarsi pulled at my light.

She wanted me back inside.

Sighing, I tugged the cowskin off my shoulders. It was too warm now to wear it.

Despite the insistence of Tarsi's pull, I stalled a few seconds longer, letting the sun warm my face, eyes closed as I listened to the birds.

I had a feeling it was the last I'd see of the sun for a few days.

Turns out, I was right about that.

CHAPTER 17

FIRST JUMP

T arsi began formally. She even told me where to sit.

Accommodating her wishes, I plunked myself down cross-legged on a prayer rug that covered the stone tiles in front of her fireplace.

I waited for her to sink to her own prayer mat, accepting a cup from "the girl" and watching fire eat through a pine log one of them had shoved into the grate.

I am old, Bridge, Tarsi sent. *I see some things because I remember them. When I said last night that this thing with the children bothers me, it is partly because it feels the same. The imprints in the Barrier are similar.*

"Similar?" I frowned. "To the last Displacement, you mean?"

She chuckled. "I am not *that* old, Bridge."

I flushed, but she only smiled.

There was another attempt to begin the human Displacement, she explained. *In this cycle. That time, the attempt was thwarted. The rise of Syrimne during World War I could very well have precipitated the Displacement early. The danger was averted, mainly by the being himself. It is fortunate that he did.*

It took me a few seconds to process her words.

"You mean Syrimne? He stopped it?"

In part, yes.

Relief infused me. "So we can stop it this time."

"No." Tarsi mirrored her words with a finger. *It is dangerous to assume that, Bridge Alyson. The Displacement cannot be kept off forever.*

I felt my mouth pull into a frown.

"Look. That's crap, if you don't mind my—"

It is possible to stop it, Bridge Alyson... in the way that anything is always possible. But I do not see signs that indicate any likelihood of that outcome. It is best to prepare to play your usual role in the coming events.

She was starting to remind me of my grandmother a little.

My grams had that edge when she was annoyed, too.

When I was younger, it always surprised me because of the sweetness of her little old lady exterior. But that contrast was less fascinating to me now, sitting in the dark in the middle of the day, talking about the world ending.

I clenched my hands, looking at my fingers.

"I should tell you," I said, still looking down. "I don't believe in prophecies. I'm sorry, but I don't. Vash convinced me it was better not to argue with you all about this, but that doesn't change how I feel."

Seeing the old woman smile, I let anger seep into my voice.

"I'm also not just going to roll over and plan for the end of the world like it's all a big party. I might have been raised among 'worms,' but I've seen enough vids to know war is an ugly, pointless horror-show most of the time. If I can prevent that happening, I will. I resent the implication that whatever I do is 'inevitably' going to bring about that end."

Grunting, I added,

"Truthfully, I wish more of you seers would help by advising me on how to *avoid* war instead of reciting prophecies from however-long ago."

I understand. Tarsi broke into my thoughts easily, with no discernible reaction. *I am not here to persuade you, Bridge. I'm not even here to advise you. Only to educate you as best I can.*

"But why?" My frown deepened. "I've told you. I don't believe in your myths. If you don't want to help, why not just let me be a figurehead?"

Her eyes grew shrewd, and a little impatient.

Alyson, you have been leading. For months now. The time to 'play figure-head' is long since past. Do not play little girl with me, and I will not play old woman with you. Fair?

Feeling my face tighten, I nodded. "Fair."

She followed my eyes to the fire. *If you truly wish to thwart the prophecies outlined in the Myth, you must first know what it entails. The Bridge is not believed to be evil. No more than Syrimne is believed to be evil. In your case, we got to you in time, before you could be made into something truly dark by Galaith or whoever else.*

She shrugged with one hand.

Syrimne was not so lucky. The Sword is often delegated the hard path.

I glanced at the girl, wondering what she thought of our bickering.

I motioned with my mug, silently asking for a refill of the thick drink. As she began preparing to make more in the clay teapot, I turned back to Tarsi.

"It's still a little hard for me to hear good about Syrimne," I admitted. "It's like saying Hitler was an okay guy, he just had a rough childhood."

"No." Tarsi made a line in the air with one finger, frowning. *He was not a good human at all. Not at all. It is not a good comparison, Alyson.*

I smiled in spite of myself.

"Okay," I said. "So what's the difference? Did Syrimne have a change of heart?"

No. Her eyes remained flat. *He did not have, as you say, 'a change of heart.' His handler, a seer named Menlim, warped the development of his mind and his* aleimi *to such a degree that we found it nearly impossible to communicate with him. We were the enemy in his eyes. Not credible. Syrimne, you see, believed he was saving the world.*

"Great," I said. "What whack-job doesn't?"

Alyson. The old woman's thoughts grew flint-like. *You have no idea of the reality of seers' lives back then. We watched hundreds of thousands of our people butchered practically overnight. Our children stolen and experimented on. Our most respected artists and religious scholars enslaved as sideshow entertainment. Our females systematically raped and sold away from their mates. Do you know that even now, rape of any seer, male or female, is not considered a crime in the human world?*

Briefly, I contemplated reminding her that her own people had a pretty liberal view of "consent," then decided I was being pointlessly argumentative.

Rising to my feet, I stood by the stone mantle.

"So what now?" I asked, my voice subdued. "How do we investigate who did that to the kids in the camp? That's what we've been asked to do, right?"

She shrugged with one hand. *It is ironic, given your aversion.* Her eyes flickered up. *I thought we would start with the last critical incident. See if we could map comparisons to what happened in Sikkim.*

"The last critical incident?" I thought about her words, then felt the blood leave my face. "You mean Syrimne? We're going to look at Syrimne?"

She gestured to the right and up, a seer's yes.

"But what would that prove?" I asked. "Syrimne died almost a century ago."

Tarsi slurped her tea. *Think of it in terms of strategy. Which the Dreng have, in abundance. This is a strategic moment for them. It is good to look at their first attempt to alter the game in their favor, even if it failed.*

The idea made me sick.

Sick enough to wonder why I was taking all of this so personally.

But I did take it personally, and not only the death of those kids.

Symbols of the sword and sun decorated half the walls in Seertown. I'd always wondered why this, the symbol for Syrimne—who had personally murdered thousands of humans and suspected "traitor" seers—decorated an entire wall in Vash's temple.

To me, it was like painting swastikas all over your living room.

Maybe Tarsi was right. Maybe being raised human caused the reaction, and having that symbol beaten into my head as a proxy for death and fanaticism. Even so, it still struck me as more than a little morbid.

Maygar had the same mark tattooed in blue and white ink on his left bicep. He'd called it the mark of a "real" terrorist.

"He is alive, that one?" Tarsi asked politely. "You did not kill him?"

It took me a second to understand what she meant. Then I frowned.

"He's alive," I acknowledged.

"You must be relieved."

I didn't answer, but found myself thinking about Maygar anyway.

Was I relieved? I guessed I was. I couldn't exactly wish for his death, even apart from my being responsible for it. Besides, I still wanted to know why he'd done it.

I couldn't believe he'd rape me just to jab at Revik.

Despite all his barbs, he'd been almost protective of me when it came to Revik. He acted like he didn't think Revik was good enough to be married to me, especially after he learned of his infidelity.

What was it he'd said? Something about how he'd be a good husband to me.

Or at least, better than Revik.

A sudden, sharp pain slid through my chest, strong enough to make me gasp. It felt like anger, but enough lay behind it that I stopped breathing.

When I recovered, I realized I knew the presence.

Christ. How long had he been there? And why hadn't he said anything?

Even as I thought it, he evaporated from my light.

Turning when the girl offered me a steaming mug, I took it from her more abruptly than I should have, biting my lip.

It is easier to show you, Tarsi sent, causing me to turn.

She had gotten up so quietly I hadn't heard her, and now she stood behind me. If she noticed anything, no hint was discernible in her color-less eyes.

May I? she asked.

I hesitated only a second. "Sure."

You should sit again, Bridge.

I sank down to the prayer rug, scooting closer to the fire. The girl immediately knelt behind me, holding a hairbrush in one hand. She held it up, indicating shyly towards my hair. Sighing internally, mostly from the guilt I couldn't quite shake at having her wait on me, I nodded. I'd slept on it wet, so it probably looked like two cats were mating on my head.

"Okay," I told Tarsi, as the girl began carefully detangling my hair with her fingers and brushing it out. "I'm ready."

As soon as I said it, everything went dark.

I had never before been brought into the Barrier so quickly, so completely without warning or transition…

…AND I AM STILL TRYING TO BREATHE AS DARK SURROUNDS ME.

I hang motionless in the black of three a.m. on a moonless night in a pit.

I stand, sit or fall.

Here, it is impossible to tell if any of these are true. No stars live here, no embers or remnants of fire. I can't see myself, in my light form or in the flesh. I exist in the deepest, most silent nothing I have ever known.

Light implodes, in the center of that dark.

It paralyzes me.

The shocking white ring draws inwards, then, after a moment where time stops… it explodes outward. The fountain is so brilliant, so filled with teeming presence, I cannot look away. I watch it plume up and out in rising crescendos of light.

Color pours into the black.

It looks like a volcano from orbit, a high, shimmering fountain on a starless ocean.

I glance to where Tarsi floats beside me.

Her outline is vivid, filled with so many rotating geometries and thinner-than-hair structures I struggle not to lose myself in her.

I realize that is simply her *aleimi*, the way she looks inside the Barrier.

The fountain spins outwards, expanding clouds of energy and gas.

Soon, molten chunks fly past us in the dark. I flinch as the cloud continues to grow, fed by whatever implodes at its core.

Buffeted by giant expulsions of heat and light, we begin to spin outwards with all else, moving through space. I see the sparks forming into denser pools. Spirals turn to smaller clocks, moving in distinct, individual rhythms. I watch hundreds of these spirals form, thousands. A kind of wonder breaks through the events of the past days and weeks and months, and I know why Tarsi starts here.

She starts with birth.

It is the first thing.

We are closer now, closer to one of those spirals of light, and I feel the familiarity of that grinding motion, as if it lives somewhere inside the code of my DNA. I watch stars form pinpricks throughout windmilling arms of molten fire, and I know that I am home, or the vicinity of home at least, in the galaxy where everything and everyone I've ever known has lived.

Wonder again washes over me, this time at the smallness of me.

That was neat, I tell her.

She doesn't answer in words, but I feel her smile.

Here, watching light form inside that expanse of liquid black, I begin to understand, at the very least, what I will never understand.

...THE CAVE MATERIALIZES.

It happens quickly, before I recognize the fading of stars into embers.

It isn't her cave.

Meaning, it's not the same one where my physical body sits on an elaborately woven rug, where my hair is being patiently combed into straight lines by a woman who deserves better, a woman whose face is creased by wind and sun and whose opaque eyes are far-seeing.

This new cave is exponentially larger.

I see no furnishings apart from a fire pit and a dense, rectangular rug that covers most of the cave floor. I stare at the rug's detailed designs, lost in fish, whales, anemone, octopi, horseshoe crabs, starfish.

I don't look up until Tarsi tugs my light hand, leading me deeper.

The fire-lit walls open to a cavern so large it would take my breath if I had any here. It is so high I cannot see the ceiling despite a ring of burning torches and a fire pit that reminds me of beach parties back in high school.

Where are we? I ask.

The Pamir. The caves of our ancestors.

I am impressed. I have never been to the Pamir, not even in the Barrier.

Is this still here? I look around me at the sheer magnitude of the space. *Now, I mean? In the physical?*

She tilts her hand, like a bird banking in flight, a gesture in seer sign language that means "more or less"...more or less. She leads me to a flat expanse of cavern wall, worn smooth by countless hands and tools.

There is a shockingly detailed painting there.

I stare at the images on volcanic stone.

Some, I recognize. All feel strangely familiar.

At the top, a white sword blazes, intersecting the center of a pale blue sun. The sun is like a cross between Native American and Tibetan images. Almost Japanese, I think—before realizing I am trying to categorize something as human that is distinctly seer. I look at the other figures depicted in painstaking detail around a rendition of Earth that could have been painted by Bosch on painkillers.

The old woman points up, to a central image above the planet.

It is an old man. His staff spins up into the heavens, forming a white arc of cabled light that reaches from Earth to a shimmering, deep gold sea. He wears all white and stands in a night sky, holding light between both worlds.

His face is serious, a little bit frightening.

One of his feet balances on the earth.

The Bridge, she says.

Her eyes are stars, so bright I can't look at them directly.

I gaze up at the old man.

Why male? I ask. It is a bit of a sticking point with me. *Is it always male?*

She chuckles, pointing at another image, this one of a female holding a cloud of what looks like lightning inside a patch of black sky. The female figure wears white, as well, and also has one bare foot on the Earth.

Also the Bridge, Tarsi says.

I study the image, strangely placated, although her eyes are as frightening as the male's.

There are countless other forms woven into the drawings.

Who are they all? I ask. *They can't all be the Bridge?*

No, she agrees. *This mural is meant to be a depiction of the intermediary beings. The ones we know of.* She smiles again. *They are your family, Bridge Alyson. Your true family. The last of your kind to incarnate here.*

I glance over at her, once more startled by the brightness of her light.

What does that mean, my kind? What kind would that be?

You know the myth, do you not? The Myth of Three?

I nod. I am uncomfortable, though. I don't know it, not really.

It would be more accurate to say I know *of* it.

The Myth is one of those things that separates me from the other seers. They were raised on the Myth and I was not, and no amount of having it summarized to me now would make it a part of my living and breathing reality the way it was for them.

Tarsi smiles as if she understands. Or at least, as if she hears me.

She begins to recite.

From her mind, the Myth is poetry.

More than that. It is living presence.

The phrases fill me with light, resonating with fine structures in my *aleimi*. Music unfolds from inside collapsed pockets of meaning, expanding like opening flowers.

I see the world's history as she sings:

Love's breath ignites in pools of gold, but it is not the first...

...Nor the last, nor even the beginning. A people swim the surface of Muuld, in a world marked garden for the chosen. We breach simple with flat tails and fingered toes, revel in the brightness of young light.

Numbers swell, our limbs extend, exiting gentle waves. We conquer worlds alarmingly fast. We cover creation with our works, both ugly and wondrous. As time brings new, as every cycle of birth and chaos has beginning...

It cannot last. The first race consumes itself inside itself. It calls to Death, and Death listens. But Death could not be left in his loneliness, nor the first in our pain. Compassion brings tears, a wondrous Bridge to touch the sky. They watch, afraid.

For with her, Death leaves bones to feed the new. Love softens Death, brings hope between them. The others come, to weave the next, and...

Those of us who stay must grow, or perish. We make magics beyond what any sees after. But the gods closed doors to those other worlds, and they are left with only one, and it is alone. And in that one, there is Second race born, from trees and under rocks.

They grow to our likeness, yet believing they are alone. Their works cover that lone world, until they meet us and fear. Fires burn black a second time, a second life. Death listens as the Bridge spins down, illumines a path to the sky.

Love song beckons, leaves them alone. The gold ocean covers all wounds.

Second race follows the path of the first, and those left behind, fated to watch the fires burn yet again. For time speeds up, and all histories fold inside themselves.

As for the first, the youngest and most foolish, most magicked and most childlike, the gods call us from the stone. And a great wail rose when the gods spoke, for the door to that other place must need be lost, and those on the other side forgotten.

For when Third Race comes, they bring with them the stars. We leave them, our Guardians of the Middle. And the Bridge spins her light…

…Until we come to live here no more.

CHAPTER 18
ELAERIAN

S ilence falls as her words end.

In that construct cave, I realize I have never heard the Myth before, not like this.

I can only stand there as the lines reverberate through my *aleimi* like shivers of current. The words themselves hold a light that doesn't look like light to me; I feel it as presence filled with the import of time, of timelessness.

I let it wash over me, waiting for some kind of... I don't know.

Understanding, maybe.

It's not there. Not in a way that makes sense to my mind.

Tarsi breaks the solemnity and chuckles.

You see? she says. *Female. In the old myths, the Bridge is always "she," never "he."*

But I'm going over specific words now, in my head. *The Myth. It kind of implies that I'm not, I mean, that I'm not actually —*

You are not Sark, she agrees.

Her words are matter of fact, as if she were relaying a fact of little consequence.

Not second race, she reiterates. *You are first race. All intermediary beings are first race. We call them Elaerian. Second race is Sarhacienne, "Second"... Sark. Third race calls itself human. The old names for them are immaterial now.*

I hear only part of this. I repeat her words back to her like a myna bird, as if hearing them again might change her mind about what she'd said.

I'm first race. Like actually a different species? Biologically?

At Tarsi's raised light eyebrow, I see red and orange sparks course through the veins in my *aleimi.*

I ask her again. *Not only am I not human, I'm not even Sark?*

She smiles. *You were aware you had differences from us. The light in your eyes—it is visible to humans. Your blood is not like ours. There are other things. You are telekinetic. That is not a Sark trait. You came to physical maturity much too fast to be Sark. You were able to adapt your early growth cycle to that of humans, to pass. Sarhaciennes cannot change their biology to accommodate their environment. Raised among humans, they continue to resemble human children until well past their twentieth year.*

She gauges my eyes.

It strikes me that she has converted our appearance to match that of our physical bodies. It happens so seamlessly I barely notice.

She adds, *You likely have other differences we are not aware of. Much of our knowledge of your race has been lost.*

But I am stuck in a mental loop I can't seem to escape.

Something Revik said to me once repeats in my head.

It is illogical to have an opinion about what species one is.

Of course, when he said it, I thought he was talking about his own species.

But who gave birth to me? I ask.

She shrugs with one hand.

Isn't that kind of an important detail? I ask.

It is said that Elaerian reproduce differently than Sarks and humans. That they are able to manifest their offspring inside the embryos of other beings, from the Barrier. It is also said that some always live among us, but keep their presence unknown. Some say they are able to appear here just long enough to breed and then expire. It is possible your parents did any one of these things. It is equally possible you birthed yourself from the Barrier. Or were born of a Sark, and the difference is in your aleimi.

That makes absolutely no sense, I send, fighting anger.

She shrugs. *I cannot tell you what I do not know.*

Wait, I say, holding up a hand. *Revik said my blood is a 'type' among Sarhaciennes. He said it's rare, but that it does occur.*

Her smile is patient.

Is it so important, to be the same race as us? She quirks an innocent eyebrow. *Or is it to him you are so determined to be alike?*

I force myself to pause, to think.

Maybe, I concede. *Or maybe it's just a little much, thinking I knew what I was... twice... only to find out I was wrong both times. Is this how the elders came to believe I was the Bridge? These biology things?*

She makes another of the "more or less" gestures.

The markers in your light are even more telling. If you were more accustomed to looking at people by their aleimi, *rather than by physical appearance, you would realize there are some distinct differences in yours.*

So Revik knew?

She gestures affirmative. *Most certainly he knows. He conducted the final confirmation.*

Confirmation? Meaning what?

Tests. Aleimic *assessments, mainly. Imaging. Barrier examinations.* She waves dismissively. *You would not have noticed these things, not then. But they are partly why you were able to bond with him so easily.* She smiles. *In a sense, you already knew one another. Far more than you probably realize.*

I feel like I am back on the ship, discovering all over again what he'd done to me behind my back. Even now, he keeps me in the dark about how much he knows.

I found out on the ship, after practically prying it out of him at gunpoint, that he'd invaded my privacy numerous times while protecting me for the Seven.

He'd been through every room of my flat in San Francisco, as well as my mom's house, my brother's, Jaden's, my friends' apartments and houses. He'd stashed weapons, money and headsets at my place, and at Mom's and Jon's. He'd created a hiding place in my ceiling in case he ever had to get me out of there without using the door. He'd read my mind and the minds of just about everyone with whom I came in contact regularly.

He went through my drawings, medical records, school records, police records, all of my online accounts. He had open access to anything I did on the net, any VR portals I visited—any porn I looked at or read.

He conducted surveillance on my work and school, my bosses, my family, anyone I slept with, worked with, or befriended.

Why didn't he tell me? I ask finally.

She sighs. *You wish me to decipher the intricacies of my nephew's mind?*

Feeling my anger rise, she clicks again, softer.

There are many possible reasons. To avoid frightening you. To avoid losing your trust so early in your relationship. Disclosures of this type tend to operate better in stages. That you are the only known living representative of your species… that you did not realize this because you can shape-shift to match your environment… this is not comfortable information, either to give or to receive.

Thinking further, she made a dismissive motion with one hand.

And yes, the telekinesis alarmed him a bit.

At my silence, her amusement returns.

He also likely did not expect to find himself married to you within a week of having awakened you.

She chuckles, her humor sending ripples through the Barrier.

…I imagine a lot more of his attention was consumed with how to relay that particular piece of information to you, Bridge Alyson.

Still smiling, she studies my eyes.

I feel a faint worry under her humor, though. Like Chandre, she's concerned she's harmed my view of Revik. This bothers me for reasons I can't quite articulate to myself, not at first. I feel ganged up on, I realize.

I feel like his feelings are being prioritized.

Alyson, she sends, before I can say anything. *We are simply aware that, given your current condition, you are likely to overreact to any new information about your mate. In this case, it is completely unwarranted. He was under strict guidelines as to approach and disclosure. He asked us—many times—for permission to approach you directly so that he might start training you. He was refused, repeatedly. Mainly because we did not know how violent your awakening would be. Blinded, you were safe. Relatively speaking.*

I pause on this.

So why didn't Vash tell me? I ask. *Once I got here?*

I am telling you, she says.

Fighting to keep my temper in check, I pull a childhood trick I used when I got angry at my mother. Holding up my hand, I stare at the reconstructed flesh.

It works, in part.

I am amazed at the detail—down to a cut I got the previous morning on the helicopter door, as well as bruises on my knuckles from the fight with Maygar.

I wonder if I added those details, or she did.

You did, she says. *You see? It is one of your gifts. To become like those around you. You have only been partially successful at this in the human world.*

Again, I remember something Revik said to me.

Like blood on a white sheet. They notice you, then make up a reason why.

At Tarsi's smile, I focus back on the figures drawn painstakingly on the cave wall. I count twenty-five, maybe thirty forms other than the two she's said are the Bridge.

They're all intermediary beings? I ask. *All Elaerian?*

She points at particular images.

The first stands below the image of the sword bisecting the sun. A young boy, he holds the blue sun in his arms and laughs.

His eyes are kind, startlingly innocent.

Death, she says. *You know him as "Sword" or "Sword of the gods."* *Syrimne d' gaos.*

Her finger moves to another, a female figure all in red, woven into and standing behind the image of the sword and sun.

War, she says. *Also "Cataclysm."*

Her finger moves to one made of bones, in the shape of a crow-like bird.

Rook. He is also called Famine. The Starver of Souls. She glances at me. *These are imperfect translations, of course. But your knowledge of old Prexci is insufficient at this time, so I am providing the English. It is only roughly equivalent—*

I know those names, I say, interrupting her.

Looking around a little uneasily, I remember a conversation Revik and I had, what seems a million years ago now, about the Four Horsemen of the Apocalypse.

I'd blown him off at the time, thinking he was just explaining seer religion.

Now, however, I am reasonably sure Tarsi just listed off three of their names, one after the other: Death, War, Famine.

The fourth is their leader, who rides a white horse. That is the one about whom no one can agree—whether they are supposed to be evil or a force for good.

The first time we played chess, Revik told me I had to be white. It was his idea of a joke. He said the Bridge was always white. He even called me "the white horsewoman."

I look at the images of the Bridge.

In both, the figure is dressed in all white.

It is not so simple as the humans portray it, Tarsi says gently. *Let us say for now that much was lost in the translation.* She gestures towards the painting with one hand. *What else do you see, Alyson?*

I re-focus on the images.

It is like chess. I point to the image of a centaur in a helmet, carrying a sword. He wears chain mail, his expression fierce. *Knight?* I ask.

She nods. *Warrior. Knight is also good.*

I point to an image of an older, Saint Nicholas-looking man wearing a crown.

King? I ask. When she gestures "more or less," I point to his female counterpart. *Queen?*

Again, she makes the "more or less" gesture.

We call the King "Shield," she says. *The queen is "Arrow." But essentially you are right. They are stabilizing forces. They provide structure when it is needed.*

Shield? I stare up at the kingly form. *Galaith?*

She gestures assent.

So he was good?

She gestures dismissively. *Good, bad... at base, he was neither. He aligned with the Dreng, Alyson, so no, he was not good.*

Her light eyes focus on mine. Their complexity makes me stare.

As with Syrimne, she adds. *It did not have to be that way. And he still served his purpose... more or less. Dark consequences came of that stability Galaith designed, many more than were strictly necessary. But he did help to thwart that early attempt at bringing the Displacement, prior to his recruitment by the Dreng.*

I stare up at the face of the being there.

I imagine I can almost see Galaith in it.

He, too, is your brother, Bridge Alyson, she says. *It is part of why you were tasked with curbing his excesses.*

I give her a wry smile. *If by "curbing his excesses" you mean bringing about his death, well I guess I fulfilled my task well enough.*

The old seer merely shrugs.

Not all of your brothers and sisters made it to the human chessboard, she adds, gazing up at the mural. *But many make their appearances in other places.*

She points to the image of a dancing rabbit.

Fool, she says. *Trickster.*

I point to the image of a turtle, under the earth. *That one looks familiar. What is he?*

Wisdom, Tarsi says. *And traditionally, it is she.* Tarsi points to a being I hadn't seen, woven into the fabric of the oceans. *"Dragon" would be close in English. Not quite that. Not quite fish. Perhaps it is more accurate to call him "Birth." He and Wisdom are creation, male and female. Closer to the Chinese meaning of dragon than that of European humans.*

Her eyes turn towards mine, pale as stars.

Some of these beings do not incarnate down here in an individualized form, Bridge Alyson. Not in the way you or Syrimne have, at least. They are much more Barrier beings, unable to function in a stable way on this plane.

I look around at the other images.

We haven't covered a third of them.

Do you understand now? she asks.

Understand? I look at her. *Understand what?*

Why Death is your responsibility, she says.

CHAPTER 19
NOT SO EASY

I didn't sleep well that night.

Piled high in furs, mostly yak and cowskins, I didn't want for warmth, and the bed wasn't hard.

It was him. The separation pain came back as soon as I closed my eyes.

Mixed with that came a paranoia I hadn't experienced since he first left for Egypt. I knew it was irrational. Whatever Revik did to skirt the truth when it inconvenienced him, I'd never known him to lie to me outright. He made it pretty clear he expected monogamy from me, and that he had a fairly all-encompassing definition of what that meant.

Besides, if he wanted some before I got back, he was smart enough to do it somewhere other than Seertown.

That train of thought didn't help my mood much, though.

Nor did the realization that I'd left him with a hell of a hard on, not unlike both times he'd turned to others in the past.

Somewhere in all my worrying, I did fall asleep, though.

I know this, because I was awakened by the girl the next morning.

I finally got a name out of her—Hannah, of all things—right before she handed me a cup of that steaming brown drink. I dragged myself out of the pile of furs only to be handed another mug, this one holding the requisite yak-butter tea.

That, and the freezing cold air coming through the open windows made me scowl. One lovely thing about seers in Seertown was that most were westernized enough to have a healthy appreciation for espresso.

Tarsi didn't waste time.

After I stretched and sluggishly pulled on clothes, I felt a nudge in my mind. She sat on the same rug that lay on the flagstones by the fireplace. Now I noticed the rug was a smaller and less elaborate version of what I'd seen in the Pamir cave.

She patted the wool, her eyes pointed.

Dragging myself to my feet, I walked over to sit cross-legged beside her. I tried to ignore the tendrils of light I felt encircling me tentatively from somewhere else.

He was in bed. I felt him lying there, staring up at a whitewashed ceiling.

It struck me suddenly that wherever he was, it didn't feel like Seertown.

A whisper of panic bloomed in my chest.

I backed off before it fully blossomed, trying to keep it from him. I didn't try to determine where he was—or whose bed he might be in.

I glanced at Tarsi, still feeling him in the edges of my light. I knew he wasn't asleep, and that was enough to make it difficult to keep my focus.

I watched Tarsi motion to Hannah, who crouched by the stone fireplace, stirring something in a hanging iron pot. Hannah smiled at me shyly with those straight, white teeth as she handed me a second bowl of the coffee-like drink.

"So where do we start?" I asked Tarsi.

Tarsi held up her hand.

As soon as she unfurled her fingers, I…

…AM SOMEWHERE ELSE.

I stand in a field.

It is so still and peaceful I am startled.

I had expected violence, I guess.

Scenes of war, people shouting or screaming.

Instead, a shockingly bright sun pierces the clouds.

I am alone. Mountains rise in high walls on all sides. Tall grasses wave at my thighs, floating down a hill and around a lake so pale it appears to be made of ice. Above the lake, more jagged, snow-covered peaks cut the horizon.

I recognize this place, but I don't know why.

The world feels different here.

It is more alive. Or maybe less broken.

Cries break the silence. The wind fills with the dark stutter of birds' wings, more than I've ever seen in one place. They rise up in a cloud, a dark spiral that banks in blue sky. Bees pollinate wildflowers around grasses that brush my thighs. A mongoose hops through the grass. I see those scruffy, donkey-like horses the old humans call Kiang.

Then, in the midst of all that peace and tranquility—

I hear a shout.

I drop to a crouch.

I am somewhere else, deep inside a dark-green forest.

Dense trees crowd around me, blocking light, leaving it cathedral dim. Moss-covered rocks litter the sloped earth. I puzzle over where I am, how it connects to where I was an instant before, when the stillness is broken by another yell.

"Get him!"

A lithe form sprints past me down the sloped forest floor. He whoops as he leaps a fallen trunk. More figures bound by. They fan the hill in a jagged line like wolves, rushing headlong down it, shouting.

They are children.

"Head him off, Stami! Don't let him get too far ahead!"

The owner of the voice stands above me on the same hill.

His words bring my eyes to his perch on a gray boulder.

His rounded cheeks and pink lips belong to someone maybe twelve years of age, but his chest is already barrel-shaped, his hands large enough to cover my face. His eyes and bone structure are vaguely Asian, but his hair is white as chalk, his irises a deep black.

He is too large for his age, I think.

There is something wrong with him.

"Head him off!" he shouts. "Stami! Don't let him get to those thorns!"

I see their prey as I follow his stare.

Darker than the forest, the smaller form flicks between the trunks of trees like a deer. He runs silently but all-out, his entire being focused, an inhaled breath. Unlike the other children's, his feet are bare. His skin is dark.

Black hair sticks to his head with sweat.

I let my eyes follow his winding trail through the trees.

Then I am seeing *through* him, through his eyes.

Then his mind.

He knows these woods.

If he can shake Stami, the fastest of his pursuers, he might get away on the other side of the stream. If he has even a few seconds' lead, he might make it.

He has done it before.

Not often. But he has done it.

I think of Brer Rabbit and his briar patch—

When a tall boy slants out from behind a cluster of brush and leaps. He catches hold of the smaller boy's shirt. He drags at him, flinging him sideways and into the dirt, tripping his legs like a wolf bringing down a deer. They tumble in pine needles and moss and mud by the edge of the stream.

They struggle.

The black-haired boy fights to get up, but the taller boy grabs his hair, clothes, his ankle, slowing him down until the others arrive. A few jump into the fray with abandon, flattening the black-haired boy in the mud just a yard from the stream.

I hear a cry from him.

It is heartbreaking. A defeated cry.

They jerk him upright.

He reaches his feet, panting. Alone. He wears the aloneness like a cloak, and it pulls at me, resonating with my separation pain.

I cannot help but feel for him.

I want to intervene, to pull him from the hands of these other children, who feel like animals to me, randomly cruel, endlessly hungry. I want to protect him, but I can't reach him through the time that stands between us.

My light feet disappear inside a cheerful stream filled with colorful stones.

The place is so beautiful, the fear vibrating the air doesn't quite compute. It doesn't belong in this cathedral of sun and leaves and distant birdsong.

The dark-haired boy stands unsteadily, his leg hurt.

Three larger boys hold him while he struggles, each a head taller or more. Almond eyes look out from behind shaggy, black hair. His face is round and bruised, his skin tanned from long exposure to sun.

He looks tougher somehow than the others, like he's spent more nights outdoors. Like he's gone longer without food. The boy who first tackled him cocks his fist and punches him inexpertly in the mouth. The same boy, who I know is Stami, hits him again.

The white-haired giant arrives.

He does the talking.

I don't know what language they speak, only that, if I wasn't in the Barrier, I wouldn't understand them.

"Lesson one, Nenz." He clicks his tongue in feigned sympathy. "What happens when shit-blood worm-fuckers break rules?"

The dark-haired boy stares at Stami, then at the giant kid with the white hair.

My vision flickers back and forth, from his to my own.

Again, I want to stand between him and this strange, albino boy with the cruel, deep-black eyes. But this has already happened.

It already exists out there, as a recording in time.

Gerwix, my mind whispers.

That is the giant's name.

Gerwix laughs. "Nenz! Is it my birthday? Are you giving me an excuse to beat you until you piss blood? Do you love me so much, runt?"

The dark-haired boy's face flinches.

For him, I don't get a name, not apart from what the giant calls him.

Yet somehow, I know he is the one Tarsi and I have come for.

It scares me that he is so real, so vulnerable.

"I didn't break any rules," he says sullenly.

"You were talking to her. We saw you."

Stami jerks a knife from a sheath on his leg, holds it to the younger boy's face, showing it to him. Gerwix, the white-haired giant, smiles.

"You want her, Nenz? Is that what you were doing? Trying to get into her clothes?"

Stami, the taller, handsome kid lays the knife on his bare arm.

Fear returns to the darker boy's face. "No! No... I wasn't doing anything!"

"Liar. She's Stami's girl. Leave her alone."

"She talked to me!"

Stami presses down viciously with the knife and the dark-haired boy screams. Stami keeps cutting, twisting the blade up his arm and shoulder to his neck. The dark-haired boy screams again, struggling against their hands.

Blood runs down his side, wetting the top of his pants.

A few others laugh, but their laughter is nervous now, tense.

Only Gerwix's chuckle sounds real.

Stami's voice is lower, and I hear real anger there. "Your uncle pays girls to lie with you, freak. Stick with the unwillings. Leave the real girls to us."

The white-haired boy steps forward.

Still smiling, he motions for Stami to lay off with the knife.

Stami hesitates before pulling it off the darker skin. He makes a show of wiping the blade on his pants, as if he got it dirty skinning an animal.

Gerwix's laugh is ugly; it belongs to someone much older.

"Don't be greedy, Stami." He motions them to turn the boy around, untying the front of his pants. "I think we can give Nenz what he wants."

The laughter grows nervous.

Despite some shuffled feet, no one leaves. Two back off as they stare, fascinated as the white-haired boy grabs the smaller one by his hair, forcing him to his knees.

They are already ripping down his worn pants when my mind catches up with what is happening. I just have time to see the dark face grow resigned as he is forced prone over a log. Even with his head, shoulder and arms bleeding from the knife, he fights them, his thin arms and legs jerking and writhing in a futile, animalistic panic.

Despite his struggles, it is clear that this ritual is familiar, that it's been played out already, that it will play out again, that he lost the moment Stami caught his shirt and dragged him into the mud...

I SNAPPED OUT.

I sat cross-legged on the rug, fighting an overwhelming urge to cry, to beat at the old woman sitting across from me with my fists.

Instead, I sat there, fighting to breathe, breathing too much.

It had been cruel, what she'd shown me, the kind of brutal animalism that always crushed some part of me.

But it wasn't only that. The grief coming off that boy, the awareness behind his eyes, the depth of depression he carried… it was more than I could bear.

It was more than I could even feel all at once.

A part of me had been crushed inside his small frame, and I couldn't get out.

It was enough emotion to break someone's mind, if they lived in it long enough.

Tarsi studied me carefully.

"You see, Bridge?" she said. "Killing him not so easy as you think."

I still fought to breathe. "That was him? Syrimne?"

"Long time ago, yes. When he was whole."

"Whole." I looked at her, fighting my way through emotion that still contorted my light in knots, causing spasms in my arms and neck. I fought to process it, then, realizing I couldn't, I let it run through me instead, like waiting for a storm to pass.

After another moment, my voice leveled.

"What does that mean?"

"He was broken, Bridge." Her eyes studied mine. *Death is just one facet. It is a role, traded from life to life, possibly even among different beings. Much like Bridge.*

Her eyes sharpened, looking for understanding.

The person moderates the role. Keeps it in check. On its own, Death can be incredibly destructive. It is important that you remember that boy. He was whole once. He was a real person. Death is a hard path. The hardest of all.

A kind of dread washed over me as I took in her words.

We'd only just started. That glimpse of childhood brutality had been the prelude to our hunt, not the hunt itself. It was simply her way of introducing me to our quarry.

I could feel from her that it was also a test.

She wanted to know if I could handle this.

Thinking about how that one scene likely fit into the longer timeline of this being she called Death, I honestly didn't know if I could.

Again, I remembered something Revik said to me.

To find anyone or anything in the Barrier, he'd said, swallowing a mouthful of omelet as we sat on the ship's balcony. *You must become what you seek. The Barrier is resonance, Allie. It is what we seers do. We resonate with things.*

To find him, I would have to become Syrimne.

CHAPTER 20
CLAUSTROPHOBIC

R evik stood on the rim of a burnt-out crater.

The scorched pockmark ate through two thirds of a fortress-like structure made of black stone. If he hadn't seen the pirated feeds of the building exploding outward, he might have thought a meteor hit the mountain.

The crater still smoked.

Trees had been knocked down as far away as a mile from the center.

Leaning carefully to gaze over the edge, he tracked body parts stuck in poses from where they'd been embedded in rock. Easing back so that his weight stood more securely at the rim, he glanced at Balidor.

The gray-eyed seer frowned without returning Revik's glance.

They'd only been there an hour, and already, Revik was getting used to the smell. It brought back memories of wartime, especially the ovens.

Wincing, he tracked the movements of the rest of the infiltration team.

Adhipan members spread out along the rim of the crater.

A few had begun to climb down to get a better look.

Revik recognized a number of faces, both from the flight from India and the training camp outside of Darjeeling. Others had flown in from China or elsewhere just the day before. Around forty operatives now cased the site, all of them Adhipan.

Revik understood why they were climbing into the hole.

Not only would they be collecting physical evidence, but the best and easiest way to collect imprints of the bomber was to get as close to the bomb itself as possible. Whatever fragments may have survived could be anywhere from the blast point to a few thousand yards from there, but they would start at the center and work out.

So he understood the logic, but he still wasn't looking forward to that portion of this exercise.

Given the sheer level of devastation, they might have to do it the human way, at least in part. Meaning they might have to conduct an analysis and search based on the chemical imprint and other physical properties of the blast. Explosions had a habit of obliterating *aleimic* fingerprints even more thoroughly than the physical kind.

Something else struck him as he looked around.

"This isn't where it started." He spoke English, unthinking. He turned to Balidor, switching to Prexci. "Was there any evidence that this might be a secondary site?"

Balidor gave him an odd look. "Yes."

"Can you show me?"

Balidor motioned for Revik to follow him.

He stepped back from the crater's rim, and led them across the broken field.

Revik followed as Balidor picked his way through cracked stones, ripped up earth and body parts, bone fragments and parts of skulls. Most of these last were small enough that Revik didn't let himself focus on them too closely.

He kept his eyes focused forward instead, on the furthest of the three stone towers that remained standing after the attack.

Balidor pointed to the other two towers, in turn.

"Training cells. A few of the older kids survived in there. Standard protocol was to move them inside once they were clearly salable. Meaning, old enough to pass for human, making progress in their studies, talented enough to effect at least a mid-range sale. It protected them from being stolen by local bandits. It's also where they brought high-end customers… those with enough connections to skip the auctions and buy wholesale."

Revik nodded, gesturing that he was familiar with such things.

Balidor pointed to the other tower. "Quarters, for the staff."

Revik continued to focus on the third tower, where Balidor's feet aimed in a nearly straight line.

It looked dead compared to the other two.

The windows had no glass.

Revik could see no light inside, and no sign it had been updated since whatever warlord built it several hundred years earlier. The heavy wood and iron door looked like it could be original to the structure. It came with a lock, now broken, like something from a lower-level exhibit in the Tower of London.

Revik's steps slowed as they got nearer to the entrance.

Balidor noticed, and slowed to pace him.

"Yes," he said grimly. "You feel it, too."

He gestured at the broken door.

"We thought this area had been abandoned at first. An old disciplinary center. Possibly even a torture chamber, left over from some particularly despotic human. The imprints there are intense... but almost impossible to nail down. We next thought whoever did this had perhaps put up some kind of Barrier field. To obscure themselves, obliterate evidence and so forth. But the construct we found woven there was much older. Close to a hundred years."

Balidor gestured again towards the gaping maw of a door.

"Two of my people went inside. They said it's worse in there. The imprints are older, as is the construct... or what remains of it. They were able to determine this was the primary blast site, as you said. But not much else."

He glanced at Revik. A flicker of surprise touched his eyes.

He caught the younger man's arm, staring into his face.

"Are you all right?"

Revik shook his head. "I want to go inside."

"Are you sure, brother? You're white as a ghost."

"I'll be all right." Revik extricated his arm, and once again began picking his way across the courtyard, until he was at the tower's door.

"Be careful," Balidor called after him. "There's not much warning before the drop."

Glancing back, Revik saw the Adhipan leader had remained where he was. Raising a hand in acknowledgment, he hesitated only a second longer, then grabbed one of the torches burning outside the broken door.

Taking a breath and instinctively shielding his light, he walked inside the stone foyer.

Stepping carefully across the broken flagstones, he started down the only available route, a staircase cut directly into the fire-blackened rock. He held the torch out in front of him and descended one step at a time.

He fought a gradual closing around his chest and throat.

He'd always been a little claustrophobic.

The close, pitch black corridor amplified the imprints emanating off the walls. Both made it difficult to breathe. He tried to get a lock on the imprints, to understand their source... but all he got was more of that feeling. A throbbing, sick pain, it resembled the worst kind of separation sickness, so warped and broken by deprivation it had turned into something else entirely.

He might not even have recognized it, if he hadn't been buried in separation pain himself for over a year. It combined with his own problems, twisting his need into something that made him want to die—literally.

He found himself reaching for Allie...

He stopped it.

Taking another breath, he forced his light closer to his body.

The pain worsened. Out of nowhere, anger suffused his light, intense enough to blank his mind. Feelings rose, and thoughts. Things he'd been suppressing for days, ever since that morning he'd returned from Cairo.

He should have told her.

He should have told her the second they left the construct.

Hell, he should have taken her with him right then, found a place in town, torn her goddamned clothes off.

He fought that out of his light, as well.

Why hadn't anyone explained the marriage rites to her? Chandre? Yerin? Vash? He'd been gone for months... and hadn't exactly been in a position to explain anything to her in the period before he left. He'd nearly blown everything, just because he'd assumed she understood the basics of their condition.

Gods, even before she'd asked him, her light pulling on him was enough to change his mind about waiting. She'd probably been pulling on every seer in a five-mile radius—likely for months, the whole time he'd been gone.

Before that, when he'd been with Terian.

They'd been watching her masturbate.

Pain turned liquid in his light, ratcheting the intensity of emotion.

She'd agreed to engage in a full contact sport with a rival seer who wanted to bed her—assuming he wasn't bedding her already. Why? Why would she do that, unless she wanted to hurt him? Had she lied to him?

Was she still angry with him for what he'd done?

The pain cut his breath, a helplessness he briefly couldn't control.

The son of a bitch had touched her. He touched her in places Revik hadn't touched her. Places he'd restrained himself from touching her for over a year. He'd gotten into her light. He'd had his goddamned fingers in her. He'd also scared the hell out of her. Revik felt it through those other seers.

He felt her terror. He'd seen it in her eyes.

Her face had been bloody.

She'd been screaming.

Gripping the rough stone, he forced his mind to shut down. It was something he would normally only do if he were being attacked.

He forced himself to breathe…

Until, slowly, slowly, the feelings unwound.

He remembered where he was.

He could feel the tower as something outside of himself again. It still reeked of suicide, slow madness, the kind of prolonged powerlessness that he'd never coped with well… but he could distinguish those feelings from his own light.

He made himself walk.

He moved one foot, then the next.

He was still struggling with his light when he reached the third corridor landing. Turning the corner carefully at the bottom of the steep stairs, he walked through an arch and then the length of the flagstone corridor.

He rounded another turn, expecting another set of stairs.

Instead, a sheer drop greeted him.

There'd been no warning, not even a change in the quality of light.

Whatever occurred there had happened far enough down that the aboveground structure remained intact.

A deep blackness stretched beneath Revik's feet.

Waving the torch over the chasm, he tried to get a sense of its depth and width. He was unwilling to relinquish his torch to satisfy his curiosity—especially since Balidor's men likely already mapped out the physical disposition of the scene. He turned the torch to either side of the hole, and saw burn marks flaring around the mouth.

He began walking back up the corridor, sweeping with the torch, scanning the floors and walls. Shoe marks scuffed the dirty floor, and what looked like bare feet, too small to be anything but a child.

Wedged in a crack between flagstones, something reflected back light from the torch's flame. Sweeping the fire back and forth again, he located the exact spot and bent down to pick the object up.

It was a key. It had an organic coating on it, but the skin was so old and hard that Revik barely recognized it as an organic at all.

It looked like it could be World War II. Maybe even earlier.

Holding it up under the torch, the sick feeling came back, this time stronger. He found he didn't want to hold the key with his bare skin.

Covering his hand with his sleeve, he stuffed it in a pocket.

He made his way slowly back up to the surface.

When he reached the doorway and outside, he walked away from the tower at about twice the speed he'd walked towards it. He climbed over broken stone and debris to where Balidor stood, smoking a *hiri*.

After being crammed inside that black hole, Revik inhaled the air outside in relief, despite the still-strong odor of burnt hair and skin and rotting flesh from the crater a few hundred yards in front of him.

He waited until he stood alongside Balidor, then reached into his pocket for the key, using his sleeve again and holding out his hand for Balidor to take it. He didn't say anything while the other seer examined the organic metal. He just stood there, taking deep breaths of the cold air, trying to get his equilibrium back.

"Where did you find this?"

"Third landing," Revik said.

"Do you know what this is?" When Revik glanced over, Balidor's gray eyes were hard, the color of steel. "It looks exactly like the keys we used on the early restraint collars. The ones the Germans used in World War II."

Revik nodded, gazing out over the courtyard. "That's what I thought, too."

"What do you think it means?"

"I don't know," Revik said, his voice close to normal again. "But I know what crossed my mind." He gave Balidor a grim look. "Whoever they were holding down there was stuck in that pit for about ninety years. Maybe longer."

Balidor studied Revik's face.

"That's what I thought too, brother," he said.

Touching Revik's arm, Balidor gestured towards the desolate tower.

"They weren't able to determine what caused the first blast," he added. "No residual powder. The only incendiary is natural gas present in deposits in the mountain bedrock itself... but there's no way that could have been ignited without some way to pierce the stone. There's no sign of drilling. Surveys show it would have been trapped behind several feet of solid granite. We checked for seismic activity and found none."

Revik looked up at the sky. It stretched blue overhead, despite dark clouds pooling over the mountains.

He glanced back at Balidor.

"Could we be talking about a seer?" he asked.

Balidor didn't move for a moment.

Then he whistled softly, giving him a sideways smile.

"Brother, I am impressed. My own people haven't come up with that yet, and many of them have been here for several days. As unlikely as it seems, yes, I believe that is a possibility. One we should explore, at any rate, given the evidence."

"A manipulator?" Revik said in Prexci. "Telekinetic?" he added in English.

"Possibly, yes. It would explain a number of factors."

Revik felt himself fighting to breathe again.

After a moment, he shook his head.

"Someone would have felt them behind the Barrier." He looked at Balidor, fighting the remnants of pain lingering in his light. "There was a child down there. After the blast. Could someone be breeding manipulators?" He frowned. "Terian's always had that thing with genetics."

Balidor shrugged with one hand, his face unreadable.

"Your observation about the child is troubling. But a lot in this incident is troubling." He gave Revik a thin-lipped smile. "I must remind myself that the Displacement is coming. That perhaps it is not so strange that more than one intermediary being might be on Earth at this time."

At Revik's frown, his eyes grew thoughtful.

"Do you still think Terian is connected to this somehow?"

Revik glanced at the tower.

He felt the nausea return, the feeling of despair. Brushing it out of his light as best he could, he rested his hands on his hips.

Instead of answering Balidor's question, he asked another.

"Why children?" he asked.

Balidor shrugged with one hand, his face impassive. "Perhaps the children were incidental. Or," he said more gently. "Perhaps he thought he was helping them. Freeing them, perhaps?"

Revik stared out over the broken courtyard.

His eyes traveled back to the edge of the crater where members of the Adhipan could still be seen picking through body parts and rubble.

Whoever the seer was, if there had been a manipulator locked down there—or any seer, for that amount of time—they would be insane.

Seers didn't do well alone.

In fact, they usually died. Whoever that seer had been, if they'd been locked up alone for seventy-plus years, they should be dead.

Yet, if it was a manipulator, and they'd been found in the forties, or even the thirties—after Syrimne, or even while Syrimne was still alive—it would explain why someone had hidden them away so thoroughly. Someone could have figured out a way to clone Syrimne. The child could be the product of that.

Or perhaps it was just someone from the school who wandered down there after the blast, looking for a place to hide.

He thought of Allie, and the separation pain grew debilitating.

A manipulator. Whoever they were, they would be interested in her.

He shook it off, clenching his jaw before he looked at Balidor.

"Yeah," he said finally. "Maybe."

Taking another deep breath, he began walking back over the rubble to join the remainder of the search team. As he did, he felt the hunter's mask fall back over his mind, stripping his thoughts of emotion.

That time, when Revik walked, Balidor followed him.

CHAPTER 21
HELLO, LOVER

R evik lay on a single bed in the temporary barracks Balidor set up
outside Darjeeling.

This would be the last night in these accommodations—for
him, at least.

He would be joining Balidor's ground team for the next few days,
which meant sleeping in tents on partially frozen ground, at least until
the helicopter picked him up, which Balidor promised would be within
four days.

Five at most.

He'd still had no word from Allie.

Staring up at a whitewashed ceiling, head resting on his arm, he
found himself thinking about the last message from Balidor.

Tarsi had extended her timeline. No reason given, not even a hello
aimed in his direction, not from either of them.

Whatever it meant, it spurred his offer to stay on with the Adhipan.

He wondered now if that had been such a great idea. Despite Balidor's assurances, he wanted to talk to Allie himself. Obviously, she
wasn't going to ask for him, so he needed to make it clear to her that he
wanted to see her.

He couldn't leave India with her without breaking the law. Hell, he didn't even know if he could take her from Tarsi's legally, not without formal permission.

He could probably convince Tarsi to let him talk to her, though.

He'd shared all his various imprints of Terian and Terian's different bodies with the Adhipan already. No one knew Terian's light as well as he did, so they'd welcomed his offer to help, but they were all better trackers than he was.

They didn't really need him.

It had been nine days since he'd reached Seertown from Egypt.

He'd been delayed in Cairo, too.

First by the paranoia of the infiltration team, then by Maygar and his ridiculous attempts to buy him off, then to piss him off. Since he'd left her at Gatwick, pretty much nothing had gone the way he'd planned. He'd thought he would be lying in a very different bed right now—not surrounded by half-clothed infiltrators, staring at a water-stained ceiling, wondering if he should take a shower just so he could jerk off without one of the other seers making a crack, or worse, offering to help.

Because he'd focused on her and sex in the same breath, he felt her.

She backed off the instant his light coiled into hers, but the pain lingered, making it impossible for him to disconnect. He stayed with her, like he did every time they bumped up against one another in that space, pulling at her for fleeting impressions, but they weren't enough to calm his paranoia.

She was busy. Working. Tarsi had her hard at work on something.

It was stressing her out, whatever it was, upsetting her—

Tarsi appeared.

Unapologetic, she slammed him out of their Barrier space.

Revik was left lying there, half-crippled as the connection severed.

He lay there a few minutes longer, fighting to slow his breathing as the pain gradually dissipated. When he recovered enough, he sat up. He gripped the blanket around his waist as his feet touched the floor.

He found a female seer also awake, and watching him.

She smiled when she caught his gaze, humor in her eyes.

When he looked away, she laughed aloud.

"Hey. Newlywed," she said in Mandarin. "What the hell are you doing out here? Why aren't you at home? I'd be pissed off, if I was your wife."

Without answering, Revik pushed the covers aside, getting to his feet.

"Hey," she said, laughing. "Can you walk?"

Grabbing a towel off the chair at the end of the bed, he headed for the shower without giving the female so much as another glance.

Her laughter followed him out.

...at least until the closing corridor door cut it thankfully off.

REVIK BLINKED BACK SWEAT.

Reinforcing his grip on the Chinese-made QBZ-97 assault rifle they'd given him, he held it in both hands as he walked through the trees.

It had been a long time since he'd done this kind of field op.

He'd also never favored this particular gun.

He preferred the LR-300s and M16s, where he could fire sighted from full cover. He couldn't do that easily with the 97. He also didn't like where the magazine sat on the gun. It made for a slower reload, and the safety was oddly placed.

Not like he'd need that much out here.

The Adhipan moved fast, and nearly silently through the forested hillsides.

Revik was less than a third of the age of most of the seers tracking with him, but out-of-shape from his time with Terian and no real exercise in the months since. He found himself limping along like a late middle-ager, fighting to keep his breathing quiet enough to avoid pissing off the rest of the team.

His muscles had started to protest less than halfway through day one.

Now, on day three, he was doing marginally better. He'd been going out of his way to eat a lot and then powering through, pushing himself when it hurt. The least he could do was start building back some muscle while he was out here.

They hadn't had a lot of solid hits, but they'd had a few.

Those might have been intended as misdirection.

If so, it hadn't worked. The Adhipan still maintained a consistent track.

That fact alone told Revik one thing: whoever and whatever they were following, it likely wasn't a Terian body. If a telekinetic seer really had been housed in that underground dungeon, Terian wouldn't do anything to risk losing custody. He wouldn't expose himself out here at all. He would have gotten out via air transport immediately or, barring that, he would have gone dark, waited for a way out.

Well, unless Terry wasn't the one calling the shots.

Only two seers left the Sikkim school on this particular trail.

The Adhipan picked them out initially because among all those who survived, they alone telegraphed emotional signatures that didn't match. Also, instead of heading south with the other refugees, towards Nayabazar or Darjeeling, they headed north, into the mountains. They also brought human guides.

Then, just the day before, Revik walked the interior of a cave with several other Adhipan infiltrators.

They'd found evidence of a campfire and discarded bedding, as well as imprints from humans and seers having slept there. The imprints were already a few days old, but blood stains on the cave floor made a trail into the trees.

At the end of that trail, they found two rough graves, only half-finished, illustrating the end of the human guides. Revik and several in the Adhipan found child-sized footprints in the dirt. They'd done extensive scans, but came up close to blank.

Sensing movement, Revik glanced sideways.

Balidor met his gaze, then motioned to him with his eyes.

Revik followed the seer's fingers as they indicated up the nearby bank.

He was being asked to scout the ridge.

Nodding once, he kept his feelings to himself as he turned and began vaulting, as quietly as he could, up the hill.

He knew he was clumsy by Adhipan standards, but he'd already gotten better in the days he'd been out here. Balidor made it pretty clear he wanted Revik along for his own reasons: both to test him, and to get a sense of how he fit with the group. Given how rarely they admitted new seers to the Adhipan, as well as Revik's reputation with the Rooks, Balidor also likely hoped Revik might prove himself to his team.

Maybe because he was genuinely beginning to like the Adhipan leader—or maybe just pride—Revik found himself trying to meet Balidor's expectations.

Or, at the very least, to not embarrass himself.

Reaching the top of the hill only slightly out of breath, he remained in the trees dotting the steep edge of the highest point. He kept his silhouette off the ridge line as he scanned the valley below.

Splitting his consciousness between his eyes and the Barrier, with some small portion still with the Adhipan in the ravine on the other side, he looked for movement. From the Barrier, he looked for any sign of life bigger than your average monkey.

He got nothing.

He made roughly the same sweep twice, just to be certain. He was about to make his way back down the same incline—

When something pinged his consciousness.

It was sharp enough, and near enough, that he jumped.

He turned his head as if pulled by a puppet wire...

...and found himself looking at a very young, very dirty seer.

Maybe twenty years of age, so appearing around thirteen in human years, the boy stared at him from less than fifteen feet away. His face wore strong, Asiatic features, framed by thick, black hair.

His black eyes seemed to bore into Revik's.

The boy gripped the bark of a nearby tree with corpse-white hands that might have been completely untouched by sun. He wore what looked like misshapen adult's clothes, also Asian, and human in style. He'd belted the shirt and pants around himself to keep them up, but his feet and head were bare. Red with scratches and coated in mud and bits of greenery, his feet had swollen from walking.

Revik blinked in surprise, sure he was hallucinating.

When his blink ended, the boy had gone.

Revik felt the seers in the valley below reacting before he fully believed what he'd seen. He hadn't lost his connection to the Adhipan throughout the brief encounter, and now he felt them vaulting up the hill behind him, faster than he had.

A lot faster, he realized.

The part of him that had felt a brief flush of pride at how quickly he was regaining his speed realized he'd been kidding himself. Now that they were motivated, they moved through the trees too quickly for his light to track. He'd need to train every day for months to be able to match even the slowest of them.

The female, Laska, reached him first.

Without a word, Revik pointed to where the boy had been, sending her a more detailed snapshot with his light.

She disappeared into the trees.

Revik stood there a second longer, then followed to cover her even as four other seers reached the same part of the ridge, Grent and Balidor among them.

Embarrassed now that he'd hesitated, Revik fanned out with the rest of the team down the opposite hillside, following Balidor's commands from the Barrier, doing his best to move as quietly and quickly as the rest of them. As the fan spread down the hill, he kept his consciousness split, scanning and shielding more tightly as he was forced to cover more ground.

Then Laska signaled all of them, and he got an image of the boy again, standing on the branch of a tree, on the other side of a grassy clearing.

He was maybe thirty yards away from her.

Like the rest of them, Revik shifted direction at once, running through the trees at top speed to reach where she stood. He'd been closer than over half of them, but he still reached the clearing dead last, and the most out of breath.

He approached the area where Laska and four others had their guns trained on the kid.

He moved cautiously as his eyes pulled the boy's outline from the trees.

He studied the dirty face.

That feeling of familiarity was back, though still vague, more of a flicker than anything concrete. He was still trying to decide its source when he realized the boy was staring at him, too.

In fact, the boy stared at him alone. He ignored the Adhipan seers.

That fact didn't go unnoticed by the others.

They looked between him and the boy.

Revik felt a few in the Adhipan scan him—less than politely, in that they neither asked nor were they open about it—in an attempt to discern if Revik recognized the boy. He let them in, partly in irritation, but mainly to see if they could determine the nature of the connection.

None did, at least not that they were willing to share with him.

The boy's expression remained flat, but the intensity of his interest in Revik shimmered off him in waves.

Revik found himself moving closer in reflex, when Laska and then Balidor each held up a hand, motioning unmistakably at Revik to remain where he was.

Hold your position! Laska sent, sharp. *Look at the structures!*

Revik focused above the boy's head.

Blinking his way from the Barrier to his physical eyes then back again, he focused his *aleimi*, sure he'd scanned him wrong. Convinced at his second look, he watched the crystalized geometries rotate in awe.

When the boy didn't seem to be blocking him, he went in for a closer look.

He recognized some of the basic shapes from Allie's light, but not in the configuration he could see now. *Aleimic* structures changed from use; they grew, but they also reconfigured and clustered when specialized functions were exercised, particularly if those functions involved using more than one structure at the same time.

The geometries that spiraled up from the boy's head looked like a fountain of mathematical fireworks, highlighted from recent use... but also from repeated use, over a long period of time.

From the Barrier, he looked like Allie would look after about fifty years of manipulation training, followed by twenty more in the field.

There was no way the boy standing in front of him could be old enough for what lived above his head.

STOP! Balidor sent sharply.

Revik hadn't realized he'd taken another step.

His eyes remained on the boy.

Somehow, the emotion that rose in him came closest to pity.

Laska took a step forward, too, shielding Revik.

The boy switched his focus to her.

Revik tensed. He watched Laska rearrange her hands on the gun. Her aim never left the boy's head. Revik looked between Laska and her target, then focused on the boy.

He studied the black, mirror-like eyes.

Laska took another step and Revik felt it—without knowing exactly what *it* was, or where it originated above that small head.

He lowered his own gun reflexively, raising a hand.

"Stop!" he said aloud. "Laska! Don't move!"

Holding his own gun out, away from his body, Revik raised his other hand, straightening out of a combat crouch.

He stepped out from behind Laska.

"Hey!" he yelled in Hindi, drawing the boy's eyes. "Over here! Will you talk to us? We won't hurt you!"

For a moment, no one moved.

Revik felt the charge of light snake around the boy's head.

He felt the other members of the Adhipan focus on those same structures, watching light flicker in concentric rings through minute geometries above the small, dark crown. Revik felt the same tension in the other infiltrators that had risen in his own light. Like biting a live wire, it flowed from one of them to the next, sparking their own *aleimi*.

Revik held the gun further out from his body.

On impulse, he tried sending to the boy.

Are you all right? he sent. *Are you hurt? What can we—*

You, he sent. *I know you.*

Revik felt the Adhipan looking at him again. He swallowed thickly, but kept his thoughts even, and unshielded.

Are you sure? he sent.

The boy smiled. His eyes looked cold, predatory.

Okay, Revik sent. *Okay. I don't remember everything. I—*

You can't hurt me. Not anymore!

Revik gestured in agreement. *We won't try. I promise.*

Anger curled out of those detailed structures.

We? he snarled. *You're a "we" now? You left me there!* You *did it!* You *promised you wouldn't, and you did it anyway!*

Revik tensed.

At a loss, he glanced at the Adhipan hunters.

He didn't have to scan them to know what they were thinking. But explaining to this kid with the nuclear bomb hovering above his head that he had probably left him while he'd been working for the Rooks—and that since then he'd had his memory wiped and had been doing everything he knew to try and make amends—probably wouldn't help.

Not given what they'd found at that burnt-out school.

Not a school, the kid sent. *You know it's not a fucking school! You lied about that too! You lied about everything!* The older look returned to his dark eyes. *But I'm not alone now. So you can tell your dogs to go home. I won't go* anywhere *with you.*

A tremor rippled Revik's spine.

Yes, he sent to the boy. *I understand. I saw that place. I felt how terrible it was.* He fought to think. *I'm sorry. I really don't remember—*

I should kill you.

Revik felt light spark around him dangerously. Holding his free hand higher in the air, he set his gun down on a flat rock near his feet.

I've got a mate. Do you want to kill her, too?

The boy's eyes narrowed.

Revik hesitated at the look there.

No cave, he sent after that pause. *No guns. No wires. No schools. No one will take you anywhere you don't want to go. No one will hurt you, I promise—*

Liar, the boy sent. *You're a liar!*

Not this time.

You killed me! You destroyed me!

His words hurt Revik somehow. *You're still here,* he sent.

You're a bad man! A bad fucking man!

Not anymore, he sent. *Whatever I did before, I'm sorry.*

The boy gave a thick laugh, older than his body's years. The hatred in his thoughts grew more palpable.

Nervous, Revik glanced at Balidor. The older seer signaled with his hand for Revik to keep going, but to be careful. Revik gestured in affirmative.

Then the woman, Laska, rearranged her hands on her gun. As she did, she took a half-step forward.

The movement swung the boy's eyes back to her face.

Before Revik could warn her, something slammed at his light.

His energy dropped so severely, his knees crumpled. It came out of nowhere, pulling at him from above—like a vacuum to his light from above his head. Out of his peripheral vision, he saw several members of the Adhipan stagger as well. He held out a hand in a daze. His knees hit the dirt as his fingers smacked the same rock where he'd placed his gun.

He heard Laska give a strangled cry...

Just before there was a loud cracking sound.

Then something flew past him, pushing air out of the way so quickly he ducked, flinching from its path. When he could focus again, another seer was running between him and the downed female.

"Laska!" the male screamed.

Grent ran for his mate.

He moved so fast Revik couldn't follow the motion with his eyes. He watched the other male in shock as his mind replayed the sound of bone cracking.

He realized what Grent had already felt.

Laska lay where she'd fallen in the undergrowth, blood on her lips. Grent cradled her in his arms, her neck hung at a wrong angle. Her eyes remained open, staring up at the trees. The male screamed, a sound that stabbed at Revik's heart.

None of the Adhipan moved.

Then, slowly Revik staggered to his feet.

Dazed from the hit to his light, he stared at Grent and Laska.

Fear, then rage wound through him.

He saw the shock hit Grent's light in concentric waves. Unable to watch the male's realization of what had occurred, he looked for the boy. Finding him standing motionless on the same branch, Revik focused on the smile playing at the bow-like lips. Without thinking, he snatched his gun off the rock and raised it to his shoulder...

The metal stock ripped out of his hands.

Something slammed him in the middle of the chest.

Whatever it was, it had the weight of a thick, oak plank. The force behind it was almost mechanical, like being hit by a wrecking ball.

It threw him off his feet.

Arms and legs pin-wheeling, he tried to slow himself. Greenery streaked by as he experienced another sharp drop in his light.

Then his back hit something hard. His head, too.

His body crumpled to the wet ground.

Protruding objects met his back, legs, and arms as everything around him started to gray. Warmth covered his head and neck; he smelled his own blood. He looked up, fighting to focus his eyes as a tall form stepped out of the trees.

The female seer looked down at him.

Her eyes shone a turquoise blue that was nearly iridescent. Like the boy, her face was Asian, with high cheekbones. She held a long rifle fitted with organics that made the Chinese models carried by the Adhipan look like children's toys.

Blowing *hiri* smoke through straight black hair to get it out of her eyes, she walked over to the tree where he lay.

She dropped the thin cigarette, grinding it out with the toe of her boot.

"Hello, lover," she said in Russian.

Raising her heel, she aimed it at his face.

Everything went dark all at once.

CHAPTER 22
FAMILIAR

F ire blooms out in crimson waves over a field.

I watch the bodies blown back, the ghosting whisper of light trails around the second tankard before it ignites.

He is here, with me.

It bothers me, how familiar he feels, how much I know him already.

He watches the devastation from above, directing like a mathematician conductor, his focus lost inside elaborate geometries of light. They rise above us in a column, sparking and igniting as he combines and recombines their intricate threads.

It is beautiful. My admiration is heartfelt, almost shy.

He is beautiful, in his orchestration of this precise work.

The work is still work to him. It requires concentration, will, purpose. Yet it fills him with such freedom, of muscles flexing, utilizing complexities in himself that are still new to him, that still fill him with relief, almost longing. The work allows him to breathe. After years and years of repression and hiding and pretending to be what he is not, he lets it exhale outwards rather than eating him from within.

It makes my heart hurt, this freedom.

An explosion rocks the ground near to where he stands in the physical world.

Shrapnel flies towards him and the two seers protecting him.

I fear for him for an instant—

Then he throws up a shield of white light.

It is dense; it pushes the force outward, protecting him and the two males beside him. Fire and iron and wood slide over and around them in a hot wind of explosive air. They are like rocks in the midst of a fast-moving stream.

I feel the gratitude of the two seers with him.

They adore him. They positively adore him.

It is what he is born to do.

He knows nothing else for which he is suited. Here it is less a question of right or wrong, good or bad, but of untapped functionalities expressed outwards to some purpose, even if that purpose is not fully his own.

He knows now, that this force in him had to come out eventually.

In one way or another, he would have expressed the power living in his light. While he cannot trust those for whom he exerts himself now, he trusts himself even less. So he works for them, and considers himself lucky.

He has a purpose.

He helps to make the world better.

If only temporarily.

Memories break inside my mind, pieces of him mixed with pieces of myself, or maybe just memories of his memories. A historical moment lives here. Something of import, that lives beyond what any seer or human remembers. A knowing imprints all of us, like a notch in our collective DNA.

Somehow, we are all responsible.

He is not born. He is created.

He is made through indifference, through patience and intention.

A man holds a gun to his head.

It is a small head, only slightly larger than the one I know from the forest. Dark hair obscures his round face and pale eyes. I can't see his eyes though; they are invisible to me, as are most of his features.

It is not only seers who work to break him.

This one is human.

Young. Mean. He works for the other, but he is devoted, not a slave.

"Disarm!" the human snarls. "Disarm, you fuck! You think he'll let you live if you don't? Disarm or I'll blow your head all over this wall—"

It shocks me, to hear him talk that way to the boy.

The boy is both strangely old and strangely young for his years. He copes and shuts down and learns and strategizes, all in turn. Sometimes he does all at once.

He fights them, too. His mind fights, for his body is fragile.

His tormenters writhe through his *aleimi* like metal snakes, but he fights them anyway. He holds onto memories of parents, some glimpse of what it was to be loved. He remembers affection, but it slides out of his grasp so easily.

It isn't long before he questions if any of that had been real.

The human's name is Merenje.

"You snot-nosed prick. Don't care about your life, eh? What about your little girlfriend? How many of us do you think it would take to break her?"

I feel something in the small chest give out.

They find his weakness. They always find it.

I see her then. Large eyes, dark hair. A prostitute they brought him; she is young, almost as young as him. He knows she was sold to them. He knows she doesn't want to be there. She doesn't care about him, but she is all he has.

She begs him for protection. She begs him, touches him when he wants it. She tells him lies. She knows. He is her only hope of getting out of there alive.

They beat her, too. They beat her, and use her, but she is...

The cave wavers, breaks apart.

A wall of windows appears. A burnt-out factory in a field.

He is there, young again, though not as small as when I saw him beaten and cut and raped in the woods. He is a teenager now, a young man. The emotion remains intact but it is more focused from the years.

Structures spark around his light.

Fear lives there, a crushing grief covered over in blinding rage... and something else, a feeling of purpose. It all mixes with a darker wildness, the temperament of an animal.

Emotion pulses out in erratic bursts.

I feel his mind reach out. I feel it start, the folding sensation.

The power behind it terrifies me.

I've glimpsed that fire-like potential before. I've seen it in me, this fire. I am careful as I look at it, like a giant picking up a snail.

The boy is past that.

He uncaps that force, a writhing, boiling pit below a thin membrane he uses to hold it back. When he slides back that veil, he screams from the power of it. It feels fucking good. It feels so much better... better than he's felt, in longer than he can remember... and I lay there, panting in the dark, remembering that feeling somewhere inside my own being, jealous of him for not caring.

He exhales it out, and...

Windows explode inside rusted frames.

They shatter outward.

The release is so profound he is filled with something akin to joy. The folding turns into a merging, a oneness with all lights, everywhere, and he sees inside every atom, every moving and shining particle.

He's held it back for so long.

When it finally goes he laughs and laughs and can't stop laughing...

CHAPTER 23
HUSBAND

I sat hunched over a cup of chai, staring into the fire.

My mind felt excavated, spent.

I could no longer think. I lived there now, inside our jumps. Both relief and irritation accompanied every break between sessions.

It was like a drug.

It frightened me a little, to know I was living vicariously through the boy. I was exercising that part of myself through him—siphoning off the excess, so to speak, like watching porn instead of having sex.

I was aware enough to be disturbed by the idea.

Day followed day, mostly the same since that first introduction to the boy in the woods. Tarsi and I weren't any closer to finding the connection to the current day massacre—assuming one even existed—but I felt like I needed to scrub my brain with steel wool and Comet for about a month.

I don't think I fully knew it was morning until the old woman came in, holding an armful of wood. Stacking pieces by the stone fireplace, she turned and looked at me, her light eyes appraising.

"You need break," she announced in her choppy English.

I nodded, vaguely grateful. The irritation came a few seconds later. I pushed it aside, glancing hopefully at the pile of skins that had become my bed.

"Yes," I agreed.

"Good." She smiled. "Husband here. Waiting for you."

I stared at her for several full seconds.

"Revik's here?"

"You got different husband?"

Taking a long drink of the tea, I set down my cup, noticing only then that my hands were shaking. I couldn't believe I hadn't felt him.

Then, thinking about it, I could believe it.

But that made me wonder again why he hadn't come before now.

He hadn't felt angry the times I'd managed to touch his light, but he hadn't exactly felt normal, either. Tugging my boots closer, I shoved my socked foot inside the first one and began knotting it up. I blanked out my mind.

"He mad at me," Tarsi said cheerfully. "He say he no leave until he talk to you."

My nerves worsened. "Great. Okay. He's out there now?"

"He no leave," she repeated. Her pale eyes smiled at me. *Take the yak skin. And keep the clothes. I'll get them from you when you come back.*

Once I got my second boot on and tied up, I stood, letting the blanket drop to the floor as I looked for where I'd left the coat. Finding it by the door, I fumbled into the arms, and then I felt him, looking for me. A sharp ribbon of pain sliced through my chest, sucking in my breath. I lay a hand on the whitewashed stone, fighting to keep the chai down.

Once I'd recovered enough, I looked at Tarsi.

That time, I saw kindness in her eyes as well as humor.

"Do I need to come back here?" I said. "I do, don't I?"

She gestured fluidly with a wrist flick up, a seer's yes.

She added, "Go with him now. Both of you are useless." Smiling, she went on in the more fluid words of her mind. *It is better that we let the two of you be married for a while. You are both becoming a liability in your current state. Him even more than you.*

At my skeptical look, her eyes sharpened.

"You need to tell him something, Bridge. Before you leave. I'll know if you don't. I'll come after you, tell him myself." *Use my exact words,* she warned. *Before you go anywhere with him. He won't hear it later.*

I nodded, but that last part puzzled me. I finished fastening the coat, standing by the door.

"Okay. What is it?"

She told me. Her words didn't clear anything up, so I repeated them a few times in my head, trying to make them make sense.

"What does it mean?" I asked.

Alyson, tell him exactly what I said.

"But you're talking about me, right? Why can't I know what it means, if—"

She clicked at me, loudly enough that I fell silent.

Alyson, she sent. *I am not playing games. Tell him. Or I will.*

After a slight hesitation, I nodded. But I wasn't happy. Reaching for the wooden door handle, I stopped a last time, looking over the interior of the small cottage. It had become my whole world in the past few weeks.

"Say goodbye to Hannah for me," I said. "Tell her thanks."

"You stalling, Bridge?" She smiled.

I sighed. "Maybe."

Steeling myself, I jerked the door open and entered the clearing, putting the old woman and the stillborn images of war and glass shattering and dead children out of my mind... for a short time, at least.

I should have known he wouldn't wait in the open.

And yet, it still made me pause when I couldn't find him right away with my eyes. I scanned shadows, half-using my sight, and made out his tall form, standing unmoving by a clump of dark, hard-skinned trees. He stood at the opposite edge of the clearing, not far from where I'd last seen Chandre.

He wasn't looking at me.

He hadn't been so heavily shielded around me since we'd been together on the ship. His visibility behind the Barrier existed only in what wasn't there, not what was. His outline constituted an empty spot in the living light of the forest.

As soon as I thought it, his light changed.

Within a blink, his light matched that of the woods with an exactness I couldn't help but find impressive.

I began to walk.

His long form remained motionless as I crossed the grass.

Shadows stretched alongside strips of early morning light, dappling his face under the trees. He didn't look over as I approached, but continued to focus on the sky past the edge of the cliff. It occurred to me he must have left in the middle of the night to get here at this hour.

When I stood directly in front of him, he turned his head, but still didn't quite meet my gaze.

For a moment, we just stood there.

It was almost easier to be with him like this, with his light so closed.

I looked up at pinkish clouds, and realized I hadn't been out of Tarsi's cave in what must have been a few days.

When I looked over next, I caught him watching me. His eyes traveled down my body before he felt me looking and averted his gaze. His face was blank, the mask I remembered from when we first knew one another. He had a bruise on one cheek, dark enough that I knew it had to be a few days old, at least.

Tentatively, I tried to read what was going on behind the mask.

He didn't exactly push me off, but I felt him move, sidestepping my light.

His voice made me jump. He spoke English, his accent thick.

"Are you staying?" he asked. "Here. With Tarsi."

I took a breath. "She said I could go."

He didn't meet my gaze, but nodded. "What will you do now?"

I hesitated, suddenly unsure.

"I'm leaving," I said. "With you. Aren't I?"

I saw his shoulders abruptly unclench. His light remained firmly closed. He seemed about to say something more, then looked away again.

"Are you ready?" he asked. "Do you have everything you need?"

I studied his eyes. "Yeah," I said. "Revik, your face. What—"

He shook his head. "Not here." He held out a hand. He didn't try to touch me, but stopped, palm open, offering it to me.

I stared at his hand, seeing my father's ring on his index finger.

Feeling him react to, and misunderstand, my hesitation, I reached out, but before our fingers touched, I hesitated again, retracting my arm.

"Wait," I said. "There's something else. Something I'm supposed to tell you. Before we leave." I felt my face warm, and realized I was embarrassed. I wasn't sure why I was embarrassed, but I fought to block my reaction.

In the end I looked away, towards Tarsi—or her door, at least.

When I turned back, I saw him waiting.

"It's ridiculous," I said. "But she wanted me to say it word for word. Before I went anywhere with you." His face remained patient, so I ran fingers through my tangled hair. "Okay. She wanted me to say this: 'He lied to you. In Cairo. She doesn't know. I...'"

I hesitated. His face hadn't moved a muscle.

"'...I agree with you. But you need to be... careful.'"

I felt him waiting still, so I held up my hands.

"That's it," I said. "That's the message."

He didn't meet my eyes. I saw him look towards Tarsi's house.

For a moment, he didn't move. His light remained tightly shielded, but I felt some kind of conflict on him, or maybe it was an emotional reaction of some kind.

Hell, he could have been talking to her.

He nodded a second later, seemingly to himself.

I saw his throat move in a swallow, just before he offered me his hand again, giving me a bare glance.

"Okay." He cleared his throat. "Are you ready?"

"Revik." I studied his eyes. "What does it mean?"

He shook his head. "We can talk about it later."

"Is this about Maygar? Because he didn't..." I saw him flinch and stopped.

Pain rippled off him. For a moment he didn't move.

"No," he said finally. "It's not about that." He looked me full in the face. "Allie." He struggled with words. "Allie... are you all right?"

He had opened his light, so much that I found it difficult to hold his gaze. Grief spiraled off him, but worse than that, guilt, and a pain that was hard to deal with.

Looking away from that expression, I tried to smile, backing off.

"I'm fine." Still trying to get that look off his face, I joked, "I'm pretty sure *he's* not."

He didn't smile back.

When the feeling on him intensified, I caught hold of his arm.

"Hey." I bit back the flare in my light when he looked down. For a moment, I could only return his stare. "I want to go with you." I released his arm, taking a half-step back. "I've missed you like crazy, and we can talk about whatever you want. But I really don't want to go back to Seertown. Much less the compound, or—"

"Not Seertown," he said, his eyes still on mine.

"Then where?"

"I found us a place, Allie. It's safe." He cleared his throat. "We'll be alone."

I thought about that for another breath, then I nodded. I took the hand he offered a third time. When his fingers wound into mine, I felt it down to my feet.

"Okay," I said. "Then I'm ready."

He walked with a slight limp again, I noticed.

We hiked for hours, and I watched him walk.

I wondered if his injuries from Terian were acting up again, or if this was something new, something related to the bruise on his face.

I almost asked as we walked uphill.

In the end I didn't, aware of his probable reaction to my bringing it up.

It felt at first like we were retracing the steps I'd taken to Tarsi's, but at a certain point, Revik deviated.

He brought us through a ravine I didn't recognize, then further south, towards a different crest of mountains. Helping me up onto a slim trail once we reached the other side of a narrow, heavily forested canyon, he took me past a broken wall of cliffs made of granite-like boulders.

I gazed out over the canyon, watching birds skim along the roof of the canopy.

Hearing the thundering crash of water over rocks after we'd been walking a few minutes longer, I looked around until my eyes found a high waterfall of glacier runoff. The sound grew even louder once we rounded another jutting section of rock. He took my hand again when we reached a section where the rocks grew slippery, leading me up to a snaking path through the trees.

The air felt colder within minutes, and thinner.

After we'd been walking another hour, I struggled a bit to breathe and stopped to rest.

Laying a hand on a tree beside the path, I looked down at the zig-zagging trail roping below, half-obscured again by trees. I saw someone on the trail then and froze, just before the figure disappeared.

"Revik," I said quietly.

From behind, he touched my shoulder, almost tentatively.

"Adhipan," he said. "Females only."

I glanced up, but he didn't return my gaze.

My eyes drifted to the bruise on his face. "So much for being alone, I guess." I tried to mask my bitterness with humor, but didn't really succeed. "I'm amazed they're bothering to be sneaky."

Revik touched me again. Again, his hand didn't linger.

"They won't be able to see us where we're going," he said. "Balidor promised me. They're only escorting us there, then they'll leave... monitor the construct from afar."

I nodded, but didn't quite believe it.

Seers could lie as well as human beings. Better, I'd learned, especially when the truth interfered with their warped sense of "duty." Funny how everyone was so concerned with me now. Where was all that overbearing male concern when Maygar decided to do his wacky claim thing, and in full view of the entire compound?

My anger deflated when I saw Revik's eyes brighten.

It shocked me, even with what I'd felt off him before.

I had to look at him twice, and even then I couldn't make up my mind if I was right. His light closed, and I watched him, disbelieving as he wiped his face with the back of his hand, avoiding my stare.

Seers weren't human, I reminded myself.

The men had zero stigma around getting openly emotional. Actually dangerously emotional. Tightening my fingers in his, I tugged on his hand. He still wouldn't look at me.

"Hey," I said.

"Allie." His voice was thick. "The Maygar thing..."

I shook my head. "No, Revik... please. Please don't." Feeling him tense, I shook my head again. "It's not you. I swear it's not. I just don't see any point in talking about it. It happened. It's done." When his face tightened, I tugged on his fingers. "Look. Everything came out okay. More or less."

He still wouldn't look at me.

I quieted my voice.

"Please, baby."

I felt him react to the endearment, glancing at me.

I caressed his fingers, feeling my touch ripple through his light.

"I already yelled at Chandre, blamed you, blamed myself. I don't have the energy to do it all again. We're good. Aren't we?"

His jaw hardened, but he gestured a "yes." He looked like he wanted to say something anyway, but feeling me push back against his light, he didn't.

We didn't talk again for a few hours.

By then, we were on a high plateau.

A long, grassy field spread out before us. White-capped mountains stood on all sides. The view before me of low-seeming clouds and the strangely polarized, blue-white sun brought a chill to my spine.

Feeling suddenly like I'd stumbled into one of my dreams, I slowed my steps, my breath a little short. I glanced around at the wildflowers dotting the thigh-high grasses, feeling the sense of familiarity like a physical blow.

It could have been that same field, from the jump with Tarsi.

What were we doing here, anyway? Was there an airstrip nearby?

The sky was darkening. When Revik tugged lightly on my hand, his fingers questioning, I followed. We walked through the thigh-high grass without talking, until we reached the top of a small rise.

Below, a fence ringed one portion of the field. It delineated the edges of a mown space around a low ranch house with a tile roof.

"Here?" I looked at him. "You want to talk here?"

Revik nodded. He glanced up at the sky, like I had. I don't know if he noticed the look of bewilderment on my face or not.

"I bought it," he explained. "We needed to modify the construct pretty extensively. It was easier to buy it, then we could rework the whole thing." He hesitated, studying my face. "The house is pretty simple, Allie."

I nodded, looking up at the mountains, but my mind was clunking and jerking disjointedly into its own gears, trying to chew through this new information, and the information he'd just piled on top of it.

He'd *bought* it?

And how could this possibly be a good idea, the two of us alone up here? I'd assumed we were heading towards a town, or an airstrip. When he'd said we'd be alone, I'd pictured us going to Delhi, maybe even to Europe.

Separate hotel rooms. That kind of thing.

Keeping my light tightly shielded, I let go of his hand to walk down the hill, wading through the tall grasses. In almost no time, I reached the gated fence.

Entering through the opening across from the cabin's door, I strode in a rough circle around the lawn-like clearing, and its ring of packed dirt around the house.

I knew I was stalling. I felt myself gathering imprints as well.

I felt traces of the old human who lived here before. He felt like a nice man. I saw hoof prints, what looked like at least one dog's. He'd had grandchildren. I wondered if he'd gone to live with them. There was an old-fashioned water pump, and a trough.

Revik followed me.

It occurred to me he was watching my reactions minutely.

"It's beautiful up here," I said, and I meant it.

I followed with my eyes as wind rippled the grasses outside the fence. New, sharp green shoots dusted with wildflowers turned the plateau into a mosaic. A tall windmill, the old-fashioned wooden kind I liked from when I was a kid, stood behind the house, spinning evenly in a higher breeze. Beyond it, I saw what looked like horses grazing on the slope. They stood not far from a river.

"You own the horses, too?" I asked.

"Yes."

"And the river?"

Revik gave a short laugh, making a seer's "more or less" gesture with one hand.

"Enough of it," he said.

"I'm starving," I said, looking at him again. "Is there food?"

He made a hospitable gesture towards the front door.

I followed the motion of his hand, walking in front of him. He hung back as I reached for the handle.

It wasn't locked.

Twisting it all the way, I opened the door.

I'd expected something western, I guess, from the horses and the windmill. I was pleasantly surprised when I saw colorful wooden furniture like you might find in a Tibetan home. It had been cleaned recently, maybe even re-furnished. Thick rugs covered a flagstone floor, all the way up to the fireplace, which stood near a dining area and a heavy wooden table, also brightly painted. Behind that, I was surprised to see a real kitchen with a gas stove, a full-sized refrigerator and a sink, more brightly colored cabinets and a woodblock cutting board in the middle. I wondered what powered the electricity.

"A combination," Revik said from behind me. "Solar and wind. There's a fair bit up here. The generator kicks into oil when it gets low. That's mostly for the winter."

I glanced back to where he stood by the door.

He was watching me again. He motioned towards another door, which led to a shadow-darkened back area.

"Take a shower if you want," he offered. "I'll do something about food."

"You don't have to—" I began.

"Just go, Allie." He quirked an eyebrow. "I won't poison you. Promise."

I laughed. When he smiled, I headed for the back room. Right before the door, I stopped, remembering I hadn't brought anything with me.

He must have felt that, too.

He paused on his way to the kitchen.

"I had Cass pick out clothes." He rubbed the back of his neck, seemingly embarrassed by my surprise. "I didn't look, but there should be things in the closet. They did all of that in the last week." He met my gaze. "When I got back, Allie."

Hesitating only a second more, I nodded, trying to relax.

I didn't miss the opening he'd left me, in telling me he'd been gone, but his words raised a whole host of other questions, too.

I entered the darkened room, still a little thrown that he'd involved Cass.

Shutting the door, I faced the dim space, trying to get my bearings.

The room itself was pretty simple. A large wardrobe made of wood and painted in bright colors, Tibetan style, stood in one corner, across from a heavily curtained window. A door to a small bathroom stood to the left of that. The floor had been covered in thick wool rugs, and I saw candles on a wooden shelf over the bed.

I was still looking around, trying to collect myself, when something else occurred to me.

There was only one bed.

CHAPTER 24
PROPOSAL

I was staring into the fire when, a few hours later, Revik emerged from the bedroom, letting out a dispersing cloud of steam.

We'd finished eating.

I was still at the table, one leg drawn up to where my arm circled my shin, holding my foot on the seat of a wooden chair.

Revik had surprised me, by being able to cook at all I guess. What he made definitely fit the "unusual" camp, in terms of a human/western palate, but it had been good—some kind of mango curry thing with nuts and spinach and a few things I couldn't identify.

I knew it was seer food from the way he ate it.

When I did the same, the textures grew even more subtle.

In fact, they did so well past my tongue, creating a warm flow in my light from my throat down to my thighs.

Just when I'd started to wonder if maybe there was an ulterior motive for all of this, he disappeared into the other room without a word. I heard the shower start up a few minutes later and sighed, settling myself in to wait.

Now I gave him a fleeting smile as he sat down in the wooden chair he'd vacated before, directly across the table from me.

He returned my smile, leaning back and running a hand through his wet hair. He'd shaved I noticed, and wore clean clothes, a loose shirt that was almost Chinese in cut with those rope-like, knotted fasteners, and jeans. From Cass's pile for me, I'd found a silk kimono, black with a gold bird on the back.

I wore it all through dinner. It was long, embroidered and hardly revealing, but now, glancing under the table at his jeans, I wondered if maybe I'd been pushing it.

He reached into a pocket and produced a *hiri,* which I'd never seen him smoke, although I'd smelled it on him more than once on the ship. He lit it with a wooden match, which he shook out and left on his plate.

I considered asking him for one as well, then decided I hadn't quit smoking like a human only to start as a seer. When I glanced up, he was watching me through a cloud of sweet-smelling smoke.

"Does it bother you?" he asked.

"No," I said. I was telling the truth. Unlike human cigarettes, *hiri* smoke actually smelled good.

He looked at the end of the *hiri,* then at me.

Leaning my arm on the table, I tried, unsuccessfully, to blank out my mind. I had nothing to say, really, but I couldn't seem to stop thinking about it.

I wasn't up to talking about the war, or even asking where he'd been for the last few weeks, or about the limp I'd noticed again as he crossed the room. I wasn't ready to think about tomorrow yet. I didn't really want to know details about what was going on at the compound, or how long we had before someone made us go back there.

The very last thing I wanted to do was revisit our aborted conversation about Maygar.

I didn't want to try to make small talk, either, which both of us completely sucked at.

I didn't want to talk at all, when it came down to it.

I wasn't sure where that left us, though.

"Do you want to sleep?" he asked.

Before I'd thought about why, something in my chest constricted.

I fought it, keeping it out of my light, or at least away from where he could see it.

"Sure," I said. Without my willing it, my eyes flickered towards the bedroom. "You can go ahead, if you want."

I focused on the bruise on his face, then looked away.

When the silence stretched, I glanced around us surreptitiously. There was a low couch with a stack of thick blankets on one end, and a pile of pillows on the other. I tried to decide if I should just come out and ask him.

He rose to his feet, grinding out the *hiri*.

I held my breath, thinking he was going to disappear into the bedroom again, leaving me even more lost as to what I should do.

But he didn't.

He walked around the table. I didn't look up as he sank to the chair beside mine, moving it closer with his feet so that our knees touched.

He took my hands in his, and I stared down at our fingers. His knuckles were still bruised, but the marks had faded.

"Allie," he said. "What's wrong?"

Removing one hand from his, I pushed back my hair, and was horrified to realize I was crying. I wiped my eyes, smiling in embarrassment, and more than a little bewilderment. I wiped my face again.

"Wow," I said. "I'm sorry." I clutched his hand where his fingers wound around mine. "Is this that irrational thing you warned me about?"

He moved closer. "Yes," he said, soft.

I couldn't bring myself to return his gaze.

I remembered how he'd felt all those days I'd been at Tarsi's. He hadn't come for me, or even asked about me, for almost three weeks. He'd avoided me in the Barrier. As I sat there, I realized how much I didn't want to talk to him about that, either.

When I started to get up, he caught my arms, holding me in place.

"Allie." His voice held an edge of panic. It brought my eyes to his. "What am I doing wrong? Tell me."

"You're not doing anything wrong, Revik. I'm just tired, I—"

"Allie!" His light hit at mine, forcing a gasp from my lips. He pulled me closer. "You said to let it go, so I did! Are you angry with me?"

"No." Biting my lip, I shook my head. I held his gaze with an effort. "I'm not angry. I swear I'm not, Revik."

He just looked at me, his light eyes showing incomprehension.

Pain circulated in my light veins. I realized part of it was from my light interacting with his. I bunched my hands into fists, focusing on our fingers, the differences between our hands... in size, in skin color.

Shaking my head, I took a breath.

"I'm sorry," I said. "I just don't understand. This seems like a bad idea, us alone up here." I looked around the fire-lit room, feeling my skin warm. "What are we doing here?"

Understanding reached him.

I felt it click in. Then his mind whispered past mine, remembering the last morning we'd been together, in Seertown. His pain shivered through me and I winced, pulling away from his light. I felt him react to that, too.

Staring at the fire, I was trying to decide how to get out of this awkward mess, when his hand slid into my hair.

"Allie." His voice was soft. "Allie. *Gaos.* You're so beautiful. You're so fucking beautiful..." He kissed my face.

My skin warmed.

Disbelief hit as his words sank in, and he kissed me again, caressing my cheek with his. He'd never complimented me before. Not my looks, anyway. Come to think of it, he hadn't complimented much of anything about me.

He wasn't really the complimenting type.

"I wanted to come earlier," he said. "I wanted to." His fingers stroked mine. "I had hoped you would ask for me. I waited, Allie. As long as I could."

Before I had time to think about that, he kissed my face again, leaning across the space between us. He leaned closer when I let him into my light, resting his head on my shoulder, caressing my hands. Everything about him was warm, merging into me, into my skin. His light was more open than I'd ever felt it.

I honestly had no idea what to do with him like this.

He raised his head, looking at me.

"Thank you," he said. "For the ring."

My skin flushed more.

"You don't have to wear it," I said.

But I fingered it on his hand anyway, stroking the inside of his wrist when he moved it deeper into my lap.

I looked up, feeling him pull at me.

His eyes were intense in that way that was foreign to me still. When I caressed his fingers, looking again at the one with my father's ring, his pain ribboned out at me. I felt more of him in it that time, a flood of feeling that slid deeper into my light.

After the barest pause, he leaned towards my mouth.

Seeing where he was going, I touched his chest, pushing him back gently.

"No." Moving my head aside, I shook my head, fighting for breath. "No," I said. "I need more than that. You need to tell me… something."

His eyes glowed faintly with firelight. He closed them, longer than a blink.

He leaned back in his chair.

"All right." For a moment, he didn't speak, caressing my fingers with his. I watched his eyes, saw their focus aim inward before he looked up. "Allie." He took a breath. "Allie, I wanted to…" I felt him form words before he spoke, as if translating. "I wanted to request, formally…"

His mouth hardened, just before he shrugged.

"I suppose you'd view it as a proposal," he said, more in his normal voice. "I want to consummate. Tonight, if you're willing."

I was positive I hadn't heard him right.

At the same time, pain tried to infiltrate my light, making it hard to replay his words in my head. I almost couldn't hear him when he spoke next.

"…It's an open offer, Allie." His face darkened as he studied mine. "I know this isn't very, well…" He gestured vaguely with one hand.

"I tried to find out from Jon and Cass, but they didn't know. What you'd want. If you'd expect a more…" He met my gaze. "Human ritual. I didn't know if you'd want anything."

He cleared his throat, gesturing delicately with the same hand.

"…A ceremony. There are seer versions. I'm open to a human variant. In India. Or somewhere else." He cleared his throat again. "We could bring your people here. Or we could travel… if you'd rather do that. I don't know if you want me to explain more about… you know. How this works with seers."

I must have blinked.

I continued to stare at him, wondering if he'd possibly been replaced. It actually crossed my mind that Terian had replaced him.

I realized then, that he was waiting.

He expected me to speak.

"Revik." I found I was stammering. "Revik, I really don't need—"

"Just think about what you would want," he said, quicker that time, as if heading off something he saw on my face. "I know I'm springing this on you, but just think about it." His fingers tightened on mine. "And where you'd want to live. We've never talked about any of the logistics. We should. I'd like us to share a home. I'm open as to where, Allie. Really open. There are probably safety considerations, but we can negotiate with the Council."

I swallowed again, staring down at our hands.

"Allie, I don't want you to think—"

"Revik. Stop." Holding up a hand, I took a breath, fighting to control my light.

Finally, I shook my head, closing my eyes.

"Please don't take this the wrong way. Please. I really, really appreciate that you were willing to do this. And yes, I know we're both in pain... a lot of pain." I hesitated, forcing myself to look up. Wincing a little at his expression, I added, "But I can't... I really can't let this be your solution to what Maygar did."

He stiffened.

For a second he didn't move at all.

Then his face changed, his features bleeding rapidly into shock.

"Alyson... d'gaos!"

"Please! Don't be offended. You know why I'm saying it."

He continued to stare at me, his face frozen in an expression that didn't seem to know what I was saying at all.

I bit my lip. "Revik, please. This is exactly the opposite of what you said to me the last time we talked." Swallowing, I waved a hand towards the fire. "I'm not letting that whole... thing... force your hand. We should just go back to the original plan. Make sure this is right."

When I glanced back, he was staring at me, his eyes still buried in a kind of disbelief.

It had progressed from earlier though; I saw him thinking now, maybe trying to decide what to say. In any case, his silence, mixed with that lost, puzzled look on his face, made it hard to look at him for long.

"Maybe you were right before," I said. "Maybe we should talk tomorrow."

"Allie, you've completely—"

"Revik." I cut him off again, speaking before I'd thought. "I'm sorry. I really am. But I don't think we should do this tonight. Let's just... sleep on it."

Feeling another ripple of emotion off him, I searched my mind for some neutral way to end this. I only found one.

As casually as I could, I started to regain my feet.

Grasping my arms, he pulled me down again.

"Allie, no." He softened his voice, but I heard tension in it. His fingers were warm as they clasped mine. He touched my face, turning my chin so I would look at him.

"Please. Listen to me. *D'gaos*.... have I fucked things up with us that badly?" Feeling something off me, or maybe just feeling me pull away, he clutched me tighter. "Alyson! This isn't about Maygar!"

He was breathing harder.

His light seemed to spark at me, reminding me of all that time ago, when he was first teaching me sight, the few times I saw him upset or angry or afraid.

A little alarmed, I clasped his fingers in return.

"Revik... hey," I said. "Calm down, all right? It's okay. You didn't mess anything up with us. It's really nice what you're doing. I mean it."

"*Nice?*" he said. "Alyson! *Dugra ti le ente...*"

I felt something rise in his light. I flinched at its intensity.

He withdrew, all at once.

Shielding from me, he took a breath, forcing whatever it was back.

"Look," he said. "I am hearing you, Allie. I'm listening." He motioned towards the low couch. "...I'll sleep in here. I'll sleep outside if you want. But please, gods, listen to me. This has nothing at all to do with Maygar! Maybe I haven't been clear about—"

"You were clear," I said.

I flushed after I spoke, realizing I'd cut him off again.

I felt his light spark around me, disbelieving once more, and I fought to relax, extricating myself gently.

"Revik," I said. "I believe you. I do. But you're confusing me. And I still think it's a bad idea."

"Which part?" he said. "What's a bad idea? Us? The sex?"

I stared at him. "You honestly think we should have sex right now?"

I saw something flicker in his eyes, but he wiped it away, leaving me with the mask.

His voice came out neutral.

"I'll wait," he said. "...as long as you want for that. Please, Allie. Just tell me if that's what you meant."

Fighting to read past that mask, and to think, to wade through his words and my mind, I realized this was going to a bad place. I tried to think how to back us off of the pit we were circling. I stared at his hands, fighting separation pain, wishing I could just leave the house, wishing I'd slept with someone during that year he'd been gone, or done anything other than wait for him while he figured out how he felt about me.

But that was ridiculous. And borderline insane, really.

I shook my head, still staring at our hands.

"I'm sorry," I said. "Revik. I'm really sorry about this. Maybe I just need some time to think."

When I looked up, he was staring at me.

His face was utterly blank now, his light closed. It crossed my mind to wonder how much he'd heard of what had just gone through my head.

"I'm not talking about us," I said. "To be clear, I didn't mean us. I'm talking about sex. Tonight. It just feels wrong. I don't want to do it like this—"

"So we won't," he said quickly. "We won't, Allie."

I heard relief in his voice, and that brought the pain back, bad enough that I couldn't answer him at first. Lowering my head, I clenched my jaw, waiting for it to pass. As it began to subside, I felt him caressing my fingers with his.

"I'll sleep out here," he said, quieter.

He still sounded relieved.

I got a little too quickly to my feet.

He stood with me. I didn't want to risk walking, not with my light halfway outside my body, so I risked looking like an idiot instead, and stayed by the table until I calmed down. I didn't move when he stepped closer.

He touched my hand lightly with his fingers.

I was just standing there, not looking at him, when he lowered his face so that our cheeks touched. I felt his breath by my ear.

"Allie," he murmured. "Please. Please don't leave me because I'm clumsy with this. Please."

The pain in my chest worsened.

I looked up. His clear eyes held that intensity again, making them hard to look at. I felt myself softening at the expression there. I was still staring up when I felt myself reacting again: to his nearness, to his light, noticing the shape of his mouth.

He flinched.

I took a reflexive step back.

Disentangling my light, I didn't look back as I walked out of the room.

I DIDN'T THINK I'D SLEEP.

I lay on the bed wearing the kimono, thinking I'd lie there most of the night, staring at the same patch of ceiling. But something in the stress… or, more likely, the eight plus hours of hiking, most of it up steep, mountain tracks… knocked me out cold. I had a passing glimmer of guilt that he got stuck on the couch with his height, but it didn't even last long enough for me to get up and brush my teeth.

The next morning, I didn't know where I was.

I looked for Tarsi and Hannah, expecting to see them crouched by the fire.

Instead, sunlight peered through the cracks in the curtains of a real window, and the only thing across from the bed was a bureau with several wooden boxes on top. I lay on something indescribably soft, feeling the cleanest I'd felt in days.

I raised my arm and the sleeve of the kimono fell to my elbow.

Remembering the night before, I didn't move for what was probably fifteen minutes, riding out the morning dose of separation pain while trying to shield it from view in the construct around the small house. Eventually, though, I climbed out of bed, untying the front of the kimono and hanging it on a bedpost.

For a moment I looked at it, and felt like a jerk.

I'd been wearing makeup last night, too, after the shower.

Biting my lip, I went through drawers, found a pair of jeans and a long-sleeved shirt. Tying my hair back as best I could, I washed my face in the freezing cold sink water, getting off the remnants of the makeup and scrubbing my skin.

Cass, being Cass, had supplied me with enough cosmetics, skin creams, perfumes, and hair products for the entire cast of *Cats*.

I decided to skip that for today, with the exception of moisturizer and deodorant.

Pulling on socks, I took a deep breath and ventured into the other room.

He wasn't there.

Looking around, I wondered if he'd slept in the cabin at all; the couch didn't seem any different than it had the night before.

I was reassured slightly when I smelled coffee and located the pot steaming on the counter. It was still hot, and didn't smell old, so I poured myself some, after rummaging through the cabinets for a mug.

Still clutching the mug, I headed for the door to outside.

I figured he'd done his usual and wandered off.

Knowing him, I had a few hours at least, to sit outside on the bench, stare at the mountains and wake up. Shoving my feet into my unlaced boots by the door, I pushed it open with my hip and peered outside.

Once I could see through the morning light, I stopped dead.

Two horses stood in the mown space around the house, tied to the fence.

Revik stood beside the larger one, a pale-colored horse with a dark-red face. I watched him cinch some kind of makeshift saddle to its back with what looked like a macrame seat belt. The saddle itself, upon closer inspection, was a sheepskin blanket.

These weren't the small Tibetan horses, either, but the full-sized variety I remembered from home.

He glanced over when he saw me. He wore his careful face.

"Good morning," he said.

He motioned towards the horses, as if that explained everything.

I looked at the smaller, nearly all-white horse standing next to the one with the red face. Both wore rope bridles that had real-looking bits.

"Good morning." Feeling even stranger, I ventured closer, still clutching my mug. "Are they from that herd we saw yesterday? Down by the river?"

He nodded, still working the blanket on the roan, yanking it further up its back. I watched him arrange it over the high, bony withers.

I noticed the white one already wore a similar blanket and seat belt, and seemed to be staring at me, chewing in some irritation on the bit in its mouth. Its shaggy mane made it look like an annoyed teenager.

"They're okay to ride?" I asked.

He made the "more or less" gesture with his hand.

"They've been ridden before." He glanced at me. "It's been a while, especially for this one." He patted the roan. "But they seem good-natured."

The roan jerked its head up, flattening its ears when the white one sidled closer. When the smaller horse nipped its shoulder, the roan stamped its leg, snorting before thrusting its forefeet, stiff-legged, into the dirt and leaping a little into the air.

Revik sidestepped the dancing feet absently.

"Okay," I said. "You know I've been on a horse, like, twice. Right?"

He smiled, but I saw him studying my face.

I looked at the horses again. The white one was rubbing his head blissfully on the fence now, eyes half-closed.

Revik cleared his throat.

"You don't have to come, of course," he said. "But I think they'll be okay." He patted the roan on the rump, looking at me. "I thought we could explore. See the river. Map out the valley a little."

Meeting a direct gaze from him was harder than I thought it would be.

His face was still guarded, but on closer inspection he looked, well… tired.

Exhausted, really.

He seemed to hear my thoughts.

"I'm fine," he said, making a dismissive gesture. He smiled more genuinely. "It took me a few hours to catch them." He motioned towards the roan. "I haven't done anything like that in years. It was fun."

Not exactly reassured, I nodded.

He met my gaze, and I saw him again, at least in his eyes.

I knew on some level what he was doing.

I knew he was old-fashioned enough that this made sense to him, given what we'd talked about the night before, how we'd left things. Even as I wondered about his first wife, what he'd done while courting her, I was also touched, more than I really wanted him to see, at least right at that moment.

I looked at the white horse instead of him, trying to think.

He cleared his throat. When I glanced over, he was looking at me. That intensity was back in his eyes, but I saw a faint thread of nerves beneath.

"Are you coming, Allie?" he asked.

I only thought about it for another second.

"Sure," I said. "I'm in."

After the barest pause, he smiled.

CHAPTER 25
MARRIED

We didn't get back until nearly dusk that first day.

By the end of it, I could already tell I was going to be sore from riding, but I didn't care.

It had been one of those really great days that only come every so often, the best I'd had in as far back as I could remember.

Definitely the best since I'd left San Francisco.

I couldn't remember the last time I'd done something like that, just hung out in the sun under a blue sky with someone I wanted to be with. Exploring. Eating a picnic lunch. Wandering along a river. Lying on the grass. Swimming. Laughing over dumb jokes. Talking.

We circled the property from his memory of the boundaries, then rode along the river for a few miles until we reached an area with more trees and wider pools. Fording in a calmer spot, we took the horses up into the foothills before coming back to the shade by the water.

The next day, we followed the river upstream, walking the horses up the river itself, through a narrow canyon surrounded by sheer cliffs. Breathtakingly beautiful, the ride that day had mostly been to look at scenery, although we stopped then, too, once we found a spot that made a good picnic area.

The third day, we went straight for the mountains, taking the horses up a steep, winding trail until we found an even bigger waterfall than the one we'd passed on the way to the cabin. We hung out there most of the afternoon, alternately hiking, sitting around, talking, even playing around with some sight stuff.

Each day, he brought food. I didn't know if he was getting up early to cook or what, but the food supply seemed endless.

I went swimming each of the three days, despite the freezing cold water. I swam in the river itself, not far from where he lay on the grass, trying to nap while the horses grazed. I also swam in the pool formed by the waterfall higher up, where we stopped on the opposite side of the valley.

I didn't know if he was still on that kick, wanting us to get to know one another without sex, but I really saw the logic to it by the end of day two.

We'd rarely had time together when we weren't in some kind of crisis. People trying to kill us, time pressures of whatever kind, him stuck in the role of bodyguard or teacher, me depressed about my mom or the new life I blamed him for, at least in part. Then there'd been the rest of it—the separation sickness, fear, misunderstanding-one-another's-intentions, paranoia crap that seemed to dog us from the beginning.

I found him easy to be with when neither of us was trying to communicate anything dire. We were both a little overly cautious maybe, and we both probably looked at one another longer when the other one wasn't paying attention.

But other than that, yeah... it was easy.

I'd forgotten he had a good sense of humor.

The white horse had been his idea of a joke—the whole "white horse of the Apocalypse" thing and the Bridge. Apparently he'd been up half the night chasing horses because the white one had been so difficult to catch.

Still, he'd experimented with riding it for a few hours to make sure it was safe, so when he offered that one for me to ride, he'd been fairly confident, he said, that he wasn't actually putting me in danger.

After the first hour, I nicknamed the horse "Bait and Switch."

The white horse seemed like the easygoing one at first, maybe because he didn't fidget or startle as much as the roan, and didn't react at all when I first climbed up on him. Once we left the fenced area by the house, however, he had a tendency to take off at a gallop without warning, and stop on a dime... also without warning.

The third time he did it, I went flying over his head and landed in a heap on the grass.

Once he realized I wasn't hurt, I saw Revik fighting to suppress a smile as I cursed at the horse while it cantered around us in a circle, tossing its head and mouth with the metal bit.

Revik offered to ride the white one after that.

I tried again, weathering a few more of Bait's attempts to unseat me, but after he dumped me a second time, I gave in, giving Revik a turn.

After he'd gone flying over the white mane to meet a different piece of field, I watched him tumble into a seated position as Bait galloped off, kicking out his heels.

Riding up to him on the red-faced horse, I leaned over the pale neck to tell Revik, who was still sitting on the ground, that I'd renamed Bait yet again... and that he would henceforth be known as "Karma."

That actually made him laugh out loud.

Things stayed easy at the house.

By the third night, we got into a rhythm. We took turns showering, changed clothes, ate. Then I sat cross-legged in front of the fire while he leaned against the couch with a notebook and a pen. After a few hours of watching him sketch that first night, I finally asked him what he was doing.

He'd been vague about specifics. Something about mapping a Barrier structure he'd seen. He'd shown me how he did it, though, explaining his system of using different patterns in the lines to demonstrate where the structures stood in relation to one another dimensionally. Borrowing his sight, I could see how he was translating from the Barrier into a two-dimensional diagram. It was actually pretty neat. The structures even looked vaguely familiar, but I couldn't place where I'd seen them before.

Things only got weird when we went to bed, and then mostly because each night I'd try to get him to trade me for the couch. Each night, he refused.

I slept fine that second night. Even after the third, I woke up feeling good.

Well after midnight on the fourth, I was still awake.

The house was warmer, maybe because the weather kept getting warmer, or maybe because he'd turned on the steam heat to test it out the night before, while in one of his tinkering moods. In any case, I didn't need the blanket.

Wearing a long, silk, pajama shirt that might have been meant for him, I lay on top of the covers and stared up at the ceiling.

It was dark with the drapes closed, but a swath of moonlight made its way through a crack in the curtains. I distracted myself, finding faces and animals in whorls of plaster and wondering what the stars looked like.

An hour later, I realized I wasn't going to sleep.

I was in pain.

I'd known that, of course.

Suffering from separation pain was hardly noteworthy, after months of that… over a year if I counted the time on the ship and before that, in Seattle. It was such a constant in my life, it took me a while longer to realize it was the reason I was still awake.

I wondered if he was sleeping.

I let my mind toy with his offer that first night, and whether he'd meant it when he said it had nothing to do with Maygar.

I believed him. Or, I believed that he believed it, anyway.

Still, it made me wonder what he told himself about why he'd changed his mind.

I still struggled with the whole pain-light-marriage thing in general though. It was easy to convince myself that most of our "feelings" were somehow biologically wired, due to the way seers reacted to the light-bond. I'd been told by a few of them, everyone but Revik himself, really, that it didn't actually work that way.

In fact, they claimed it was the opposite.

Unlike humans, seers just happened to hardwire their feelings biologically.

Well. Sort of.

I knew I still didn't see it quite the way they did.

With Revik and I, it all happened so fast, it was easy to doubt the feelings that rose for me in the wake of the bonding itself.

I was told that happened sometimes, too. It didn't mean the pairing was a mistake, or "random," or related somehow to a form of seer sexual frustration… all of which I'd worried about with us, to lesser and greater degrees.

Neither Revik nor I had mentioned our talk that first night.

He hadn't kissed me since then, either, or touched me at all really, even to hold my hand. After replaying the conversation in my head, I realized he wouldn't come near me, not unless I gave him a reasonably clear signal.

I could just wait.

We'd both tacitly agreed to wait, and it had only been a few days.

Sooner or later, we'd have to talk about it.

There'd been a few tense moments that day. I'd jokingly shoved him on the picnic blanket during lunch, and it nearly turned into a wrestle when he grabbed my arms—right before he abruptly backed off.

He reacted when I took down my hair. I felt it before I saw it. I wasn't even sure I'd read him right until I glanced over and saw the look on his face.

He reacted to my announcement that I was going swimming, too.

He was possibly angry about my reaction to his offer. Or maybe he was embarrassed because I'd essentially turned him down. I didn't know if he got embarrassed about things like that, though. He seemed pretty open about sex in general, with everyone but me, anyway.

I got the impression he was still holding onto the Maygar thing.

He wasn't happy that I'd fought him. I definitely picked up on that at least once.

Hell, we probably needed to fight ourselves… which we'd still never done. Just spar it out until one or both of us cut the crap. Given his record in that area though, it might not be much of a match.

And that brought me back around to his original offer.

Was I being stupid?

I still didn't completely trust him.

There was that.

But he'd acknowledged that, too, in his way. And I was pretty sure the only thing to fix it would be time. Truthfully, at that point, I didn't really think he'd cheat on me. My mind didn't, anyway, when I reasoned it out. Now that he'd decided to be married, I believed him that the rules had changed for him.

He was a seer, after all.

But believing him and trusting him still weren't fully aligned in my head.

Gritting my teeth, I sat up. I slid off the edge of the bed before I really thought about what I was doing.

I'd leave myself an out.

I'd see if he was awake, ask if he wanted to go look at the stars.

Walking to the door to the other room, I stopped again, second-guessing everything for another few seconds. He'd never buy that. On the other hand, did it matter? I'd seen through his attempts at meeting me halfway.

Taking a breath, I pushed the door open as softly as I could.

I listened to the quiet, wondering at first if he'd left again.

Then I heard him breathing.

I couldn't tell if he was asleep, not at first. His breathing wasn't exactly regular, but it was heavier than usual, so he was most likely asleep and dreaming. Before I could talk myself out of it, I crossed the rug-covered floor on my bare feet.

I told myself I was just going to look. If he really was awake, maybe he would want to go outside with me.

Or fight me. Whichever.

But he wasn't awake. Sprawled on his back, he lay on the couch fully dressed, an arm hooked around the cushion behind his head. An old paperback book lay on the floor by the couch, as if it had fallen from his fingers when he dozed off. I glanced at the title, saw that it was some Russian writer, and fiction.

He read a lot, as a general rule, but I couldn't remember ever seeing him read fiction before, not even on the ship.

His face rested against the back cushion, leaving its outline in profile. His other hand lay on his stomach. He didn't look wholly relaxed, though; whatever he was dreaming about, it left a vague tension around his eyes.

The couch was wide. Even with him lying flat on his back, I could fit there, next to him.

Staring at that foot and a half of fabric, I hesitated. I wondered if he would mind waking up with me next to him.

More likely, I'd startle him and end up in a headlock, or on the floor.

After a brief tug of war in my head, I sat down... carefully.

He didn't wake.

His light shifted though, once I'd been sitting there for a few seconds.

It moved like a living thing, separate from the rest of him. I felt it change, right before it snaked around my outline, dancing in pale eddies as it explored. I fought not to react, but, looking at him, I felt the pain deepening, flickering at the edges of my awareness. I watched it rise, knowing it would only get worse the longer I sat there.

I should leave. Now. Before I did something stupid.

I watched his face tighten as he resettled on his back. Somehow, my mind returned to that first morning, in Seattle. Despite all the horrible things that happened with us afterwards, I'd woken up wrapped in his arms.

He'd wanted sex that morning, too.

I wondered how different things would be with us now, if I'd taken him up on that initial offer.

I continued to sit there as his light wound up liquidly through mine.

"Revik?" I whispered.

He didn't move. His breathing didn't change.

I stroked his forearm, tracing the line of muscle with my fingers. His arms were bigger than they had been in Seertown. Wherever he'd been these past few weeks, he'd gotten exercise. His face had filled out more, too, and his skin was tan from being outside. It had been even before our excursions of the past few days.

I watched his expression relax as I touched him.

I cleared my throat. "Revik?"

He'd been a light sleeper on the ship. Half the time when I woke up, he wasn't there. I caressed his fingers, pausing on the ring he wore, thinking about what it meant, his wearing it. I'd been afraid to ask, but I wondered if the finger he'd chosen meant anything, either.

I tried to make up my mind to leave.

I laid a hand on his chest. His light opened more, the longer I left my hand there, until his pain gradually bled into mine. I saw his face tighten as I slid my palm up to his shoulder. I massaged the muscle there slowly, watching him relax deeper into the couch. When he still didn't move, I found myself doing the same to his chest through his shirt.

I did that for probably far too long.

Finally, I made up my mind to leave.

When I took my hands off him, I felt his breathing accelerate.

He was awake.

I hesitated, looking at him, watching his face. My eyes had adjusted to the dark, so I could see him almost clearly. He hadn't opened his eyes, or done anything really, but he was awake. I could feel it. His light felt different, too.

I could just leave. He probably wouldn't say anything if I just got up and left. But I found myself sitting there anyway.

"Revik," I said, quiet.

I felt his reluctance. He didn't want to talk. He also didn't want me to leave. He wanted me to touch him. I felt him wanting it.

"Revik," I said, softer.

Slowly, he turned his head.

His eyes were glassed to the point of being opaque. Watching him look at me, I fumbled with words, trying to decide if there was anything I could say that would explain this, what I was doing. I was still looking at him when he lowered his hand, stroking my calf gently with his fingers, using his light to pull on mine.

It felt like a question.

I thought of all the b.s. I'd considered feeding him, about looking at stars and getting up because I'd been bored.

I found myself lost in his open expression instead.

We gazed at each other's faces in the bluish light from the window, and I couldn't help but think about his explanation for why he'd brought me here.

I felt his shock that I'd woken him, but he didn't let me close enough to see much past it. I could still feel him not wanting to talk, almost aggressively not wanting to talk to me. Despite his shields, I was lost inside his light, further in than I'd realized.

He wanted me to keep touching him.

He thought if we talked, he'd say something and I'd stop touching him.

I understood. I really did.

I also felt the part of me that still wanted to hesitate, that was still waiting for him to say something or do something, something that probably wouldn't even reassure me.

...until I let that go, too. Finally.

And then I was just looking at him, biting my lip against the pain in my chest. It bled slowly into a coiling nausea when I didn't move.

He caressed my hand, threading our fingers.

Pain flickered around the edges of his light, but he had it under control again. Briefly, I saw the predator thing rise to his eyes. I saw his throat move, just before his gaze shifted down. He focused on my mouth.

I felt the question on him again, but further away that time.

Taking another breath, I shifted closer to where he lay.

Without dropping my gaze, I slid a hand under his shirt, pushing the soft fabric up his body. His skin reacted to my fingers like they carried a faint electrical charge. I watched his eyes though, and they didn't move. His body didn't move either, while I caressed him. He seemed to hold his breath, leaning into me gradually as I explored his skin.

It occurred to me that I'd only really seen him without a shirt once, in Seattle.

I pushed the one he wore up further, so I could look at him. I saw the tattoo on his arm, a blue and black band of writing he'd told me on the ship he couldn't remember how he'd gotten. His chest was covered in fine, dark hairs and still muscular, though not as large as I remembered.

I massaged him slowly, exploring him with my hands.

I felt his breathing grow heavy when I didn't stop.

His fingers tightened on my arm, but otherwise he didn't move, not even to look at me. I tugged the shirt up past his shoulders.

After the barest pause, he sat up, helping me take it off his head and arms.

When I dropped it to the floor, his fingers found my hair. His body softened, right before he tried to pull my mouth to his.

I stopped him gently with my hand.

I felt pain on him, a caught breath.

"Allie," he murmured. His voice tugged at me gently.

He seemed to want to say more, but didn't.

Easing his hands out of the way, I slid into his lap.

He didn't move as I unhooked his belt, tugging the leather tongue out of a loop, then away from the silver prong. I felt disbelief on him as I pulled it out from around him—just before he caught hold of me. He clenched a hand in my hair.

I pulled back briefly, but just to drop his belt on the floor.

When I slid deeper into his lap, he let out a low groan.

The sound stopped me, cold.

I looked at him.

"You said it was an open offer, right?" I asked, quiet.

His eyes flickered up, off my body, where he stared at me in his lap like he couldn't believe it. He gazed back at me for a few seconds more, at a loss. His eyes studied mine in the half-dark, as if trying to read me without reaching out.

Then his fingers tightened in my hair, pulling my mouth roughly to his.

He kissed me, using his tongue, his skin flushing hot.

After a few seconds, he groaned against my mouth.

I found myself trying to calm him with my light, but he pushed my attempts away, nearly frantic. The urgency on him completely threw me. I tried again to compensate, to slow him down, but he pushed at my light, gasping against my mouth, his hand under my shirt.

When I opened, half in shock, he wound into me until I gasped, until both of us were half-blind with pain. He let out another groan as his body melted under mine, just before he arched against me.

Trying a different tack, I took his hand, bringing it to my breast, and his pain worsened. He slowed though, caressing me gently as I kissed his neck. He pushed up my shirt, using his tongue and his light until I couldn't think straight, until my fingers clenched in his hair.

He took one of my hands, bringing it down past where his belt had been. He kissed me harder, holding my palm and fingers against the part of him that was now straining his pants. When I massaged him there, he groaned again, louder, his pain rippling out at me until we were both sweating.

"Allie... gods..."

He fell silent. Again, I felt him wanting to say more. He fought to pull back, to control his light. I curled my arm around his neck, caressing his chest.

"Revik, it's all right," I murmured. "Baby, it's all right... let go..."

"Tell me. Please, Allie. Tell me what's all right..."

I slid deeper into his lap, kissing his face. "I want this," I said, soft. "I want you." I kissed him again. "Do you want me?"

His fingers tightened more. I felt a flicker of disbelief on him again.

He didn't move though, and he didn't look up.

Biting my lip, I eased off with my light, sliding backwards on his legs.

"Do you still want to wait?" I asked. "Revik, just tell me."

I didn't realize my eyes were glowing until he looked up.

I saw his face lit with a greenish cast, my eyes reflected in his.

I could feel more off him now, but in layers, sliding in and out of the edges of his light. Behind his eyes, mine reflected sunlight; my lips curved in a smile, clothing plastered to my body as I waded out of the river, laughing. I felt desire on him... dense... enough that my hands hurt, my mouth, even my tongue. It worsened when I saw him mastur-bating in the shower, eyes closed, fighting to keep his light from mine in the other room.

He leaned against the shower wall, fantasized about fucking me in the field by the river, in front of the fireplace, on the kitchen table, on the bed in the other room.

The image faded even as I realized he was trying to shield from me once more, and only half-succeeding. It wasn't shyness exactly. Whatever it was felt closer to fear, an uncertainty of how I saw him, of how I might react if he went too far.

I felt a consciousness on him of difference between us, in background, in age, in how I was raised, along with an awareness and memory of how most humans saw him. Hitting me in odd pieces, it brought the pain back, connecting his mind with the look on his face now.

We were kissing then.

He leaned back on the couch, pulling me against him, and I shifted deeper into his lap, moving so that I sat astride him. Everything hurt. His hands tightened on my hips, holding them flush with his as he bled his light deeper into mine. I felt intention behind it, a flicker of caution as he wound deeper into me, opening me further.

A blank stretch of time passed before I realized he was taking off my clothes.

He worked the catches of the silk shirt with clumsy fingers, still pulling on my light, still trying to bring more of it into his. I sat back on his legs as he eased the last of the shirt off my arms. Then he was looking at me.

He stared for a full minute before his eyes closed, longer than a blink.

"Allie," he said. "Allie... if you're not sure about this... tell me."

"If you want to stop," I said. "...just stop, Revik. Please."

He picked me up, bringing me with him to the floor.

I felt disbelief in his light again, folded into an urgency that worsened as he lay on me. I stopped him, long enough to help him the rest of the way out of his pants. Circling my waist gently with one arm, he lifted my hips, hooking my underwear with his fingers to ease them down my legs. He paused again once he got them off… long enough to take in my naked body in the light from the window.

His pain turned liquid, sliding deeper as I caressed his chest.

"Please," he murmured. He was sweating. "Allie. Please… do you really want this? I may not be able to stop."

His pain flared, sparking in my light as his slid deeper, trying to open mine more. The reality of what we were doing hit me, snapping me back to where I was, who I was with.

He pulled on me harder with his light, trying to loosen my hold on mine.

Guilt lived there, mixed with a desire that shifted into a near desperation. He wanted me to lose control, I realized; he was trying to work his way under my defenses, one by one, in any way he could… trying to seduce me even as I was lying naked under him. Some part of him was hedging his bets, tying me to him, fighting to get me to submit.

I caressed his face, kissing his jawline. "I'm not going to tell you to stop," I murmured. "I'm not, Revik… I promise you."

I opened so that he felt more of my pain, enough that his jaw hardened. A thick flush of heat pulsed off him as he looked at me again.

He sank his body into mine as he kissed my mouth.

For what felt like a long time, that was all we did.

I forgot where I was until it started to hurt again, starting with his hands on my upper arms, moving through my stomach, my chest, the light in my throat. His pain worsened, winding up into me until I was nearly frantic. I felt him losing control over his light, thinking about what he wanted, how much he could ask me for… how gradually he should work his way into asking for more.

I was asking him then. I couldn't tell if it was aloud or inside my head, but I asked him again. He made some kind of sound…

…right before his voice rose.

"Allie… wait," he murmured. "Wait."

I looked up. We were both naked. All I could feel was his skin, a wool rug at my back. He was hard. I could feel him fighting not to press it against me, even as his legs held mine apart. His arm was wrapped around me, keeping me motionless as he started to pull back, to extricate his light from mine without really letting any of it go.

My pain turned to desperation, grief. I felt myself recoil as what he was doing sank in. His hands only tightened more, holding me under him.

He pulled on me again, hard enough that I gasped, clutching his arms.

"Allie." I felt reluctance on him, another flush of pain. "Was Tarsi right?"

I stared up at him, still trying to piece my mind back together, to deal with the reality of what we were doing.

"About what?" I asked.

He caressed my face. "Please, honey... tell me." His jaw hardened. "Have you been with a seer before? I won't be mad." His pain worsened. "I need to know. I need to know the truth, Allie. Please tell me the truth."

Confused, I watched him look at me. Why wouldn't I tell him the truth?

"No," I said. "I haven't."

His face tightened. It took me another second to realize my answer turned him on, enough that he was fighting to hide it from me. He shook his head.

"We shouldn't," he said, his accent thick. "I should show you first... show you... it could hurt a lot, I don't know..."

Reaching down, I curled my fingers around him. He fell silent.

He was right; he didn't feel quite like a human.

Before I could say anything, his pain blinded me.

He let out a kind of startled cry as he leaned into my hand. His back arched as I continued to stroke him, exploring until he was fighting to breathe, his fingers clenched in my hair. His other hand caressed my fingers where I touched him.

I didn't feel anything on him that would hurt me, not physically anyway. I wanted to tell him that, too... but I felt the silence in him again, the unwillingness to talk, to do anything that might make me stop.

When I tried to read him, he groaned against my neck.

"Alyson... gods. Please." Pain spiraled off him. I felt his restraint slip as his muscles clenched. "Let me. Let me… please. Please… gods. I'll be careful."

My hand clenched in his hair. He groaned again when I caressed the end of him. I was still trying to understand, to know what he was afraid of doing to me.

"I could do it like you were human," he said.

I looked up at him. "Like I was human? What does that mean?"

"I don't want to hurt you." His pain hit at me again. "I can do it so it won't hurt. Baby, gods, stop… stop…"

I let go of him. I waited until his breathing gradually slowed.

"Do it like I'm a seer," I said.

The pain coming off him worsened. "Are you sure?"

"It has to hurt eventually, right?"

After a pause, he nodded. "Yes." His fingers tightened on me, his weight growing heavy again. "Allie… do you love me?"

I closed my eyes, caught off guard by the vulnerability behind the question. His other hand was on my hip, but he didn't take his eyes off my face.

"Tell me," he murmured. "Tell me. Please, Allie… tell me. I adore you…"

I felt him against me. I realized what he was doing.

"Yes." My voice softened. "Yes, Revik… I love you."

He let out a low groan.

…then he was inside me.

Everything stopped.

It wasn't pain. Disbelief hit both of us; I saw his face change, just before he clenched his jaw.

He felt different. Not a lot different, but enough. The angle was different. Having him inside me did something to my light, almost that folding sensation. After days of feeling that with Syrimne, I was terrified I'd trigger the telekinetic thing… hurt him on accident. I fought to hold it back, to control it in some way, but his light only pulled on mine harder.

Then he arched into me for real.

I cried out. I struggled to hold back my light, but only managed halfway.

He angled into me again, slower, and I whimpered, hearing him groan as he went deeper. When he did it a third time, I found myself saying his name, my fingers clutching his back. It felt good, so damned good, good enough to forget about—

He stopped dead, gasping.

"Allie... gods..." He was sweating. "What are you doing to me..." For a split second, he seemed to be fighting something again. His fingers clenched in my hair. "Relax," he said, kissing me. He groaned softly. "Relax, love... please. I'm going to try. I'll hurt you if I don't try now. I'm barely holding it as it is..."

"Try?" I fought to breathe. "Try what?"

"Look at me. Please... Allie. Please... look at me..."

I did.

He arched deeper, until the end of his cock seemed to fit into a part of me, almost like a puzzle piece. I let out a low gasp of surprise, staring at his eyes, then gripped his back tighter, more turned on than I knew what to do with.

I let out a whimper when he didn't move.

"Are you ready?" he asked, soft.

I fought pain, an almost uncontrollable urge to pull on him with my light, to make him do something, anything but press against me there.

"Please," I managed. "Please. Whatever you're going to do... do it, please..."

After the slightest pause, his shoulders visibly unclenched.

...and pure, physical pain stopped my heart.

It threw me out of my mind, out of any rational part of myself.

Some part of him glided up into me like a thin blade, through an opening I hadn't known existed. Nothing could have prepared me for it. Nothing.

He let out a heavy cry, clasping my back.

I felt so much pleasure on him it nearly blacked me out—even as pain forced a low moan from my lips. Whatever it was slid deeper, until I could only lie there, panting, fighting panic as he held me, trying to calm me with his light.

I felt disbelief on him again, a near-animal feeling as he held himself back... but I felt love there, too, a tenderness that made my heart hurt... relief, fear, and that hot, liquid pleasure that was more like a drug than any drug I'd ever taken.

He shared it with me, even as he fought to control it, sending a dense warmth through my light, stroking my hair and face until slowly... slowly... my muscles started to unlock.

His desire nearly blinded me then. His hands started to hurt.

"Allie," he groaned. "Allie... gods, you have no idea how good this feels." Desire spiraled off him, enough to blank out my mind. He let out another low groan. "Are you all right? Baby... tell me. Tell me now, before I—"

"No." I gripped his arms. Thinking, I fought to breathe. "Yes. Yes, I'm all right. Revik, I'm okay—"

"Do you want me to stop?"

"No." I shook my head. "Don't stop." I kissed him. "Don't stop."

He went deeper. The folding sensation came back.

I yelled for real, unable to hold it back, and then he was all the way inside, and I wasn't even trying. It felt better than anything I'd ever felt, better than I could stand. I wrapped my legs around him and heard him cry out, gasping, saying my name.

I opened my light...

...and he came, all at once.

It shocked me.

Hot and liquid, almost painful, it seemed to go on for a long time.

His hands gripped my hips, holding me against him, his light completely entwined in mine. He let out a low cry as it peaked, pinning me to the floor, his whole weight on me as he fought to go deeper. His light flooded mine with that mind-numbing pleasure, and relief... more relief than I could process.

I watched his face as the wave crested.

Then, as it slowly began to roll back.

After a few more beats, that other part of him retracted. It left in a single, smooth pull—and I gasped.

Then we were just lying there, panting.

I couldn't believe it. I couldn't believe what we'd just done.

It took him longer to pull back, to slow his heart rate.

He lay his face against mine, and he was sweating, fighting to calm down. Gradually, I felt him pull his light back into himself. He tried to withdraw his *aleimi* from mine... then stopped, relaxing into me again when the pain worsened. He closed his eyes.

Embarrassment shimmered off him.

It grew into something closer to guilt as he retraced our steps.

He wasn't shielding from me at all.

That vulnerability grew more pronounced as his fingers caressed my face, but relief still spiraled off him in waves, and he didn't seem to be trying to hide that, either. That non-human thing rose to the forefront of his light.

Before I could get a bead on the difference, he kissed me. Merging his light into mine, he deepened the kiss, caressing my face.

"Gods, Allie," he murmured.

"Revik, wait—"

"Allie, I'm sorry."

I shook my head. My mind seemed to be coming back, slowly, like crawling through mud. "No... can we just..." He kissed me again, pulling on me achingly with his light. "Please. Wait... what was that? What happened?"

"Seers are built different."

"Yeah." I gave a gasping kind of laugh. "Yeah, okay. I got that part."

Raising his head, he closed his eyes, longer than a blink.

His light slid further into mine, growing more cautious as he felt me react, until I clutched at him.

His voice lowered, pulling on me along with his light.

"I thought about what I would say," he murmured. "The whole way here. I was going to show you, ask you to shower with me, but we got here and..."

He gave a short laugh, kissing me again. "Then all I could feel was you wanting to leave, wishing you'd slept with other people. Telling me I was being 'nice'." He leaned his forehead against mine. "*D'gaos*. Alyson. I just came in you like an adolescent."

Pain wafted off him as I stroked his sides, feeling his ribs.

I was still wound up, still halfway inside him with my light, but I felt shy touching him. He leaned his body into my hands, which helped. So did the fact that he was still inside me. A part of me couldn't get past that much reality.

When I kept exploring him with my hands, his fingers slid into mine.

He separated us seconds later, and I had to fight to keep from protesting, biting my lip as he shifted to his side.

"Give me a minute, honey. One minute," he murmured. Kissing me, he rubbed his face, blinking to clear his vision. "I want to do this better for you," he said, gesturing vaguely. He sounded calmer though. "Can we forget that one?"

"No," I said.

Looking at his body distracted me.

Fascination with his physicality mixed with a growing unease as I realized the condition it was in. Cuts and bruises that hadn't fully healed stood out to my eyes and fingers on his chest and sides. I knew some were from Terian, but older ones stood out alongside injuries that looked more recent. A thumb-thick line circled his throat above a stretched, white scar that wound up from under his arm, ending in a pale question mark on his neck.

I traced his ribs, noticing dark areas that must be newer bruises.

Pain hit me, a different pain.

"Revik, where were you the last few weeks?"

"With Balidor." He met my gaze. "In Sikkim."

I felt myself pale. So he knew about the kids. But that's not what bothered me. "Revik," I said. "Please. You said you'd let the other infiltrators handle him."

"Terian didn't do that, Allie."

"I don't care! You're getting too close."

"I was careful."

"Not careful enough!" I laid a hand on one of the bruises. "Jesus." Pain hit me again, worse. "Who kicked you in the face?"

Sliding closer, he rested his belly against mine, studying my eyes.

His light spread through me. Warm. Softening my fear.

"You're different," he said, soft. "Not only because a virgin."

I knew he was distracting me. I also knew he was right, that this was the absolute worst time ever for us to talk about Terian or dead children.

Also, his distraction was working.

I forced a smile. "Virgin? You race-centric seers. It's all about you."

He smiled back. Pushing me gently so I would roll to my back, he rested his weight on me more fully, propping his jaw on a hand. With his other hand, he ran a finger over my jaw, then my cheek.

"Alyson," he murmured. "You seduced me."

I felt my face warm.

His fingers brushed back my hair.

He kissed me again, slower that time. When we paused, he rearranged his weight, pinning me under his arms and legs. I felt the deliberateness behind the pose as he looked at me again, as if asking me if it were all right.

When I didn't push back, he smiled. His voice remained soft.

"You almost gave me a heart attack." He caressed my arm with his fingertips, making me shiver. "I couldn't believe it when I woke up." Pain touched his voice, and he fell silent, looking at me. I felt him getting hard. "Gods, Allie. I hope you're not tired. I'm really, really turned on right now."

Flushing more, I caressed his chest to avoid his eyes, running my fingers over muscles and skin, the fine coating of dark hairs. I shook my head.

"Not overly tired," I said.

He was still watching my face.

His voice lowered, getting deeper again.

"We'll need to stay here now," he said. "You know that, right?"

I looked at him. "How long?"

"I don't know." Caressing my fingers, he looked away, glancing towards the window. "But I'm feeling possessive, Allie. Very possessive." His hand slid back into my hair, clenching there briefly as he kissed my face. "I want to give you a lot more reasons to want to be faithful to me. A lot more."

I smiled. "Really? What kinds of reasons?"

"I don't know yet," he said.

I felt another flush of that wanting, a sharp intensity in his light. He kissed me again, murmuring, "But I'm going to want to fuck a lot. A *lot*, Allie. I'll probably drive you crazy, not let you sleep."

I laughed. I couldn't help it. "Who are you? This is like a different Revik. Are you drugged from having an orgasm?"

He smiled, but it didn't touch his eyes.

"You don't like it? I'm talking too much? Presuming too much?"

I touched his face. "I do like it." Thinking, I added, "...A lot, actually. But I don't want you to feel like you need to."

"You think I'm insincere?"

I laughed again. "No."

He pressed into me. When he lifted his head, his eyes grew more serious. "Allie, I never…" He hesitated. "I don't remember ever being with a virgin before."

I glanced up, hiding my embarrassment with an effort. I smiled.

"Never? Aren't you like a hundred?"

He raised an eyebrow, then smiled back. "Yes. But then, I don't remember being with any seer who wasn't a pro until I was at least forty."

I nodded, not looking up as I continued to touch him. I wasn't sure how much I wanted to know about that, at least right then. Or really… ever. He'd had a lot more years to collect notches on his bedpost than I had, and he hadn't exactly wasted them.

Beyond that, pros would know what they were doing.

I, on the other hand, hadn't known the basic facts of my own anatomy.

I could tell it had shocked him.

Whatever I'd said, whatever Tarsi told him, the reality that I'd never slept with another seer shocked the hell out of him while we were in the middle of it. I thought about what he'd said about never being with a virgin, about me seducing him, his worries about scaring me when we first started… and my face warmed again.

No, I definitely didn't want to hear about his past.

"You said I was different," I said, to change the subject. "Do you mean actually, physically…" I hesitated. *Different*-different? Like down there?"

Amusement touched his eyes, but I saw something else there, too.

"Humans didn't notice?"

"Well, yeah. I didn't think I'd be a weirdo in the seer world, too."

He slid a hand around my face, but I saw his mouth harden.

Looking at him, I found myself wondering just how much he'd seen while following me all of those years. His eyes tightened perceptibly, and I decided talking about past lovers wasn't a good idea for either of us right then.

I felt another shiver of pain off him as he watched me look at him.

"And?" I said, smiling. "Okay different? So-so?"

The tension on his face broke. He laughed.

"More like, 'I'd better get used to this before my wife leaves me,' different." He smiled, but I felt his embarrassment again. "It's not only the physical, Allie. Your light does something."

He sent the rest carefully, trying to show me.

It was that folding sensation I'd been fighting. A liquid heat drove down from a structure in my *aleimi*, starting in my abdomen before it ran into his—until a part of us entwined, like two sinuous tails.

I felt his breath catch, his weight grow heavy again.

"Stop," he gasped. "I know I started it, but stop... Allie. Please."

I fought with my light, shutting it down with an effort.

After a few seconds, his hands relaxed.

I swallowed as he caressed my cheek with his.

"Gods," he murmured. "You're going to have to go easy on me, wife."

I felt my face warm again.

"Revik, are you..." I couldn't find the right words. "...all right? Now, I mean. Do you feel all right?"

"No." He kissed my face. "Better, I'm embarrassed to admit, but no." He hesitated, looking at me. "What about you? I know it wasn't much..."

I tried to think past whatever was going on with me.

I clutched his back, too hard I realized, but I couldn't seem to make myself let go. I felt scars there, too, marring his skin, more than what I saw in front. Remembering how he'd looked in London, after Terian, I clutched him tighter, fighting emotion that wanted to rise with it, an irrational grief mixed with fear.

I couldn't have explained any of that to him, so I didn't try.

"I feel different," I said. "Already, I mean. Do you?"

His eyes didn't waver. "Yes."

"Do we need to talk? About that?"

He kissed my cheek. "Yes. Do you want to now?"

I hesitated, thinking about whether I did.

"We're really married now, aren't we?" I said finally.

His fingers tightened, right before his pain grew sharp.

"Yes." He pressed against me. His voice grew soft. "But I thought of myself as married before, Allie. I have since the ship."

Remembering what else he'd done on the ship, I fought another irrational flare of emotion. I was still struggling to control myself when he wrapped his arms around me. He kissed the nape of my neck, just before he melted into me, sending me... god, it felt like love. It came wrapped in a dense wanting, a near-surrender I couldn't think past.

It touched me deeper than anything I'd ever felt on him.

Deep enough that briefly, it washed out all the rest.

Slowly, as I calmed, that quieter version of him seeped back over his light, the one I'd always known, the one who felt like an infiltrator.

I felt that part of him focus on me. I felt something different in that, something almost predatory.

Whatever it was, it turned me on to a disturbing degree.

He lowered his mouth, kissing me. He took his time, exploring me with his tongue. A flicker of that animal feeling sharpened as his lips and tongue lingered, grew less tentative.

He sent me questions, cautiously at first.

He got more explicit as he felt me react.

Before long, pain made it difficult to think, to remember where we were. My eyes started to glow, a pale, iridescent green. They reflected in his, and I felt that do something to him, too.

But he still hadn't touched me.

He'd barely touched me at all.

He raised up his weight, angling his body to lie next to me, and I felt a dense flicker of frustration.

His hand wrapped around my cunt.

I gripped his arm... right as his fingers slid inside me.

I groaned, caught off guard, and I felt him reading me, stroking as he went deeper, his mind restrained. I felt his intent, that harder, denser want, right before he bit my neck, shocking me again. He didn't do it gently. I fought for breath, fought for control, clutching at him as his thumb pressed down, as he massaged my clit. His light wrapped into mine, and the playfulness was gone, replaced by a question that wasn't really a question.

Possessiveness lived there. Pain.

God. A desire to fuck until it hurt.

I felt the intensity behind that want.

I felt the demand there, and I couldn't breathe.

Instead of pulling away, I opened to it, in so much pain I'm pretty sure my mind stopped working altogether.

After that, things got pretty blurry for a while.

CHAPTER 26
DEAD

Cass studied the broad, Asian-featured face, and wondered what it would be like to kill someone.

Not at a distance, like most deaths seemed to happen these days, but to really do it, the way Revik had done when he killed Terian in that cave in the Caucasus.

Sticking a knife into someone, having them die right in front of you, the blood flowing on your hands… it had to feel different than firing at gun from behind cover at people you could barely see.

It had to feel different.

The man's muscular chest moved with slow, even breaths on the thick pallet. His skin shone an eerie pale under the deep tan. His lips were cracked from dehydration, yet the bruises had faded from his high cheekbones in the intervening weeks. The cut on his scalp had healed, along with the marks that once decorated his muscular arms. Now they lay soft and brown on wool blankets on either side of his thick torso.

He wasn't dead. Or even dying.

The seer medical-types said he'd gone into a kind of coma, something seers did to heal themselves when seriously injured.

The bunker-like room, lit with candles, held wisps of mist from the open windows to the forest outside. Cass looked out the nearest of those, watching two monkeys climb into the higher foliage of a fern-like tree, chattering. One had a baby clinging to its back. It swung a little from its mother's tawny fur as she climbed nimbly up a thick branch.

Cass looked back at the man lying on the pallet.

She laid a hand on his chest, feeling him breathe.

After another pause, she sat back in her seat, scrutinizing his still form.

Reaching into her bag, she pulled out a book with a black leather cover. Flipping it open to a series of pages filled with painstakingly drawn hieroglyphs, she traced some of the more delicate ones with her fingertips before letting her eyes drop to the text itself. She read the first sentence, written in what looked almost like calligraphy-styled English.

"Feigran is alone now."

She paused, glancing back at the trees.

"I wonder if it will bother him," she read. *"Terian assures me there is nothing to worry about, that he prefers to live in this way. Yet I am not certain if his word can be trusted in a matter such as this, and not only due to his apparent callousness towards any but the most dominant and aggressive segments of his own personality."*

Cass turned the page.

"What remains of him down here seems to lack empathy almost entirely. So much so, I cannot help but fear the eventual consequences of this experiment. I also wonder how much of his true utility is being sacrificed, when his mind is of such limited composition."

Cass told herself, every day, she would give the book back.

The minute she heard Allie and Revik were on their way to the compound, she would return it to the exact spot she'd found it in Allie's room.

Flipping to a new page, she read on.

"Terian seems so patently determined to cut off all feeling in the parts of him that remain. I do not think this is self-punishment. In many ways, Terian is more of a child than Feigran himself. Like a child, he confuses lack of feeling with strength, and does not see how it limits him. It makes me wonder again if he is stable enough to act in the capacity Xarethe wants of him, even if we watch over him to the degree she suggests."

Cass's fingers traced the new name.

"Xarethe," she murmured.

Her eyes moved to the next paragraph.

"Yet, it must be Terian. There is no one else. I will not risk such a procedure on Dehgoies. Honestly, I am relieved to have Dehgoies watching over him for the length of this experiment. He seems to have strong protective instincts. I will remember that, and see if I can encourage this trait in him. He is not blind to the emotional limitations of his new friend. However, instead of fear, it seems to evoke compassion in him. He has already taken it upon himself to keep young Terian safe, if only from himself."

Cass felt her jaw harden.

She flipped to the next page, glossing over the line of symbols to the right of the words written in English.

"Xarethe thinks the process will help him. That it will provide a healthy means of taming him, and the war that rages forever in his mind. I hope she is right. If not, I may be guilty of creating a monster..."

Cass bit her tongue, then read the last line.

"...a monster the likes of which no one has seen, not even in Syrimne."

Rubbing her eyes, she laid the book on the edge of the bed.

She hadn't slept well in days.

The truth was, she hadn't slept well since Allie and Revik left the compound.

She didn't like to think about it, but she could hardly deny how much more uneasy and anxious she'd been, with both of them gone. It started when Revik left for Sikkim. It worsened when he left to find Allie.

Cass tended to lean on one or both of them pretty much all the time now. She knew it was probably unhealthy but couldn't bring herself to care.

But then, she'd always depended on Allie more than Allie seemed to realize. Since her time with Terian in that cage, some of that dependency had been transferred to Allie's husband, and to a lesser extent, to Allie's adoptive brother, Jon.

Lowering her head to her arm, Cass closed her eyes.

She had to find her way out of this.

She had to, before she drowned.

SHE IS BACK THERE. SHE IS BACK.

Green glass surrounds her, running with water and blood.

Tools hang from hooks in the ceiling. They spark the wet floor, dripping blood from glass-like blades and metal wands.

A man is chained to the middle of the room.

His dark head is slumped, his back covered in scars. He doesn't move, but sleeps there, his face taut as he murmurs words into the damp floor.

"I'lenntare c'gaos untlelleres ungual ilarte... Y'lethe u agnate sol..."

In his own way, he is alone here.

Untouchable.

Behind him, two cages stand, large enough to house a set of big dogs.

Jon lays in one, his hand bleeding where his fingers have been removed. His body is marked with razors and knives, bruised by fists and boots. He is so thin she barely recognizes him from the man she knew in San Francisco, who taught Kung Fu and ran a tech start-up and drank lots of green smoothies.

She sees herself. A naked woman with a mutilated face, she lays broken, black hair smelling of blood and piss. Her body is like Jon's. Burns cover her pale skin, marks where his hands have been, where he cuts her.

He's been inside her.

More than a few times. Over and over.

He enjoys it. She feels it, the whispers and flushes of pleasure as he gets off. He even calls her name once, his cries thick with juvenile release.

He'd been affectionate after.

Seers are made different, she discovers.

He uses that, tries to make her like it. He tries it on different parts of her, using his mind to confuse her, to manipulate her until she asks for it.

In the end, she can't tell the difference.

The jungle grows back, around the cages, around the man covered in scars.

He will return one day. She feels it.

From inside the jungle, two bright turquoise eyes stare at her, framed by black hair.

She struggles, fighting to move, to scream—

SOMEONE GRABBED HER SHOULDER FROM BEHIND, SHAKING HER ROUGHLY.

Cass jerked violently, turning, gun in her hand.

Panting, heart thudding in her chest, she raised her head from the foam mattress. She aimed the Glock—the same Glock Revik gave her and taught her to use almost seven months ago, while they were still in Russia—directly at Chandre's face.

Chandre didn't move.

She didn't change expression.

Her reddish-black eyes narrowed though, as if measuring Cass's expression, the breadth of her intent. A seer's eyes, they showed very little white. Red-tinged irises filled most of the visible orbs, making her always seem to be staring. Long, black braids hung around a sharp, feline face. Sculpted lips added a sensual femininity to her otherwise hard features.

She reached out, placing her hand on Cass's gun.

Without looking away from her face, she lowered the gun slowly, until it pointed at the floor.

Cass exhaled.

As she did, a soft, reassuring wave washed over her like a breath. Shaking off Chandre's hand, she flipped the safety on, laying the gun on the bed.

The calming influence immediately retracted.

Cass had warned her not to use her seer crap to push her around unduly, or their relationship would come to an abrupt end. Chandre seemed to have taken that warning to heart, at least as far as Cass could tell.

Which, admittedly, wasn't far.

"What are you doing?" Chandre asked. The seer's red eyes slid slightly out of focus, which meant she was probably reading Cass's mind.

It occurred to Cass only then, that she'd been asleep.

She looked down at the cot, at the depression where her head had been, nestled against the side of the man who'd tried to rape her best friend. A man she'd shared a train berth with, who'd joked with her as he taught her sharpshooting and how to swear in Mandarin, who'd flirted with her when Jon wasn't there, hovering over her protectively when they broke into buildings to retrieve records left behind by the Rooks.

Who'd been her friend.

Tucking the gun and the leather-bound book into her shoulder bag, Cass glanced out the window, making her mind carefully blank.

The forest stared back at her, empty and quiet, even of monkeys.

"What are you doing here?" the seer asked.

Her eyes looked worried, hidden behind a flush of anger.

"Why, Cass? Why would you come here? With a gun? What are you doing?"

Cass combed her long hair out of her eyes. "I wanted to see how he was."

Chandre's gaze narrowed. "With a gun?"

"The gun was incidental. I always carry it. You know that."

"What were you doing? Just now?"

Cass made a dismissive gesture in seer sign-language.

"Sleeping," she said. "And why are *you* here? Aren't you supposed to be guarding Allie?"

"They relieved me." Leaning over the bed, Chandre shut the open window. "It is a tomb in here. Are you trying to freeze him to death, human? Or just yourself?"

Chandre stepped back from the bed, hands on her hips.

Her eyes grew hard, hunter-like. "Just now, what did you do? It is illegal to touch him. You should not be touching him."

Cass snorted. "Illegal? Give me a break. I wasn't going to hurt him. I'd hardly be asleep in here if my master plan was assassination. Would I?"

Chandre sat on the second chair beside the pallet.

For a moment, she looked only at the man on the bed.

Then her eyes flickered sideways, meeting Cass's.

"I understand, cousin," she said. "But you must let it go."

Cass contemplated playing dumb for about a half-second before she shrugged, letting her tone go flat.

"Yeah," she said. "I've been hearing that a lot lately. From Allie. From Jon. Probably would be from Revik, too, if I'd seen him for more than five minutes since he got back. Maybe I should take up heavy drugs. That might help."

"Let it go," Chandre advised. She gestured at the man on the pallet, her voice and hands dismissive. "Whatever happens to him… it is nothing. Save your emotion for your friend."

"What *will* happen to him?" Cass asked.

The dark-skinned seer shrugged. "Dehgoies will be even less rational once they are bonded. It should make things quick for this one, at least."

"What about his family?" She looked at Maygar's sleeping face. "Friends?"

"His mother is a Rook." Chandre gestured dismissively, as if that, alone, explained everything. "He has friends, but they will not intervene. Maygar attempted a claim on the Bridge. Even if they did not fear her mate, they would not defend him for that."

She looked down at the slow-breathing seer.

For a split second, Cass saw compassion in the dark red eyes.

"Forget him, human," she said. "He is already dead."

Looking at the corpse-like seer surrounded by candles, Cass nodded.

But he wasn't dead, not really.

CHAPTER 27
TATTOO

Cass stood inside a different building now.

Sunlight wafted through gaps in water-damaged wood, making patterns across a dirt floor strewn with sawdust and straw. Swallows and smaller birds flitted in and out of the wide door, leaving and returning to nests high in the rafters above.

Cass knew the seer was reading her.

Chandre stared at the bare skin showing on Cass's arms, her own, more muscular hands resting on her hips. Cass knew where the seer's mind had likely gone—to Allie, and what Allie would say if Chandre let this happen.

A lot of seers had been sensitive lately, after the thing with Maygar.

"Are you sure?" Chandre asked again. "It will hurt you. More than me." She gestured around at the other seers in the barn, who watched the proceedings with no small amount of curiosity. "...More than any of them. And it is a seer's mark."

Cass focused on a butterfly fluttering through a shaft of sunlight.

She watched it dip and circle lazily, as if confused by the dust-filled beams.

Chandre frowned, tapping Cass's shoulder with one dark finger.

"It will hurt," she repeated. "It will hurt a *lot*. The ink they use... it is not human ink. It is treated, Cassie. It burns. It burns the body, so it will last through our longer lives."

Seeing that Cass was already impatient, Chandre raised her voice.

"They use more of it on this mark, as it is religious to us. It will scar."

Cass smiled wryly, turning on her with a raised eyebrow. "I have a few scars already, Chan. At least this one, I'm putting there myself."

Chandre's frown deepened.

"It is a seer's mark," she repeated. "You are a fool to wear it."

Cass folded her arms under her breasts, pushing them up slightly. "I'm not asking to be a member of the club. I'm just asking to wear one of your T-shirts. Figuratively speaking."

"But why?" Chandre asked. "It puts you in danger. Unnecessarily!"

"Well, that's the point, right? I'm not going to hide behind my human status."

Chandre waved off the males by the wall as some nodded, murmuring in approval to Cass's words.

"...It is stupid," Chan said, turning on her. "Worse than that, it is worm logic. Not the logic of *my* people." She glared around at the other seers, daring them to disagree. "A people who *have* to hide. Who make a lifetime of not being seen."

"Well," Cass said, throwing her hands up. "I'm not one of 'your' people. As you feel the need to remind me constantly."

Frowning harder, Chandre stared at her.

Her dark-red eyes slid perceptibly out of focus, which told Cass she was probably reading her again. Biting her lip, she waited for the seer to finish, reminding herself that this was the other's way of showing concern.

Clicking out, Chandre folded her arms, clearing her throat.

"Your friend," she said stiffly. "Alyson. She is my friend, too."

Cass snorted. "Pathetic, Chan. I mean, really."

"You would have her hate me? She is the Bridge!"

"Great. And your precious Bridge believes in *free will*, in case you hadn't noticed. She's never tried to talk me out of *anything* I wanted to do. Well," she said, folding her arms tighter. "Except Jack. And she was right about that."

Laughter rose in pockets around the room.

Chandre paused to glare the others into silence.

Cass remembered they were speaking Prexci and felt a little swell of pride that hers was good enough to carry on a conversation... much less an argument... in front of a bunch of infiltrators.

Staring her down a last time, Chandre shrugged, motioning for the male seer standing behind her to proceed. Cass caught the subtle gesture she made to him though, telling him to move slowly. It occurred to Cass that Chandre thought she'd ask him to stop before the mark was finished, if it hurt enough.

Biting her lip, Cass plunked down defiantly in the chair next to the tattoo artist's stool.

"Don't expect me to be sympathetic later," Chandre warned.

Cass was surprised to hear real emotion in the seer's voice.

"You want to kill yourself? Go ahead, worm. Fine with me. Enough worms in this world already." Chandre folded her arms. "Don't need another one... a dumb one, too."

Cass rolled her eyes, but couldn't help smiling, just a little.

The male with the organic tattooing needle looked dubious as well, but he stepped forward when Chandre motioned him sharply the second time.

He wore a leather apron over a threadbare black T-shirt, his dark blue eyes rimmed with a line of pale pink. Grunting a little, he sat on a low stool by the beat-up recliner the other seers had lined up behind, waiting their turn to be inked.

Cass tried not to look at the bloody rags strewn on the dirt.

She knew it would hurt.

She'd seen young seers crying during their turns under the needle. Chandre made her watch half a dozen getting marked ahead of her, so she'd see how much it hurt.

The seer with the tattoo needle glanced at Chandre again.

"You'll take responsibility?" he asked the hunter.

But that was too much.

Cass rolled her eyes. "No. The Bridge will eat your spleen. And I'll watch. Laughing. Laughing and singing my 'I hate seers' song..."

The other seers laughed louder at this, until Chandre glared them all into silence.

Cass arranged herself on the chair, holding out her arm. Carefully, the male leaned over her skin, aligning the needle before giving a last glance to Chandre.

Steeling herself, Cass held her arm still, the way she'd seen the other seers do it. Before the needle lowered all the way, a young male approached silently on Cass's other side.

He bowed respectfully, asking permission with his eyes.

Cass nodded, feeling a rush of gratitude.

"Thanks. That would be great."

He positioned himself behind the chair to hold her still, pressing his shoulder into hers and gripping her arm. The seer holding the needle gave Chandre a last, fleeting look with those odd-colored eyes.

Then he pressed the end of the organic needle to Cass's skin.

He began to work, and every seer in the place fell silent.

Chandre hadn't been exaggerating. The pain was bad.

Bad enough to blank out Cass's mind, to make it difficult not to struggle, or cry out.

She couldn't think at all as she fought to adjust.

Yet she'd dealt with a lot worse. She found something familiar in that, enough to allow her to brace her mind and body. The pain ratcheted up slowly as more of the acid-like ink got under her skin, until it felt like her arm was on fire and being eaten at the same time, but it still wasn't anything like the worst thing she'd experienced.

She found something oddly satisfying in that.

She'd survived a lot worse.

Worse than most of the seers watching had ever come close to.

She bit her lip, eyes tearing, but didn't struggle against the male seer's hold. She didn't make a sound, not even when the tattoo artist pulled the needle away, ripping away part of her flesh and skin.

She watched him change the color of the ink, filling the organic holder with a pale blue.

Then he started again. That time, it hurt more.

But again, not as bad as what she'd endured under Terian.

Pain alone couldn't break her—not anymore.

By the end, she stared up from the chair at the light flooding through the barn doors, watching the birds flit to and fro, feeling the seer's calloused fingers on her arm as well as the white-hot end of the organic needle.

About an hour later, the artist hung the needle up on the metal stand.

Dabbing her skin with antiseptic, he winced a little when Cass moaned, fighting not to pull away. She'd gotten so relaxed under the steady fire of the needle itself, the dabbing of the wound with an alcohol compound caught her off guard, since it was a different kind of pain. She made herself look over when he dropped another blood-soaked rag to the sawdust-covered floor. Then her eyes fell to her arm, staring at the blue and white sword and sun burned into her skin.

White and blue flames came off the orb in the middle, bisected with a white sword detailed in black ink.

It was stunning.

Even now, surrounded by red skin, it practically glowed.

She staggered slowly to her feet, and the young seer caught her around the waist, holding her up. She bowed to the tattoo artist, a little stiffly, but with her hands in the proper position.

The male seers cheered, stomping their feet on the wooden floor.

When she turned in surprise, they cheered louder, whistling and applauding.

Stepping closer, Chandre looked at the tattoo, and frowned.

Cass had almost forgotten she was there, waiting. Now she saw that the seer had stood there the entire time, unmoving, while the organic needle marked her.

Peering down at the fine lines of the tattoo, and the color already visible under the red flesh, Cass smiled. Blowing on it a little and wincing, she bowed again in thanks to the old seer, then to the male who assisted by holding her arm.

Then, grinning, she raised both of her arms in a victory salute to the other seers in the barn.

Laughing, the males cheered louder, thumping the wooden floor with their feet.

"Shut up!" Chandre yelled.

They did. Cass grinned at her, but it didn't change Chandre's expression, which remained worried, and visibly upset. Ignoring the rest of them, she began speaking to Cass rapidly by motioning with her hands, then seemed to remember that she was human and switched seamlessly to verbal.

"...be sure to cover it tonight," she finished in English. "I have a cream for this. It is herbal, so it won't hurt you. I will bring it by later, and some tea. And drink lots of water. At least three or four glasses before you rest."

Stepping closer, Cass caressed the muscular seer's arm.

The males in the room quieted, staring at them.

"So I'm a dumb worm now, huh?" Cass asked.

Chandre's jaw tightened. "I did not deny you."

Cass smiled. She tossed back her black and red-dyed hair.

"No," she said. "You did not." She squeezed the seer's arm, kissing her on the cheek. "Are we eating dinner together?"

Chandre nodded. She didn't meet her eyes, though.

Releasing her, Cass walked past the line of male seers to the doorway.

She ignored the stares. If ever there was a town with a shortage of females, it was Seertown. Some of those by the wall had already propositioned her... politely, of course, given her relationship to the Bridge.

They hadn't just been testing the waters, though. She'd definitely sensed frustration and disappointment off them when she'd said no.

If nothing else, she'd never suffer from a sex shortage here, even with the ugly scar on her face.

It didn't help really, knowing that.

CASS SAT AT A TABLE IN A ROOFTOP CAFÉ, SMOKING A HAND-ROLLED *HIRI*.

She listened to rain hitting the corrugated tin roof.

It rained a lot in Seertown.

It rained more here than it did in Seattle. More than Portland, even, where two of her cousins lived. Mist would float into the valley between rains as well, making the buildings and even the colorful prayer flags invisible.

She'd been sitting there for what felt like hours, with only the old human who owned the place coming up periodically to replace her cup of chai. He let her play the record player, which had a motley stack of vinyl left behind from tourists and oddball pilgrims.

Right then, she had on The Stooges.

It had been Maygar's favorite record.

She glanced down at her upper arm, blowing lightly on the sun and sword tattoo that stood out on her skin. The colors seemed to brighten every day, growing sharper as the red of her skin faded. The flames around the sun's orb also got more detailed.

Chan was still unhappy about it, although she'd stopped grumbling overtly.

She'd been getting more possessive lately, Cass noticed.

Then again, a lot of the seers seemed on edge.

It didn't help, what had happened to Grent.

Grent got back to Seertown a few days after Revik left to go find Allie. He'd been practically dragged there bodily by the other Adhipan seers following a burial ceremony for his mate, Laska, in Sikkim. Cass almost wondered if they'd deliberately waited until Revik left before they brought him back.

None of the mated seers wanted to talk about Grent.

Everyone knew he was letting himself die in the basement of the Seven's compound. Vash and others in the Adhipan went to see him daily, but he wouldn't eat.

Jon went to visit him, when Dorje asked.

He told Cass it reminded him of watching a friend of theirs in San Francisco, Justin, trying to quit hard drugs. Grent had been panting, his face etched with pain. He'd sweated off half his body weight, and couldn't lie down, or sleep, or even relieve himself normally. He sat in a meditation pose for most of the visit, looking anything but serene.

Cass thought about visiting him too, but she didn't really know Grent. She couldn't quite bring herself to go down there, knowing at least half of it was curiosity.

She didn't want to think about maybe having to see Allie like that one day.

Or Revik, for that matter.

Grent's condition couldn't help but leave a pall over the whole group. Everyone knew he was down there, dying. She'd heard Yerin talking about burial rites, so Cass knew no one expected him to live through this.

Given all that, getting a tattoo seemed pretty minor.

"Does it hurt?" a voice asked.

Cass jumped, turning towards the stairwell.

A middle-aged seer stood there, just past the doorway. He had chestnut brown hair and the lightest, most piercing gray eyes she'd ever seen.

Cass recognized him, vaguely.

He was one of the new ones, who came from the mountains.

In fact, she was pretty sure he was their leader.

He didn't look particularly Chinese though, except around the cheekbones, and then only if you were looking for it. He was like Revik—one of those seers whose ethnicity was impossible to pinpoint with any real accuracy.

Their similarities ended there, however.

Where Revik had a striking angularity to his features, and eyes that stood out even more than this man's did, he wasn't really stereotypically handsome. He definitely fell into the sexy camp, in Cass's view, and she totally got why Allie was so attracted to him, but his features didn't reflect the symmetry that this man's did.

This man had the chiseled, perfect face of a movie star.

Almost shockingly handsome, he wore it as unselfconsciously as he did the uniform-like dress shirt and dark pants.

If human, she would have pegged him at about forty. Since he was seer, she had no idea what that made him. Likely, at least twice Revik's age. Maybe more.

"Does it hurt?" he asked again.

Cass looked down at the tattoo on her arm, following his eyes.

"A little," she said. When he didn't move, she held up her cup. "Chai?"

He glanced at the record player.

"It's Iggy," she said. "You can change it."

"No." His eyes cleared. "No, it's fine."

Approaching where she sat, he gestured with a hand, a request to join her.

When Cass gave the appropriate countersign, he sank into the opposite chair. She watched him in some curiosity as he relaxed deeper into the wooden seat, propping his arms on the water-damaged armrests and stretching out his legs.

He gazed out at the view, squinting past the rain.

Old buildings cascaded down the hill, strung with prayer flags.

"I am Balidor." He turned. "You are Cassandra?"

Cass smiled wanly. "No one but my mother's called me that in about twenty years, but yes, that would be me."

"Interesting name." He smiled. "It is not Thai. You are Thai, are you not?"

"I'm a mutt," she said, answering with a shrug. "A real one. Thai, Ethiopian, Irish. Scottish." She took a sip of the chai. "I think my mom named me after the Greek Goddess. You know. Apollo's babe."

"Ah yes." He clicked softly, as though remembering. "Cassandra. A great beauty. She could see the future, could she not?"

"Yes." Cass leaned back in the plastic chair. "But no one ever believed her."

She blew bangs out of her eyes. "It's always sounded pretty stupid with my last name. That's Jainukul," she added. "In case you wanted to do a security check on me. That's Thai, by the way."

He nodded, seemingly without noticing her jab.

She found herself watching him curiously again, really thinking about his age. He had a kind of leonine grace that reminded her of the way kings were portrayed from the Middle Ages. He wore authority with an assumed air that made it seem almost genetic.

He also seemed vaguely stiff, as though his manners came from a different era.

"I lead the Adhipan," he said. "The infiltrators tasked with protecting the Council." His eyebrows drew together as he glanced at her. "That includes the Bridge. In fact, protecting your friend Alyson is our primary responsibility."

Cass adjusted her body in the chair. "Cool."

She waited, still surprised a seer had any interest in her.

Maybe it was sexual. If so, he wasn't doing it like the others had. Subtlety wasn't generally a defining trait for most seers when it came to sex, she'd noticed.

Balidor smiled faintly. "I could use your help. Or your advice, perhaps."

She hid her surprise. "Sure."

"I know you helped Dehgoies prepare for their..." His eyebrows scrunched, as if he was searching for the right word in English. "...For his time with Alyson," he finished.

He studied her with those light gray eyes.

"I wondered," he said, after another polite pause. "When you spoke to him, did he tell you what hurt him in the woods?"

She stared at him blankly.

Then she raised an eyebrow, snorting.

"Revik?" Relaxing somewhat, she folded her arms. "You know him. Or, I assume you do. He was vague. He was also a little preoccupied. I asked him about it, sure. He said you..." She gestured towards Balidor, seer-fashion. "The Adhipan... had reason to believe Terian or someone else might be 'engineering' something. He didn't say what. He also didn't say what that had to do with his face."

She paused, giving him the chance to fill in the blanks.

When he didn't, she cleared her throat.

"Well? Is it true?" she asked.

Balidor hesitated. He made a "more or less" sign with his hand.

"Is it some kind of weapon?"

"No." Balidor's brows drew together. "Not exactly."

He hesitated, and Cass found herself studying those gray eyes.

"I have noticed a tendency," he said next. "Of Dehgoies Revik's. He seems to not, well... share things. With his wife." He studied Cass's expression. "Do you know what I mean?"

Cass looked at his serious face, and realized he wasn't reading her.

He was waiting for her to tell him.

Something about the unspoken politeness of that gesture disarmed her completely.

She dropped the guardedness of her tone.

"Yeah," she said. "I do know what you mean. So does Allie. It drives her crazy, actually."

"So... do you think it unlikely he would have told her what happened to him?"

Cass thought about that.

Again, she felt the Adhipan leader waiting.

If he was reading her, he was really damned good at hiding it.

"I don't know." She picked up her tea, propping her elbow on her arm. "Honestly, I don't think he hides things from her on purpose. He just avoids telling people things that might upset them... and he worries about upsetting Allie more than anyone. He also doesn't seem to think it's important a lot of the time. Sort of an unspoken 'need to know' rule. He's not the chattiest guy in the first place, if you hadn't noticed." She smiled, putting down the tea. "He can give a lecture like nobody's business, though."

Balidor nodded, his face respectful. "You think it unlikely he told her, then?"

She frowned. "I didn't say that. She's his wife."

Remembering his face when she'd last seen him, she snorted. "... Although, to be honest, I think he had other things on his mind when he left here."

Balidor gazed out over the rain-filled valley.

He looked up then and smiled, accepting a cup of tea from the old man who owned the restaurant. He bowed before speaking a few polite words to the human in Tibetan. The human smiled in return, speaking back with a nearly toothless mouth.

Cass watched the hunched, white-haired human disappear back through the cloth-covered doorway. She turned to Balidor.

"Whatever it is... do you *want* Revik to tell her about it? Or not?"

Balidor gave her a sideways glance, sipping his tea.

"I will be honest," he said, clicking softly. "I wish for them to enjoy this time together. And yet, it is imperative that she understand the current risks. I also do not want to find myself in the unhappy position of being forced to tell her things about which her mate did not see fit to inform her."

He paused, giving Cass a serious look with those light gray eyes.

"He is likely to be... touchy. When they return."

"Yeah," Cass said, grinning. "I can understand that."

He met her gaze. Then he smiled in return. "Yes. I see that you do."

"So what happened in Sikkim?" Cass asked. "Can you tell me?"

There was a short pause.

Balidor sighed, his eyes concerned as he stirred his tea.

"It is difficult," he said. "You are human."

Cass's smile grew stiff. "I'm aware of that."

"I believe you are a trustworthy person," Balidor added. "But any hunter could read you for information if they wished. In addition, you were already targeted once by our enemies, due to your closeness to the Bridge."

After a pause, she shrugged. "I appreciate the honesty. I guess."

There was a silence while she looked over the valley.

Her eyes scanned the increasingly limited view of the town now that a thick mist settled over the buildings and trees. She focused on a monkey climbing down a string of prayer flags, its dark eyes concentrated.

Balidor smiled.

"You likely have not witnessed this yet with seers? This bonding?"

"You mean Revik and Allie?" Cass shook her head. "No, but I've heard people joking about it. Are they both going to come back crazy?"

Balidor clicked humorously even as he gestured in the negative.

"They will be different. Some of this is biology." He gave her a sideways smile. "Also, I think you are right. Sharing information about his time in Sikkim is unlikely to be his priority, given the circumstances. If Dehgoies did not tell her what happened when he first saw her, it is unlikely she will know anything before they return."

Cass shifted in her chair. "What do you mean? They'll have to talk for part of the time, right? Go for walks. Play backgammon."

He made a line in the air with a finger, a seer's "no."

"That is unlikely," he said. "Not for a few weeks, at least. Given the amount of time they waited, it could be longer." He gave her another faint smile. "They will talk, yes. But not in the way you mean."

"A few weeks?" she said. "Seriously?"

He shrugged, stirring his tea. He laid his spoon on the rickety table.

When his eyes met hers next, they were serious.

"And you, Cassandra?" he asked. "How are you doing... with all that has happened to you?"

Interest rose to his gray eyes, and it was more than polite.

She hesitated at the look there, then shrugged, letting her gaze return to the rain sheeting over the valley.

"I don't sleep well," she said.

He clicked sympathetically, a near purr.

When she glanced at him, she caught him staring at her. The stare didn't make her nervous, or seem to require anything from her in answer.

She felt herself start to relax.

Copying his pose, she stretched out her legs, crossing her ankles. He took another sip of tea before his eyes flickered back to the valley.

They sank into a companionable silence.

The sky had just begun to darken, the clouds to turn scarlet and paler shades of pink.

Together, they watched the sun set over the mountains.

CHAPTER 28

HONEYMOON

*I n the distance, windows shatter in an old and rusted factory. I see a boy
with black hair laughing, screaming into the sky—*
I lifted my head, squinting to see through the pitch dark of the
room.

I could still hear the sound of breaking glass.

We'd made it to the bed.

I didn't know how or when. Revik lay wrapped around me, my legs
curled around and between his. He held me tightly, rearranging his long
form, and—

I hear voices, as if from far away.

*The clearing lay in darkness but for a few lights swinging in a half-ring,
obscuring shadowy forms. The sun has already disappeared. I don't remember it
leaving and the rain hasn't stopped, but it has grown colder. I try to move…*

…and let out a short gasp.

My whole body hurt, seemingly from my hair down to my feet, but
my light wound into his as soon as he responded to my body's jerk. The
pulling started again, somewhere in the area of my navel.

Images rose from before we'd passed out on the bed. My fingers
coiled his wrist. I'd lain below him, on my stomach, both of our bodies
slick with sweat and he'd been reading me, fighting not to lose it as I got

close. I looked back, and for a moment, we were somewhere else, and the trees closed in around us.

Open, his eyes glowed a brilliant, emerald green in the dark.

It had taken him longer than me to really let go.

He was a lot stronger than me, for one thing.

He'd been afraid he'd hurt me, he said.

What he didn't say was, he'd been afraid I wouldn't react well to him, if he really let himself go. He'd worked as a pro. He worried I'd think he was perverted, that I'd be unfamiliar with the inherent kinks in seer sex, his sexuality in particular, which he seemed to think might be different in some way, or maybe just more extreme than most.

I couldn't quite discern his reasons from his fleeting thoughts, but I got glimmers of intensity there, violence and control, resonant with that demanding want for my submission I'd felt on him when we first started this.

What I felt turned me on… a lot, which only seemed to confuse him more.

The virgin thing turned him on.

It touched him, too, more than he seemed to feel comfortable admitting to me, at least at first, something about seers leaving imprints during sex, and him only feeling me there.

It also made him nervous.

When I finally got him there, it didn't result in kink, per se.

I saw it in his eyes first.

His control slid away, tumbling faster until his whole face changed, growing more open than I'd ever seen it, nearly unrecognizable just before he rolled me to my back. His pain wrapped into me, thick and nearly desperate. He felt lost there, an aloneness that bordered on self-hate, a wanting that felt old, yet somehow still specific to me.

He fucked me like he was trying to break something in himself, holding me down so that I could barely move, going so deep I cried out at each thrust.

His fear paralyzed me.

Fear that I would leave him… that someone would take me, that we would be separated again, that he would drive me off. It grew nearly violent by the time he came, until he bit my shoulder and neck, fighting his way deeper inside me, asking me over and over with his light if I loved him.

We'd been in front of the fireplace.

I'd just given him head for the first time, and somehow, that seemed to affect him more than our earlier intercourse.

He'd wanted sex again before we'd even finished.

Instead he held me down, returning the favor until I couldn't form coherent words.

He wouldn't let me come.

He used his light to hold me on the edge for hours.

By the end, both of us were crying, and I was begging him. He got me to make promises, to admit to things I'd never told anyone, to open my light and heart until I could barely tell us apart. He wanted me to tell him about everyone I'd ever loved before him.

He wanted to know every time I'd had sex.

When I was half out of my head, at the point where I'd do anything he asked, he pinned me on my stomach and fucked me with the hard end of his cock. He brought me to climax after climax before he came himself.

His body wracked with something that seemed to break him in half toward the end. I couldn't hold everything he sent, everything he wanted of me. Guilt wrapped into the pain he sent, guilt around what he'd done... and around a kind of mind-numbing possessiveness he couldn't seem to control.

He said a lot. During, and after.

One thing he told me explained a few things.

Apparently, Maygar went to Cairo to tell Revik that we'd fallen in love.

He'd claimed I wanted a divorce.

He even tried to pay Revik off to bring severance proceedings against me. When Revik refused to do anything until he heard it directly from me, Maygar taunted him about our supposed sex life, giving out enough detail to be pretty convincing.

Eventually, Revik lost his cool.

He'd believed Maygar, though.

He'd gone back to Seertown believing that, until I told him I loved him and seemed confused about his references to my screwing other men. He'd still more than half-believed we'd had sex—pretty much up until the instant he was fully inside me.

He'd been ashamed of that, but it more bewildered me.

When I asked him why in god's name Maygar would do *any* of that, Revik looked at me like I was the crazy one.

"He's in love with you, Alyson! *Gaos.* Don't tell me you didn't know? Half the fucking compound knew... even before that stunt he pulled. Or do you think he wanted you as a wife just to hurt *me?* That he'd risk his life just for *that?*"

I didn't have an answer for that, either.

He wasn't the only one who acted less than rational.

I found myself crying at one point, even apart from what he'd done.

I hit him, too, right in the face... so angry about Kat and the woman on the ship that I didn't actually feel sane. He held me down when I swung at him again. Then he cried, too, when I told him I'd never forgiven him.

I traced scars on his skin, letting myself really see them, and see how many he'd collected while he was young—really young, long before he'd been a soldier or infiltrator. White with age, they stretched and changed shape as his back and shoulders broadened.

He'd been small as a kid, he said, even for a seer.

Under me, he made a sound, coiling an arm around my shoulders. He pulled me against him, kissing my neck, and I bit my lip to keep my mind focused.

I need the bathroom, I told him.

It took him another second of thought to let me go.

I separated us with an effort, then climbed to my feet, stumbling to the bathroom door. I walked like I was drunk. It felt like something inside me had been smashed and was slowly knitting itself back together into a different shape.

Closing the door, I sat on the toilet.

After wincing my way through that experience, I pulled the flush chain and stood. I found myself staring at the bamboo-enclosed shower, fighting to think as I did, knowing only that I wanted something. After another moment of concentration, I figured out how to run the water. I had just put my hand into the stream when I heard a creak and turned.

He stood there, eyes unfocused, dark hair sticking up around his head. He glanced around the small space, as if not quite sure what he wanted.

I found myself looking at him.

I'd never seen him naked in full light.

"Are you okay?" I asked.

Thinking, he nodded. He saw me looking at him then and moved closer to where I stood. For a moment we just stood there, and I felt him prodding me to keep looking while he kissed my shoulder.

I glanced up after a moment, almost shyly.

"Is that another tattoo?" I asked.

Clan mark. He kissed my mouth, tugging my hand to the blue and black series of curved lines. I watched his cock harden as I stroked them.

"Do you have any others?" I asked.

Thinking, he turned around, pointing to his shoulder.

Sword and Sun. A fairly elaborate one. He wore Syrimne's mark.

"When did you get that?" I asked, touching it. "It looks different from the ones I've seen other seers wear. A different design. And it's in a different place."

I don't know. Before. Sometime before the memory wipe.

Like the arm band?

Yes. He tugged my fingers back to the clan mark. I let him pull me closer. I was still caressing the tattoo on his groin when he kissed me.

For a long moment, we stood there, kissing.

He brought me to the floor.

…until he raised his head, looking back over his shoulder.

I heard running water, loud in my ears, and blinked around at where we lay, confused by the murkiness of the room. I was astride him, immersed in clouds of steam. He looked up at me, gesturing towards the shower, using seer sign language, probably out of habit since I still only knew about half of the words.

Even so, I understood. Sliding up and off him, I gasped, standing shakily. I took his hand when he reached up, leaning backwards to help him to his feet.

I brought him with me into the bamboo stall.

The water was still warm, since it was the Asian style of heater, one that heated water right before it came through the nozzle. I wondered how long it had been running.

It was hard to care.

Once inside, we left each other alone.

…until he shampooed my hair, which led to my back, then the rest of me.

When I started to return the favor, we ended up against the back wall, and he supported me with his arms as he entered me again. He started slow… we both did… but like every other time since that time in front of the fire, something kicked in, and by the end I was holding onto him and the wall, asking him for…

…I closed my eyes, falling backwards into a sprawl on the bed.

My hair was wet from the shower. The sheets were cool on my back and legs.

Intensely comfortable, I felt myself starting to drift off.

Then he left the room.

I sat up, alarmed.

Anxiety made it difficult to think, about its cause or even where I was, where I'd been for what felt like an odd blank stretch in the dark, a time-lessness that confused me only when I tried to pin it down.

I'd just made up my mind to go look for him when he reappeared in the doorway.

His arms and hands held a pitcher of water, a bowl of something, and what looked like a glass with utensils stuck inside. He set the pitcher on a night table near the headboard and dumped the rest of it on the bed, crawling in next to me. I kissed him, and he kissed me back, stroking my skin as though weeks had separated us.

A few more passed before I remembered that he'd left at all.

At my thought, he raised his head, glancing at the part of the bed he'd covered in kitchenware.

We have to eat, he sent. *We have to, Allie.*

I was kissing his chest as he eased my leg from around him.

Rolling to his back, he grabbed the bowl and the glass, setting the former between us. He scooped up the utensils that had spilled out on the bed and put one in my hand, then jerked the wooden cover off the bowl, handing the bowl to me.

The room was still dark, but I could see white, curling things inside the container that looked like noodles. I wondered why I could see so well in the dark.

"Practice," he said. *Combat, Allie.*

He motioned between us, a half-finished thought, but I got the idea.

I could see better in the dark because he could see better in the dark. I didn't think on that for very long though, distracted by the smell coming from the bowl.

My stomach gurgled.

"Where did you get this?" I asked.

I tried to imagine him in the kitchen with a candle, cooking, but even with my confused sequencing, I didn't think he could have been gone that long. Leaning towards me, he stabbed a spear-like fork into whatever filled the bowl, withdrawing the utensil impaled on something soft and white. Wanting in part to encourage me to eat, he put it in his mouth and chewed, motioning for me to do the same.

"Tradition," he said, as I stabbed my own spear into the bowl more cautiously. "Seers get sick… forget to eat. A lot of food, Allie."

His words were accented, half-jumbled.

He kissed me between them, but again, my mind filled in the gaps. Other seers had stocked the house with food, knowing we'd be too weird to be able to feed ourselves.

Somehow that struck me as funny and I laughed.

He smiled, raising an eyebrow.

I pushed at his chest. "No wonder they made you a spy! Here I was intimidated, thinking you could cook, too."

He smiled again, kissing my fingers. *Can you cook?*

"No." Laughing a little, I shook my head. "Not well, anyway. We'll have to send our kids to culinary school."

Pain swam through my light.

The intensity behind it shocked me, made it difficult to breathe.

Realizing it was his, I studied his face cautiously.

He slid his fingers into mine, kissing my palm.

Children? I sent tentatively.

His pain worsened. He met my gaze and we kissed again, longer. When I started touching him again, he pushed my hand away gently.

Eat. Please, Allie. Please.

Taking a breath, I put the whatever-it-was in my mouth and chewed, preparing myself for the worst. Seer food still had a tendency to taste like dirt wrapped in moss to me, but after a few chews, I relaxed.

Then my hunger kicked in for real.

I started filling my next forkful before I'd finished swallowing the first.

Revik leaned over me, pouring a glass of water from the pitcher.

He took a long drink while I ate, then handed it to me. He watched me drink it, and I felt another sliver of pain from him before he took back the glass, filling it again.

That one he motioned for me to drink on my own.

When I finished off the second glass, he nudged my attention back to the bowl.

I took another mouthful of food, and for an instant, it almost distracted me from watching him eat. Even cold, the noodle-things tasted mind-blowingly good. Better than anything I'd eaten in a long time, like really good macaroni and cheese, only with some kind of meat, and a few spices I didn't know. As I took another mouthful with barely a pause between bites, I realized I was ravenous.

"Better?" he asked, after he'd swallowed again.

"This tastes like human food," I told him.

"It's seer food." He kissed me lingeringly. "You're going to take on my palate some. Maybe you'll like it more." He kissed me again. "I've craved that disgusting human coffee since Seattle."

"Seattle's a coffee town," I said, smiling. "Can't blame me."

"No, it's your fault," he assured me.

He watched me eat, and I felt his pain sharpen. "Fuck, I want you to give me head. I want you to kiss my cock while I eat." When I slid closer, he pushed me gently away. "No. *Gaos*. We can't. We fucking can't." His eyes closed, even as he held me off him. "*Gaos*. I think it's getting worse, Allie."

"It's getting worse," I agreed, stabbing another forkful of food.

"We have to remember to eat," he said. "We have to, Allie."

But I couldn't get my mind off the noodles.

"I can't believe how hungry I am. I could eat this whole thing."

He grunted in a flat kind of humor, leaning over me to stab another forkful for himself. "Allie, it's been at least three days. We were both getting weak."

I halted my fork halfway to my mouth. "Three days? But last night—"

He shook his head, his eyes shining faintly in the dark.

"At least two nights ago. Maybe more." He glanced towards the covered window. "It's dark again. I think we got up right after sunset this time."

"This time," I said, only now it wasn't a question.

I fought to piece together the last few however-long-it-had-beens, and realized I did remember waking up. The first time we'd been by the fireplace. Another time I remembered us on a tile floor somewhere, covered in a quilt.

The same or a similar quilt half-covered me now.

He was still eating, his free hand caressing my fingers that lay between us. He offered me his fork and I ate the noodles off the end. Feeling another whisper of pain from him, I leaned closer, kissing his mouth. He pushed me back gently with his hand, jabbing his finger towards the bowl.

"Eat," he said. "I'm not starving my wife to death."

I laughed, taking the glass from his hand after he refilled it again.

We each drank about half. I had a few more forkfuls of noodles before I realized I was full... like, really full, probably because he was right, and we hadn't eaten in a few days. He handed me another glass of water, indicating with a gesture for me to drink it.

"We need to keep the windows open," he said, worried.

He didn't finish the thought, but again, I followed where he was going.

He meant the drapes.

He wanted to see the sun come up and go down, so we'd have a reminder to eat. I felt the worry on him intensify as he looked at me, and forced myself to take a few more bites of food. Finishing my water, I left the empty glass on the bed and climbed over where he lay, massaging his back while he ate more.

He was still smaller than when I'd met him.

He hadn't gained the weight back, or all the muscle after Terian.

I remembered the thing about drapes and craned my neck, looking for a cord, when it occurred to me that we might freeze if—

"No." He swallowed what was in his mouth. "...There's glass, Allie."

Getting up, I studied the heavy cloth.

I yanked on one end.

I pulled down the curtain rod by mistake and leapt back as it crashed to the floor. I burst out in a laugh, but Revik had already reacted to my startle. I couldn't help but marvel at how fast he got up.

Then I noticed the bluish light flooding the room.

"The moon," I said, pointing. "Hey. Look at that."

A moon over three-fourths full stood in a sky deeply blanketed with stars. Stars shone like hard diamonds, despite the moon's brightness. They receded so far into the distance they could have belonged to the Barrier instead of the physical sky. I stood there, mesmerized, when Revik joined me at the window, curling his arms around me from behind.

"No," I said, looking up at him. "Eat more."

He shook his head. He was full, too.

Caressing my bare belly with his fingers, he started kissing me. His mouth tasted like noodles when I leaned into his chest to kiss him back.

Seconds later, I was pushing him towards the bed. He let me, laying down on his back, wincing and knocking utensils to the floor.

I started giving him what he'd asked me for before.

I watched his eyes start to glow.

That time, he didn't push me away.

CHAPTER 29
LOST

With a jolt, I looked up. I heard voices.

This time, they sounded far away.

The sun was rising, filling the room with gold and pink light, deeper than what colored the fields outside.

I didn't remember it setting.

I remembered eating, though. I remembered eating more than once.

Was it time again? I couldn't remember whose turn it was to remember. We'd worked out some kind of system, but forgot it not long after. I remembered laughing in front of the fridge, him holding a hand over my eyes as he had me point at containers.

I sat in his lap now, arms wrapped around his neck and shoulders.

He held me even tighter than I held him, one hand clasping my back as he braced himself with his other arm. He was reading me, slowing as I got close, going deeper, breathing harder as he used his light to keep me on the edge.

Eyes half-closed, he gripped my thigh as my light wound into his, until his teeth sank into my shoulder. He let out another heavy groan.

I felt him losing control.

I understood. I was doing it again. I could feel it.

Asking him for… something.

I couldn't help myself, not anymore.

I could feel it in him, just past the edges of my sight. As sure as he was that he couldn't give it to me, I was equally sure that he could.

Frustration rose in my light. It triggered another wave of aggression in him. I tried to calm him down, but his hands only gripped me harder, his eyes glowing as he looked at my face. He was asking me, first in German, then in some language I didn't recognize, caressing my neck and jaw. He switched to English.

"...Wife." He kissed me, his voice low, threaded with pain. "Tell me what to do. Please. *Gaos.* Allie. *Please.* Tell me what to do. Tell me how to give you this..."

But I didn't know how to tell him. I tried to show him.

I'd been trying, for as long as he had.

I leaned on his chest. I helped him go deeper, pulling on him with my light, and he groaned again. His pain worsened, and I could feel him reading me for it, but it didn't help. He held me on the edge for what felt like an endless stretch of time, focused on that pull in my light, stopping me as he tried to find it, first in me, then in himself.

He stopped me again, holding me until I fought him.

Somewhere in that, I heard them.

Alarm didn't reach me, not yet.

Changing the angle, he went deeper and that felt even better.

He was losing control. Pleasure rippled off him as my nails dug into his back. Relief suffused me when I saw his face go soft, when I realized what his expression meant. Our thrusts grew harder and deeper and less precise.

I read him and he opened, his arm tight around me.

That time, when the folding thing started, I was so far in him, he couldn't stop it when...

Everything went away. All but blood rushing in my ears, feeling I couldn't hold.

I cried out. He made some kind of sound.

It felt so utterly, unbelievably good.

For a moment, at least, I felt that intensity in both of us unclench, turn into something so heart-achingly soft...

He was there when I came back, holding me still through the last tremors. He kissed my throat, murmuring against my skin.

"I love you," I heard him say. "*Gaos.* I love you, Allie."

I wanted to keep going. He'd been waiting for me.

But I felt it again, some presence I knew. Even more I didn't know.

I raised my head from his shoulder, still fighting to slow my breathing as I tried to level my light enough to scan the room. Still cradling me in his arms, he copied me, helping me look. I got lost there, briefly, looking at him.

The angles of his jaw and cheekbones stood out, highlighted by sun. His eyes glowed faintly, reflecting that same light. Forgetting whatever had distracted me, I stroked his face, kissing his mouth. I tugged on his hair as I dug my fingers into his back—

Something cold touched the skin of my neck.

I turned around, but couldn't see past the light in my eyes. My eyes grew brighter, blinding me. Revik's fingers tightened on my skin—

Arms came out of nowhere.

I cried out, terrified when we were separated. Strong hands dragged me off him, pulling me across the floor. I twisted around...

...and punched someone who yelped.

My scream echoed in the hollow space, sounding like an animal.

Someone else hit me then. In the face.

It hurt. I blinked back tears, trying to focus on the man standing there. I didn't know the features that stared back at me, couldn't focus on them enough to make sense of them.

Yet, something there was familiar.

Whatever it was, it was almost enough to snap me out.

I groped for him, trying to push him away, but he only tightened his hold. I saw him looking at my body. I saw a faint smile...

Then small arms slid around my neck, tightening before I could focus on their owner.

"Allie!"

He nearly strangled me. His eyes glowed, sharp in the dark, blinding me. I wanted so badly for it to be Revik, but I already knew it wasn't.

"It's all right," he said. "You're all right, Allie!"

I was dreaming. I had to be dreaming.

The boy looked back at me, eyes wide in a round face. His lip bled.

I'd punched him in the mouth.

"Nenzi," I managed.

The man next to him visibly jumped, staring at me.

I barely noticed. Fighting to breathe, I grabbed the front of the boy's shirt with both hands, reassuring myself he was real. "Nenzi, where's Revik?"

The round face grew suddenly hard. Shadows flitted around me, nearly physical. They slithered between us. Above that, I saw deep clouds, a golden valley I recognized.

I heard sounds. A thud of flesh on flesh.

I screamed…

I tried to move, to crawl in the direction I could feel him, but pain crippled me, and the blond man held me by the throat. I'd never been claustrophobic before, but it felt as if the walls were closing in on me.

I felt like they might bury me, leave me alone in the dark forever.

Hunched by the wall near the bathroom, I fought for air, ignoring the fingers holding my wrists, the airplanes flashing across the sky behind my lids. Bombs fell in the darkness. Buildings burned. I saw monks screaming, their robes on fire.

The boy spoke. His voice was barely a whisper, but I heard it above the sounds of helicopter blades, shouts, fire… the scream of airplanes overhead.

"Allie?"

I stared at that round face, fighting tears.

"Allie?" His fingers grasped at mine. *Allie, are you hurt?*

I watched his eyes brighten. I knew who this was, but he couldn't be here.

He'd been dead for nearly a hundred years.

Somehow, though, I wasn't afraid.

The feeling that rose in me was closer to relief.

"Nenzi?" I asked. "Is it really you?"

His light flared, blinding me in the Barrier.

I felt my recognition touch him, nearly incapacitate him with feeling, even as his relief expanded over me. Tears rolled down his face. His mouth contorted as he looked at me from my face down to my feet, slowly, as if memorizing every part of me. He looked at me with something like reverence. No, that wasn't it.

He looked at me with love. A love so intense it hurt.

It filled my eyes with tears.

This had to be a dream. I was back in Tarsi's cave.

Everything that had come after—swimming in the river, the horse with the red face, Revik's eyes glowing with their own light, making love in front of the fireplace, our soft confessions in the dark, everything I'd felt and been—it couldn't be real.

"Nenzi?" I asked again. "Where's Revik?"

The small seer's light touched mine, expanding over me until I couldn't breathe. Feeling a sudden burst of protectiveness, I motioned him towards me.

"Nenzi! Come here!"

…when something hit me in the thigh.

It felt like a sledgehammer.

My leg seemed to smash apart, even as force threw me to my back.

I cried out in shock.

He couldn't move.

It was more than pain.

Beyond the pain was the other. The knowledge that he was down, that he wouldn't get back up. He called my name, and I heard him, deafening, in my head.

GET OUT ALLIE! GET OUT! GET OUT! USE THE TELEKINESIS AND GO! PLEASE BABY! PLEASE!

I groaned, my back pressed to the wall.

I hadn't moved.

Clutching my leg, I tried to understand what had happened. My leg felt physically fine. I couldn't see anything wrong with it.

My light scattered like errant flame, useless.

Then the pain hit for real. I fought to move, to stand up, and agony ripped up my back. I writhed, gasping, trying to use the wall for leverage.

"Revik!" Tears came to my eyes. "Gods. What did you do to him?"

Nenzi was with me. He clutched at me with small hands.

His pale, sunless face glowed. He looked anguished.

His eyes continued to shimmer at me like iridescent fish. He clutched my hair, kneading it in his fingers. The fingers of his other hand caressed my face, my shoulder, touching my cheeks, my hands, my arms.

"Allie!" He gripped me tighter. *I'm sorry! I'm sorry, Allie!*

I touched the boy's hand. He was real. He was really there.

Tears filled my eyes. "What did you do?"

Allie, it's all right. He won't hurt you. He promised!

I followed his gaze to the larger shape squatting beside him.

My mind felt suddenly much, much clearer.

This was real. I wasn't just lost in some nightmare.

They'd taken Revik.

A sparking sound rose. I recognized it as an organic *yisso* torch.

Staring up, I focused on the new seer's face. An adult male with the white-blond hair glided smoothly to his feet, standing over us. Tall—nearly seven feet—and Scandinavian-looking, he could have been human but for his height. Focusing on his amber-colored eyes, I understood suddenly why he'd felt so familiar.

My skin turned cold as recognition filtered through my light.

I knew who he was. I knew—even though I didn't know this particular body.

I lunged at the bureau where I knew Revik kept a gun.

The Scandinavian darted after me. With cat-like speed, his hand gripped my ankle, yanking me roughly to the floor. I landed hard on my stomach. I tried to kick his hand away, but he dragged me backwards.

I fought with my light, reaching for that folding sensation, trying to find it, recalling jumps with Tarsi. I fought to remember what I'd done to Maygar—

The giant Terian punched me in the face.

The boy turned on him, hissing.

"Sorry! Sorry!" The Scandinavian held up his hands. "But you saw what she was doing! You don't want her killing us, do you?"

I struggled with my light again, fighting to control it. I pulled my body across the floor until his fingers gripped my ankle, dragging me back.

"Terian..." I barely managed the name.

I looked at the bureau, then around at the room.

They'd taken Revik. They'd *taken* him.

Terian caught me by the neck.

"You won't like this much," he muttered. "Neither will he." He glanced at the boy. "But your mind will start working again eventually, my dear. I'm afraid we have no choice."

I fought him, frantic now.

I understood, finally, how badly I'd blown my chance.

The collar wasn't activated.

I put every ounce of my energy towards using the telekinesis, wanting nothing more than to throw him off me like I had Maygar. I concentrated. I willed my light to break his back, make his head explode. But the reality was, I'd never been able to invoke it at will, despite months of practicing with every seer in the compound.

I fought my way clear of the Scandinavian's giant hands, tried to heave myself towards the bureau once I felt his fingers loosen, but he caught hold of the collar easily.

I felt the boy stiffen, but Terian gave him a sharp look.

"We talked about this," he said. "Nenzi, you said you understood. You *agreed* with me, that it was necessary... just for a short while."

I saw anger rise to the boy's eyes, but he didn't move when Terian bent over me again.

I shrieked when he turned me around, hitting out at him with my fists and elbows, fighting to writhe free, but Terian caught my hair in one hand, yanking my head forward. He held me expertly, bending my neck until I couldn't move. He held me against his chest, ignoring my hands and feet frantically shoving and hitting at him.

Then he pinched a nerve in my neck and shoulder. It paralyzed me briefly.

I grew completely still.

So did he. Light flashed from the retinal scanner as he hung over my neck.

I heard a click.

...and Terian released me, gliding smoothly to his feet.

"There, there," he murmured. "That wasn't so bad."

Teeth bit into my skin.

I let out a shocked cry, clawing at my neck.

Whatever it was dug into my flesh. Then it burrowed deeper. I shrieked as it worked past muscle to bone, wrapping around my spine. The strands wormed their way around every contour, coiling around nerves at the base of my neck. I started to shriek again, but Terian crouched, grabbing my arm.

"Be silent!" he hissed. "I'll kill him! I'll kill your mate! I won't hesitate, Allie, so do not test me in this!"

Gasping, I met his gaze, forced silent by his words.

A shudder ran through me as it ended.

The cold strands locked into place.

The sharp touch of metal on bone not only hurt, it had a nauseating flavor that forced a gasp from my lips. I hung my head, sucking in breaths, swallowing down the bile that filled my mouth.

"Fuck," I gasped.

I gripped the metal in my fingers, panicking as I realized I couldn't see.

I couldn't see my light.

The room flattened. It whited out, then grew at once dead and frighteningly two-dimensional. The collar no longer hurt, not other than that sickening feeling of metal flush against bone. I blinked my eyes, trying to focus.

I realized I was trying to scan… couldn't.

I couldn't feel him anymore. He was gone.

Before, when I thought I'd lost him, he'd still been there.

Every time I'd looked for him, I could feel him. I could find him in some measure at least, however faint. He'd never been gone entirely before. Never. Even before I met him in the flesh, he'd been there, like an imaginary friend.

Until now.

Gasping, I fought full-fledged terror.

The anxiety I'd felt whenever he left the room—it was nothing compared to this.

I couldn't breathe. I couldn't think. I didn't feel human or seer, or remotely sane. If I'd known in which direction he lay, I would have crawled over broken glass. I yanked on the collar with both hands, screaming. I fought the Scandinavian Terian and the boy as if my life were at stake, but my mind was nearly blank.

Terian pried my fingers off the collar, one by one.

I felt the cold shock of more metal as he forced my wrists behind my back, locking cuffs around each one. I felt a sharp sting as a needle sank into my throat. He pinched a nerve in my neck with one hand when I started to struggle more violently.

My muscles stopped working right. I slumped on the wooden floor, breathing too hard. I didn't move as he finished pushing down the stopper on the syringe.

I looked at the boy.

The world remained dead.

The drug seeped a kind of artificial calm that worked over the edges of my awareness, but it didn't help. A feeling of vulnerability came over me, so profound I couldn't stop breathing, even after I was hyperventilating.

I yanked against the cuffs, struggling irrationally to get them off.

I lay my neck on the door jamb, trying to rub off the collar, oblivious now to the pain, to the vulnerable feeling in my neck. It was nothing compared to how lost I felt. I hooked the metal ring on a piece of wood, bracing my feet and yanking until my neck hurt for real. I felt it tearing where it penetrated my flesh.

I groaned, but only fought harder, unable to lose the panicked feeling at not being able to feel him, or anything else.

Terian jerked me off the door and turned me around, punching me in the face. The force of the blow sent me falling straight to my back, on my cuffed wrists.

I lay there, winded, a flipped turtle.

The boy whimpered, watching me.

I looked up at him, and saw him tugging at Terian's arm. The tears in his eyes looked fearful, almost frantic.

Terian caressed the boy's head. "There, there. It's all right. She'll be all right." He exhaled, out of breath, combing disheveled blond hair out of his eyes. "We got what we came for. Be happy about that."

"Revik," I managed. I could only repeat his name, until I wasn't sure if it was aloud or in my head. "Revik…"

Terian stared down at me with those unnerving yellow eyes.

"Don't fret, love," he said. "We can't kill him. Not anymore. Personally, I'd like to bring him along, but I'm afraid Nenz here won't stand for it."

I struggled backwards, my cuffed hands digging into my back.

There was no place to go. I tried to fight the Scandinavian off, but agony ripped through my spine when he grabbed me by the collar, yanking me to my feet. The drug made my legs wobble, but it still hadn't knocked me out.

He shoved me towards the door, still holding the collar. I stumbled across a floor half-covered by rumpled wool rugs, littered with plates, clothes, a towel, what might have been broken glass.

"Busy little bunnies you've been," Terian muttered.

He used the collar to steer me towards the living room, and straight for the front door.

It occurred to me only then that I was naked. I struggled against his hands, but he barely hesitated before forcing me outside. He shoved me down the wooden steps, holding the collar to keep me from falling.

Then I saw him.

Revik lay in a heap on the dirt below the wooden stairs. He was naked, too. His skin looked white but for the tattoos and his catalogue of scars… as well as what I'd done to him over the past however-many days. Four men stood over him. They must have drugged him, either before or after they shot him in the thigh.

I saw the collar on his neck as his eyes met mine.

"NO!" He screamed when he saw Terian holding me. "NO! NO!"

He fought in an open panic, struggling to get to his hands and knees.

One of the seers kicked him in the side and I shrieked, fighting like a wild person against Terian's hands. Half picking me up when I attacked him, Terian turned me around, yanking me backwards by the metal cuffs.

He caught me around the throat, holding me against his chest.

"Revi'!" Terian shouted. "Revi'! Calm yourself!"

"Get your fucking hands off her! *Get your fucking hands off her!*"

"Do you want her to kill herself? She already tried once inside!"

"Let go of her! *Let go of her!* I swear to the gods I'll kill you—"

"Did you hear me, Revi'? You must see reason, my friend!"

"LET GO OF HER—"

"Calm, Revi'! Calm!"

"I'll kill you! *I'll fucking kill you if you hurt her!*"

Terian held me tighter. I felt tension in his hands.

"We will not hurt her!" he said. "But we can't have the two of you ripping yourselves apart, do you hear me? You know it's a risk… you know it! Will you make her die for you?"

He waited for that much to penetrate, for Revik to be looking at me again.

Once it did, I felt Terian relax, but only marginally.

"Good. Yes." He took a breath, his voice still loud, but calmer. "You will get your chance, Revi'," he said. "I promise you that. The boy doesn't want you with us. We can't kill you, which means we have to let you go. I'll even call your friends in the Adhipan once we're safely away, if you—"

"No!" Revik struggled to get up, but one of the seers placed a foot on his shoulder, forcing him down. "Don't take her! Please... gods, I'll give you anything you want. Anything!" He fought against the seer holding him. "I'll help you rebuild it! I'll help you, Terry!"

He looked at my face, then back at the Scandinavian holding me.

"I'll do whatever you ask! Anything... I'll fucking *work* for you, Terry! As long as you want! Don't take her... please! *Please*, goddamn it!"

Tears were running down my face.

I felt Terian's fingers tighten at his words, but I couldn't take my eyes off Revik. The panic in his face debilitated me, even when I couldn't feel his light. The collar he wore was hurting him; I could see it, but he barely seemed to notice. When he began fighting openly again, Terian slid a hand around my waist, holding me against him more deliberately.

With his other hand, he cupped my breast.

"Revi'... behave yourself! Or I'll give you reason to complain."

Revik froze, his body taut, animal-looking once more.

But it was the boy who spoke first, making me jump.

"Get your hands off her!"

The blond Terian turned his head at the same time I did. I stared at the boy, bewildered at the fury I saw in his eyes—well before it occurred to me to be grateful. He stared up at the tall Terian, hands clenched at his sides.

Terian hesitated a second longer. He looked between Revik and the boy.

The boy stepped in front of him.

"Let go of her," Nenzi hissed. "Or I'll kill you."

There was the barest pause, then the Scandinavian-looking seer took a step back. He released every part of me but the collar.

"Thank you," Revik said. "Thank you..."

The boy looked at Revik, his fingers still balled into fists.

"*You*. You disgusting *shit!*" His words held so much hatred I flinched. Like Terian had, I looked between the boy and Revik. "You don't say *anything* about her! I should *kill* you for touching her..." He looked at me, breathing harder, then back at Revik. "Rapist! Fucking pervert *rapist!* I saw you hurt her!"

"Nenzi!" I said, stunned. "He didn't hurt me!"

Revik looked at me. His eyes grew pained, just before they ran down the length of my body.

"No," he said, hoarse. "No. I didn't mean to."

"Yes, you did! *Look at her!*"

"He didn't hurt me!" I said, angry. I turned on Revik, my voice warning. "Revik—look at your own body before you start complaining about mine!"

My words seemed to snap him out, briefly at least.

"How do you know this kid?" he asked.

"Tarsi. It's a long story. He shouldn't be here—"

"Shouldn't be here?" Revik said. "What does that mean?"

"Stop talking to her—" the boy began angrily, but I cut him off.

"Nenzi! He's my *husband!*"

Behind me, Terian chuckled, but his eyes held a sharp interest when I glanced back at his face. He was looking between Revik and the boy and me, listening to us.

I kept talking, struggling to balance on my toes.

"Nenzi, *you're* the one hurting me. You and this psycho friend of yours! If you cared about me at all, you'd let Revik go. You'd kill this sonofabitch and let us *both* go!"

Nenzi remained focused on Revik.

"I know what you did," he said. "I saw it."

Revik snarled, "Listen to *her*, you little psychopath! If you really want to help her—"

"Is *this* why you had me imprisoned? To *steal* her from me?"

"What?" Revik stared from me back to him. "What are you talking about?" He looked at me and stopped, pain softening then hardening his features—until both of us were lost there. I saw his eyes blur, realized he was still trying to reach me. Pain stood out in his eyes as he strained against the collar.

Eventually he stopped, gasping, as the collar shocked him harder.

His gaze dropped to the one around my neck—right before he lunged.

A male seer caught him by the hair, holding him back. Fear exploded over his features again as he looked at me, a panic he aimed at the boy.

"Boy, please!" Tears came to his eyes. "He'll hurt her!"

"No. He promised."

"He's a fucking liar! Are you really that stupid?"

The boy's eyes glowed brighter. Staring at his round face, I realized I recognized that look. I'd seen it at Tarsi's.

"No!" I screamed. I fought Terian, trying to get between the boy and Revik. Terian released me and I managed to get down to my knees, in front of the boy.

"No! Don't hurt him! Nenzi, please. I'll go with you. Just don't hurt him!"

Revik's face contorted in pain. "Allie! Baby... don't!"

I tore my eyes off him to plead with the boy. "Please, Nenzi," I whispered. "I'll go with you. Please... just don't hurt him... please..."

The boy continued to stare at Revik, but I saw the light in his eyes flicker, then dim, right before he glanced at me. Looking down at my body, he took in the length of me, his lips pressed together. He seemed about to say something, when he turned towards Terian, his gaze suddenly sharp.

"No," he said coldly, in response to something Terian had thought.

The Scandinavian Terian's voice grew cautious. "They've consummated. I assume you won't want to test that by letting him die of exposure."

"Boy," Revik said. "Please! Listen to her! You can't trust him!"

Nenzi caught hold of my arm, gripping it tight enough to hurt. I winced, avoiding his eyes as he looked at my body again. His dark eyes shifted up, meeting Terian's behind me. His voice grew cold as ice, and suddenly much older.

"You touch her like that again, and I'll cut off your cock and make you eat it." His black eyes glimmered a faint green. "Understand?"

"Of course, my friend. Of course. It was only to annoy Dehgoies."

Nenzi looked at me. The expression there made me nervous.

"He'll come after us," Terian said. "He won't be able to help himself." His voice grew cajoling. "If you bring him with us now, we could control him. You would still get what you wanted, my young friend... only safer. For her, too."

Nenzi gestured an emphatic "no," still staring at me.

"He doesn't have anything I want," he said. "Not anymore."

I met Revik's gaze, trying to think past the screaming in my mind.

I couldn't decide if there was anything I could do, anything I could say that would make a difference. They had him chained to the steps. He'd been shot in the thigh. His face contorted in pain whenever he tried to move—or use his sight. He was bruised, beat up, probably malnourished from however long we'd been out here.

The wound in his leg looked like it had already cost him a lot of blood. Blood seemed to be everywhere, shocking against his pale skin.

Terian said he wouldn't let him die.

I saw Revik looking at my face, almost as if he'd guessed what I was thinking. His eyes filled with tears. His voice thickened.

"No, Allie." He shook his head. "No. Please, baby. No."

Terian grasped me by the collar from behind.

With a single, sharp pull, he yanked me ungracefully to my feet. I cried out, losing my balance so that I hung from his fingers.

The boy grabbed my arm, glaring up at Terian.

"Stop hurting her!"

"If you're not going to bring him, we have to separate them!" Terian said. "It's time to go. *Now*, Nenzi!"

Nenzi looked at Revik, then at me. He nodded towards Terian.

"All right."

"No!" Revik screamed, fighting the hands holding him.

Jerking me sideways by the collar, Terian dragged me towards the gate and the field. I heard Revik's anguished cry and nearly lost my mind. Craning backwards to look at him, I let out a scream as well, struggling against Terian's hands.

The scream turned into a sob as I saw him fighting the other seers.

Terian dragged me forward despite my struggles. In a matter of minutes I couldn't see Revik anymore, though I could still hear him. I willed my light, every part of myself in his direction. Half dragged and half shoved through the thigh-high grass, I eventually opened my eyes on what looked like a Jeep parked on one side of the field, a few dozen yards away.

Something in me broke.

I lunged against Terian's hands, leaping off my feet to throw him off balance.

He caught me around the waist, dragging me forcibly through the grass.

I lunged again at each step, fighting harder the further we went, trying to get free—until he gave up and simply picked me up. Slinging me over his shoulder, he held my waist with one arm, clamping my legs with the other. When he motioned to one of the guards, I felt metal on my ankles as he chained those together, too.

The boy followed, but that time, he didn't protest.

I glanced down and found him staring at me, his eyes still holding that faint glow. The look in them remained hard from his conversation with Revik.

I begged him to let me go.

When that didn't work, I begged Terian.

The latter forced me into the back of the Jeep. One of his men cuffed me to the door with a third set of handcuffs.

The boy sat next to me, his hand on my leg. I stared at his small fingers, then back at the cabin, screaming when Terian started up the Jeep's engine, throwing myself against the metal cuffs. He put the vehicle in gear and hit the gas, bumping and driving across the field.

I watched the cabin grow smaller in the distance.

Terian ground gears as we bounced over holes and hillocks, accelerating until he pulled up alongside a helicopter parked in a flat area by the river.

Seeing where we were, I burst into another sob, fighting until my wrists bled.

The boy tried to stop me, but I elbowed him off angrily.

It was the same place Revik and I picnicked the first day we'd taken out the horses.

By the time Terian unlocked me from the Jeep, picking me up and carrying me across the grass and through the helicopter door, the drug was finally taking its toll. I managed to keep my eyes open while he locked me to the bench in the back of the military helicopter. In the front seat, I saw a woman with black hair and the bluest eyes I'd ever seen.

She smiled at me, but those eyes remained cold as ice.

"Everything go okay?" she asked Terian.

"Well as could be expected," he grunted.

She looked me over, lips pursed. "She's a little underfed. Pretty, though. I suppose that's why you forgot her clothes?"

Terian smiled. "The boy didn't seem to mind."

The woman chuckled, exhaling smoke. "No, he doesn't seem to." Glancing back at the boy, she motioned towards me with the hand holding the *hiri.* "And Dehgoies?"

"He's alive." Terian shrugged. "Not much I could do. They'd been fucking for at least a week." He put on headphones, raising his voice above the cycling blades. "I left Tor and David to patch him up. I'll call when we get a little farther south."

She nodded, but a hardness touched her mouth.

I watched, numb, as the boy slid closer, leaning against my side.

A few seconds later, the rotary blades got louder as the helicopter began to lift off the ground.

I managed to stay awake a few seconds longer as we rose over the fields. I stared down until the river looked like a winding snake through the plexiglass window near the metal bar where I'd been cuffed. I could no longer see the house.

I was crying, but I held onto what I'd heard Terian say.

Those seers were patching him up. Terian would call, and someone would find Revik before he bled to death or died of exposure under those stairs.

Feeling eyes on me again, I turned.

I found the blue-eyed woman staring at me. Her eyes examined my body in detail, lingering on different parts of my skin. Barely glancing at the bruises she was focused on, I leaned back on the cushion.

More tears ran down my face, making it hard to breathe.

Not long after that, I must have passed out.

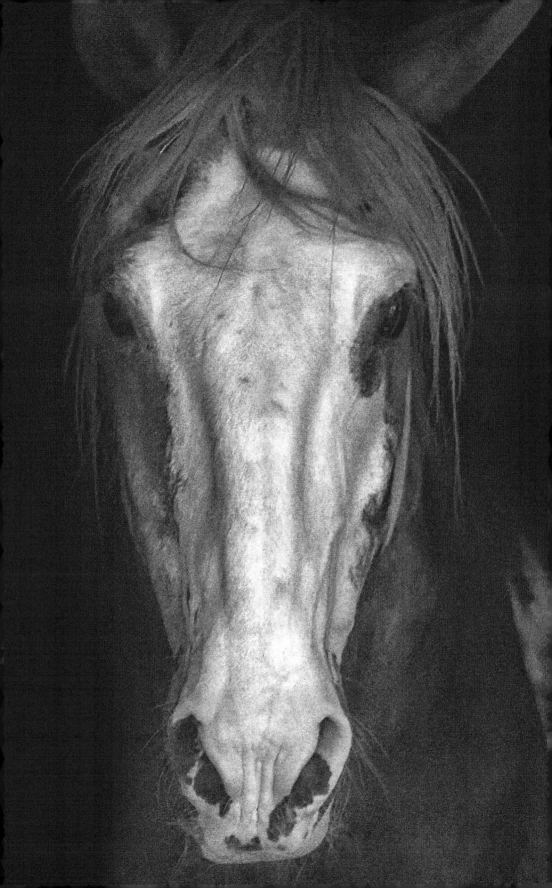

CHAPTER 30
WVERCIANS

R evik woke up in the dirt, unable to breathe.

His arms felt wrenched out of their sockets. His throat hurt. His head felt like it was being crushed in an iron vise, his pulse throbbing against the skin of his temples from whatever drug they'd given him.

He looked up to where the cuffs he wore locked to a chain that wound around the bottom supports to the wooden stairs. Looking around where he lay, he tried to scan in reflex. The organic collar shot pain up through his skull, temporarily blinding him.

It was nothing like the pain he'd endured in that glass and tile dungeon in the Carpathians... but with how he felt, it briefly knocked him out.

The second time, he was more cautious.

Extending his light, he tried to find the boundaries of where the restraint kicked in. He tried to get a sense of what type of collar it was, where the limits had been set. The second jolt was less severe.

It broke him out in a sweat, temporarily blinding him, but didn't knock him out.

Even so, it was effective. He couldn't get past it.

He tried anyway, testing it again, using a number of different kinds of scans. He fought for any glimpse through, any means of sending out a flare to someone who might be looking for him. He couldn't tell if any of it worked, but he doubted it.

All he knew for sure was she was gone.

He wasn't ready to feel that yet.

He tried to move, to sit up, and liquid fire shot down his spine, hurting him enough to make him sick, nearly blacking him out. He threw up, vomiting bile on the dirt from his empty stomach, just before he crumpled back to his side.

He'd forgotten about the leg.

He needed water.

After that, food.

He was too weak to do much of anything for long, if he didn't deal with those two things. Staring up at the lightening sky, he fought not to feel, ignoring the smell of his own vomit. No matter how many times it tried to rise, he forced the image of Allie, collared, naked and covered in bruises, out of his mind.

Minutes passed with him lying in the dirt, fighting to control his mind, before he realized the seers bandaged his leg before they left. So they'd only meant to hobble him after all... not kill him.

He supposed he had Terian to thank for that.

He wondered if Terry actually called the Adhipan, like he said he would.

He also wondered why Terian hadn't sent someone back to collect him yet. The boy must have him on a short leash. He'd obviously been displeased with the kid's decision to leave him behind.

He tried to think through scenarios, if only to occupy his mind.

Terian might take her to a cave, like he had with him and Jon and Cass, but Revik doubted it. He would feel safer in the United States. Most of the Rooks in Europe and Asia would be off the grid still; some would still resent him for his coup of Galaith, if not blame him outright for the demise of the Pyramid.

Galaith, whatever his faults, always had the gift of engendering loyalty.

Terian did not.

The sun rose over the valley. Revik watched every incremental movement of its path off the horizon, feeling his breath come short.

The star was most of the way in the sky when he found himself choking again, fighting to breathe. His skin hurt, every part of him. He forced her out of his mind, her face out from behind his eyes. He fought out every stray thought about where she was, what might be happening to her.

He spent the next few hours trying to get out of the cuffs.

He considered biting his wrist, trying to squeeze out of them that way.

The same thought seemed to have occurred to Terian's guards, though. They'd cinched the organic metal cuffs all the way down, until they bruised the bone. He couldn't risk bleeding out in the dirt if it didn't work.

He used the chain to saw at the wood instead, working in hard bursts until his arms were so exhausted he had to rest.

The sun was higher in the sky by then.

He was thirsty, hungry, and the sun was starting to feel hot. He felt sick from pain, and increasingly, from the wound in his leg. He wondered if they'd bothered to dig the metal out before they bandaged him up.

He decided they must have, or he'd feel even worse.

He went back to sawing at the wood, until again, after five or six more bursts of muscle and intent, he was forced to stop.

It seemed like time went on like that forever.

Lying in the dirt, half-dead with pain, fighting emotions that tried to rise… then forcing himself to move, sawing at the wood until his muscles could no longer stand the strain… then back to lying in the dirt, trying not to feel.

The sound crept up on him.

He'd taken another break from fighting the wooden support.

He guessed he'd made it about a fifth of the way into the segment of wood he would need to shave off before he could crack the base of the step with his arms and foot. He almost didn't notice the sound at first.

Then, he wondered if he was dreaming.

The sound got louder.

Horses.

He opened his eyes. Turning his head, he squinted through the glare, and saw three horses enter the gate at a canter. They seemed to come up on him fast, given how gradually the sound rose in his awareness.

The first one pulled up near the steps and Revik found himself looking up at a broad, wind-burned face. He didn't know it specifically. He didn't know the others, either, despite their similarity to one another.

Anyway, he would have expected a helicopter from Balidor—not these three giant brutes on shaggy, long-maned mounts.

Looking from one face to the other, he tensed more and more. He recognized the broad, Asian-like features, the deep black eyes. Apart from the color of their irises, each of them had identical, almost-albino coloring, with white hair matted and greased to a darker yellow in thick braids down their backs.

Wvercians.

Revik hadn't seen any like them since he was young, maybe an adolescent.

He watched them take turns looking at him from their horses.

Hand gestures passed between what appeared to be their leader and the other two riding with him. Then the youngest-looking of the three jumped off his horse with a graceful slip of his leg, and ran up the stairs.

Revik felt the seer's feet shudder the wood he was chained to, just before the door to the house slammed. He looked back at the others.

"Help me," he said in Prexci. His voice came out hoarse, a thick whisper. He spoke to the leader, seeing the dark eyes focused emotionlessly on him. "Please. They took my wife. Please. Help me."

The leader swung off his saddle, leaping down as lightly as the first man, despite his considerable girth. As he stood over Revik, it occurred to the latter that the man could probably kill him with one sharp kick to the throat.

Wvercians were generally nomads, and warlike.

Smugglers. Opportunists. For the most part, they didn't follow Code. When they did, it was a different version from the one Revik was raised in. They'd been known to smuggle children, and women. They tended to form their own tribes, ignoring the clan laws of the other seers as they competed amongst themselves. They'd aligned with humans as often as their brother-seers over the past one hundred or so years.

From the well-bred horses he could see under the shaggy manes, and the organic rifles he saw slung in their saddles, these three must be doing well for themselves.

"The house is mine," he said in Prexci. "I give it to you. Everything in it. It will be legal." He pointed towards the river. "Horses down there. Those are mine, too. Full-sized. One draft. At least one thoroughbred. Ten in total."

The leader smiled.

He looked at the other man, who leaned over the pommel of an over-sized Tibetan-style saddle, peering at Revik's face. He pointed at the organic bandage, saying something Revik didn't catch. The leader smiled, saying something back in a language Revik recognized as a bastardized form of Prexci mixed with Mandarin.

Their accents were so thick he only picked out words, a few phrases.

The one who remained on his horse spoke the most.

(some kind of insult) "...here to rob him." (the man laughed, and said something else Revik didn't catch) "...knows about the...?" (something else) "...Bridge? Same person as..." (something else he didn't catch).

Revik stiffened at the mention of Allie.

The leader didn't seem to notice. He grunted, motioning in affirmation.

The one on the horse spoke again.

"...leave alone if the..." (something else that sounded insulting) "...orders?" (something else) "...dead? She couldn't have..." (something else he missed) "...few thousand in his own..." (Revik was pretty sure the word was "army").

He looked between them. He'd started grinding at the wood of the steps again with the chains, almost unconsciously.

If they knew who Allie was, they might not be here to help him.

Where the *fuck* was Balidor?

The third Wvercian exited the house, half-running down the steps.

At the leader's level look, he gestured negative. The leader grunted, then looked down at Revik, his black eyes devoid of feeling.

"You are Dehgoies Revik?" he asked in heavily accented Prexci.

Revik hesitated. He looked between the three of them, then decided he didn't have the luxury to be coy.

"Yes," he said.

The leader looked him over, then motioned towards the youngest of the three Wvercians. Revik stiffened, trying to push his body backwards when the smallest giant pulled his heavily modified organic rifle off his saddle. It had organics in the stock, too, which likely meant some kind of high-caliber ammunition. Revik stared at it, watching as the man clicked off the safety and raised it to his shoulder.

"Wait!" he yelled, holding up a hand. "Wait! The Bridge!"

The man with the rifle lowered it slowly, his eyes puzzled.

Revik spoke faster, louder. "You're looking for her… right? If you kill me, you kill her! She's my mate! I swear to the gods she is! Take off the collar, and you'll see. Check the telltale. She and I are one…"

The man with the rifle looked at the leader, his eyes bewildered.

The other two laughed. The one on the saddle motioned at the one with the rifle. A thick scar ran across his forehead and down beside one eye.

(a string of run-together words) "…thinks you're going to kill him!"

The leader motioned for the young one to proceed, then turned to Revik.

"Hold still," he said, pronouncing the words deliberately.

Revik did. He watched the youngest of the three seers aim at the chain around the base of the stairs.

Realizing what was happening, he closed his eyes, turning his face away.

There was a metallic clang, and hot metal burned his arm.

He winced, but when he moved, the chain came free. His wrists were still cuffed, but no longer to one another… or, more importantly, to the stairs.

He sat up with an effort, gasping a little when he jarred the shot leg.

"Thank you," he said, gesturing respectfully. "Thank you."

"Can you walk?" the leader asked.

Revik winced, trying to pull himself closer to the stairs.

"I don't know," he said.

They looked at one another. "Can you ride?" the leader asked.

Revik nodded, looking between them. "Yeah."

He started to pull himself up the first stair towards the house. He heard them talking amongst themselves. Then the one with the gun got in his way, motioning him off with his hands, his gestures adamant.

"No," he said in Prexci. "Stay!"

Revik pointed towards the house. "I need clothes." He looked at the leader. At the blank look on the giant seer, he gestured in sign language. *Clothes. There are some inside. I need my gun.*

The one on the horse laughed, saying something in a joking tone.

But the smallest one vaulted up the stairs again, past Revik and into the house, once more letting the door slam behind him. Revik lay there on the wood, happy to be out of the sun. He was still slumped with his back against the steps, when the leader pulled a canteen off his horse. Walking over, he offered it to him.

Revik nodded in thanks, and drank for a full minute.

He was still drinking when the youngest Wvercian clomped back down the stairs, holding out clothes. Revik saw he'd gone into the refrigerator too. He handed containers to the man on the horse, then walked back to Revik, handing him a shirt and a pair of loose, cotton pants, both Chinese in style. Revik struggled into them while the three Wvercians talked amongst themselves in low voices.

The younger one handed him a container of food when Revik tried to get up.

Revik waved it off, but the young seer thrust it forward again.

"Eat," the leader said. "We will go soon." He used his hands to indicate a person falling off a horse. "Ouch," he said, smiling.

"Yeah," Revik said. "Ouch."

Reluctantly, he took the container off the young seer, fighting impatience as he dug his fingers into the thick pile of greens and pasta in the wooden box.

He was still putting fingers-full of the casserole in his mouth, swallowing without a lot of chewing, when the leader approached him with what looked like a pair of bolt cutters, made of some kind of organic.

"Hold still," he told Revik.

Revik froze as the giant fitted the cutting tool under the collar he wore. He felt the round loop of the collar drop into the notch inside the shears. Then the massive seer squeezed the handles together, his trunk-like arms flexing. Revik flinched as the cutters grazed his skin, nicking the side of his throat. He gasped a little as he felt the organic in the collar die, just before it broke apart on his neck.

The two prongs at the top of his spine unwound.

The mechanism clunked open.

Wincing, Revik pulled it out of the holes in his neck, letting it drop to the dirt. For a moment, he only rubbed his neck, nodding again in thanks to the other seers, unable to speak. The world gained dimension around him as he flexed his light.

He could see the seers now, and relaxed a little.

He still couldn't feel her.

He forced it out of his mind, even as the pain worsened briefly, making it hard to see at all. He looked up at the broad-faced seer. His outline appeared less flat, but if anything, the three of them looked even more intimidating.

"Thank you," he said, nodding again. Gratitude briefly closed his throat. "Will you take me as far as Seertown? I will pay you. Well. Very well."

At their puzzled looks, he looked around at each face.

"I will pay you very well," he repeated in Mandarin. "I will pay each one of you, for even the loan of a horse, if you cannot take me. Simply tell me how best to make arrangements with you."

The leader glanced at the other two.

The man in the saddle shrugged, gesturing vaguely, nodding towards Revik.

The leader sighed, facing him.

Seertown is gone, little one, he sent, speaking directly into Revik's mind. *They bombed it into the ground. Just this past night.*

Revik halted in mid-motion, about to take another clump of greens into his mouth. He could only stare at the hulking seer. His mind tried to reject the information, then to make sense of it. He couldn't get his mind off Allie, even for this; he couldn't help but think about this in terms of her.

It explained why Balidor hadn't come at least.

"Who?" he asked finally. "American?" He made the correct motion in sign language. "The planes? Were they American?"

The giant seer smiled, but his eyes grew flat.

Who cares which worm flag they fly? They came in their dead machines and they bombed the town until every seer in it was run away or murdered.

Taking his canteen from Revik's hand, he took a long drink, gesturing up towards the house.

We are here for you, brother. We come seeking the Bridge and her mate.

Revik fought the pain in his chest. He clutched at the cotton shirt, forcing more food in his mouth, if only to distract himself.

Did Balidor send you? he asked finally.

The giant seer smiled, but Revik once again saw him exchange looks with the others. They still weren't telling him something.

He kept his nerves out of his light.

"Does any of you have a smoke?" he asked, to dispel the tension. "*Hiri?*"

The one on the horse threw him a stick.

Revik put it to his lips. He inhaled on the end while the one who'd shot at his chains leaned close, cupping his rough hand around a flame housed in a silver lighter.

We were sent by friends, the leader told him. *We will take you there now.* Smiling, he gestured towards the wooden bowl. "Eat!" he said. *We ride soon.*

Where are we going? Revik asked. He kept his thoughts neutral.

The larger seer made a vague gesture.

To base camp first. We will get supplies, fix your leg. He smiled, his dark eyes flat, doll-like. *Then we go looking for her, yes?*

Revik smiled, bowing politely in gratitude, but he felt his mind growing sharper as he scanned around the giant's light.

The youngest of the Wvercians motioned for him to hold out his arms. Using the same cutting tool that broke the collar, he cracked the bracelets of the handcuffs, one by one. Revik continued to focus his light on the other two, rubbing his wrists.

The thing about Seertown appeared to be true.

He got glimpses of burning buildings, the town's evacuation sirens going off while planes screamed overhead. He'd felt something earlier, anyway. When Terian's guards were kicking the crap out of him on the steps. Whatever it had been, it made the Wvercians' story ring true, even apart from what he felt in their minds.

None of the three seemed to be trained as infiltrators, but he was extremely careful as he scanned their light. He couldn't afford to anger them.

For now, it was better to pretend he believed everything they told him.

In any case, he was reasonably sure they weren't taking him to Balidor.

THE RIDE ACROSS THE FIELD AND DOWN THROUGH A NARROW, ROCK-FILLED canyon via a winding goat trail wasn't comfortable.

Even when they reached the green meadow at the other side of the canyon, every step of the horse jostled his leg, sending harsh stabs up to his hip.

He'd broken at least one major bone.

On his instructions, they'd brought him the roan with the red face, and saddled him with a few of the sheepskin blankets, thinking a regular saddle would be too rigid. They were likely right, but having to grip with his legs to stay on was its own kind of torture.

He felt sick within an hour from pain.

He was having a harder time not thinking about Allie.

Away from the house, it seemed to worsen.

The worse the physical pain got, the more it confused him, blending in with wanting her. A part of his light scanned for her compulsively, even as he fought out the images that wanted to play out in the forefront of his mind with her and Terian.

Or, more perversely, her and the boy.

He tried to get the three Wvercians to talk.

He tried to learn more about Seertown, where they were taking him—anything to feel he was using the time, not just wasting it while she got further away.

They didn't avoid his questions entirely, but they circumvented them in odd tangents, giving vague answers whenever he tried to pin them down on details.

After multiple queries, he finally learned that the Americans had, indeed, been involved in the bombing of Seertown.

Revik always assumed most seers knew of the infighting in the seer community between the Rooks and the Seven, and that the Rooks had heavily infiltrated the United States government, as well as SCARB and the World Court.

The Wvercians seemed to find such details unimportant.

To them, the source of the problem was clean, straightforward, and could be encompassed in a single, all-inclusive word: humans.

Revik wondered if there'd ever been a time when the world seemed so simple to him.

He was unable to find out from them if the Council of Seven escaped intact, or even if Vash had lived. They were able to tell him the compound suffered multiple and direct hits, and that the old House on the Hill had been hit as well. The stone structure predated First Contact with the humans, and was one of the oldest known seer-built structures standing in nearly its original form. The catacombs underneath housed irreplaceable artifacts, even bodies of the first race prior to their extinction.

It was also home to an extensive archive that housed original scriptures and other documents brought from the Pamir.

Revik had never been invited down there, but the place was considered sacred.

He tried to think if he had any other contacts living nearby.

His mind drifted to Tarsi.

She wasn't exactly a soldier these days, but he didn't have a lot of options.

The reality was, Revik didn't have many friends in India or China anymore. He hadn't spent much time in Asia at all since his "rehabilitation." Since leaving the Rooks, he'd only come here once, to live in caves with reclusive monks, in a kind of hell of his mind and light, with only monthly visits from Vash to monitor his progress.

He certainly hadn't made any friends.

Those years consisted of meditation and light restructuring under the guarded eye of a sect of monks who, with only a few exceptions, rarely spoke to him.

When that phase of his penance ended, Vash relocated him immediately, initially to Russia, where Revik spent more years alone.

At the time, Vash made it sound like that was part of his penance, too, so Revik hadn't felt he could exactly refuse. He'd been out of the Pamir's caves for less than a week before he was handed a new passport and a bus ticket to Delhi, followed by a flight to Berlin and then on to Moscow where housing for him had already been arranged.

After Russia, he didn't return to Asia, either, but flew straight from Moscow to the United Kingdom. At that point, his surveillance of Allie required more on-the-ground work, which meant he needed to be accessible. Not so close that the Rooks might use him to find her, but near enough to reach her if needed.

The Seven found him a paid position in London, working for humans.

He hadn't been back to Asia since, not until now.

Galaith never had him working in Asia much, either, at least from what he could remember. Well, apart from Vietnam, but even that was a short tour.

Not long after Revik left those monk caves, he'd been formally tasked with protecting Allie, so that was part of it. They didn't want it to seem he was doing anything important, much less working directly for Vash. They encouraged him to keep up the façade of a "normal" seer life, one unaffiliated with either the Seven or the Rooks.

That life primarily involved paid sex, his job for the humans, the odd infiltrator job, occasional recreational travel, some socializing with other seers.

Nothing that would call attention to him, in other words.

Vash didn't explicitly forbid him to return to Asia, but it was strongly implied that he wasn't welcome there. He definitely wasn't welcome in Seertown, but he was also strongly discouraged from visiting any other part of India, China, or Southeast Asia.

Eventually, Vash didn't want him in Russia, either, or even Eastern Europe, not even for visits.

When necessary, Revik met Vash in the Barrier, inside one of Vash's many constructs.

When Revik got restless, he headed west, not east.

He'd tried not to take it personally.

It had to have been a controversial decision to allow him back at all, given who he was. He knew he was chosen to guard Allie partly because no one would have believed Vash would give him such an important responsibility. And there was Allie herself. Her security had to be a priority, as well as the necessity of keeping her, and therefore her protection, anonymous. He couldn't be a regular fixture in Vash's circle, or someone might decide he was worth monitoring a little more closely.

The cover had worked well. No one came near him in those years.

He'd worked for the humans dutifully, and that felt appropriate, too.

He woke up when the roan splashed into a stream.

Jerking his head, he looked around in some alarm, realizing he'd dozed off. From the horse walking beside the roan, the seer with the scar on his face was watching him, curiosity in his dark eyes.

After a pause, the man grinned, pointing vaguely at Revik's crotch.

"Married?" he said, leering. "Good, eh? The Bridge?"

Revik stared blankly at the seer. Biting back what he would have liked to say, he pulled the canteen off his belt, taking a long drink of water. He was a little feverish. He couldn't afford to get sick, not for any reason.

How long? he asked the leader.

Not long, Small. Not long now.

Where are we going?

Not far. They are waiting for you already.

Waiting for me? Revik felt a brief flicker of hope. *Who? Adhipan?*

The man made a "more or less" gesture with his hand. *Some Adhipan. We save who we can. Of the worthy.*

"The worthy." Revik repeated the words aloud. He fought his voice neutral. "Aren't we all worthy... friend?"

The leader smiled. *Can't save everyone, little brother. Victory without quarter, yes? Have to keep your eyes on the end point.*

Revik didn't answer, but his nerves rose. Something in the wording of that response hit a less-often accessed part of his mind. The energetic after-tone of the words resonated in his light in a way he didn't much like.

He glanced down at his leg, wincing as the horse jostled it.

Blood was starting to seep through the organic bandages.

Whoever they really were, it didn't matter.

He didn't much care whose side he played on, not anymore.

CHAPTER 31

MEN

The explosion flared up out of the darkness under the trees.

Cass watched it go, feeling a part of her go silent inside.

She'd never been in a bombing before. If someone had told her a year ago that she would be in the mountains of Asia, living among seers and running from bombs dropped by American planes, she would have laughed.

She wasn't laughing now.

The explosion seemed to originate from the area of town Balidor called the 8th District. Cass had seen bombs fall on the 8th earlier, so the fires must have found something larger and more flammable. It looked like half the district was on fire now.

Chandre had been going there.

She would have heard the planes, though, Cass reasoned.

She was an infiltrator. She'd probably been in lots of things like this.

Well, maybe not *lots*, but she hardly compared to members of the barista and musician slacker crowds Cass hung with back home. Anyway, Chandre had her seer powers. She could sidestep an explosion, just like Balidor had steered Cass away from that castle-like building right before the upper windows blew out from heat and flame.

Cass's bigger worry was Jon.

He'd been asleep in the compound like the rest of them when the bombs first started to fall, but he took off somewhere before the groups started to check in, and Balidor hadn't been able to locate him. Knowing Jon, he was probably pulling babies out of burning buildings or something equally nuts.

She just hoped the idiot didn't get himself killed.

Even as she thought it, a formation of planes came around for another pass, veering lower to aim missiles at the town of Seertown proper.

Cass winced as rockets screamed towards the main market, leaving white trails. They connected with brick and tile buildings in precise, symmetrical patterns, and explosions mushroomed out of the walls and roofs, collapsing whole stories, trembling the ground.

The rumbling concussions echoed through the small valley.

The whole thing felt unreal, but for the smell, the screaming and the people she saw—like the monk now running down the street below them, his robes on fire, his dark face covered in blood.

Swallowing, she looked up as another formation flashed overhead.

Gripping her gun tighter, she blinked sweat and smoke out of her eyes, fighting to block out the screams.

It already felt like this had been going on for days.

The planes themselves still looked American to Cass, but she'd heard seers arguing back and forth about that over the virtual network. The one advantage to being in a firefight; Cass could actually hear what was going on as seers dropped out of the Barrier to hide from other seers. They relied on regular old human technology to communicate instead, ironically because they were less likely to be overheard.

The castle-like building seers called simply "The Old House" or "The House on the Hill," burned high above Seertown. The castle's ancient, symmetrical gardens burned as well, including the bare white trees with their animalistic-looking branches. They decorated the manicured lawn along a spiral path, interspersed with moss-covered statues and benches made of white stone.

It had been one of Cass's favorite places in Seertown.

Now the castle and its grounds looked like something out of an apocalyptic fairytale.

She watched fire blow out more windows on the upper floors, ribboning tapestries. It climbed higher when a breeze caught hold of the flames, jumping them to the next set of rooms. Down the hill from where she and Balidor stood, a second, significantly heavier explosion trembled the ridge, shaking the ground under their legs.

Then a third.

That wasn't from a missile.

They must be back to dropping bombs. It had been dark when they started, and now the sun had passed the zenith in the sky.

They were trying to annihilate them. To kill off the seers for good.

"Maybe," Balidor said quietly, looking out over the same scene.

Cass looked at him. He'd been so still beside her, she'd forgotten how close he was.

Her eyes returned to the 8th District. Plumes of fire rose, staining the black smoke and clouds briefly red. She saw a second burst of flame follow the first, blinked in the sudden radiance as it lit the disjointed array of brick buildings.

"It ignited something," she said, unnecessarily. "Just how much ammo and fuel do you guys have stored up here?"

Balidor focused on the same area of the 8th, his face granite.

Cass studied his expression. "Allie. Have you heard anything from—"

"No," he said.

Cass was still watching Balidor's face when the shots came.

Two of the nearby Adhipan dropped at once, ducking behind cover to return fire. Balidor grabbed Cass's wrist before she could turn her head.

He dragged her into a small grove of trees, pushing her up against a wide trunk. He held his gun but did not fire, shielding her with his arm and holding her against the thickest part of the tree. She touched her own gun, but he gave her a warning look.

Sighing, she took her hand off the holster.

More protection.

He didn't want to be responsible for killing the Bridge's human.

It occurred to her also that he might be not-firing himself to disguise their numbers. She'd heard infiltrators talk about how they often tried to obscure their forces in one direction or the other during military engagements.

Either way, she just stood there, wincing whenever bullets struck near enough to throw up chunks of wood. She watched Balidor's face. He held her against the trunk with one arm, using hand-signals to communicate with the other seers.

Then he froze, as if listening.

Cass saw shapes whisper by them, running down the hill so fast they looked like ghosts. She watched two in the Adhipan run after them. Balidor hesitated, then gave her a fleetingly apologetic look.

He leaned his mouth by her ear.

"Find cover. Don't go into Seertown. And be careful! I don't feel any more, but don't stay here. Go higher. I'm leaving Pradaj with you."

He kissed her on the cheek, startling her.

Then he released her, running down the slope after the others.

She saw him briefly silhouetted as he ran off the edge of a small cliff. She heard a faint crashing sound as tree branches swayed in the ravine below.

The sounds receded. When she glanced to one side, she saw Pradaj, another middle-aged seer, but a bit more beat up than Balidor. His dark face was scarred, and he looked East Indian. She raised a hand in greeting and he smiled wanly in return, as if amused with her wave in the aftermath of a gunfight.

She was about to speak, when a shot rang out.

Pradaj collapsed. Falling to his back, he lay there and didn't move.

Cass froze, paralyzed. She stared at his body.

He'd been shot in the head. Panting, she looked around, heart hammering in her chest as it hit her she was alone. She looked out over the ravine, wondering if she should try to sprint after Balidor and the others.

She was still standing there when the voice spoke.

"Men," it said, clicking ruefully. "They're just not reliable, are they?"

Cass turned, feeling something twist in her belly.

She found herself facing a smile she recognized, on a face she didn't.

"Your friend Chandre wouldn't have left you in the lurch like this." He pointed a gun enhanced with organics at her chest. "...now would she?"

Cass felt her belly knot so violently her bowels nearly voided.

She gripped the tree's trunk, staring at a face she'd never seen before, but that she recognized nonetheless. The Asian man smiled at her, his black hair twisted into a clip at the back of his head. His trench coat was stained white with ash and smoke.

"How are you, Cassandra? You're looking well."

She fumbled frantically to unholster her Glock.

"Uh, uh... no." He motioned with his hand.

She looked down to where his gun already pointed at her.

He waited for her to make up her mind, smiling as he studied her eyes.

"We're old friends now, you and I," he said. "...and while we could do this the usual way, with me shooting you, or overpowering your feeble worm mind, I'd rather have you see reason." His voice grew cajoling.

"Lose the gun, lover. I won't hurt you this time. Promise."

Staring at his hand holding the gun, she tried to disobey.

She would rather be dead than go anywhere with him.

But her hand wouldn't do what she wanted. She stared at him, fighting to breathe, gasping with the effort of trying to lift the gun higher, to aim it at him.

He'd been lying of course, like he always lied.

He was in her mind, controlling her.

Saying it was her choice was just another of his headfuck games.

He reached out, closing his hand around the Glock.

He took it from her, his fingers surprisingly gentle.

Cass watched her gun disappear to an inside pocket of his coat, feeling every nerve in her body scream. Adrenaline coursed through her limbs, causing them to shake. She wanted to attack him, to rip at his face with her bare hands.

He clicked at her. The sound held a tinge of amusement.

"Give me the book, Cassandra," he said.

Reaching into the bag slung across her shoulder, she opened it, her hands shaking. After a brief battle between her limbs, mind, and heart, she gripped the thick, leather-bound book and handed it to him wordlessly.

"Good girl," he said. "Now turn around. We're going for a little walk."

For another collection of seconds, she struggled to disobey.

She was still standing there, half-panting from the exertion, when a massive form appeared from behind the largest of the nearby trees.

Cass looked up at him, doubting her senses.

The giant put a thick finger to his pink lips.

Black eyes stared at her from a flat, Asian-featured face with pale skin. He looked like a Viking. A half-Chinese albino Viking wearing animal skins, with some kind of fancy organic headset wrapped around his skull. She focused on the Viking's hands.

He carried what looked like…

Holy bejeesus, it was a sword.

She was still staring when the Viking plunged the four-foot, serrated blade through the middle of the new Terian's abdomen.

Cass could only stand there, paralyzed, as Terian screamed, lifted off his feet by the sword with the jagged teeth. The blade glowed, as if surrounded by some kind of faint electric field. Whatever it was, it allowed the Viking to cut him nearly in half, using the sword to slice up through his rib cage and solar plexus.

The blade got jammed on something around where his neck met his shoulders, and the giant grunted, shaking the body like a dog might shake a rat.

Eventually, impatience won out.

Shoving Terian forward to brace his body against a tree, the giant propped a heavy, fur-lined boot on his back.

With another grunt, he yanked upwards to free the blade.

Whatever Terian had been using to hold Cass's mind released her the instant the sword vacated his flesh.

Right about the same time, the body stopped screaming.

What remained of Terian collapsed to the ground.

Cass watched it twitch, still spurting blood from the long cut bisecting the Asian man's body. Eventually, the spurts of blood slowed.

She looked up at the giant.

For a moment, the two of them just stood there.

Then, reaching down, the giant picked up the leather-bound book and brushed it off with his thick fingers. Smiling, he handed it back to Cass. He patted her head affectionately, gesturing at her upper arm. Cass looked down at where the blue and white sword and sun tattoo stood out on her tanned skin.

Lifting his own shirt sleeve, the giant showed her the same mark.

His was a brand, not a tattoo, and much older, but he grinned at her when she stepped forward to brush it with her fingers.

Studying his black eyes, Cass felt herself relax.

The albino motioned at her, using his hands, head, and arms.

Making the seer gesture for "yes," she tucked the leather-bound book back into her shoulder bag, fastening the leather straps.

Without a word, she followed him into the trees.

CHAPTER 32
REBELLION

Balidor stood inside a circle of white-skinned trees. Moss-covered statues lined a path of white stones dotted with cairns and granite benches. The garden beneath the House on the Hill was almost as old as the structure itself.

Thankfully, it had started to rain.

The rain came down in sheets—one of those late-in-the-day summer storms that were so common in this part of the Himalayas.

As for the meeting itself, United States General Gregor Cardesian, nicknamed "The Apostle" by the American press, chose the location. Balidor found it an odd one, but this had been a day of things he couldn't comprehend.

Exhaustion was starting to wear on him, and he knew most of it wasn't physical. He let his gaze run over lines of blue and camouflage uniforms, only half-seeing them.

He shouldn't have left Cass.

He wouldn't have, but Vash made the request.

Balidor understood the request, given what happened, but he didn't fully agree with it.

He also felt dangerously low on people at the moment. He'd sent a few Adhipan to the 8th to ascertain the severity of the situation. He had a few more working to aid civilians and monks in Seertown itself. Of those senior infiltrators remaining—those who weren't dead or injured from the carpet bombing—he'd sent over half to find and protect Allie and her mate.

Balidor was still convinced this bombing was about her.

His eyes paused on burning strings of prayer flags over one section of the garden. Looking up the hill at the blackened, white-trunked trees and ash-filled sky, Balidor found that the gardens looked positively ancient to him suddenly.

So did Vash.

The Apostle parted lines of infantry, gazing perfunctorily around at fires dotting the water-logged buildings of Seertown. He'd gotten the name "Apostle" in the last set of seer purges. It struck Balidor that even if he had been an extremely young man at the time, that put Cardesian northward of seventy human years.

He looked a great deal less.

His iron-gray hair managed to remain absolutely in place to spite the wind and rain. His close-set eyes sparked with intelligence, and not a small amount of arrogance.

Ignoring Vash, the Apostle strode directly up to Balidor.

He laid thick fingers on his shoulder and squeezed in a friendly manner.

"It is good to see you, Mr. Balidor," he said. "I do wish that the circumstances were less... formal."

Balidor sighed internally at the implication that he should feel honored to be so singled out. Human politics were so heavy-handed as to be entirely obnoxious.

That is, when he couldn't afford to find them amusing, like now.

"Formal?" He stared at the human. "I think we can preclude with pleasantries, Cardesian. Your presence here alone violates at least three post-war treaties. As for the bombing—"

"We didn't do that."

Balidor raised an eyebrow. "Really? So those weren't American planes I saw dropping bombs just now? Killing monks? Our elderly? Refugees? What about the human children you have killed? Does that not matter to you, either, friend?"

The Apostle frowned, removing his hand.

"I see that your species' penchant for dramatic overstatement hasn't lessened." He looked around, as if assessing the location anew. "We have a few choppers nearby. We came to offer assistance."

"Assistance?" Balidor looked at Vash.

The ancient seer stood unconcerned, despite his bound wrists.

Near him stood three seers Balidor recognized.

There weren't many at their level he didn't know, no matter who they worked for. One, Eldrake, he remembered in particular. He'd worked under Galaith since the time of the Nazis. Balidor ran into him a few times in Eastern Europe, including at the death camps.

"Yes," Balidor said. His eyes swiveled back to Cardesian. "Your intentions seem perfectly friendly. That's why you have bound and collared the most respected holy man in our city." He gestured pointedly at the lines of troops. "And pardon my asking, but if they were not *your* American planes, whose American planes were they, General?"

"We're working on that."

"What does that mean?"

Cardesian adjusted his belt, in a way that might have amused Balidor under different circumstances. It was obviously some sort of male dominance display.

The human's voice grew into a warning.

"We got here by tracking the groundies you're fighting. They aren't flying the Chink flag, but crossed our lines close enough to be a threat. Our icebloods tell us most of them are seers. So we had to take an interest." His frown deepened. "No one's claiming responsibility, at least not yet. But we can't just wait for them to head back north, to Bei-fucking-jing."

"General," Balidor said, clicking in irritation. "I have no idea what any of that means."

Cardesian held up a hand to silence him.

Frowning, he seemed to be listening to something through his headset.

When he looked at Balidor next, his voice hardened.

"Intelligence is telling me now that this 'unprovoked attack' was an attempt to gain custody over a highly dangerous and illegal seer," he said. "I don't suppose you'd know anything about *that*, would you, Mr. Balidor?"

Balidor started to open his mouth, but Cardesian cut him off.

"After that mess last year, I would have thought you'd help us *contain* the situation, Balidor. Not hide her up here like some kind of prize whore."

"General." Balidor sighed. "I have absolutely no idea what you're—"

"Just how stupid do you think we are?"

Balidor paused, uncertain at first if the human wanted an answer. He glanced at the seers protecting Cardesian's light.

"Compared to what, General?"

"Do you think we haven't known… for *months* now… that the little girlie you have running things up here is a goddamned fire-starter?" He spat on the ground, his hands on his hips. "I'm real sorry you were attacked, Balidor. I am. But I can't say I'm surprised. It was only a matter of time, with the roulette you've been playing. You can't keep a goddamned *weapon* like that out in the open and not expect someone to try and take it."

Balidor spread his hands. "General, I have no idea to whom this grand conspiracy of yours refers, and—"

"You know damned well who I mean! The *girl,* Balidor! The one who blew up a goddamned *ship* in our waters, killing God knows how many civilians! The one who led that nightmare in London, who likes playing pattycake with our men in Russia and keeps starting shit on the feeds. You know *exactly* who I'm talking about!" He gestured jerkily with a hand, frowning. "She's got one of those… you know… rebel types as a boyfriend."

Balidor frowned. "Boyfriend?"

The Apostle eyes turned to glass.

"Yeah. We know he's alive. Caught him on surveillance when he crossed back over into India. So don't even bother to deny it, Balidor. I've seen the tapes."

He stepped closer, close enough that Balidor felt himself tense.

"Are you going to deny the little bitch is alive, too?"

"We did not try to hide this from you, General."

"Bullshit! You changed her name!"

"A common practice among my people. She was raised among humans. We sought only to reunite her with her heritage. To bring her into her proper clan—"

"Okay, okay." The general held up a hand. He smiled at Balidor indulgently. "You can play your polite little bullshit seer games all you want. But know this. We *let* you keep her, Balidor. We tried to keep the peace, give you a chance to come clean."

Placing his hands on his hips, he aimed a level stare.

"It's out of my hands now. If you can't protect her, then we'll just have to do it for you." He frowned, making another of those jerky hand-gestures. "Unless you'd prefer we ask SCARB to step in, do a whole rundown of your little facility here."

Balidor glanced at the seers standing guard around Vash.

Eldrake had a faint smile playing at his lips.

"I see," Balidor said, turning back to Cardesian. "What is it you wish me to do, General?"

A distant rumbling caused Balidor to turn.

Another line of fire and smoke broke the overcast sky, tongues of red and yellow reaching heavy clouds. Balidor stepped up on a stone bench to see better over the trees.

A second hangar must have ignited.

He touched his link, about to speak, before he remembered the Americans would have hacked his local security network by now.

Hesitating when he felt the seer on the other end, Balidor said only,

"Did you see that, Yerin?"

"Yes." Yerin did not elaborate.

When Balidor glanced back, Cardesian returned his gaze narrowly, likely nonverbal on a secure link that was actually secure.

"Say hello to Chan," Balidor said, stepping off the bench. "Send someone to watch over my kids." Without waiting, he terminated the link.

Cardesian said, "I think we can dispense with the pretense that the girl is harmless, Balidor." A smile touched his words. "I've just been informed that a World Court representative will be here shortly. No doubt, they would like to investigate for themselves the exact cause of these sudden 'disturbances' in your supposedly neutral zone."

"Very diplomatic, General." Balidor kept his voice even with an effort. "You know, I am beginning to think the other humans are right. That we should not base our views of humanity on the American model. That you would use a disturbance you yourselves created as excuse to rip our settlement apart—"

"Careful, Balidor."

Cardesian stepped closer, his eyes hard as stones.

"Can we dispense with the usual Sark indignation? I know it's expected, but perhaps we can speed things up a little. Yes, we Americans are imperialist scum. Humans are worms. We live only to torture, kill and destroy all life on Earth. If we would just all sing *kumbaya* and evolve, we'd be drowning in beer and candy and hot seer pussy. May we all rot in the halls of your Ancestors..."

He waved a dismissive hand, then put it back on his hip.

"That part of the program finished, I wish to know if your people will assist mine in looking for the girl... and *securing* the bitch without a goddamned international catastrophe of some kind. In exchange, I might be able to call off the dogs at SCARB, at least in the short term. Maybe we can even get you some real aid up here."

Balidor gestured in the negative. "If you bring SCARB in to start looking for illegals to collar, you will start a war... a real one. Maybe tell your new president that. Tell him that a lot more of our people will die. Maybe more than we can recover from."

Cardesian smiled. "What makes you think he cares, son?"

"It'll be a little hard to control seer trade if you kill off all the seers," Balidor said bitingly. "It'll be a little hard to corner the market in seer tech, too. Or come out the winner in your battles with the Chinese. Somehow I think they've been a little more careful about not killing off all of *their* seers."

At the Apostle's narrow look, Balidor clicked at him.

"Don't tell me Wellington doesn't care. I know he does. In your own, limited, worm-like, planet-killing way... so do you."

Smoke billowed from behind the hill in the direction of the 8th.

Another dozen or so American troops had joined the first group as he and Cardesian conversed, but Balidor knew this to be only a show of strength.

The real forces were already deployed, looking for Alyson.

"You realize Seertown just got in the way of the front lines, don't you, son?" Cardesian said.

"I do," Balidor said. "Please do not make it worse by declaring martial law. You must know by now that they will assume my cooperation. Whether I am named coward or traitor is immaterial for either of our purposes. They will look for a leader who does not cooperate with those who collar them and *shoot their mates*... and when that happens, things will get bloody fast. You have no idea what kind of grudge my people can hold when their families are involved."

At the other's bored look, Balidor's voice grew to an open warning.

"Cardesian, this is no longer the old generation of peaceful seers you handily conquered in the Pamir. You successfully changed our culture in that respect, at least. You've never really faced my people as a mobilized, military force."

Cardesian shrugged. "You should have better control over your people."

When Balidor turned away, Cardesian caught his arm.

"Balidor, I am trying to *help* you!"

He extricated his elbow. "Help us? How?" Seeing the anger in the human's face, he quoted, *"Can you make us care for that which is transient? Or only fear what might occur if we do not obey? You speak only for the blind, pointing and crying out."*

"Do not quote your scripture at me as if I were a child!" Cardesian's eyes held a dangerous light. "I know the same passages you do... likely better! Do you really wish to see your precious Bridge's body displayed on the Castle walls, covered in blood and runes from your damned holy books? Give me another reason, Balidor. I dare you!"

Balidor was genuinely surprised.

"General," he said. "I merely meant that my people won't hear yours on this. Honestly, I doubt they'd hear me. They definitely won't if they see me helping humans to collar the Bridge. She is a symbol here, as well."

"Symbol." The human's mouth tightened. "You think I'd betray my people for your goddamned symbol... you don't know jack about humans, son."

Once again, Balidor noted, Cardesian seemed oblivious to the fact that Balidor had a good 350 years on him.

The human shook his head. "I've made my offer. I can call SCARB off with a single transmission. Bring her to me, and I'll help you hunt down the scum who did this to your city. I promise you that."

Balidor gave him a puzzled smile. "You speak as though I had such a thing in my power. I assure you, I do not."

"Then get your holy man to do it!" Cardesian gestured towards Vash. "If he's the big boss around here, have him tell the others—"

"He's not."

Cardesian took a step closer on the wet grass. For the barest instant, real anger flashed in his dark eyes. Then Balidor saw them change.

A silvery sheen fogged the dark irises.

A bare pause lived between one state of consciousness and the next.

Then a different cadence came from those human lips.

"Balidor, I would like to know what's happened here."

Hearing the human's voice shift, Balidor studied Cardesian's light, his own cautious. It took him only seconds to ascertain that Cardesian himself was gone; his light had been hijacked by a seer's.

It occurred to Balidor that he knew with whom he now spoke.

"I have told you already," he said. "I do not know."

"Where are the books?"

"What?" Balidor said, genuinely confused. "What books?"

"Who attacked you? Who are the Chinese aiding?"

"We don't know that either," Balidor said. "We thought it was you."

"Convenient." The Apostle took another step towards him. The silvery glow remained in his eyes. "Someone killed my man in the forest. Was that one of your 'mystery attackers,' as well?"

Balidor shrugged with one hand, his voice flat. "My infiltrators tell me you killed my man first. Further, one of our people has disappeared. So tell me, General, why should I care what happens to yours?"

Cardesian's eyes grew more birdlike.

"You honestly think I would do this? Kill hundreds of our people? I kept the front *away* from Seertown!"

"Then why are you here now?" Balidor said.

"I came for the books. I want what is mine. I want what she stole from me."

Balidor continued to measure the light of the other man, without getting too close. He knew Terian's light well enough to recognize it, given all the work they'd done tracking him. He didn't believe he was looking at a Terian body, per se; any human body and mind could be "borrowed" by a seer of sufficient structure.

The conversation so far hadn't illuminated much.

Balidor watched the silvery eyes appraise him, as if the being behind them was doing its own mental inventory. The Apostle was still staring at him when two Sarks approached, dressed in Air Force uniforms.

"Let's see how our famed leader of the Adhipan likes his own collar," Terian said through the human's lips.

Abruptly, Cardesian's eyes snapped back to focus.

The silver leached out of his irises, just before his voice changed, once more carrying a human accent from the United States. The general gestured towards the uniformed seers, his expression hard.

"I'm tired of screwing around with this iceblood." He grunted, giving Balidor a hard stare. "Hook him to wires, if you have to. Just give me everything he has on that girlie of theirs. I want to know where she slept, who she fucked, who she was friends with, how she spent her time... any hidey-holes she might have. Find out where she might have kept any materials she stole in her intelligence raids."

He gave Balidor a hard look.

"And find those human traitor friends of hers. Put a trace on her boy-toy, too. He might know something." Adjusting his belt, he gave Balidor a withering look. "Those materials didn't get up and walk out of here..."

He gestured up towards the House on the Hill.

"And put out that fucking fire! She might have stuff hidden in there."

Balidor exhaled in relief, even as it occurred to him that Terian had done that, too. Apparently he was more of a sentimentalist when it came to ancient seer artifacts than Balidor would have credited him.

The uniformed Sarks bowed. One, a bald male with a tattoo covering half of his face, Balidor recognized as well. His light had a particular bluish tint to it, and structures with an unusually delicate flavor.

His seer name had been Starlen, once.

Balidor glanced at Vash. Within a heartbeat, he made up his mind.

Reaching for the top of his boot, he jerked out a narrow throwing knife.

He flung it at the bald one's chest.

Starlen slid liquidly out of the way, but Balidor darted forward as the seer next to him reached for his sidearm. Using his arm and momentum, he slid his body so that the bald seer stood between him and the other's gun.

He grabbed hold of his hips and trip-threw him into his companion, pivoting his body. The two uniformed seers tangled into one another. It bought Balidor seconds, which was all he needed.

Pulling a handgun from a holster inside his own jacket, he aimed it at the legs of the two watching seers, squeezing off three quick shots to bring them down.

A fourth shot came from his left.

He felt the bullet before he heard the sound.

Then he was staring at the grass of the garden lawn, which was abruptly eye-level. Green shoots stuck up sideways as his breaths moved them in short bursts.

Holding his side where the bullet impacted his armored vest, he rolled as someone grabbed his wrist, sliding a syringe into the hinge of his elbow. He managed to punch whoever it was in the face.

He broke the syringe with his fingers, jerking out the needle.

When he looked up, at least five rifles pointed at his head.

None were held by humans.

Assessing their collective *aleimi*, Balidor went after the youngest.

He took control of his light within seconds.

The youngster swiveled his gun up, aiming it at the other uniformed seers. Balidor was about to speak, to try and reason with them—when Starlen shifted the direction of his own gun. Before Balidor could let out a sound, Starlen shot the young seer in the temple.

The bullet exploded out the back end of his skull.

Balidor watched, disbelieving, as the seer's body crumpled.

For a long moment, no one moved.

Balidor continued to stare at the downed seer, doubting his eyes, having an emotional reaction even as his eyes flickered up to the murderer, Starlen. As much as Rooks and the Seven fought back and forth, they rarely killed other seers.

Humans, yes—humans taken over by seer *aleimi* being the most common casualties in their longstanding intra-species war.

But they didn't kill one another.

Their long lifespans and dwindling numbers made the consequences too dire. Their decreasing birthrates, particularly for those seers forced into some form of sight-slavery by humans, made it a matter of species survival. Such considerations transcended any factional struggles, no matter how bitter.

It was one of those unspoken rules.

After what had happened already that night and day, as well as losing Pradaj in the woods, Balidor found he couldn't look away from yet another broken seer body, especially one so young.

At Balidor's shocked look, Starlen smiled, crinkling the tattoo on his face.

He gave Balidor an apologetic shrug, just before he swiveled his organic rifle, aiming it at Cardesian.

"Victory without quarter," Balidor heard him mutter.

He squeezed the trigger, dropping Cardesian with a single shot to the face.

The human fell unceremoniously to his back, where he lay, nerves jerking.

Starlen's eyes returned to Balidor. He smiled again. That time, it held more genuine friendliness. Pivoting the assault rifle skyward on an organic harness, he held out a hand.

Balidor stared at it, unmoving.

"Join us, Balidor," Starlen said. "We're not with Terian. Nor his human puppets. We serve the Bridge."

Balidor watched as two seers put guns on Eldrake, the seer who'd been guarding Vash.

Once they'd separated the ex-Rook from his weapons, one of the youngsters cut the bonds holding Vash's wrists behind his back. He used shears to cut the collar Vash wore next, flinging it to the grass, where another broke it with his heel.

Starlen watched, then smiled at Balidor, his voice and eyes serious.

"Are you hurt?" he asked politely.

Balidor looked down at himself. Opening his shirt where the bullet hit, he saw it mashed to an unrecognizable shape on the organic vest. He'd have a hell of a bruise, but it wouldn't be the first time.

"No," he managed.

Starlen said, "There is no need for us to fight on opposite sides, brother. We want you with us. The days of collaring seers is over."

Balidor looked around the suddenly silent garden.

Seers held guns on human troops.

More seers appeared to be coming out of the woods.

Balidor scanned their light, looking at their physical bodies in case he'd run into them while they were masquerading their lights to appear human. Most he didn't recognize personally, although a few *aleimic* signatures were familiar. He noticed a large number appeared to be from the mountains.

If so, they might even be unregistered under SCARB and the World Court.

Balidor fought to process this, but his voice held nothing but bewilderment.

"Who *are* you?" he asked.

"We are the Rebellion," Starlen answered.

The sound of planes grew audible overhead.

Balidor stared up at the wings of passing aircraft. The planes themselves had their origins from places all over the globe, from different time periods all the way back to World War II. But it wasn't the planes themselves that riveted Balidor.

He paused on the colors they flew instead.

A blue and gold sun broke the dull flash of metal and organic skin on each wing, pierced by a narrow, white sword.

It was a symbol he hadn't seen since the end of World War I.

Balidor knew without scanning that seers, not humans, flew them.

When the bombs began to fall that time, it wasn't on Seertown, or its occupants.

Balidor heard it when the first American transport went up in an explosion of metal and glass. Bombs hammered down over the landing strip below the town, where the American fleet had parked several dozen of their planes. The explosions ran into one another, shaking the ground under Balidor's feet.

He watched, feeling a strange numbness fall over him.

He knew somehow, it was already too late.

The war had started for real.

CHAPTER 33
WREG

R evik woke abruptly, in a state of panic.

He wasn't reassured when he found himself inside what appeared to be a cement and clay holding cell, lying on a cot in one corner. Someone had collared him, and cuffed his hands behind his back, locking them both at his wrists and his upper arms.

His panic worsened.

Pain rippled through his body, keening upwards, sharpening until he was gasping, half-groaning as he leaned his face into the cold cement wall. He fought to shield himself from it… then to force his way past it when the collar made that impossible… but the pain didn't lessen or die away like it had all those months before.

Nor did it get worse.

It remained, confusing him as he stabilized somewhere within it.

He assessed what he'd been collared with.

Standard issue, one-way.

It wouldn't do much for the separation pain. He'd have some physical pain if he tried to fight it, but nothing like the ones Terian used.

He didn't have time for this.

It was the only thought that truly helped.

He forced his eyes around the cramped space, feeling like a trapped animal. The other corner had a spigot for water, along with foot platforms over a covered hole, like most of the common toilets in rural Asia. He doubted he could even get his pants off though, not with the way his arms and wrists had been bound.

Water dripped down an algae-covered wall.

Given the way the walls bled, he was likely underground. The room reminded him of interrogation cells he'd witnessed in at least three different human wars.

A rusted metal table stood in the center, framed by dented folding chairs.

He could smell blood.

His jaw hardened. He wondered how long he'd been in here.

He didn't remember arriving, so he must have passed out.

Writhing out from under the thin blanket someone had thrown over him, he examined his leg. A thick organic cast now covered most of his thigh, attached to a splint on a moveable joint. It was stiff, and he could tell the painkillers they'd given him were wearing off, but he should be able to stand, walk… maybe even jog if he really had to.

Not for long, though, or very quickly.

Inevitably, he thought of Allie.

He fought back pain that worsened in a sharp rise. Dragging himself up to a seated position, he stared around the cell, still fighting nausea.

Desire slid to the front of his mind, in spite of everything. He wanted her, even scared out of his mind. He didn't know how to reconcile the two feelings, so fought to blank out conscious thought.

When that didn't work, he tried simply to endure it.

He'd known the bonding process would fuck with both of their heads.

He hadn't expected to have to deal with it without her.

He had to get out of there. Now.

Anger fought to replace fear. Mostly, he was angry at himself.

He should have gone after Terian from the very beginning, before returning to Seertown. Hell, Galaith had already done most of the work for him. Killing whatever remained of that psychotic prick would have been relatively easy compared to what they'd faced in him before the Pyramid collapsed.

He'd known Terian would target Allie.

He'd practically promised Revik he would.

And Allie, from what Revik determined, had been up to something too.

She'd been busy in the months he'd been gone. No one would tell him what, precisely, she'd been up to, but he read between the lines of enough with Jon and Cass to know *that* involved Terian, too.

Whatever it was, Jon hadn't liked it.

Of course, Revik avoided Terian mainly out of deference to Allie herself.

She'd asked him to stay away from him, to not seek revenge. She'd asked him to let the Adhipan deal with him. She'd been worried about him, and he understood that, but now he couldn't for the life of him understand why he hadn't refused her request.

She would have forgiven him—eventually.

The kid, on his own, they could have handled.

Without Terian there, holding his leash, providing him resources, the kid would've been too young and isolated to do much damage before they brought him in. He wasn't Syrimne, who'd been an adult seer with a whole army behind him.

One way or another, they would have neutralized him.

Instead, he'd let Terian and the kid take her.

His pain worsened, twisting deeper.

He'd let his guard down. He'd let the Adhipan handle security instead of telling the Council to go fuck themselves and taking her someplace on his own. He could have waited a few weeks, set things up right, made sure no one knew where they were, not even Vash.

Instead, he let his dick make the decisions.

That and his paranoia about Maygar or some other jackass trying to pull something on her when she was already vulnerable.

Anger and pain mixed with fear, making his head throb.

He stood, shakily, and bit his tongue, almost thankful for the pain in his leg.

Walking the edges of the room by balancing his shoulder lightly against the wall, he limped to the door. Turning around, he tried the handle clumsily with his bound hands.

It was locked.

Reaching out with his light, he fought to scan, trying to get above the room. Gritting his teeth against the thread of pain from the collar, he saw faint walls, more cells, a corridor of iron doors set in rock.

He didn't see anyone. No humans.

The whole complex appeared to be underground.

Glancing up, he saw a tiny eye of God camera in one corner of the ceiling.

"Hey!" He yelled at it, though he doubted it had audio. He slammed the door with his shoulder, yelling as loudly as he could. "HEY! LET ME OUT!"

He tried several languages.

None of them worked.

His shoulder started to hurt when he continued to slam it against the door. Eventually, he forced himself to pause. Sitting heavily on the floor, he leaned his back against one of the legs of the table, and tried to think.

He had to get out of here.

He stared at the rusted bolts that held the table's legs to the cement, wondering if he could pry them up. The table was the only thing heavy enough that he might be able to use it to batter down the door. Then again, they'd likely chained him this way precisely so he couldn't do what he was contemplating doing.

After pulling at the bolts for another span of minutes, he decided it wasn't getting him anywhere. Water had rusted them to the metal plates, and the angle of his bound hands made it impossible to get leverage.

Leaning against the table leg, he closed his eyes—

The door opened with a squeal.

He jerked upright, muscles clenched.

By then, he fully expected a Terian body to walk through that opening.

Instead, the leader of the Wvercians who'd found him walked in, wearing a clean set of clothes. Revik moved his feet to straighten his back against the iron table leg. When more seers entered the room, he tried to decide if he should risk trying to climb to his feet.

Then he got a good look at the man entering behind the Wvercian, and his throat closed.

He remembered him—somehow.

Tall, with strong seer features and a broad, muscular body, he wore a uniform Revik knew mainly from historical sims. Military. Everything about him said career military, especially the way he carried his body. Still, the familiarity went deeper than that.

Even the man's scars looked familiar.

He looked Revik over with opaque, nearly-black irises. He seemed to take in every part of him, though his expression remained incurious.

Finally, the man smiled. It didn't touch those odd-colored eyes.

"Dehgoies. That's your name now. Isn't it, runt? Dehgoies Revik?"

Two more seers walked in behind him.

They stopped just inside the door.

Revik glanced at them. Another of those two looked vaguely familiar. The one with him looked young though, obviously a new recruit.

Neither shocked him like the face of the black-haired seer standing over him.

Revik's eyes returned to him.

He took in the man's thick black braid, the corded muscle of his arms. A tattoo of the sword and sun stood out on his bicep, the inks scarcely faded, although the tattoo itself looked old, and had been done in the highly stylized traditional style.

It looked similar to the one on Revik's back. Too similar, maybe. A slight tint difference in the inks was the only difference he could discern.

Whoever he was, he looked exactly as Revik remembered him, even down to the uniform.

He decided to take a chance.

"Hello, Wreg," he said.

The giant Wvercian frowned, looking at the military seer.

The latter only smiled, pulling a *hiri* out of his coat pocket. He lit it with a silver lighter, and even the lighter struck a note somewhere in Revik's mind.

"Wreg? A little informal, wouldn't you say? 'Revik?'" The opaque black eyes glanced up, doll-like, shining as if made of obsidian glass. "Are you trying to piss me off? Or is that the kind of crap they tolerate in the Adhipan? I'd heard Balidor was a bit on the informal side, compared to his predecessors."

"I don't know your current rank, sir." Revik felt his jaw harden. "I didn't know you still *had* a rank, sir... or that I fell under it. The war ended. Maybe you heard." He motioned with his head. "Rebellion uniforms? A bit melodramatic, don't you think? Do they have Halloween in India now?"

"You're not in India anymore... *Revik.*"

The dark eyes stared into his. They betrayed no emotion at all.

"Since we're on the subject," Wreg continued. "What brings you to Asia, *Revik?*"

He ashed the *hiri* on the cement floor, gesturing fluidly with the same hand.

"We knew of you, of course. The infamous defector, Dehgoies Revik." Wreg grunted, giving him a wry smile. "We had you tracked as a Westerner. Worm food, and a traitor who played both sides of the fence. Now that we know who you *really* are, can I assume you simply avoided returning to Asia until now?"

The thin smile returned.

"...I'm fairly certain I would have noticed."

There was a silence.

Revik looked around at faces, then at the whitewashed walls.

His mind ran ahead of his facial expression. Something was wrong here. Did these people know him from when he was a Rook? Something didn't feel right.

He matched the other's tone.

"I guess I did. Too many bad memories, maybe." He did his best to keep his mind still, knowing that was about all he had by way of defense. "Did I do something wrong? I didn't realize my birth status had been revoked. Or that my being in Seertown would piss you off so much."

Relighting the *hiri,* the older seer exhaled smoke, clicking his heat coil shut.

"You're still a ballsy little shit. You're on the ground in manacles and you're asking me questions." Taking another drag of the *hiri,* he waved a hand around at the mold-smelling room.

"I thought you were dead... *Revik,*" he said. "A lot of people did. It was one of our few compensations from that op in Trelimn. It almost redeemed you. In a few people's eyes, at least." A humorless smile hovered on the seer's face. "And yet here you are, looking just like you did then. Explain that to me, *Revik.* Tell me how you managed to rise from the dead. Without so much as a scratch."

"There are a few scratches, sir." Revik shifted his weight, trying to get feeling back in his legs. He fought to keep his mind still.

"You must know I can't answer your questions." He glanced around at faces, pausing on the Wvercian, then the two seers who stood behind him, listening. "I can guess from context, but I don't know the specifics of—"

"Yet, you remember me. Why is that, *Revik?*"

Revik shrugged. He didn't really have a good answer for that, either.

Seeing the other's scrutiny intensify, he forced his expression blank.

"I *don't* remember you, sir. Not really." He controlled his voice with an effort. "What do you want? You must know that you took me illegally. You must also know it wasn't the best timing, from the perspective of our people."

"My men saved your life." The seer spat *hiri* resin on the cement floor. "Why, is beyond me. You can pretend you don't remember all you want, *Revik,* but I can't help but think it's awfully convenient."

Revik frowned. "Why do you keep saying my name like that?"

Wreg glanced at the Wvercian, then smiled.

"Right. Because we should say your traitor name with respect." The black eyes filled with contempt. "You deserted. Right when we needed people the most. Even shit-blood pricks like you. You're going to tell me you don't remember that, either? That it all just conveniently 'disappeared' when you ran back to the Seven for absolution?"

He pointed the *hiri* at him.

"Go fuck yourself... *Revik.*"

The Wvercian grunted a laugh, folding his arms.

Revik stared at the wall, fighting to hide his impatience.

"Bet you're wishing you could scan me now, aren't you, *Revik?*" Wreg focused on the mud-streaked ceiling. "Of course you are. You never had a modicum of decency with your fellow brothers and sisters. Is that the dirt blood in you? To treat others like tools? Like pieces to move around on a game board for your own amusement—"

"Do you have a point... sir?" Revik bit his tongue. "Or did you really bring me here to rehash some decades-old grudge I don't even remember? There are places I'd rather be."

"Yeah." Wreg grunted. "I bet."

Revik stared up at him, trying to decide how far he could push this.

If they wanted him dead, he would be dead. Even so, he was having trouble keeping calm. Did they work for Terian? This couldn't possibly be a coincidence, not with Seertown being bombed, much less Allie being taken.

He was still trying to decide what to say when Wreg reached into his coat.

He pulled out a square image reconstruction.

Getting up off the stool, he placed it on the ground between Revik's feet.

"Who is he?"

Revik stared at the image, feeling something in his chest constrict. He glared up at the muscular seer. "How the fuck should I know?"

Wreg crouched down, tapping the image. "Look again, Dehgoies Revik. Think real hard before you answer."

Revik let his eyes trace the outline of the boy's round face. The dark eyes stared out of the image, still as death under jet-black hair. Revik felt his jaw harden, remembering the way those eyes had looked at Allie.

Like he owned her.

"I told you." He looked up at Wreg. "I have no *fucking* idea. Is he one of those seer kids who died recently? In the news?"

"Something like that, yeah." Wreg leaned back on his heels, staring at him. "I would have thought you would show more interest. Given who your *wife* is."

Revik felt something in his stomach grow cold.

Wreg smiled. "A reaction. At last. Hallelujah." His smile turned colder. "Where is she, Revik?"

"You're asking me that? Your goons said you'd help me find her!"

"Yeah," Wreg conceded. "They did. But I need you to explain a few things to me, first, runt." Looking between Revik's eyes, he said, "We hear she took out one of yours. Little shit who tried to claim her before you got your cock in her."

He smiled when Revik averted his eyes.

"Eye witness said she threw him a good thirty meters. Nearly killed him, too, from what I hear." He paused, studying Revik's face. "Is that true?"

Revik stared at the large-boned seer, but didn't answer.

Folding his hands between his knees where he crouched, Wreg shrugged.

"Apparently, we'd been vastly misinformed," he said. "Someone told us she was untrained." The broad face creased in another humorless smile. "Funny. I wonder who could have *possibly* trained her?"

Revik didn't answer.

Staring at the cement floor, he fought to process this, to catch up.

They had someone there, at Seertown, probably in the Guard.

They knew about Allie.

Jesus, did they think *he'd* trained her?

Sure, the thought had crossed his mind to try, especially after Maygar, but he had no idea where to even start. He'd been playing around with a few ideas along those lines, to distract himself mostly, those nights they sat in front of the fire at the cabin.

Ironically, he'd been trying to map the boy's structures from memory, to see if he could figure out which he'd used for telekinesis so he could show Allie.

Pain hit him.

For the first time, he let himself remember, to really feel what had happened over the course of however-long they'd been together.

Despite how he'd brought her there, in the end, it had been her who seduced him. Even after, it'd been her who kept pushing him to go further, to stop holding back. She told him things. Once he made it clear he wanted her to, she told him whatever he wanted to know, even when he continued to hide behind silence.

They hadn't finished.

He'd been consciously aware of that, even at the time.

He'd looked forward to more, to drawing it out. Then there'd been that thing with her light—that thing that drove him half-insane with wanting, that turned both of them nearly violent. She'd been pushing him with that, too, asking him for it even after he told her he couldn't, that he was afraid he would hurt her if they kept trying.

She hadn't cared.

He remembered the way the boy looked at her, and his pain turned to overt fear, intense enough that he barely heard Wreg's next words.

"...Needless to say," the Sark added. "We couldn't find this Maygar. But the rumor is, he's alive." He grunted, hands resting on his thighs. "I guess the wife's got a forgiving nature, eh, runt? Come to think of it, why didn't *you* kill him? I would have. If someone pulled that shit on my mate, I would have torn them to pieces."

When Revik didn't answer, he prodded him with a foot.

"We found her, Dehgoies." He waited for Revik to look up, then smiled a little at his expression. "You should have told us that ex-Pyramider has her. Terian. We now know he has the boy, too." He gave Revik a half-smile. "You want to tell me again how you don't know who he is?"

Revik stared at the floor of the cell without seeing it.

He didn't think he was moving until his wrists started to hurt, and he realized he was grinding the chains together, his heels dug into the floor.

"Are you going to tell me where she is?" he asked finally.

"Ah." Wreg smiled. "A bit touchy about the wife." Still studying Revik's, the black eyes turned shrewd. "I have to say, that surprises me. Back in the day, you seemed pretty willing to stick your dick in anything that didn't try to cut it off. I guess even shit-bloods like you can grow up. A little, anyway."

He straightened fluidly.

"That's good," he said. "That's really good."

Before Revik could answer, Wreg kicked him, hard, in his good leg.

Revik sucked in a breath, gasping. The kick caught him off guard, so it hurt like hell. When he looked up, fighting to breathe, the other seer appraised him again, his opaque eyes expressionless.

"You ready to cut the crap now, *Revik?*"

"Why am I here?" Revik snarled the words, still gasping in breaths. "If you knew about Terian, why take me? I'm not with them anymore. I haven't been for years!"

"Maybe it's not you we're after."

"Terian won't trade me for her. And I can't help her, not if you've got me locked up here. Let me *go,* goddamn it! I'll find her."

Wreg smiled. "Think you can rescue the missus, Dehgoies?"

"He'll kill her." Revik met his gaze, hearing emotion leak into his voice. "He could do it on accident. She's never worn a collar before. She won't know when to stop. And he jacks up the limits too high. She's telekinetic, so he'll be afraid of her. He'll overcompensate—"

"What makes you think we care?"

Revik looked around at the others in frustration, but met only blank stares. His gaze paused at the door, focusing on the young seer guarding it.

He said, "I may not remember specifics, but I know who you are. I know what you want. You want the Bridge. Alive. Let me go, and I'll get her back."

"You don't strike me as all that battle-ready, friend."

Revik bit back fury, glancing at the door.

"What do you want?" he growled. "What do you want for my release?"

Wreg smiled. "Now you're asking the right question. Finally." He picked the *hiri* up from where he'd left it on the floor, taking a drag and exhaling sweet-smelling smoke.

"Salinse wants to see you," he said.

Revik looked up, feeling his breath stop. "Salinse? He's alive?"

Wreg smiled. "Yes. He is."

CHAPTER 34
MEMORY

Minutes later, Revik limped down a passageway carved from solid rock. He focused on moving his legs, testing the limits of the one with a hole blown through it, hopefully without damaging it further.

It was something to think about. Something to do.

He'd given up trying to remember how he knew these people.

He didn't care. He'd been a kid during WWI, so whatever this was about, it must have happened while he was with the Rooks after WWII, or in the period he'd operated out of Germany before that.

It didn't matter to him.

He knew a little about Salinse.

He'd studied him and his followers while working for the Seven, along with any seer terrorist cells big enough to show up in the security documents he had access to while working for the British government. He'd retained a curiosity about what went on in Asia, maybe more so because he wasn't allowed back.

That Salinse's "Rebellion" may have had ties to Galaith and the Pyramid Rooks had been a pretty well-substantiated theory of the Adhipan's.

Yet the exact nature of those ties remained unknown.

They'd never been absorbed into the Pyramid itself.

While they claimed to be the remnants of the group that fought along-side Syrimne during WWI, there was little to prove that, either, other than Salinse's bloodline, which appeared to be relatively solid.

He was first blood cousin to Menlim, the seer believed to be Syrimne's handler.

Menlim, the true mastermind behind the original rebellion, built its hierarchy to minimize the risk of infiltration, using a design that had striking similarities to the Pyramid itself. Cells of personnel rotated in and out of the highest rungs, with those in the upper tiers exchanging places with those below and to either side in a pattern dictated solely by the person at top.

Under such a system, knowledge was transitory.

Ops, pieces of ops and even entire long-term strategies were held solely by one or more delineated cells.

No one knew when they were being sidelined. Or, for that matter, when they weren't. They might conduct elaborate operations that were mainly diversionary. Conversely, they might perform seemingly trivial tasks that were strategically critical.

Menlim's structure had been less multi-dimensional than the Pyramid, but only a seer could have designed something like it.

Of course, knowing all that didn't explain the half-scent of memory that whispered around this place, and around these seers.

But it gave him a starting point.

Revik focused on the range of his leg and cast. He tried walking normally until it hurt, stopping before he risked damaging it more.

He had maybe a full minute of regular gait.

He could probably increase that with time if he didn't overdo it.

His arms were still cuffed behind his back, along with his wrists. He let his eyes blur on the rock walls, fighting his anger, the feeling of powerlessness that lay under it.

He knew Terian. He knew exactly what he'd do.

The first thing, anyway.

He bit his tongue, hard enough to taste blood.

He couldn't let himself feel, not now. He needed his head straight. He'd listen to the old Sark, tell him whatever he wanted to hear, give them whatever they wanted.

Until they let him go.

The seer in front of him halted, keying in an access code on a wall panel.

Revik watched him do it.

Organics. Old, but definitely alive. The seer used a DNA scan to activate the final sequence. Revik grew peripherally aware of two more guards at his back. As the door lock went from red to green, the lead guard glanced at the Wvercian, the same one who had ridden on horseback with Revik from India.

Revik knew they were speaking to one another.

After a pause, the Wvercian shrugged.

"Do as he says," he said. "He's the boss."

Frowning, the guard hesitated.

Then he looked at Revik, motioning sharply for him to turn around.

Wary, Revik did as he was told. He felt the seer doing something to the collar he wore, and stiffened.

Then it popped off, leaving the skin of his neck oddly light.

Revik stood without moving for a few seconds, in shock.

He turned, looking at the three guards and the old Wvercian, until the first guard motioned for him to turn around a second time. The guard unlocked both sets of manacles. He started with the ones at his wrists, then moved to the heavier ones clamped around his upper arms. Revik exhaled sharply when his arms came free, wincing as the circulation came back to his wrists and elbows.

He glanced at the closed door with its green light, then back at the three seers.

The first one indicated for him to enter the room.

When Revik just stood there, the guard gave a short bow and turned, walking back the way they'd come. The two other guards followed.

After a short pause, the Wvercian gave him a wan smile and did the same.

Revik swallowed. He took a few seconds to scan for Allie, but still couldn't feel her.

He tried again.

Nothing. Not a trace of her light.

He contemplated just leaving—walking out. But with his leg, he wouldn't get far. He also wouldn't get anywhere in a hurry, especially if this site was as isolated as it felt. The construct here felt secure. Military-grade secure.

They were watching him, even now. Waiting for him to make up his mind.

Touching the wall lightly for balance, he limped over to the door. As soon as he stood in front of it, the thick panel opened, disappearing into the rock wall. Without spending a lot of time looking inside, he limped over the threshold and into the new room.

The door immediately closed behind him.

Once it had, he checked the organic panel.

It was still unlocked.

Exhaling, he turned, taking in the new space.

He remembered this room, he realized in some surprise. Or he remembered one a hell of a lot like it. Something about the layout and feel was instantly and intensely familiar, despite the lack of a clear memory to accompany it.

In contrast to the cement cell and hewn-rock corridors, the floor consisted of marbled stone tiles, covered over in intricately handwoven rugs. The largest of the latter, filling the center of the room, depicted a blue and gold sun intersected with a white sword.

Despite the familiarity of the symbol, Revik felt something in his heart react as he stared at it here, in this context. If Salinse's people were telling the truth about who they were, the older seers in his army may have worked side-by-side with Syrimne.

Possibly Wreg. Possibly even the old Wvercian.

Being here, Revik could almost believe it was true.

These people weren't like the make-believe terrorists that lurked around Seertown. They didn't feel like they were playing a game. They felt like the real thing.

It wasn't the same, when they ran Syrimne's flag.

A grated fire burned in a stone pit at the center of the room, below a round hole in the ceiling with a long chain to what was probably a flue. A series of padded benches ringed the pit. More were pushed up against the rock walls on either side.

A terrain map of Asia hung above a heavy, rectangular desk.

The wood of the desk looked old, and seemed to be from an unusual type of tree, like it had traveled a long way to sit in this cave. Papers lay scattered around an organic monitor, along with a few tallow candles and a number of hand-helds, also organics. A silver sculpture of the sun and sword dominated a stone shelf behind the desk.

It looked like someone's office.

Maybe it also doubled as sleeping quarters.

Revik glanced at a nearby glass case filled with guns. Most didn't appear to be working models. He saw a few Austrian Mondragons though, a Ross rifle, Mausers, Lugers, even an old Nambu pistol from Japan—

"Hello, nephew."

He stiffened, turning towards the voice.

A figure rose from the shadows by one set of padded benches.

The Sark's dark robe blended perfectly with the wall. He had been sitting so still and silent Revik hadn't seen him, even un-collared and sharing the same construct.

Revik's heart beat faster as the other's features emerged.

The long, gaunt face had an ageless quality. It appeared out of the darker rock like a wraith, smooth and white, with sunken eyes. Revik's heart accelerated in his chest. He couldn't tear his eyes off the other seer's. He fought to take in the skull-like features, to absorb the familiarity of them.

He struggled to breathe.

His heart hurt, grew heavy in his chest.

He couldn't breathe.

He felt cold and hot all at once.

Claustrophobic.

He reached for Allie in reflex, panicked when he couldn't find her.

He didn't realize he'd taken a step backwards until his back connected with an outcropping of rock by the organic door.

He fought to control himself, to pull back his light.

He realized dimly he was having what amounted to a panic attack.

He clutched his chest. His heart hurt, his lungs.

He wanted desperately to run, but couldn't breathe.

He watched the Sark cross the room, realized the other male was taller than him, by at least a few inches. The difference stretched, grew into feet in his mind. He saw concern in those clouded, pale eyes, and felt about fifteen seasons old.

"Get away from me," he managed.

He watched helplessly as everything around him began to gray.

Consciousness slid from him so quickly that he didn't have time to reach for the door, or even to send out a final call for help.

REVIK OPENED HIS EYES.

He stared up at a gaunt face, sure he was dreaming.

Dark, yellow-tinted irises stared back at him, the color of urine… only the urine of someone sick, or extremely dehydrated.

His vision clicked back into focus.

The eyes above him now were an opaque white, the color of bleached bones.

The Sark reached for his arm. His cultured voice held concern.

"Nephew! Nephew, are you all right? Breathe, my son. Breathe…"

Revik fought to work his tongue. He pushed the wasted hands back, not wanting to touch them. He struggled to pull himself off the floor.

The Sark immediately got out of his way.

He watched Revik with those white eyes, long fingers clasped in front of his robe as Revik pulled himself to a seated position.

Revik leaned against the rock wall, not looking at the Sark at all as he brought his breathing under control. Pulling his body upright with his hands and his good leg, he slid up the stone wall to get himself off the floor.

Then he just stood there, supporting his weight on the wall as he tested his balance.

He forced his expression flat.

What came out of his mouth still sounded aggressive.

"Are you Salinse?"

When Revik glanced over his shoulder, the gaunt seer tilted his head in assent. He continued to study Revik's face. Whispers of concern flickered around Revik's light, but he avoided them, fighting the impulse to cringe from the old man's *aleimic* touch.

Salinse asked, "Do you remember me, nephew?"

Revik's throat tried to close.

The familiar manner in which the old seer spoke to him, even the exact dialect he spoke, hit at Revik strangely. It was Prexci, but unlike any Prexci he had a conscious memory of hearing.

This must be from when he'd been a Rook.

It had to be.

Looking around, doubt tugged at him, though.

"No," he said. "I don't remember you."

Revik felt the silver light touch him again.

He recoiled, even as parts of him responded to that touch.

"You don't look well, nephew," Salinse observed, still looking him over with those white eyes. "Even apart from the leg. Have you been ill?"

"No." Revik stepped sideways, putting more distance between him and the old seer. "Do we know one another? Is the 'nephew' more than ceremonial? If we truly have some blood-family tie, you have a hell of a way of renewing acquaintanceship."

He couldn't bring himself to call the old seer "uncle."

He knew it was the correct form of address in the old system, given their relative ages and the fact that Revik was technically a guest in the old Sark's home.

He still couldn't do it.

"Salinse," he said instead. "Why am I here?"

The old Sark exuded mild distress. Letting out a purr that amounted to a sigh, he turned on his heel and walked towards the fire pit.

Revik stayed where he was.

He noticed the old man was barefoot.

He watched as Salinse sank gracefully to one of the padded benches around the hole housing the fire, then motioned for Revik to join him at an opposite bench. Hesitant, Revik stepped deeper into the room, conscious of the limp, of how slow he moved.

He'd just passed out cold. Jesus.

Wiping sweat off his forehead, he scanned every corner, looked for more doors, not only in the walls, but in the floors and ceiling. He noticed a trapdoor in one wall and put himself between it and the old Sark. He contemplated a bench nearer to the trap door, then decided it didn't matter. He wouldn't be able move fast enough anyway.

He sat stiffly across from the old seer and stretched out his leg.

Salinse smiled. His voice gentled, holding a near-kindness.

"I understand your caution. Revik, is it?" When he received no response, Salinse went on as though he had. "I heartily apologize for how you were brought here, nephew. I regret that I could not afford the usual courtesies, and that I was forced to rely on Wvercian... how do you say... 'the muscle?'"

He smiled, but the milky eyes remained still.

"There was simply no time," he added. "I heard about the attack on Seertown, and immediately suspected they might be after your mate."

He paused at Revik's flinch.

"I hope you know," Salinse said. "I do not myself have the same opinion of you as does Commander Wreg. While I am sympathetic to his passions, I understand very well the circumstances around which you left us."

Revik tightened his hold on his light, feeling the Sark's probe.

The intensity and subtlety of the scan unnerved him.

It also made him feel soft, out of practice.

Salinse's eyes shimmered faintly.

"You caused quite a stir, I hear," he said. "Marrying the Bridge. Of course, I did not know who you were, when news of the happy event first reached me."

He gestured delicately with one hand.

"I had heard the name Dehgoies Revik, of course. You have a reputation even within your assumed identity. I knew the basics of your story, and your record as an infiltrator. But other than a fleeting thought that you might one day make an interesting recruitment opportunity, I had no cause to think about you beyond that."

Revik didn't speak. He found himself listening though, trying again to place the familiarity of the room, of the old Sark.

"An auspicious event," Salinse said, smiling. "The Bridge taking a mate... it is auspicious indeed. Such a thing could not help but be an occasion for gossip. And it is important who is chosen, certainly."

The old seer grunted, folding his robed arms.

"Those clan seers of Seertown. I suppose they think she chose badly? Or that you forced her in some way?"

Revik felt his jaw harden. "Again. If this is a social call, I have to question your timing. And your tact, Salinse."

The Sarhacienne inclined his head. "You are right, of course. We must discuss business."

Once again, he studied Revik's face.

"This… Terian. He has a grudge against you that is personal, is that true? If grudge is really the word, with one so obviously insane."

Revik made a "more or less" gesture with one hand. "Yes. But that's not the main reason he would have taken Allie."

Salinse continued to study his eyes, as if lost there.

"Yes… of course." He clicked softly, as though rousing himself back to the present. "Well, I suppose we cannot waste time."

He turned that odd gaze back on Revik.

"What do you need? You are welcome to any amount of weaponry, of course… and air transport. We have intelligence we could share. But what do you think would be wise, in terms of numbers? You have dealt with him before. Is he likely to overreact?"

There was a silence.

Then Revik nodded, almost to himself.

"I appreciate that," he said, and meant it. "I think a moderate-sized group for the main assault, with an equal or larger force as backup. Maybe…" Out of habit, he asked for more than he thought he'd get. "…Forty?"

"Done."

Revik blinked. "I'll want to leave at once."

"I assumed so, yes."

Revik nodded again. "Fine. Do I need to agree to terms now, before we go, or can we settle that later?"

The old Sark smiled. "You do not wish to know what we want from you?"

"Not really, no," Revik said. "Now that I've married the Bridge, everyone seems to want to recruit me for something. Whatever it is, it's fine."

He began to use his hands to push himself back to his feet, but Salinse signaled for him to remain where he was. It was the polite form of the gesture, but Revik felt the command behind it. After a pause, he acceded reluctantly.

"You can do better than that, nephew," Salinse said.

Revik felt his jaw harden.

After another pause, he gestured assent.

"Fine," he said. "I'm assuming you still believe the Seven's claim to leadership is 'illegitimate'… ever since their treaty with the humans after the wars? So you want me to, what? Swear off my allegiance to them and fight for your side? Provide intel, use my position as the Bridge's mate to gain access to the Adhipan? Recruit from their ranks?"

His anger swelled, darkening when Allie's face whispered past his sight.

He let a pulse of light reach his eyes.

"…You're probably thinking I married her to gain some kind of leverage, maybe even to get my penance revoked. You'd be wrong about that, but since I'm assuming that's what most in the Seven think, I don't hold it against you. If you think I'd turn on her, you'd be wrong about that, too. If you ever give me reason to think you pose a threat to my wife in any way, I'll kill you."

He paused, then gestured in a conciliatory way.

"But I'm assuming you know that already," he said. "Or you wouldn't be using her to get to me, and vice versa. If you know me as well as you pretend, you also know I don't much care what you want, as long as you give me a gun first and let me go after my wife. I'll accept any terms, as long as they don't harm her in any way. I can't speak for her, but I'll relay any message you have."

The Sark's narrow lips formed a near-smile.

"Ah. Yes. I see you are still a pragmatist. You want your wife back. This is you 'playing along,' yes? You don't much care about anything or anyone else… or even whether our intentions are 'good' or 'bad' in the wider scale of things. Not until your goal is reached."

Revik bit his tongue to keep back a retort.

Finally, he shrugged with one hand. "Fine. I am playing along. Is it important to you that I seem to care? Fine."

He nodded, gesturing politely with a hand.

"Salinse," he said. "What is it that you would like me to do to fulfill my end of the contract with you?"

"No, no," Salinse shook his head, clicking softly. "I would not dream of playing such games with you, nephew. And perhaps you are right, this is not the time for us to have that discussion. But it pains me to see you so willing to hand your freedom away, whatever the ultimate purpose behind it. I wished only to appeal to your reason… and the ideals I knew us to share in your youth."

Revik gave him an incredulous look.

"Yeah?" he said. "And what were those, exactly?"

"To ensure the safety of your people," Salinse said. "To fight for a cause that is just. One that would improve the plight of all the races."

Revik didn't answer at first.

Folding his arms tighter, he sat up straighter, adjusting the position of his hurt leg.

"I thought I was pretty clear. I don't remember much of my early years." Letting out a low snort in spite of himself, he looked at the old seer. "And for whatever it's worth, this 'glorious ideals' version you're referencing is a new one on me. If I can believe what others have told me… including your own men… my youth consisted of a lot more drinking and fucking than selfless posturing."

The old seer purred in the back of his throat, a sound of sympathy.

"Nephew," he said. "I recognize that you are angry. I recognize also that you fear deeply for your mate. I am asking you to rise above the traumas of your youth, as well as any that have occurred since. There is more going on here than a simple rescue operation. The world has changed in very dark ways since those early years. Surely you see that."

He leaned closer, clasping his long hands.

"These back and forth squabbles among seers cannot continue. The Displacement is coming. We can no longer afford to fight one another… over ideology, treaties with the humans, money, power, sex, or whatever else. It is time to declare a truce among our different viewpoints. We have maintained the luxury of isolationism for far too long."

The Sark paused, watching Revik's face.

"We are reaching a critical point. You must see that, too."

Revik returned the seer's gaze, then shrugged.

"You want me to trust you, Salinse?" he said. "Then tell me. Who am I to you? Why not stop with the hints and allusions to my past and just tell me?"

There was a pause before the Sark leaned back on the bench.

"No," he said carefully, shaking his head. "No, I do not think we should have that conversation now, either, Revik." Leaning back some-what, he sighed. "For now, suffice it to say, I am one of those people from your past you do not remember. I think any detail beyond that should come after you return."

At Revik's narrowed gaze, Salinse added, "I am not toying with you. I am trying to respect your professed wishes. If we begin that discussion, it will take time. Time we do not currently have. You must rescue your mate. That has to take priority."

Pausing, he folded his hands in his lap. "We now have confirmation that Terian has taken her out of Asia."

Revik stared at the old Sark's face.

In the silence that followed, a swell of pain rose that made it difficult to remain still. He tried again to find her with his light. Again, he hit a wall. He needed solitude. He also needed to be outside of the Rebel construct.

He made a polite gesture of acknowledgement.

"Thank you. As I said, I would appreciate any help your people could give me. Anything at all. Including simply letting me leave."

Salinse smiled. "I think we can help you a great deal more than that."

"Do you know where he has her?"

Salinse gestured affirmative. "You are aware of the boy?"

Revik nodded. "Yes."

"Good. This is very important, nephew." The old Sark's eyes grew deathly still. "Terian is not your problem. Not anymore. He is not the one holding your wife. It is the boy. It is essential that you understand this."

Revik didn't speak, focusing his eyes on the grate.

After a pause, he nodded. "I gathered that, yes."

Salinse's light flickered palely, skirting the edges of Revik's body. When Revik looked up, the old Sark sighed.

"You do not understand," he said. "Your experience with Terian has blinded you to the reality of what is occurring now. I do not blame you for this, but I ask you to hear me. To think about my words. The balance of power is shifting again. That which sits at the top will change once again. Very soon."

His voice grew sharper.

"Galaith had his faults. He was overly ambitious in many ways, and had no regard for the free will of our people. He was also far too committed to seeing his own vision fulfilled with the humans."

He clicked softly, making a flowing gesture with one hand.

"...and yet... and yet... he was quite effective at organizing all of our peoples. He minimized dissent, used treaties effectively. He worked out compromises with the humans that kept them from overreacting to our people's continued existence in their world. Most of all, he created order within the Barrier." Salinse smiled faintly at Revik. "I understand we had you to thank for that, in large part."

Revik frowned, still looking at the fire.

Salinse let out another clicking sigh.

"Without Galaith, we can look forward to nothing but chaos as the Displacement arrives. Terian will only make that worse. He lacks Galaith's strength. He also lacks his predecessor's ability to inspire."

Revik didn't look over, but found himself thinking.

He nodded curtly. "That is true."

Salinse said, "We are on the same side again, Revik, although that may not be so obvious to you now. Terian, by himself, would have imploded in time. He was only ever marginally a leader, even with his ties to the Dreng."

Shaking his head, he added softly,

"But if he finds a way to control the boy through your mate... if he owns *the Bridge*, in addition to the boy... everything changes."

Salinse met his gaze, his eyes sharp.

"You must kill the boy, Revik. My people can handle Terian." His fingers pointed at Revik's chest. "That is my only contract with you. Kill the boy, and our debt is settled."

Revik didn't answer at first.

He turned over the seer's words, looking for flaws, a trick of some kind.

He could find none.

"Done," he said, nodding once. "We have a contract." He gave the old seer a half-smile. "And you should have bargained more, Salinse. I would have done that for free."

He struggled to his feet, straightening with an effort.

"One last thing," he said, looking down at Salinse. "If it's relevant."

At Salinse's accommodating gesture, Revik asked, "How did you come to learn of the boy? Did you have people watching him before now? Or did you only hear of him after what he did in Sikkim?"

Salinse didn't hesitate.

"I was contacted by Terian himself," he said. "He came here, looking for materials on the first war. On Syrimne, specifically. He wanted our help. He wanted it badly enough to come in person, and we were able to get enough imprints from his light to track him afterwards."

"Why?" Revik asked, genuinely puzzled.

Salinse gave a wry smile. "Well, apart from him having the only direct line to the Dreng, he was acting suspicious. Highly suspicious. And his questions were too pointed, too specific to be wholly academic."

"No." Revik shook his head with a frown. "Not why did you track him. Why did he come to you? The records are clear enough on Syrimne. Barrier and otherwise. That's unlike him, to risk exposure."

Salinse made a vague gesture with one hand.

"I do not know the answer to that, nephew. But he was very interested in the psychological profile of Syrimne. He wanted detailed, first-hand accounts of his motivations, fears, strengths, weaknesses. Any likely triggers or instabilities."

Revik felt his throat tighten. "What did you tell him?"

"Very little," Salinse assured him. "He is not an ally, although he sought such a relationship with me. It was Galaith with whom we had, shall we say... an understanding."

Revik felt his jaw clench.

"What did you tell him?" he asked again.

Salinse sighed. "I will be blunt. He wanted to know about Elaerian mating habits. He wanted to know if finding him a female companion might calm him. Or if there was some other method that might work better."

Revik felt his face drain of blood.

He knew. Somehow he knew, even at that school at Sikkim, even before he saw the little monster lay a hand on her. The kid would head straight for Allie.

Terian was simply his errand boy.

Salinse blinked a pair of transparent lids, studying Revik's face.

As if coming to some sort of conclusion, he folded his hands.

"I am trying to help you, nephew. And to warn you. This boy... whoever he is... he sees himself as your wife's true mate. As a result, he will view you as a direct threat."

The Sark's voice grew more blunt.

"Terian has no idea what he's dealing with in this. The boy has been alone for far, *far* too long. He will not be able to control himself. There are things you probably have not yet had an opportunity to discover about your wife."

Pausing again, he gentled his voice.

"Elaerian are not Sarks, Revik. They bond with creatures differently than we do."

Revik tried to hold onto logic, to think about this rationally, but he found himself remembering her light, remembering what it had done to him.

Not just the first time, but every time after.

That part of Allie never stopped looking for its counterpoint in him, something he hadn't been able to give her. Avoiding the pain that tried to rise, he forced his eyes back on the room, pulling himself out of the Barrier.

He gestured to the old seer that he understood.

"You said they'd left Asia," Revik said. "Where are they, exactly?"

Salinse smiled wanly. "I suppose Terian thought it an unlikely place. In a way, it is. And it makes sense he would take her where he felt best able to protect her."

He met Revik's gaze with those clouded eyes.

"They are currently headed for the mainland of the United States. We haven't pinpointed a final destination, but we're working on it."

Revik nodded, backing towards the door. "Can we be out of here by the end of the day? I'd rather do any tactical planning in transit."

He was already calculating times in his head.

Twenty hours, minimum, to most parts of the United States.

Possibly more, depending on what they had by way of transport, how long it took them to gear up, how long to reach whatever served as an airstrip out here.

Revik still didn't even know where "here" was.

He figured he had to still be in Asia.

Salinse gestured affirmative. "Of course. Wreg will assist you."

Seeing Revik's hard look, Salinse clicked softly.

"He understands the importance of this mission. And he is loyal to the Bridge."

"I'm in charge," Revik said. "That's non-negotiable, Salinse. They do what I say, or I go alone."

Salinse smiled. He bowed to Revik, using the formal version.

"You are in charge. Of course, nephew."

His smile altered subtly, growing a flavor of something Revik didn't much like.

"*...As it is all entirely as it should be,*" the old Sark quoted, softer.

CHAPTER 35
FALLING

Revik left the elevator and walked out to the main floor.

Tightening his shields, he looked around the hangar-like space.

He felt conspicuous already, but didn't have time to be shy. He reached out with his light, found Wreg at once. Clicking out, he sought him with his eyes, making out his uniformed outline among a group of similarly dressed seers.

Before he could shift the direction of his feet, someone clasped his arm.

He jerked violently, turning.

He'd been half-ready to fight.

Instead he found himself staring into a pair of hazel eyes he'd never expected to see again, at least not with life in them.

"Revik? *Revik!* Jesus… what are you doing here?"

The human's voice was full of relief.

"Damn, it's good to see you! But what happened to your leg, man?"

Revik gazed blankly into the face of Jon.

Something about being face to face with the human, the adopted brother of his wife, threw him completely out of his calm, out of any semblance of linear thought. Without fully acknowledging it to himself, he had assumed Jon and Cass were dead, or at the very least, captured by the Americans.

But it was more than that.

The human's open face and light, his obvious happiness to see him, hit like a blow to the gut.

Jon released his arm.

He looked at him, his smile faltering.

His eyes took in Revik's appearance, the expression on his face.

"Revik, man... what's going on?" Jon asked. "Where's Allie? Is she here?"

"No," he said.

Revik cleared his throat, but found it difficult to speak.

He was still trying to pull words together, when two other people converged on him from the other side, throwing off his equilibrium even further.

"Revik!" Cass bounded up, her arms wide. She looked different, almost like she had before the events of the past year, even with the scar on her face.

She looked almost happy.

"Revik! You're here! Thank gods!"

Before he could move out of the way, she threw her arms around him, crushing him in a hug. He just stood there, unmoving. Without meaning to, he met the gaze of the man walking up from behind her. Balidor gave him a smile as well, but his stood out on a more emotionally complex face.

His eyes full, he patted Revik's shoulder affectionately as Cass let him go.

"It is good to see you, brother." His voice sounded like he meant it.

Revik thought a question, but never got it out.

Balidor answered him anyway.

"There isn't much left of us," was all he said.

Revik looked around the giant hangar, really seeing it for the first time. Over half of it appeared to be full of what were probably refugees from Seertown, he realized. Camped out on the floor with blankets and bedding next to piles of scattered belongings, rugs and food, cooking utensils and even domestic animals, they appeared to be bunking down for the night, probably until it was safe to return to their homes.

Assuming it ever was. Safe, that is.

"This can't be everyone," he said.

Balidor made an affirmative gesture. "It is not," he agreed. "Many went to Delhi. Others went deeper into the mountains, and to relatives and friends in China. Some were transported out by what remained of the Americans. This is only one place."

Revik looked at him. "The Adhipan?"

"Assisting refugees. I sent most of them back to the Pamir. For now." He hesitated. "...with Vash," he added. "Tarsi, too. Most of the Council. Several others among the older monks. Those we cannot afford to lose."

Revik nodded wordlessly. He understood the Adhipan's charge.

Jon's voice brought his eyes back.

"Where's Allie?" Jon asked, sharper. He was staring hard at Revik when he turned. "Revik? Where is she? Why isn't she with you?"

Cass looked at Jon, then up at Revik, releasing his sleeves where she'd still been holding onto his arms. Frowning, she did what Jon had done, taking Revik in with new eyes. Her gaze landed on the cast around his thigh, the angle at which he stood, then returned to his face, the expression he wore.

She touched his arm, gentler that time.

"Revik?" she asked. "Are you all right?"

Balidor was staring at him, too.

From the look on the Adhipan leader's face, Revik thought he might be reading him.

He didn't care. He didn't want to have this conversation.

It was one thing to speak tactically with someone like Salinse about getting Allie back from Terian and the boy. It was an entirely different thing to speak to his wife's family and friends. He couldn't deal with their emotional reactions right then, or the look that would come to Cass and Jon's faces when he told them who had her.

After what happened the year before, he couldn't predict how they might react.

And he couldn't help them with it.

He couldn't.

"You should stay here," he said, after a too-long pause. He looked at Balidor. "You'll stay? Keep things together here?"

From the look on Balidor's face, the Adhipan leader had read him, after all.

Something in his eyes had dimmed, despite his infiltrator's mask.

"Of course, brother. I am at your disposal. You do not want me with you?"

Revik thought about it for a long pause, then shook his head, glancing at the refugees huddled against one half of the hangar.

"Not for this. I could use you, but... no. I thank you for the offer."

"Any of my people? There are ten here, in total."

"Salinse has offered me numbers."

Balidor hesitated, then made a short gesture that he understood.

Jon and Cass exchanged looks.

Wide-eyed, the two of them looked to Balidor when Revik wouldn't return their gaze. Jon seemed to catch on first, which didn't surprise Revik. He'd seen a lot about Allie's two closest friends, collared or not, while all three were captives of Terian.

Despite being human, Jon had near-seer abilities at times.

Revik wondered more than once if Allie restructured his light in some way, knowingly or not, as they grew up together.

But thinking about her brought another hard pulse of pain, enough that Balidor flinched, then gripped his arm.

"Brother," he said softly. "Where is she?"

He gestured vaguely. "States," he said, his voice thick.

He glanced sideways, seeing Chandre approach from behind Jon.

He focused on her deliberately, fighting to regain his composure. It was easier facing her fierce eyes, the infiltrator's mask she wore like a skin. When he looked back at the others, he immediately wished he hadn't. Jon looked like someone had punched him in the face.

When Revik didn't say anything more, the human blurted, "I'm coming with you."

Chandre's voice rose. "So am I."

Revik turned, looking at Chandre. Balidor must have told her.

He was about to tell them no, that they damned well were *not* coming with him, when Cass spoke up from his other side, drawing his eyes.

"We'll stay here," she said.

She looped her arm through Balidor's companionably, clutching his sleeve. The Adhipan leader looked faintly surprised, but didn't step away, or try to disentangle himself from Cass's hold.

Her expression had focus. Her eyes held less of that devastated look he saw in Jon's.

"I have a job for big Adhipan man here," she said, patting his arm. "We'll help you from here, Revik. Just get Allie back."

Revik looked around at all of them, but could barely see them anymore.

He couldn't feel anything as he looked at them, couldn't comprehend what he saw on their faces. He could feel his light closing to theirs, but he didn't care anymore.

He only wanted them away from him. Out of his way.

"Fine," he said.

Without another word, he walked.

He moved through and past them, heading in the direction he'd last seen Wreg. As he made his way down the middle of a corridor between rows of fighter planes, he tried to pull his mind back on track, to get out of the spiral that started as soon as he laid eyes on Jon.

Limping, he focused on his leg, then on the rest of it.

He now knew where Terian had taken her. They'd gotten word right as he was taking his leave of Salinse.

Getting inside wouldn't be easy.

Getting inside in a way that Terian wouldn't anticipate would be even harder.

Terry would be waiting for him. He'd made that clear.

Revik approached Wreg. He waited for the older seer to look up, then cleared his throat, measuring the opaque black eyes.

"Salinse spoke to you?" he asked.

Wreg gestured affirmative, bowing.

Neither appeared to be sarcastic, nor did he display any lingering anger.

He appeared ready, listening, and respectful.

It was as if that morning had never happened.

One thing about this group, Revik thought dryly—they respected the chain of command.

Truthfully, he had missed that a little.

"You now have full access to the construct, sir," Wreg said, again with no trace of disrespect, or even undue coldness. "I took the liberty of beginning preliminary equipment assemble and tactical planning for entry into US airspace. I gather from Father Salinse that you want to leave quickly. I did not wish to wait until you were able to free yourself to ask for what is obvious."

Revik nodded. "I appreciate that." He let the other seer feel he meant it. "Have you selected the team?"

Wreg gestured affirmative. "Only first cut, of course." He motioned towards the uniformed group milling across from the refugee area. "They await your inspection. We have about eighty infiltrators in total, so you have some latitude to choose who you wish."

"Eighty?" Revik was mildly thrown by this. "That many?"

Wreg gestured affirmative.

He added, "Backgrounds, sight ranks, specialized skills all live in the secure side of the construct. I'll await the final list from you before conducting preliminary briefings."

"What do I need in the way of keys, for relevant intel?"

Wreg flashed a set of symbols at him in the space. They were complex, and multi-dimensional enough that Revik found himself giving a short nod of approval.

"Thanks."

He was about to plug into them, when he felt a soft ping from his other side.

He turned, meeting Balidor's gray eyes.

They had followed him. Great.

Balidor's eyes met his, holding a warning on the surface.

Careful, brother, he sent, barely a whisper.

Balidor's mind nudged his, indicating towards the light of the construct.

Revik followed with his mind's eye to where the Adhipan leader indicated.

For what felt like a long pause... he hesitated.

He scanned the silver strands writhing there, wound into the structure of the construct. Existing within a construct—as Revik was now, simply by being in Salinse's stronghold—wasn't the same as *using* a construct. To access the locked portions and manipulate the layered light as a tool, he would need to open himself, to resonate with the overall design.

He would need to become one with it, in a sense.

Scanning the properties of the silver strands making up the construct's meta-structure, he understood exactly what Balidor's warning meant.

The light of the Dreng lived here.

It flowed thick inside the construct, as it had in Salinse's light, almost as thick as what he remembered from the Pyramid. Whatever Salinse's claims that Terian carried the only direct line to the Dreng following the Pyramid's collapse, he hadn't been fully honest. Their power lived here, too. It came through with a slightly different flavor, but in important ways, it was the same.

The Dreng's fingerprints remained irrefutable.

Staring up at that light, he found himself seeing Allie standing before him in the dirt yard. Terian's hand clenched on her throat as she balanced on her toes. She'd been naked, covered in bruises, most of them from him.

She'd yelled at him, even with Terian holding her collar.

She'd sacrificed herself for him, offered herself to the boy.

Seeing her there, so close, so real despite the distance between them, broke everything down on top of him.

His heart hurt, more than anything in him had hurt in his life.

He'd told Terian once, he'd turn if he had to.

Somewhere in that instant's hesitation, he realized his mind had been made up before he'd really contemplated the question.

"Brother Revik?" Balidor said aloud.

Revik didn't turn, but his jaw hardened.

Brushing the Adhipan leader out of his light, he took the keys Wreg offered him, angry now. Without looking at any of them, he let the silver strands resonate with his *aleimi*. He ignored the alarm he felt off Balidor... and the tremor that ran through him at how easily that particular frequency still sat in parts of his own structure.

He plugged into the Rebel construct.

There was a silence.

For a few seconds, he simply flexed the added weight, reacquainting himself with the added structure, with the multiplication of his light. From that place of perfect stillness, he gazed down from a vantage he hadn't glimpsed in about forty years.

It was like he was meant to be there.

It was like coming home.

CHAPTER 36
OWNED

I couldn't see. Flashes erupted in my eyes, blinding me.

I felt a vague gratitude that I had on clothes, even though I knew it helped only marginally. The crush of bodies pushed up against where I tried to walk, sandwiched between guards, holding cuffed hands in front of my face.

People touched me wherever they could, and they weren't particularly gentle about it. I heard clothing rip, felt their fingers caress bare skin. I knew all this, in some part of my mind, but continued to stare straight ahead, my jaw clenched to keep my face still.

I'd become one of those people on the feeds.

I'd become a story, one of those seer terrorists and celebrities who bolstered ad sales along with viewership on the main networks. The ones with screaming headlines over their pictures, who always managed to look stoned the instant the recorders captured the still image of their real, non-avatar faces.

In my case, they'd be right.

Before the helicopter touched down, Terian slammed another syringe-full of something into my neck.

It worked on me nearly instantaneously, making me thick-tongued even before he'd finished unlocking the straps that held me in the restraint chair at the back of the military transport. When he helped me out of the sliding door, I half-fell, lurching sideways until he clamped an arm around my waist, jerking me upright.

I'm sure I looked drunk, or sufficiently wanton even for the mass feeds.

There'd be no avatars for my image, of course.

I was a terrorist; they could show my real face with impunity. Dead people had more rights to conceal their true appearance than I did. I'd never maintain anonymity in the seer or human world again.

Not like I ever had, come to think of it.

These images would be current, though.

Since my mom died, they'd been sharing the few non-avatar images of me from high school and college. My hair had been the wrong length, the wrong color, even the wrong texture. My face looked different now.

It was more angular, thinner. My cheekbones stood out more.

According to Jon, my eyes had changed color.

Oh, and I was taller.

The Scandinavian Terian remained by my side as we parted the crush of reporters waiting by the White House helipad. He kept an arm firmly around me as the guards led me across the White House lawn and into the famous building.

No one noticed the boy as he trailed along behind us.

"Could you speak up?" the sharp voice asked.

I held up my cuffed hands, spreading my fingers and blinking against the ultra-bright lights. Terian caught hold of the chain and pulled my hands back to my lap.

With an effort, I focused on the reporter.

"Excuse me?"

"How do you account for yourself?" the blond woman asked.

Her organic headset pulsed with a bright blue light, which told me anything I said would be recorded, broadcast, and heard, even if I whispered, likely by millions of people.

Account for myself? I wondered. Does she expect me to answer that?

Even on drugs, the setting was ludicrous.

Paisley couches faced one another in the Oval Office, a polished maple coffee table between them. A bone china tea set sat there, on a silver tray with cucumber and hummus sandwiches. Terian and I took up one couch, the reporter the other.

The Oval Office's most famous occupant wasn't in attendance.

The Scandinavian fingered the collar at my neck absently as he posed—serious, pensive, handsome—for the cameras running steadily in the background.

"I'm not sure what you mean…" I began, glancing at him.

The woman raised her voice and spoke more slowly, as if supposing I was deaf, or maybe mentally deficient in some way.

"Do you consider yourself a terrorist?" she asked.

I imagined the swell of dramatic music in the background at her daring question of the bloodthirsty seer, followed by a close-up on her determined, righteous face. I didn't smile, but a more cynical side of me wanted to.

Terian coached me prior to the interview, however.

He warned me that seeming amused in any way would, at best, make me appear arrogant.

At worst, bat-shit crazy.

I knew who she was. I'd grown up seeing people like her on the monitor at my mom's house in San Francisco. I even watched the feeds sometimes in India.

She was one of those journalists who had a reputation for asking the poignant questions, of *getting to the truth.* I didn't know anyone on the ground who really believed that, though, not even when I lived in San Francisco.

The news feeds were nothing but theater and propaganda most of the time.

This woman, in particular, always grated on my nerves.

She had the voice of one of those yappy dogs, and a face that had been reconstructed so many times she looked like a wax doll. During a period where I drank heavily, after Jaden cheated on me with that horrible groupie, I occasionally used this woman's channel as an alarm clock. Her voice was one of the few sounds I'd get out of bed just to shut off, no matter how hung-over I was.

Even before I knew I was a seer, I knew the feeds were full of shit. So did all of my human friends. I just didn't realize the extent of it.

My mom told me it hadn't always been that way.

"Did you hear me?" the yappy dog asked, sharper. "Are you a terrorist, Alyson? Or does that question make you uncomfortable?"

I glanced at Terian.

He sat casually in his dark suit, still caressing my neck absently with his fingers. I knew that was deliberate, too. The body he wore looked like a posable male sex doll. He was almost absurdly handsome, and so white, he had to be human.

Or so the feeds would think.

I fought the urge to yank up the front of the low-cut sundress they'd shoved me into, crossing my legs compulsively in spite of myself, although I knew that probably only sexualized my appearance more.

Sandals covered my feet, ribbons winding up my bare legs.

Terian probably would have put me into a VR-paneled, topless club dress if he could have gotten away with it.

According to the Press Secretary and others from the Department of Defense, they needed me to look harmless.

They needed me to seem as frail and feminine as possible.

I wondered how well my bruises were showing up on the national feeds.

I cleared my throat.

"No," I said. "It doesn't make me uncomfortable. I'm just not exactly sure what you mean."

"What I *mean?*" She snorted in open derision. "I mean… you blew up a ship, Alyson. How do you feel about killing all of those innocent people?"

"Errr… no," I said. "I didn't blow up a ship."

I looked out the glass doors behind her, staring longingly at the green lawns and gardens. I wiped my face with cuffed hands, then instantly regretted it, realizing I'd just highlighted those cuffs for the cameras a second time.

"Look," I said. "That was all a big mistake. I thought you knew that. I thought you proved Caine was behind what happened there?"

The woman gave the camera a knowing look. "Sure. Of course. Because we all *know* humans have access to supernatural powers."

"You have access to C-4," I said, blunt.

The woman gave me a narrow look, as if the cocker spaniel suddenly began speaking English. I saw the Press Secretary behind the cameraman, waving his arms to Terian. When Terian glanced up, the human began making "cut it off" gestures by running his finger across his neck.

"I think what Alyson means," the Scandinavian Terian said smoothly, waving the man off with his fingers. "There are other ways that accident could have occurred, Donna."

"Are you saying the Pentagon *believes* her story?" the woman snorted.

Looking at the Aryan Sex Doll, Donna was nearly panting.

Terian shrugged, smiling faintly. It was a human shrug.

"Let's just say, we are still looking into it. We have reviewed her testimony in detail, and are not yet ready to dismiss the evidence it has uncovered. Clearly, another explanation might exist for what occurred."

The woman gave him a seductive smile, then me a thoughtful look.

As if reading my thoughts from earlier, she leaned towards me, laying her arms on her lap and clasping her fingers.

"But aren't you *dating* one of the terrorists, Alyson?" She smiled.

I could tell it was meant to be a conspiratorial smile. Like we were just two girls chatting, maybe. With a few hundred million people watching.

"You know which one I mean," she said coyly. "He's been a national obsession since the attacks last year."

In the VR space behind her, a picture of Revik appeared.

It morphed into more pictures as the woman talked, showing various angles, and even one of the two of us together, in Vancouver, BC. I had to assume they had more of those images now, since they had my real face to use in facial-rec searches.

"Whole feed channels are devoted to the two of you," the woman said, her voice still sickeningly coy. "You're the Bonnie and Clyde of the seer world. Surely, you were aware that a certain, immature segment of humans also finds the two of you fascinating?"

I exhaled. "Not really, no."

I had known though, once.

I forgot all about that, mostly because when it started, Jon and Cass had been missing, my mother murdered, and I'd thought Revik was dead.

I hadn't given a damn about much of anything back then.

The woman's words seemed to mirror my own mind.

"Of course, it's easy to romanticize someone who's dead, isn't it, Alyson? It's a little harder when you're *alive* and a mass killer."

At my silence, she gave Terian a questioning look, then cleared her throat.

"So are you still dating him, Alyson? Or have you moved on since then?"

I felt my chest clench as I stared at the morphing images.

"Dating?" I heard myself say. "No."

"You aren't still sexually involved with this seer?" she asked, skeptical.

I hesitated. "Well…"

"So for seers, maybe this doesn't constitute dating," the woman said smugly, crossing her thin legs under the short business skirt she wore. "But for humans, this implies some kind of *relationship*, Alyson. Living amongst us all those years, surely, you were aware of that…?"

"He's my husband," I blurted.

I felt Terian smile. When I glanced over, his face remained still, his eyes showing a faint concern as he studied my face. Quite the specimen of deep-thinking male. If he wasn't so completely out of his head insane, it might be funny.

The woman's voice made me turn.

"Your *husband?*" she said. "*Really…?*"

I could hear the glee in her voice.

A colder anger settled over my light.

"Yeah," I said. "We're married. So not… you know… *dating.*"

"Where is he now?" The woman smiled conspiratorially. "Aren't seers known for their pathological protectiveness towards their mates?"

I glanced at Terian.

The amber eyes held a warning, even as he touched my shoulder with one hand, a gesture probably meant to appear reassuring.

"Yeah," I said. I looked at the woman, then past her, at the VR image of Revik's face. "Yeah. I guess we are."

I watched as Terian shook hands with the reporter, Donna.

I stood there like a pet dog waiting outside a coffee shop for its owner.

I felt a little sick watching her flirt with him, touching his arm more than a few times as she leaned up next to him, pressing her likely-fake boobs into his side.

Her eyes kept darting to me, too, as if trying to dissect me where I stood. Her gaze was overt, and overly intimate. She took liberties as she looked over my body, as if memorizing it for later cataloguing.

She probably assumed Terian and I were sleeping together.

Hell, most of the civilized world probably did, especially after that broadcast, but that hadn't exactly been accidental, either.

I saw the speculation in the female newscaster's eyes, and for once, found myself glad of the collar. At least I didn't have to listen to what this vile woman was thinking.

I avoided her stare while Terian finished with the news crews and walked back in my direction. Smiling at me in an almost friendly way, he motioned for the guards to lead me out of the Oval Office.

We walked down a hall to an elevator that looked like an antique—at least until I saw the organic modifications that had been made to the control panel and the double doors.

He nodded to the porter, making a gesture with his fingers that indicated down. I felt my stomach sink when I realized what his gesture meant for me.

He was taking me back to my cage.

I barely noticed the security detail that accompanied us.

I more wondered how he'd managed to talk the boy into staying behind.

As if he heard my thoughts, Terian glanced at me.

"We'll have to make this next piece quick, Alyson," he murmured, checking an antique watch on his wrist. "Our dear young friend is getting impatient, I'm afraid."

From that, I had to assume Nenzi was yelling at Terian in the Barrier.

An instant later, I remembered where we were.

"The shields?" I murmured.

The entire White House was covered in dense Barrier shields, run by a few dozen seers on the payroll of the Pentagon and Secret Service. Nenzi shouldn't be able to reach Terian at all through that maze.

"Pretty much useless against him, I'm afraid," Terian murmured. He folded his hands in front of his body. He gazed up at the ceiling of the elevator, bouncing lightly on his heels as we descended. "I'm trying to figure it out. He seems to know how to bypass the construct entirely. I thought he might be able to help me design some sort of upgrade—"

"I'm looking forward to watching your head explode," I told him.

Terian glanced at me, raising an eyebrow.

Then, he chuckled.

"I guess it's good I have a few spares." The smile widened, right before he winked. "I wouldn't be so quick to applaud this one going though, Alyson. I would think you'd prefer it to some of the alternatives."

Leaning against the elevator wall, I gave him a bored look.

Still, his comment made me nervous, and brought back memories I would rather have repressed. Looking down, I fidgeted with my cuffed wrists. It was the closest he'd come to threatening me since we'd first left India, at least in regard to rape.

Nenzi made it clear I was off-limits to anyone, human or seer, despite the number of monetary offers and other bribes I'd already overheard offered to the Scandinavian for just a few hours alone with me.

Terian only broke Nenzi's rule once, about two days into my captivity.

Giving the kid some excuse about medical tests, he took me to a locked room made of organic steel that apparently even Nenzi couldn't see past, and kept me there for a few hours.

The only good news was, I was collared.

Even so, the one time was enough.

I considered telling Nenzi, of course.

Terian told me what would happen if I did. The threat was simple, but effective. He would tell Nenzi that Revik and I hadn't completed the bonding process.

Then Nenzi would hunt down and kill Revik.

Nenzi couldn't read me through the collar. I had to assume Terian had ways of keeping Nenzi out of his own mind, as well. If I had to guess, he probably did a lot of it by moving any incriminating memories or thoughts from this body to a different one.

Either way, I couldn't bring myself to risk it.

I had absolutely no idea of how many other bodies Terian had lurking around. If that number was anything more than one, killing this body wouldn't even do me any good.

That didn't mean I didn't continue to think about it, though, imagining how Terian's brains would look splattered against the drab colors of the Oval Office wallpaper.

Still, I'd gotten off easy, and I knew it.

Without Nenzi there, I'd be going through what Cass endured.

Possibly worse, because Terian would have wanted it public, for Revik's benefit. He would have rented me out to every loser on the White House payroll with a few dollars to spare, then let rumors and live footage leak directly to the feeds.

We reached the bottom of the elevator shaft.

The door let off a low ping.

After a pause where the security mechanism scanned us a second time, it opened to reveal a dimly lit, featureless corridor.

Terian made a hospitable gesture towards the opening.

I exited in front of him. He let me walk ahead, only taking my arm right before we entered the room at the end of the low-ceilinged tunnel.

An oval table dominated the rectangular space.

Around it sat a group of humans in business suits, filling all but a few of the padded, high-backed, leather chairs. I was still standing there, feeling again like a show dog on display at the State Fair, when Wellington rose to his feet from his place at the head of the table. Smiling, he gestured towards the two open seats.

"Join us," he said hospitably.

I sat where the Scandinavian seer indicated.

I avoided the eyes of a fifty-something male human who stared at me openly.

I couldn't quite tell if the look there was revulsion or some combination of that and lust. His reddish face turned even redder the longer he stared at me, frowning, his eyes flickering from my chest to my face, then back again.

I glanced at the Vice President, an older man with white hair who sat to Wellington's left.

His appraising look was less ambiguous.

Great. I was surrounded by horny, racist humans.

Wellington's face was almost a relief after I'd looked around at the others.

"So," I said. "What's for dinner?"

The room grew, if it were possible, even more silent.

Then Wellington burst out in a genuine-sounding laugh.

The woman sitting next to him, a middle-aged, female human with dark brunette hair and hazel eyes, laughed with him. So did the Scandinavian.

Looking around at the three of them, I realized they were all Terians.

Watching them laugh together in a kind of blank incredulity, I thought my life couldn't possibly get more fucked up.

Of course, I was wrong about that.

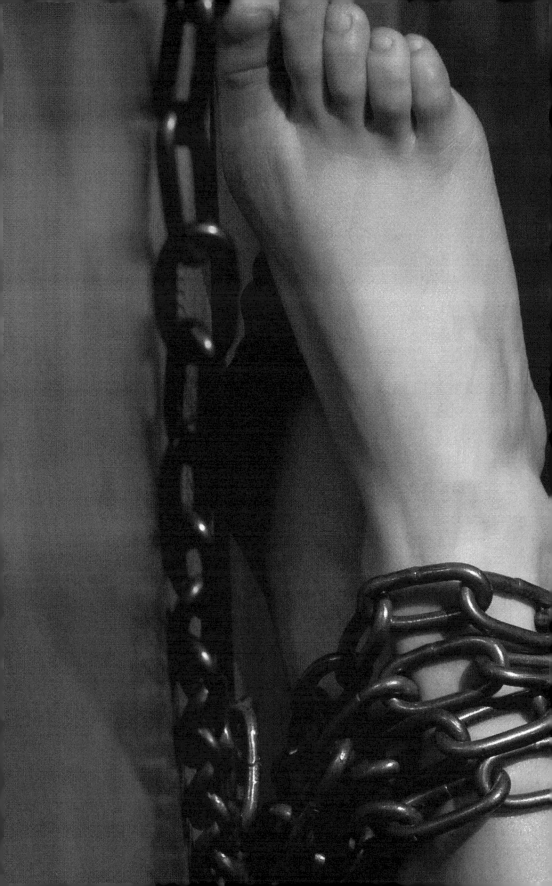

CHAPTER 37
CAGED

I woke up, my face pressed against the floor of a semi-organic cage. My wrists and ankles were locked to bars set in the same floor. There wasn't even a chain to allow real movement.

My neck and spine hurt so badly I could barely lift my head. I was thirsty. I couldn't feel my fingers, and I didn't know if the latter was from cold or lack of circulation. I was naked again, which added to the feeling of powerlessness.

It also made me angry.

But for one window in the wall in front of me, the room was dark.

The inability to use the Barrier made everything appear flat, two-dimensional.

I remembered the world this way, of course; it hadn't been all that long ago that being sight-blind was all I knew. Now, the difference was staggering, like being drugged.

Of course, it made everything hurt less, too, but it didn't do anything about the feeling of deprivation that never left, or the depression that came with it.

I couldn't feel him at all.

I watched nighttime clouds whisper by the lone window.

It took me another moment to realize it wasn't a window at all, but a virtual reality screen. My cage lived in the basement bowels of the White House. We were dug too far in for clouds, at any time of day.

The window was just another lie.

I tried to stay calm. No good would come of thinking about him, so I tried to keep those thoughts away from me, too. I clenched my hands, staring at the empty corridor, fighting not to let my mind go anywhere but my immediate situation.

I had to get out of here.

Fingers touched my foot, caressing my skin.

I sucked in a breath.

My heart beat hard enough to hurt my chest.

I craned my neck, fought for focus in the dim light.

A few seconds passed where I couldn't see anything.

It was beyond strange to not be able to use my light to compensate for the limitations of my physical senses. I was back to having to wait for my eyes to adjust as soon as they pointed away from the fake window.

Eventually, I made out his face.

He sat in the middle part of the cell, cross-legged, his face concentrated.

The longer I stared, the brighter his eyes got. They shone a pale green, ghosting the round contours of his face.

It was eerie. In part because they looked like mine.

They also looked like Revik's—at least how Revik's looked after our first few nights together in that house in the Himalayas.

Even collared, I felt some part of me react to the memory.

I forced it away. I watched this new set of glowing irises as the boy crawled across the floor. I didn't move as he reached the area by my head.

I couldn't have done much, anyway, not with inch-thick cuffs holding me to the floor.

The boy's fingers touched my face, pushing hair out of my eyes.

"Nenzi." My voice was hoarse. I cleared my throat, trying to get enough spit to talk. "What are you doing here?"

He spoke English, maybe because I had.

"He's gone. You were sleeping." He caressed my jaw, his fingers lingering on my throat. "Are you in pain? Do you hurt still?"

In reflex, I tried to look at my body.

I saw pale-looking flesh, bruises, what looked like cuts. I looked overly thin. My sense of smell was both dampened and sickeningly sharper. With the *aleimic* portion of it missing, the physical smells nearly overpowered me. I must have peed through the grate, because I could smell that, too.

But I wasn't really in pain apart from the collar.

The rest was discomfort from being tied down, from not being able to move, and having my skin chafed by metal.

After turning all of this over, I shook my head.

"Only my neck. And I'm thirsty."

The boy immediately turned away, fumbling with something in the dark.

I wasn't surprised when, seconds later, he put a cold-feeling container to my lips. I drank the water eagerly once he'd opened the top, swallowing as he held it to my mouth. After minutes passed where I only drank, pausing here and there to breathe and swallow, I nodded, gesturing with my fingers that it was enough.

He set it on the floor of the cage.

"Thanks." I looked up at him, squinting in the dim light.

He caressed my arm, then my fingers. I saw his face tighten in some kind of concentration. A little nervous at what I saw there, I averted my gaze, resting my chin on the grate. I wondered if he was reading me—or trying to.

"Nenzi, where were you today?" I asked, when he didn't move away.

The boy began to answer me in a series of complicated hand gestures until I made a negative gesture of my own. I kept my voice calm.

"I don't understand." At his blank look, I said, "You need to tell me. Speak out loud, like you did before."

I was still confused by his inability to read me.

Revik told me sight restraint collars only prevented him from using his own sight.

The collar I wore shouldn't have impacted the kid's ability to read me at all.

Revik also told me he'd been in a lot of separation pain from me while he'd been locked up with Terian. He said the collar prevented him from controlling it, so it was actually worse.

Why couldn't I feel anything?

And why couldn't Nenzi just pull answers from my mind?

For that matter, why couldn't Terian?

"Tests," Nenzi said, once his brow cleared. "They do tests on me. They want to do more. On both of us."

"What kind of tests?" I asked, although I already knew.

He pointed to his head, gesturing up towards the space above where we sat. Wearing the collar, all I could see was air where he pointed, but I understood. He meant the structures over his head. The telekinesis.

Moving closer shyly, he sat next to me, crossing his legs by my ribcage where I lay on my stomach. After another moment's pause, he placed his hand lightly on my back, stroking the skin there tentatively with his fingers.

I watched him stare at me. I closed my eyes at the intensity of his gaze.

"Nenzi, why do you look at me like that?" I asked.

He smiled. There was something heartbreaking in that smile, something that made my chest hurt. Still, I had to find some way to discourage this. Hopefully without him deciding he needed to make my skull crack in half.

"Nenzi," I said. "I think you're mistaking me for someone else."

He caressed my hair. Tentative at first, he gradually grew more bold, sliding his fingers through long, half-curled strands, working out tangles carefully with his hands. It reminded me of Hannah a little… but more so of Revik, who had done something similar a number of times when we were alone.

Both of us had our moments where we just wanted to touch the other.

There was a bit of possessiveness behind it, I guess.

But it was also loving and affectionate and sensual, and… I think with us, stemmed at least partly from the fact that we finally could.

For Revik, it had often been my hair.

I closed my eyes, pushing the memory away.

Nenzi scooted closer with his feet.

He pushed my hair aside to rub my shoulder, and the back of my neck not covered by the collar. I was so tired I could barely think, and didn't bother telling him to stop, figuring it might be better not to piss him off until I had a good reason.

I'd tried asking Terian about the boy, of course.

More than once.

The only time we had what approximated a real conversation about it, we'd been in a federal holding facility. We'd been forced to wait for over eight hours while they went through the paperwork of letting us through Sight Containment and into the United States. Nenzi took almost as long as me, probably because Terian had to falsify all his records for the first time.

I'd been naked, of course, and cuffed to a metal bench.

Terian had been his usual, charming self.

He'd plopped down next to me on the bench, smiling. His fingers touched my cheek until I flinched away.

"You're going to help me with our little friend in there," he murmured. "Keep him happy, yes? It is the healthy thing for both of us."

"Uh huh." I'd continued to look around. The room had been a ten by ten cell with white walls, a bolted down organic bench being the only furniture.

"Does he know why you really want him?" I asked.

Terian made a "more or less" gesture. "He knew well enough to bargain with me about you." The blond seer tilted his head to look at me. In that body, it gave him a kind of rakish air—again, almost cartoonishly handsome.

"And he's right, of course." The Scandinavian Terian smiled. "I can't expect him to function at his best when his basic needs haven't been met." He winked at me. "The poor lad's suffered so much already."

I snorted. "You really think I'm going to be able to bring the teenaged serial killer under control? Because why? I have girl parts?"

Terian chuckled. "Most definitely."

I decided to just come out and ask.

"Why *me*, Terry? Why does he think he knows me?"

A flicker of curiosity touched the amber eyes.

"You know, I've wondered that myself." His gaze drifted down the length of me, then turned inward. "There's your race, of course. But he seems quite taken with *you*, specifically. And he knows a lot about you, Allie-bird."

I grimaced at the nickname.

Smiling, Terian gestured in a shrug, putting his hands in his pockets.

"I'm very much looking forward to what you find out," he said. "Once the two of you have become better acquainted."

"That's not going to happen," I warned.

His lips stretched in another smile.

"Oh, I'm quite sure it will. I highly doubt he'll take no for an answer... for long, anyway. You should see all the nasty little thoughts he's had about you already."

His smile touched the amber eyes when he saw me grimace a second time.

"He's quite the little voyeur, our Nenzi," he added. "He barely took time off to sleep while you and Revi' were getting acquainted in that hovel. And let's just say, Revi' wasn't the only one who got off on some of those experiences..."

I grimaced again. I tried not to remember the look of adoration in the kid's eyes when he'd first seen me.

"You've got to be kidding me," I muttered.

"But I'm not, little bird."

"Stop fucking calling me that!"

At his delighted grin, I bit my lip.

My mother called me bird, little bird, Allie-bird. The same mother Terian bled to death over what had to have been an extremely long couple of hours. I knew why he was doing it, but it made me want to kill him with my bare hands, each and every time he said it.

He trailed fingers over my neck. I jerked from his touch.

"He was incredibly jealous, you know," he added, softer. "I can't say I blame him. I've wanted to kill Revi' more than once myself."

I swallowed, keeping silent with an effort.

"He'll calm down, I think," Terian mused. "Yes. A blow job a night from his best girl should put things right as rain in his little world."

I made an involuntary face. "Jesus. You're really sick."

He'd chuckled again.

Lying on the floor of a different cage now, I remembered thinking at the time that there was something Terian wasn't telling me.

Ignoring the boy's fingers in my hair, I scanned his words, trying to decide if he'd given me any kind of hint about Nenzi's true identity. I still had no idea if he was the same Nenzi who'd eventually turned into Syrimne.

Even if he was that being... in some, inexplicable way... it didn't explain how he thought he knew *me*, much less how he'd avoided aging in eighty-odd years.

I tried not to think about the interview with that reporter, or the fact that it had gone out live on all the major feed channels.

Two days earlier, I'd had my sentience status legally revoked by the World Court.

I was owned now, by the United States government.

There would be more hearings of course, more red tape. The other human governments were pitching fits, especially China. But no one remained in the seer world to fight it—not legally, anyway. The Council of Seven no longer existed. Terian let me watch feeds covering the bombing in Seertown by persons unknown, and the surprise attack on the American military who came to "help."

It was American media, so I couldn't be sure how much of it was true.

For all I knew, Americans themselves did the bombing.

The images of Seertown appeared to be irrefutable, though.

The official seer government was finished. Seertown was now part of the militarized zone, and basically deserted.

I knew that should be at the top of my list of concerns, and it was, to a degree. Where Vash was, whether my friends were okay, where my brother was, what Balidor had done with the Adhipan, who else might have been killed in the fight...

All those questions kept me up at night, too.

Yet somehow, what kept rising to the forefront of my mind was Revik seeing me on the feeds sitting in the Oval Office, bruised, wearing a low-cut dress and a collar, Terian's arm wrapped around my shoulders.

I knew Terian had his own reasons for wanting to provoke Revik.

It didn't help, knowing that, or that Revik would see through it.

I jerked my head, and the collar clunked against my neck.

It hurt. But it got my mind back to the present. It reminded me where I was.

It also reminded me that I was blind.

Revik wasn't gone. I just couldn't feel him. And if Nenzi and Terian were any indication, Revik couldn't feel me, either.

Which was likely the point of this collar, to keep Revik from tracking me.

At the thought, a physical pain started in my chest.

His hands were on me then, like they had been the night before.

I tried to writhe away from his fingers, but there was nowhere to go.

"Nenzi, no. *Stop it!*"

His hands caressed my back down to my rear, then the top of my legs. I felt his fingers tense as I moved as far back as the cuffs allowed. He caressed my inner thighs, then his hand slid higher...

"No!" I craned my neck. "Stop it! I don't want you to. *Please stop!*"

After a pause, he removed his hands, looking down at my face.

His eyes glowed a faint, pale green.

"Please," he said softly. He touched my cheek. "Please, Allie."

"No!" I made a sharp negative gesture with my fingers. "No!"

His eyes closed, longer than a blink.

He caught my hair, holding it tightly in his small fingers. He caressed my back with his other hand, and I saw him look at my body even as I avoided looking at his.

I was aware now that he wasn't wearing any clothes... a fact I'd purposefully avoided when I looked at him earlier. I felt the smallness of his hands, saw the whiteness of his skin in my peripheral vision, the thin chest and spider-like arms.

He looked so young.

I recoiled under his stare.

"Please," I said. "Please, leave me alone."

"What can I do?" Frustration grew audible in his voice. He sounded older to me, like he did sometimes. Less the frightened boy and more like... someone else. He caressed my face. He tried to touch my breast, but I pulled away from that, too.

"You want it," he said softly. "I can feel it. You want me to touch you." Desire thickened his voice. "What do you want?"

Tears came to my eyes, which only made me angrier.

"Please, let me *go!*"

"Go?" His voice held surprise. "Go where?"

I bit my lip. If I mentioned Revik it would only infuriate him.

I blurted, "Anywhere I'm not a prisoner! Anywhere but here, with him."

He touched my fingers again, his own soft. "Is it because you're tied?" he asked. "Should I untie you?"

"Yes," I said, nodding. "Yes. Untie me."

His eyes studied mine. He looked older again, wary, and faintly aggressive. There was something else there, too. Something I almost recognized.

"I could do it anyway," he said. "I could fuck you."

I flinched at his words. My jaw hardened.

"Yes," I said. "You could. But I won't like it, Nenzi. It'll make me feel sick. I'll find you disgusting." I paused, letting that sink in. I saw from his eyes that it had. "And I'll never like *you* again, Nenzi. Never. I'll feel sick every time you touch me. I'll want to throw up."

Seeing his frown deepen, I bit my lip.

"I'll do whatever you want," I blurted. "We can be friends. Just take off the collar. Untie me, and take off the collar. We can…" I choked a little on the words. "…make love. Then we can leave here. We can go together."

Light pulsed in his irises.

Briefly, it put me back there, with Revik.

I found myself remembering his face, the way he'd looked at me in the dark.

I saw desire in this boy's eyes, too. He might have been thinking about taking me up on my offer. I couldn't tell though, not really, and I wasn't letting myself think about it, not yet. Without access to my light, I could only try to connect the dots by what he said, by his body language, by the expression in his eyes.

It was frustrating, staring at that pale, serious face, trying to decide whether I should say more, or just keep silent.

Eventually, he released my hair, slumping to the floor beside me.

He lay there on his back, staring up at the ceiling.

His hand settled on his crotch.

I didn't look down, not exactly thrilled with the prospect of watching him pleasure himself, either… but he didn't. He looked at me instead, his face only a foot from mine, the shocking green light in his eyes beginning to fade, tendrils swimming liquidly in tiny veins in his irises.

Shifting to his side, he propped his jaw on his hand. He studied my face, then looked down at the rest of me. He reached up and began stroking my hair.

His face seemed less tense.

"I'll wait," he said. "I don't want you making bargains. Not for him."

I didn't have to ask who he meant. He was talking about Revik.

"You'll love me again," he said, softer. "You will."

Watching the faint green glow continue to pulse behind his dark irises, I let him stroke my hair. I have no idea what I could have said.

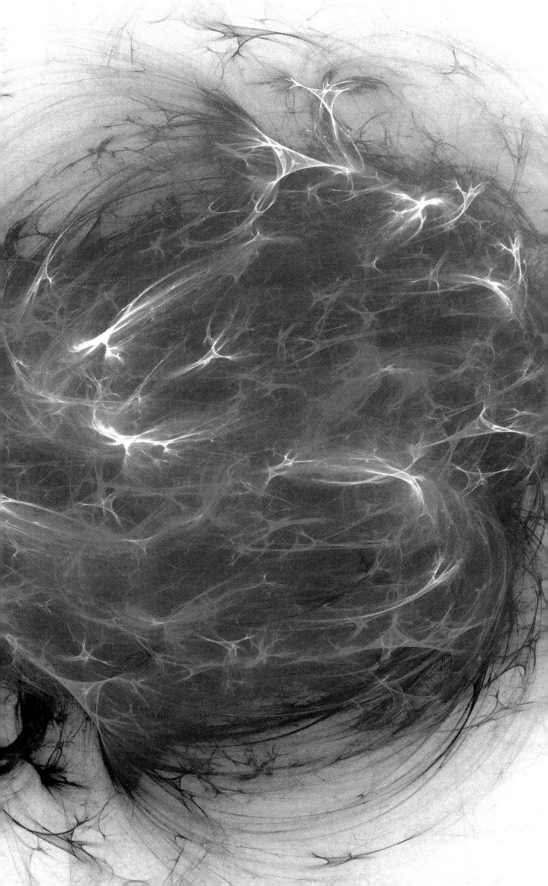

CHAPTER 38
NENZI

It was daylight.

I opened my eyes.

Someone moved me while I was unconscious. I was no longer cuffed naked on my stomach to an organic metal floor. There was no lonely seer kid groping my bare skin.

I sat by a waterfall, in a high-domed room.

It took me a few seconds to realize what I was looking at wasn't real.

Two nondescript porters watched over the doors. They ignored me while I stuck a foot in the water, watching it run over what was probably VR skin. Birds flitted by, perching briefly on the thin branches of small trees before leaving again with a flick of their wings.

My eyes drifted up to meet a giant sun dome.

Through the glass, I could see red rock cliffs, and beyond that, a deep blue, cloudless sky. Inside, a naked rock face made up one whole wall, jutting unevenly into a third of the room and curving inward towards a metal ceiling. Waterfalls ran down rocks in decorative streams, adorned with desert flowers, twisted pines, Mexican sage, cactus.

I could smell the flowers, even without my sight.

I could feel the water, cool on my bare feet.

I wore a green silk dress, slit on either side up to my thighs. Flowers poked through artistic curls in my hair, which had been wound in a loose pile on top of my head. A jeweled necklace replaced the one I'd worn in reality for months—a clunky silver chain that held Revik's mother's ring. I touched this new necklace with my fingers, eyes closed, trying to feel the other one through the mirage.

I only felt the smooth, cut sides of glass-like gems.

Briefly, I saw Revik in my mind's eye, his eyes narrow as he stared at the ring. He'd told me the first finger, the one where he wore my father's ring, meant he was owned. It was a way seers signaled to one another they were married in the human world.

He wanted me to wear his mother's ring on that finger.

I told him I'd get it resized when we returned to Seertown.

But Seertown didn't exist anymore.

I took my hand off my neck, opening my eyes.

I watched Nenzi wander by the rock face a dozen yards from where I sat. His eyes shifted up, taking in the shape of a hawk as it winged by on the other side of the glass dome. I was still watching him, my foot dipped in the waterfall, when the Scandinavian Terian sat down beside me.

I didn't look over.

When he placed something by my feet, I glanced at it, however.

A glass wand, ornately carved, rested there. It looked like antique crystal.

Staring at it, I hesitated.

I felt him watching my face, and decided not to ask.

When I finally glanced over, he smiled, his eyes flashing a dim kind of desire. I found myself wondering if it was for sex, or something else.

His eyes followed mine to the boy.

"I thought at first he needed a mother," he said conversationally, watching Nenzi over by the rocks. "Someone to pat his head, tell him everything was going to be all right." He smiled, clicking softly. "He knew you by name. It was just so intriguing. I wanted to bring you two kids together just to see what would happen."

I hid my surprise that he was volunteering information.

Nodding without expression, I glanced at the boy.

"He knew who I was."

"I believe I just said that, yes."

"Is he... real?" I looked at Terian. "Is he who I think he is? Or some kind of copy? A clone?"

"I don't know."

I watched Nenzi hold out a hand, whistle softly to a songbird with a crimson head. It landed delicately on his finger, flapping its wings to balance on its new perch. I wondered if the boy knew the bird wasn't real.

He smiled at it, making soft noises in reply as the bird chirped at him.

"It's like a dream, seeing him here." Realizing I'd spoken aloud, I felt my jaw harden. "How is it he's so young?"

"Physically, he's probably…" Terian made a mental calculation, tilting his head as he looked at the boy. "…Twenty? Twenty-one?" He smiled at me. "Are you ageist? I assure you, young seers are quite virile. Of course, he may suffer from the same stamina issues you seem to be cursed with in your mates."

I chose to pretend I hadn't heard the last.

I looked at him. "Terian, you must have a theory. What is he?"

Terian shrugged. He glanced at me. Looking down over my body in the green dress, his eyes turned momentarily hard.

"You can't refuse him forever, Alyson." The amber eyes flickered back to the boy. "Pull a stunt like that again… offering him sex to free you… offering him sex to hurt *me*… and I'll lock you in a Barrier construct and let a platoon of Wellington's soldiers have their way with you for a month."

His smile didn't touch the amber eyes.

"…I'll give them props and everything."

Taking in the expression there, I felt my chest tighten.

I remembered this man tortured Revik, Jon, and Cass for something like six months straight, beating Revik nearly to death. Jon told me Terian would try to have conversations with Revik while he did it. Not to get information, or even to feign interrogating him. No, he'd talk to him about the weather, reminisce about the old days, tell jokes.

I had a particularly brutal image burned into my brain of him cutting off Jon's fingers while asking Revik what had happened to drive a wedge between them as friends.

Jon didn't tell me that. Neither did Revik.

I got that accidentally one day while Jon stared at his mutilated hand.

I also saw him raping Cass in one of her angry moments, and one of Jon's sad ones. I caught glimpses of things related to Revik, too, but for some reason, Cass and Jon were even more protective about him than they were of themselves.

Maybe because I was married to him, or maybe because he'd asked them not to think about those things around me—or maybe for other reasons I didn't want to contemplate too closely—I rarely picked up much about Revik's specific experiences with Terian.

I looked at the boy.

Unlike Revik, I meant nothing to Terian.

I was purely an asset.

Like that prostitute the other Nenzi had as a kid, my only real protection was the boy. I let my eyes follow him as he gazed up the red rock face. The first bird had flown off, but he was watching the others, his eyes holding a fevered concentration.

"He'd never stand for it," Terian murmured. "But it is quite tempting."

When I looked up, the shark-like smile reappeared.

A deathly seriousness lived in those amber-colored eyes.

"Torturing you," he clarified. "That was what you were worrying your pretty head about just now. Wasn't it? Please tell me my knack for reading anguished facial expressions hasn't gone entirely."

I didn't answer.

His eyes once more drifted down my body.

"You've grown up, little bird," he said. "I see why our boy is smitten. And why Revi' couldn't control himself once he finally got his cock in you." He paused, probably for effect. "You're quite a lovely specimen, even banged up as you are. Not that you weren't before. But your beauty has, shall we say… matured."

I snorted; I couldn't help it.

"Gee," I said. "Thanks, Terry."

He smiled. That time it reached his eyes.

"Do you know you're even beginning to sound like him? Your mate?"

"Which mate is that?" I asked dryly, glancing at the boy.

"The other one." Patting me on the knee, he crossed his ankles, folding his arms as he joined me in watching the boy climb on the red rocks. "I made him a promise, you know. Regarding you. I haven't forgotten."

I didn't want to know what that meant.

"You know," Terian added. "I've been meaning to ask you. I'm simply *dying* of curiosity…"

"That's good news," I muttered.

He chuckled, but his eyes remained serious. "The telekinesis," he continued. "What you did to Elan's boy, Maygar. What you demonstrated last year, on the bridge in Seattle. In that diner in San Francisco. However do you do it?"

Looking at him, I pursed my lips.

Now it made sense.

He told me about the boy because he wanted me to tell him something. Inadvertently, it convinced me of something else; he really couldn't read me through the collar.

"Why do I always get the funny version of you?" I asked.

The amber eyes swiveled in my direction.

"I'm quite serious," he said, and sounded it. "It normally takes at least a decade of intense training for a manipulator to manifest the level of telekinetic ability you have done with absolutely none. I've studied your *aleimic* structures, and I see no evidence of training of any kind. I looked for markers that Revi' may have tried to structure your *aleimi* prior to awakening you—he did not. I saw nothing between the two of you, in fact, but the structure you created from taking him as a mate. There is no evidence he has trained you at all."

"He trained me a little," I said, shrugging. "On the ship."

Terian waved this off, dismissive.

"Training, despite your rather charming view of it being a sort of weekend seminar affair, perhaps with pie charts and snacks at breaktime, is a rather intensive ordeal. By training, I mean continuous work to activate your *aleimic* structures. You have done little to none of that, even for regular sight skills… much less what I am talking about. You are a complete virgin in this."

"Virgin," I muttered. Jerking my mind back from where it wanted to go, I folded my arms. "So what? People are born with abilities."

"Not this ability, Alyson."

"I can't control it," I said. "So again, who cares?"

Smiling faintly, he shrugged, and it was a human shrug. "You are incurious. You are entitled. Still, I would love to hear Revi's theories on this peculiarity of yours. I'm sure they're quite fascinating."

"What makes you think he has any theories at all?"

"Oh." Terian chuckled, patting my knee. "I'm quite sure he does."

I found myself thinking about this, in spite of myself. Terian was right, of course. If it was as unusual as all that, Revik would certainly have some kind of theory.

Sighing, I gave Terian a bored look, folding my arms.

"I'm past-life girl, right? Maybe I just remember how I did it before."

He rolled his eyes, clicking at me in mild disapproval.

"You don't believe that. Besides, even if you did believe it... which you *don't*... it wouldn't matter. Syrimne was also an intermediary being. He required training. Intensive training. Over many, many years, according to those crazy religious-fanatic Sarks I spoke to in the mountains." He smiled at me. "You know—the ones who actually *trained* him. I took the time to have a chat with a few after I ran across our boy. They said it took them decades, and those years were not gentle."

I stared at him, unable to hide my surprise. "They're still alive?"

The idea astounded me.

Yet, as soon as I thought about it, of course it made perfect sense.

Seers lived a long time.

Of course some of those same seers from the original rebellion would have survived. From a Sark perspective, a hundred years wasn't even all that long. Revik was still considered "young" by the monks I spoke to, and he'd been around that long.

Why hadn't the thought occurred to me before?

From what I'd seen of Syrimne's life, Terian's claim was essentially accurate, too; it had been at least twenty years before Syrimne could do much of anything. Twenty years of nearly nonstop training, with every type of coercion imaginable.

Winking at me, Terian called out to the boy.

"Nenzi, dear?" He waited for the dark head to turn. "Could you come over here, please? I would like to show you something."

I watched the boy approach, thinking again about what Terian had said, about Revik having a theory about me. Whatever his issues with Revik, Terian's admiration of his ex-partner's intelligence seemed sincere enough.

Vash mentioned something similar to me in passing once, about how smart Revik was—smarter than most in the Seven knew.

He'd implied Revik played dumb, actually.

I'd known Revik was smart, of course.

Anyone who talked to him for more than a few minutes could see perfectly well that he was intelligent. Still, I'd only gotten glimpses of that intelligence on the ship. There, he'd been lecturing me mostly, and often appeared bored. We'd never really talked about anything that might have intellectually challenged him.

I wondered now if I'd underestimated him, too.

The boy approached where we sat. I saw him look at the hand Terian had on my knee warily, just before Terian removed it.

The Scandinavian-looking seer rose to his feet.

Bending down, he plucked the glass baton off the floor.

He hefted it in one hand, showing it to the boy.

He let Nenzi run his fingers over the carved crystal along its sides.

The object was about two and a half feet long and several inches thick in the middle, flaring to a larger bulb on one end. It looked vaguely familiar to me from the archeological stores under the mansion in Seertown.

The boy touched it tentatively, his eyes curious.

"It's called an *urele*, Nenz," Terian said. "It was designed for sight work." Terian must have felt my eyes on it as well, because his tone shifted, growing lighter. "...although it could have its other uses, I suppose."

He glanced overtly at me, giving me a wink as he indicated towards the glass rod.

I fought back a facial expression, biting my tongue.

"This particular *urele* used to belong to our friend, Dehgoies Revik," Terian added, still smiling at me. "It won't surprise you to know that I stole it from him. After he declined my offer to rejoin our little organization."

Smiling, he looked at the boy.

"Seers used them for exams in sight schools, Nenz. Back when such things still existed. They were a way of testing one's control."

I saw Nenzi's eyes on me.

A frown puckered his forehead, making a harder line out of his lips.

He'd seen my anger at Terian.

He also didn't like the reference to Revik.

Shaking my head minutely, I rolled my eyes, nodding towards the Scandinavian. I let my expression imply Terian was a bit of a dork, an annoying brother who teased me.

Relieved, Nenzi grinned.

Still, I found myself interested in what Terian was saying.

"Back in those days," he continued. "There was a real ranking system. Not this bastardized, human-approved version the World Court uses. Just like now, seers were twice ranked in the original system, too. They had their *aleimic* rank, usually called their 'potential' rank... meaning, what they were born with. Then they had their working rank, meaning what they'd been trained to actually use."

He smiled at the boy. "I imagine some of the old timers in the Pamir even know their original scores."

I thought of Vash, and had no doubt he did know.

Tarsi popped into my head as well.

"I'd like to see if I can rank you this way, Nenz." Seeing the boy's look sharpen, he smiled. "Just for fun. The *urele* reacts to *aleimic* light. It is a bit like playing a musical instrument. You'll like it. Promise."

When Terian looked at me, I raised a skeptical eyebrow as well.

He smiled, hefting the *urele* to bounce it in his hand.

"But it's virtual, right?" I asked.

"No," Terian said, looking at me. "The superficial elements of the room are. The birds, rocks, water, glass, texture of the walls and floor. You, me, the boy—we are not. Neither is the *urele.*"

I blinked, surprised.

"So where are we really, then?" I asked.

Terian merely smiled.

"Well?" he said, turning to the boy. "How about we see what you can do?"

Nenzi made a short series of gestures with his hands.

Pausing only the slightest beat, Terian indicated affirmative with one hand.

"All right. Me first, then."

I exhaled a low snort, but Terian only gave me the barest glance.

Grasping the thick end of the *urele,* he walked to the part of the floor beneath the highest arc of the glass sun dome.

He flipped the wand over his hand expertly a few times. Then, once he reached the center of the wide circle of floor, he tossed it sharply up into the air.

With Nenzi, I watched it rise.

About halfway to the domed ceiling, the baton started to glow.

I squinted up at it, wishing again that I had access to my sight.

The fact that I could see the light at all told me it wasn't purely a Barrier toy. Assuming Terian was telling the truth about the *urele* being real in the first place.

The glass wand reached the apex of the arc of Terian's throw.

The warm glow transformed into a sharp burst of light.

I flinched back, as did Nenzi.

Our eyes didn't leave the airborne wand. A multi-colored flame flooded the dimmed room, erupting from patterned, translucent glass.

I glanced at the Scandinavian seer.

This had to be some kind of virtual trick.

When I saw his face, though, I wondered. Terian stared up, watching the *urele*. His amber-colored eyes showed a hint of concentration as he focused on the wand, until slowly… slowly… the light stabilized.

An elaborate design appeared on the floor in a wide circle.

Nenzi laughed aloud, clapping his hands in delight.

The *urele* started to return slowly… too slowly… to Earth.

As if fell, it emitted sparks, colored curls of light. The painting below our feet bled with miniature solar flares. The image continued to expand as the *urele* fell; the colored light stretched out towards opposite walls, covering my skin, the rocks, the clear waterfall. Staring at the patterns on my arms and hands, I marveled at the level of detail.

The design pulled compulsively at my eyes—a tapestry of intricate threads, each a shade off from the one before, each a separate, living pattern.

It occurred to me, in a kind of shock, that I was seeing a visual representation of Terian's light, a part of his *aleimic* body.

At that precise instant, Terian caught the *urele* easily in his hand.

The image winked out, leaving the room flat-seeming, two-dimensional.

Sparks continued to erupt off the wand in Terian's hand.

Rising to my feet, I walked closer, in spite of myself.

He held the *urele* out, so both of us could see.

Light slid liquidly from one end of the wand to the other, traveling through spiderweb cracks in the glass. His *aleimi* made colored patterns through hairline trails that hadn't been apparent before his light infused it. I watched in a kind of wonder as the wand pulsed brighter and softer as Terian reflected parts of himself through it.

"Of course," Terian murmured, glancing at me. "This isn't my whole *aleimic* body. Still. I didn't do too bad, did I?"

I shook my head, unthinking.

I wanted to touch it.

I flinched as an explosion of jeweled beads rained through the green-tinted glass, breaking apart before sliding back to a single pool of light.

I wanted to try it, too. Maybe it was the competitive side of me, or the artist in me, or maybe it just looked incredibly neat.

Terian must have seen something in my face.

He laughed, and it was the closest to a real laugh I'd ever heard on him.

"Sorry, my dear," he said. "As much as I'd love to see what you can do, I value my skin a bit more than that, I'm afraid."

Biting the inside of my cheek, I didn't look up, still watching light flicker through the transparent wand. Nenzi watched it as well, equally mesmerized. Touching my arm, he looked up at the tall, broad-shouldered seer.

He must have asked Terian a question.

"Some other day, perhaps," Terian said. Another pause. "Of course," Terian said then, answering another question from the boy. "The same way?"

The boy's eyes blurred; he didn't lift them from the *urele*.

"Well, you can leave it on the floor, sure," Terian allowed. His voice was magnanimous; he was clearly enjoying the effect the *urele* was having on the two of us. "Its design is simple, partly to accommodate seers at different levels. A normal Sark would be required to use several modalities in an exam."

He shrugged, shaking out another *hiri* stick from a pocket in his shirt.

"For example, they might require several throws, each with a different skill level. That could be anything the examiners felt like tossing the student's way, depending on what they knew of their birth rank and current level of skill. As you are telekinetic, you would have been required to hold the *urele* airborne while reflecting different parts of your *aleimi* through it. A gauge of control, you see."

Terian placed the wand in Nenzi's outstretched palm.

In the boy's pale fingers, the *urele* looked enormous.

Nenzi glanced at me. I was getting better at reading his face. I could see he wanted to do as well as Terian. He also didn't want to make a fool of himself trying.

So he was competitive with the other male. I had wondered.

I was still thinking about this when he threw the *urele* up in the air. He didn't throw it as hard or as high or as elegantly as Terian had done; the *urele* went up in a slightly off-kilter line, rising halfway up the curved walls.

But the less-flattering differences immediately grew inconsequential.

I saw the boy's fingers curl into fists as his eyes followed the *urele*.

I wondered if he was trying to figure out how it worked—

—when the crystal wand burst out violently in flaming tongues of light.

I stared up, my mouth open.

Light cascaded down, as dense as rain.

A complex, woven dome emerged. Instead of Terian's prism-like, two-dimensional reflection, this looked like real water, like shining, iridescent beads of living light. As I watched, the consistency of the dome grew more and more subtle.

Soon it was a curtain of the finest silk.

From there, it melted to perfectly symmetrical walls of thinned paint.

My heart suddenly hurt.

I felt for the kid, deeply at times; I couldn't help it. Somehow, seeing his light manifested around me only brought the emotions more sharply into relief. What he could do, who he really was—it was shockingly, heartrendingly beautiful.

He should never have been allowed to become a dark, twisted tool of the Dreng, or of that fucked up seer who'd owned him, Menlim. That someone like him could have ended up a monster, mind-fucked into believing he was saving the world…

Gods. It hurt to think about.

The *urele* floated higher.

I could no longer see the glass dome, the sun, the blue sky.

I gazed up at the waterfall of light. I knew he was floating the *urele* with the telekinesis, likely experimenting with different parts of his *aleimi* to change the qualities of light. He glanced at me then, and I saw a faint gleam in his eyes, different from the look that normally lived there.

The expression belonged to someone closer to forty than fourteen.

I remembered windows shattering in a rusted factory, a scream of triumph as the glass exploded outwards—

"You like this, Allie?" he asked.

Before I could answer, I saw his eyes squint in a tighter concentration.

When I looked up, a cluster of light separated from the *urele* in a burst.

I watched in disbelief as it transformed into the shape of a bird.

The fiery plumage looked like it belonged to a bird of paradise, or a phoenix.

Nenzi's creation winged in and out of the liquid curtain of light like a living being. I let out a little gasp of surprise as it transformed into a larger dragon with white scales. I watched it slide through the watery veil before it disappeared.

"You like it?" he asked again.

"It's amazing," I said. "Like magic, Nenzi."

"You like me?" he asked.

"You know I do."

Stepping closer, he gripped my wrist.

"Then no more husband with him." He stroked the inside of my arm with his fingers. "I will take your bargain. But not just for sex. You have to marry me. Marry *me,* instead of him. I will do whatever you ask."

Terian laughed.

I looked at the kid, bewildered, then up at the sparking lights cascading to the floor. Sometimes it was easy to see him as a kind of neurotic adult; other times, he looked, acted, and sounded years younger than even his body suggested.

The lights above his head continued to shower us in sparks, making patterns against his pale skin, hitting the clay tiles like lava, pooling in streams on the floor. I saw the colors change as he spoke, shifting from dark greens and blues to a deep orange, shot through with gold and white.

I looked at his face.

"It's too late, Nenzi," I said.

I glanced at Terian. A warning shone in his amber eyes.

"Would you like to explain... Uncle Terry?" I gave him a hard look. "Or do you want junior here to uncollar me so we can get married?"

I saw him look between my eyes.

He shrugged, as if conceding my point.

"I am sorry to say she is right," he said easily. "Seers mate for life, my young friend. Sadly, that ship has sailed."

When I looked back at Nenzi, I saw his mouth harden. The black eyes stared between mine. There was a bleakness there, a desperation that made my breath catch. Something behind that expression made me pause.

He touched my arm again. His fingers clasped my skin.

"Stay with me." His voice turned gruff. "Stay with me, or I'll kill him."

I glanced at Terian. He gave me a sideways look, but he was watching the boy intently. Looking back at Nenzi, I shook my head.

"Then you'll kill me," I said simply.

"Not if I wipe his mind!" he said angrily.

I blinked, studying the intensity of emotion in his round face.

Caution returned to my voice, but I kept it firm.

"Nenzi... this won't make me love you."

"You can't be alone forever," he snapped. "You're a seer. You need companions. You will forget about him. You'll forget... and I'll be there."

The implications behind this statement unnerved me.

He'd thought about this way too much.

"No," I said, my voice incredulous. "I *won't* forget him. More than that, I'll hate you. And if you erase him, I'll die."

"Stop being married to him! I *will* kill him!"

I flinched, looking between his eyes.

"No," I said.

A burst of light exploded over us, a small sun. When I looked back at the boy, his face contorted in rage. His voice grew into a command.

"Goddamn it, Allie!" he said. "I mean it! I know where he is!"

I stared at him, thrown by the change in tone. He sounded forty again, and more than that, I recognized the look in those black eyes.

A horrible suspicion grew in me.

Once it bloomed there, it was impossible to shove entirely from my mind.

Hearing Terian chuckle, I glanced up, seeing his chiseled face shadowed by the light cascading from above. His eyes still held caution, but he was listening to our conversation with a keen interest. Feeling my jaw harden, I blinked and shook my head, removing the boy's fingers from my arm.

"No one gets what they want all the time." I glared at Terian. "We could be friends, if you let me go. I could help you find your own mate."

Terian's eyes turned to glass. They focused lifelessly on mine.

Swallowing a little at the look there, I returned my gaze to Nenzi.

"No!" The boy's eyes filled with tears, bewildering me. "No! I love *you*. I don't want another female. *You* are my wife…"

"Nenzi…" I said, at a loss. "You don't know what you're saying."

"I watched you," he said. "I saw you in the purple house. I saw your human mother. I saw your father, and all the numbers. I *watched* you. You were like me." At what must have been a blank look on my face, he burst out, "You threw the bad man. He killed those pigs, like *Wilbur*. You made him stop!"

I felt the blood drain from my face.

That time, I knew exactly what he was talking about.

My uncle Stefan owned a farm in Nebraska. He kept pigs, and when I went to visit, I was seven years old, and I had just finished reading *Charlotte's Web*. Naturally, I'd asked him what he was going to do with the runts in his sow's litter.

I couldn't believe his answer.

I thought it was just a story. I couldn't believe anyone actually *did* that, killed something just because it was small.

They all pretended afterwards that Uncle Stefan had some kind of seizure. They said he lost his balance maybe, or that he'd been knocked over by a gust of wind.

But I made him swear.

I made him swear he would never kill another runt pig.

"How could you possibly know that?" My voice sharpened. "Nenzi… even Jon didn't know about that. I never told *anyone*."

Then, remembering my time in the cabin with Revik, I realized that wasn't true anymore. I had told someone.

One person, in fact.

My sense of unreality worsened.

I looked at Terian, fighting to calm myself.

There was another explanation, there had to be.

"My mother?" I studied the Scandinavian's face. "Did you get that from her? Did my uncle tell her about that?"

But Terian had a faint wrinkle to his brow as well.

It could have been an act, but somehow, I didn't think it was. Had he figured it out? Would he put together the pieces as he listened to Nenzi talk?

The boy took my hand, stroking my skin with his small fingers. He moved closer to me. He touched my face, my jaw.

"Please, Allie," he said. "Please. I love you."

"You don't love me." My voice came out angry, maybe because I was afraid, or at the very least, completely and totally unnerved. "I'm *not* your wife. I'm someone else's wife. You don't even *know* me, Nenzi!"

When tears rose to his eyes, my voice grew even more harsh.

"Whatever your deal is with me… it's not real. You can't read things off someone, read about their past and the facts of their life and think you *know* them—"

"You were my wife first!" he burst out.

I felt Terian staring at the boy along with me.

Nenzi's voice reflected that older person again, losing all trace of its child-like cadence. His pale face flushed under the cascading light. His fists were clenched; he was breathing harder. His eyes held a dark flame, distorted by reflected light.

I saw frustration there, grief, but also fury.

"You're mistaken," I said.

"I'm not!" His eyes ignited to a pale green.

"Yes… you are! You're confused!"

Terian touched my shoulder.

When I looked up, the amusement on his sculpted face was gone.

He was staring at the boy's eyes. His own slid out of focus, aimed roughly at the space directly above the boy's head.

That's when I noticed the *urele.*

The light had turned the color of dark blood, red with black veins.

The rain-like beads washed down around us, reflecting against the boy's pale skin before bleeding to the floor. The pale green eyes stared at mine, lamp-like, sharp against that dark red curtain.

Looking at him, all I could feel was a sharp wave of compassion.

"Do you want me to pretend to care for you?" I asked. "Someone *would* love you, Nenzi. They would love you more than anything... or anyone. But it can't be me."

Terian's fingers dug violently into my shoulder, hard enough that I twisted away from his hand. When I looked back, I saw Nenzi staring between us.

He focused on my face.

The *urele* flashed white. Light exploded out of it. The wave of light bled up the curtain-like walls in a thick wave. When it reached the top, a heavy wave of sound exploded on all four sides, like a crack of thunder.

Glass exploded outwards.

The fragments shattered to a fine powder.

I realized in shock that those weren't VR windows, but whatever lay behind them.

Even as I thought it, the illusion melted.

The domed room with the marble floors, red rock cliffs and birds, the blue sky and New Mexico landscape faded around where we stood. The waterfalls melted into a flat background, like a projector image when the light goes out.

Around us stood gunmetal gray walls, a blank, empty space.

We were in a warehouse. Or, I thought, as I looked around and up at the high ceiling, more like an empty airplane hangar.

A group of humans sat on metal bleachers behind what looked like a Plexiglas shield.

White faces aimed in our direction, round-eyed and shocked.

Guards hustled a few of the uniformed men and women off the platform, into armored vehicles parked behind the viewing area. The vehicles roared to life, taking off down the middle of the hangar towards what must be doors on the other end. It might have been comical if I'd had time to comprehend what was happening.

Nenzi didn't care about them, though.

Light from the *urele* flashed out, reaching the metal walls. More glass shards rained down around us, this time from above.

I threw up my arms as fragments nicked my face and shoulders.

Fear rippled through me, a sudden realization that what I'd suspected—what I'd *known*, somehow, all along—was really true.

Nenzi wasn't some replica of the old Syrimne.

He wasn't his offspring, a clone, an experiment, or even a confused reincarnation.

Somehow, in some way, Nenzi actually *was* Syrimne.

And he was broken, just like Tarsi said he was.

CHAPTER 39
INFILTRATOR

He stretched out on the rug beside her, head propped on one arm so he could look at her.

He caressed the hair back from her face as she talked.

He kissed her when she paused. He pressed his face to hers, fought a swell of feeling that still hurt. She smiled as she took in his expression, looking tired but heartbreakingly happy, and he wondered if she knew...

She was telling him about her brother.

She repeated something Jon said when they were kids, and all he could think about was that glimpse he'd gotten when he pushed her to confess everything, the lingering jealousy he still felt, and he felt like a bastard for wondering if—

She kissed his mouth, massaging his chest, smiling. He could feel the reassurance there... the utter guilelessness of her, of her open light.

Her eyes turned liquid and the feeling there clutched at his heart.

He still didn't quite believe it.

"I love you," she whispered, caressing his face. "I love you..."

He jerked awake.

Fighting to breathe, he stared up at a lightless ceiling in a dim motel room. His whole body hurt. Tears coursed down his cheeks and he had a hard on. The pain in his light vibrated every layer of his skin.

He couldn't move.

He fought out a thick gasp, an attempt to express some part of it.

Turning to his side, he gripped his stomach with an arm, willing it back, willing it to pass through or away from him, somehow.

Gradually, he could breathe.

He lay there a while longer. He fought his way back to some semblance of normal, an approximation of level at least. His mind only worked when he kept it going in straight lines.

He scanned for her, reflexive, but there was nothing there.

Nothing. Not even her in pain.

When he looked up, he saw Jon watching him, his eyes shining faintly from the orange lights showing through the motel window's curtains. Revik saw the sympathy there, but he couldn't deal with that either.

Rolling to his back, he closed his eyes, holding a hand over his face as he deliberately slowed his breathing. Eventually, he got his heart moving slower, contracting slower, pumping blood slower.

He didn't have time for this, he told himself.

He didn't have time.

He stared at the virtual map, studying the main and secondary structures.

Primarily, he was memorizing foundational details.

Mapping entrances and exits. Locating security tech. Rooms with external walls. Reinforced barriers. Underground spaces uncategorized on the plans, or simply empty spaces that might not actually be empty.

He looked for air ducts, server storage, sewage lines.

Anything that might provide ventilation or access below ground.

He knew Terian. He knew Galaith, for that matter.

He could expect back doors.

Likely half as many again existed in reality as what appeared on the plans, despite the fact that these were supposedly the "real" plans, meaning the version protected by the Secret Service. He had no idea if he'd be able to access any of those other doors, but he knew how to begin looking for them, at least. The plans were just a place to start.

Using them, he could look for the holes, make a few educated guesses.

The truth was, Revik didn't have a lot of options, in terms of breaking into the White House. That would have been true even if Terian wasn't president.

As it was, the usual problems had multiplied.

Still, politicians were politicians. They didn't change much over the years.

Revik had observed at close hand hierarchies spanning countries in half the continents of the globe. The human ones almost always shared certain traits in common.

When he'd proposed his plan to Wreg, the older seer laughed.

"Dignity still isn't high on your list of attributes, is it, runt?" he'd said.

Revik hadn't bothered to react.

He'd watched the other infiltrator instead, knowing he was thinking through logistics. He waited for Wreg to find some detail he had missed, some reason it wouldn't work. When the Asian seer with the thick arms adjusted his weight, eyes blurring as he retraced the steps of the plan a second time... then a third... Revik found himself relaxing.

After another pause, Wreg nodded.

"It might work at that. I assume you have some different idea for yourself?"

He motioned towards Revik's face.

Revik shook his head, then gestured in negative when the other didn't react.

"I want to go in the front door," he said.

Wreg frowned. "I don't know—"

"That's non-negotiable."

Hesitating, Wreg conceded his words with a tilted palm. "Fine, fine. It's your show. We'll need a cover. Better than the usual blood-patch and prosthetics."

Revik gestured affirmative. "Yes. I have some ideas. But what do you think, assuming that end is covered?"

"That is not a small detail," Wreg warned.

"It is a detail," Revik said. "What do you *think?*"

Wreg jerked his chin, smiling faintly. "It is good. It will work, runt. But we need to find a reputable house to affiliate with, with contacts to the houses being used now. We'll need to research the types involved, and…"

They began discussing details in earnest.

That had been a few days ago.

Wreg's formality with him may have slipped, but his ability to take and carry out orders had not. Revik even wondered if it was a sign of the other's growing trust in him, that Wreg no longer used the formal version of every response when Revik made a request.

Revik didn't want to waste so much as a second of time.

He also wasn't about to blow likely his only chance by being sloppy.

He'd run several dozen scenarios with the best infiltrators he could find among the seers he'd been given. After two days on a cargo plane, he'd come to the conclusion Salinse was right: Wreg was the best of all of them. In his way, Wreg reminded Revik of Balidor, although without the degree of subtlety in his sight.

Bringing Balidor had been out of the question.

The last thing he needed was someone preaching Code to him from over his shoulder, no matter how valuable they might be in other respects.

The hardest thing upon entry would be disguising his light.

Everything else had been worked down to the finest detail.

Money also didn't appear to be a limiting factor, even before Revik contemplated plundering his own primary stores.

Salinse insisted on covering all of it.

He had to admit, it was nice having access to real equipment for a change, not the dilapidated hunks of crap that usually fell to the Seven's Guard. Even the Adhipan could use a serious upgrade in their gear, if what he'd seen in Sikkim was any indication.

Revik knew he was skirting a dangerous edge, but he found it harder and harder to care. Strictly speaking, the parts of himself he was drawing upon to perform this op weren't the ones he should be using, from the perspective of the monks who'd taken him through his rehabilitation. Or from the perspective of Vash, for that matter.

To some extent, that was even deliberate.

Beyond what he was getting off Salinse and his people in terms of support and intelligence, Revik went out of his way to remember every detail he could of being a Rook. That included diving into memories stirred by Terian in his months of captivity, even deliberately putting himself back in that space with the help of Wreg and his team. The security construct Salinse's people used, tied to organics in their headgear and to the *aleimi* of their infiltrators, helped that along perhaps more than it should have.

Revik didn't question that too closely either.

He knew it was wrong. At the very least, it was damned risky.

He would deal with any fallout later.

Allie would help him.

In any case, he'd pretty well thrown the idea of following Code out the window as soon as Terian dragged his naked wife away in chains.

The plan as a whole was relatively simple, but played on the blind spots of the Rooks' standard security protocols—and even a few of the nonstandard ones Revik remembered. The first eight and Revik would breach the perimeter while half of the rest worked solely from the Barrier from the safe house they'd constructed. The other half would be wave two of a direct assault on the physical structure.

He, himself, would go after Allie.

That part, he wasn't willing to discuss.

She'd be with the boy.

He could even argue that going after her personally was contractual on his part, since he needed to find the boy to fulfill his end of the deal he'd made with Salinse.

The rest of them would take down the White House security system and the construct itself. Revik knew if the grid truly went down it could start an actual shooting war in the middle of Washington D.C., so they had contingency plans for that eventuality, as well.

The truth was, there was no way in hell Terian wouldn't be expecting him.

Revik could try to delay that knowledge as much as possible, but at the first sign of any disturbance, Terian would deploy assuming it was him. Revik talked to Wreg about redundancies they might build in, but he still only had two real backups for his first idea, and both were risky as hell, and none changed that naked fact.

Terian would know it was him.

Besides, a certain amount of guesswork was unavoidable without a contact on the inside. Any one of the contingencies he'd mapped would depend heavily on whatever he eventually found once they breached the perimeter.

Whatever that ended up being, it would contain at least a few surprises.

Knowing that didn't help him a damned bit, really.

Wreg still seemed to find the approach strategy for the primary team amusing, but Revik noticed he wasn't as naïve about human culture, or even American culture, as he would have expected, given the Rebels' isolation in Asia.

Revik wondered just how many ops Salinse's people had pulled on this continent over the years… then decided he didn't really care about that, either.

In any case, Wreg was fully on board with the plan now.

Leaving their main equipment store, Revik pushed aside a beaded doorway, and found himself in the parlor of their secondary safe house. This house, Salinse's people hadn't provided. Revik handled that end himself with contacts he had in the States.

Upon entering the room, he found himself face to face with Kat.

He stopped dead in front of her before he knew who he was looking at.

It had been a long time since he'd seen her in her full regalia. His eyes drifted down out of habit, settling on the high heels under the silk dress that barely covered her crotch. She smiled at him coyly and he frowned, looking away.

His eyes passed by Jon and settled on Ullysa.

"What the fuck is she doing here?" he asked the red-haired seer.

Ullysa raised an eyebrow.

She lounged liquidly on the velvet sofa, her softly curled hair spilling down over her neck and décolletage. She seemed to be artfully arranged whatever the occasion, even in their makeshift war room, but it didn't make her any less valuable of an infiltrator.

"You said to bring my infiltrators, Revi'," she said, her eyebrow still arched.

He glanced at Kat. "I didn't mean her. Why the fuck would you bring her? You know damned well I can't trust her with this." He didn't bother looking at Kat as he spoke. "I want her out of here. Now."

Ullysa clicked at him softly. "You can trust all of us in this, Revi'. You know that. Kat will do her job."

Unconvinced, Revik turned on Kat, his mouth hard. "Anything happens to my wife and you're anywhere near the cause, I'll kill you. In fact, anything happens to my wife, I might just kill you for the fuck of it."

"Or I will," Jon muttered.

The Russian seer looked hurt for an instant, but it left her face, leaving a colder mask.

She glanced at Jon contemptuously, then looked to Revik.

"So I get death threats now? Is that how it is?"

Revik didn't lower his gaze.

Kat seemed to see something in his expression. She retracted her light. Clicking, she blew bangs out of her face, shrugging with one hand as she rolled her eyes.

"Relax, Dehgoies. I am being paid, aren't I?"

Revik pointed at Ullysa. "I don't want that bitch anywhere near Allie. I mean it. I'll hold you personally responsible, 'Llysa."

"Revi'—"

"No arguments. Just agree with me and say, 'yes, sir.' She can mind-fuck Terian's humans if she needs to get her claws in something."

Ullysa looked startled, but after a pause where she glanced searchingly at Jon, she looked back up at Revik. Making a conciliatory gesture, she exhaled *hiri* smoke as she gave him a puzzled look.

"Yes, sir," she murmured.

He walked past them into the staging room beyond the parlor.

Seeing Jon rise to his feet, he stepped aside to let the human enter in front of him, but not before he heard Kat mutter to Ullysa in Prexci,

"Yes… this Bridge bitch is holy all right. Making Revi' look and act like a Rook again. Or is it only me who notices?"

"Shhh," Ullysa murmured. "His wife's been stolen, Kat."

"Fuck that. It's no excuse for—"

Revik let the door swing shut behind him, forgetting their words before he'd stopped hearing them. Watching Jon out of the corner of his eye, he focused on Wreg, wincing as he slumped into a chair to rest his leg.

He couldn't afford to be limping when they entered the building.

It was the little things that might get him caught, and he knew they'd have gait-recognition software in the White House security feeds. Knowing Terian, he might think to flag anyone with a limp, just on the off chance it picked him up.

Wreg was arranging weapons on a long, wooden table.

"You ready for your disguise?" he asked, smiling at Revik.

Revik ignored the jab. "Is the regular here?"

Wreg nodded towards a side door.

Rather than get up, Revik pinged the seer in the other room through the construct. He waited, massaging the top part of his thigh, until he appeared in the doorway.

"Okay," Revik said, grinding his jaw against the pain in his leg. "Talk."

"Talk?" The seer's sea green eyes widened perceptibly.

At Revik's cold stare, the heart-shaped face tightened, his smile wavering as he glanced at Jon, then more reluctantly back at Revik. His blond hair was long, hanging past his shoulders to the middle of his back. The unwilling identified as male, but his face was distinctly feminine, and stunningly pretty. He didn't carry the markers of a homosexual trick only, despite his obvious interest in Jon.

His body was close. Not perfect, but close.

Revik found himself thinking the unwilling was in better physical shape than he was.

Still, it was easier to modify in that direction than the other.

The young seer cleared his throat, folding his long hands.

He'd been schooled around humans all right; even his mannerisms were flawless.

Revik looked the male over again, scanning his light.

Wreg had chosen well.

He motioned for the young seer to get on with it.

"What do you want to know?" the male asked.

"Everything." Revik continued to massage his leg. "Tell me what you can, but mostly I want you to let me into your memory and your *aleimi*.

Don't keep a damned thing from me. Not out of false modesty or national security or anything else. You won't get a cent if I find out there was anything less than full disclosure. Further, I'll make sure SCARB finds out about your little operation here if I'm not completely satisfied… assuming you don't really piss me off and I just shoot off your cock and watch you bleed to death."

Letting a pause hang in the air, he held the unwilling's gaze.

"Are we clear?" he asked.

Jon flinched, staring at Revik.

The boyish face of the male unwilling faltered more. He glanced at Jon, again seemingly looking for reassurance. He gestured affirmative.

"Okay." He straightened in his chair. "Where should I start?"

"I said everything," Revik growled. "Preferences, cutesy nicknames, rituals the two of you have… all of it. Walk me through a normal visit, and picture it in your head. Don't spare a single detail, from the security guard at the front gate to whatever happens when you leave."

The boy, stammering somewhat, began to speak.

As he did, Revik leaned back in the chair, entwining his light in that of the unwilling's so he could not only hear his words, but see it, feel it, smell it along with him. He wove a map of the young seer's light as he listened, storing it in the construct as he created it, so the team could map it too, ensure he didn't miss anything. Whenever the boy's mental time-line skipped, Revik stopped him, had him rewind, take him back through the next set of sequences until he understood it all.

Once he'd gone from beginning to end, he had him describe a few more visits, noting any small variations. They were few.

About two hours later, he began to relax.

"All right." He glanced at the seer from under his hand, stretching out his wounded leg. "Thanks. You can go. But stay available."

The unwilling rose to his feet, still visibly nervous as he left the room.

He gave Jon a glance as he left, and Wreg gave him a reassuring pat on the back as he walked by. Jon had a look of near incredulity on his face as the young seer headed for the door. He aimed his bewilderment at Revik once the blonde had gone.

Revik didn't bother to answer his stare.

Most humans were surprisingly naïve about what went on in Sark fetish.

For that matter, so was his wife.

The thought brought a sharp stab of pain, bad enough to catch him up short.

For a moment he only sat there, a hand over his face.

He knew it was bad enough that the others noticed; neither of the two men tried to talk to him while he waited for it to pass. Once it began to ebb backwards he glanced to his right, looking at the bottle on the table nearest to Wreg.

Following his glance, Wreg shook his head, clicking softly at him, his lips curved in a smile.

"Maybe Salinse was right about you," he mused, wandering towards the table. He picked up the bottle. "You're quite the taskmaster when you're motivated. Did you get what you needed?"

"Most of it." Revik nodded in thanks when the older seer poured and handed him a drink. Taking a long swallow, he relaxed deeper into the chair, rubbing his temples. "There's still something that's bugging me. I want to know how Terian knew where we were, in those mountains. Either someone told him, someone in the Seven, or one of Balidor's..." He glanced up, jaw hard. "...or the boy led him there."

Jon still seemed to be fighting his equilibrium back from the interview with the unwilling. "Which do you think it is?"

"The boy," Revik said promptly, although he had no evidence to back his assertion. "What I don't know is which of us he was tracking."

"Meaning?" Wreg's eyebrow rose.

"Meaning, he might not need to recognize me, if he already knows where I am," Revik said. "If I'm his link to Allie, or if she's his to me... either way, trying to fool him with a disguise might be a complete waste of time."

Wreg pondered this a moment, his expression thoughtful.

"So you'd be walking into a trap," Jon said.

"Potentially, yes." Revik drained the glass, setting it on the side table by his chair. Taking the half-full bottle from Wreg, he refilled the glass without looking up at either of them. "Unless we plan for being spotted. Unless I'm expecting him to find me."

"He won't have your wife with him," Wreg said, skeptical.

"No," Revik conceded. "Unless..."

"Unless what?" Jon asked.

Revik frowned. He glanced up at Wreg. "He wants my wife to fall in love with him, right? The boy."

Wreg frowned back. "From what you said, yes." He stared at Revik, as if trying to read past his eyes. Suddenly, understanding flared there, as the rest of Revik's plan suddenly made sense.

"That's why you're going in like this?"

Revik shrugged, eyes flat. "It'll have to be loud. From the Barrier, I mean. Loud enough to convince him it's real... and that it's me. Like you said, he wouldn't have her with him otherwise. He'd probably even hide her away somewhere."

He went on, no emotion in his voice.

"Unless I give him a reason to want her along."

Jon's mouth fell open. He stared at Revik, his eyes showing disbelief, as if he was positive he was understanding him wrong. It irritated Revik more than he hoped showed that the human caught on so quickly.

Once again, Jon wasn't dumb. Or unobservant.

Even Wreg hesitated, as if suddenly losing the desire to laugh.

"It may not work," he warned. "You're making a leap, extrapolating what he might do faced with a particular set of variables."

"Isn't that what infiltrators do?" Revik retorted. "What about the variables? They make sense, right? Given what we've seen?"

"Who will you use? The team has to change if we're doing this for real. We need to give them a few options... and they need to be convincing."

"You don't have any pros on your team? None at all?"

"No. Well... one, maybe." Wreg gave him an apologetic look, one that told Revik he was making an effort to be polite. "We don't generally *do* that, Commander Dehgoies. It goes against everything we stand for. Hardliners especially, and that's just about everyone you hand-picked to come out here."

"Do you have anyone local?"

Wreg glanced towards the door. "You've got two pros out there—"

"No," Revik said.

"What choice do you have?" He studied Revik's face. "I understand that there's a personal element... believe me, I do. But you've asked me to advise you on execution. No way can I recommend doing this solely with novices to back you up. Or with unwillings who aren't infiltrators.

Either you use the two you've got, or we wait. Bring someone else in. You're talking a few weeks' delay at least, to weave them into the construct, establish their identity in D.C., brief them on the plan, coach them on details…"

Revik frowned, staring at the door.

For a moment, his eyes lost focus.

He tried to buy time, to think. Looking for a second opinion, he glanced at Jon. The human was watching him as carefully as Wreg, but the frown creasing his forehead held more understanding in it.

Allie must have said something to him.

Again, he couldn't think about her without pain.

"It's damned risky," Wreg said seriously. "Even if you do use them."

"Anything would be risky," Revik said, dismissive. "The boy is tele-kinetic. It took most of the Adhipan a year to best the last telekinetic seer, and I don't have that kind of firepower… or time. I need to give him a reason to—"

"Not the boy," Wreg said. "Her. *She* might kill you, runt. Did that occur to you?"

"Damn straight," Jon said. Outrage trembled his voice. "I can't believe you're even considering this! There has to be another way."

Revik stared at the door, forcing his mind over options.

Jon's voice sharpened. "You can't use Kat, Revik. You can't."

Revik didn't look at him. "It won't matter who, Jon."

"Like hell it won't! Would it matter to you if it was Maygar?"

Revik hesitated, glancing up over the glass he'd refilled.

Fighting a reaction out of his light, he took another long drink. Gesturing in acknowledgement with his fingers, he refilled the glass. He avoided Jon's eyes.

"We do it tomorrow," he said. "I'm not putting this off another day."

Jon stared at him, open-mouthed.

Wreg hesitated only a half-beat, then gestured in acknowledgment. He walked back towards the main salon.

Hesitating by the leather chair, he stopped to look at Revik one more time.

"You've got balls, runt," he said. "I can't decide if you're a genius or a fucking idiot, but you've got balls. I'll let the others know the plan."

After the door closed, Jon turned on him.

"Revik, man. You can't do this." His face looked stricken. "Isn't there some other way? Allie will freak out. She will totally fucking *lose* it."

Revik didn't answer. Even so, he found himself thinking about Wreg's comment long after the older seer had left him there with Jon and a bottle, in a beat-up leather chair in a cramped, perfume-smelling room.

The thought had occurred to him. More than once.

Then he remembered Allie being dragged away screaming, climbing on Terian, clawing at him. He remembered the dead look in her eyes as she sat on a couch in the Oval Office, Terian caressing her collared neck with his fingers, like she was a particularly expensive whore.

He took another long pull of alcohol, closing his eyes.

He set the glass on the low table to refill it.

Slumping back in the seat, he rubbed his temples as he slid into the Barrier, reworking several points of the plan over in his head, looking for flaws, running scenarios from different angles to catch anything he might have missed, anything he couldn't account for.

He couldn't afford to get too drunk yet.

That would come later, when he needed to force his body to sleep.

When Revik still hadn't answered him a moment later, Jon left the room, letting the door close none too gently behind him.

CHAPTER 40
FAMILY

In the main salon, Jon sought out the only other seer he actually knew, the only one who still felt like a real ally.

Not that Revik didn't, exactly, but truthfully, Revik was more like family.

Even apart from his relationship to Allie, Jon's relationship with Revik had entered those murkier, more complicated waters sometime during their shared captivity.

Jon loved the guy... a lot. But like all family, that also meant he periodically wanted to wring his neck.

Besides, Revik wasn't exactly running on all four cylinders at the moment.

He found Chandre in a corner, poring over a detailed schematic of the White House and its grounds. Glancing at the other seers sitting and standing around the room, Jon sidled up beside her, talking low.

"Someone needs to talk to him," he said. "He's totally fucking losing it, Chan. I mean *whacko* losing it."

He glanced over his shoulder, focusing on Kat, the Russian seer, who was staring at him narrowly from across the room.

Turning back to Chandre, he watched the dark-skinned, red-eyed infiltrator glance up from the maps, a frown on her sculpted lips. She pushed her braids out of her face, her expression unmoving as she went back to studying the detailed lines.

Jon said softly, "Do you know what he's planning to do? To get in there, I mean. To get that kid to come to him. Have you heard his idea?"

Chan didn't answer at first. Her eyes remained focused on the maps.

"Chan!" Jon said. "Did you hear me?"

She lifted her gaze, giving him a level stare.

"Did it occur to you, young cousin," she said. "That his wife is likely being raped by Terian and the boy in turns, as we speak?"

Jon hesitated, feeling his anger deflate.

"Yeah," he said. "It did, actually."

"Did it?" Chan asked. "Well, do you think maybe it has occurred to Dehgoies as well? That perhaps he isn't willing to wait for a better, more squeaky-clean plan to get inside and help her?" Her reddish irises turned to glass. "The time for soft approach is over, Jon. They fucking stole the *Bridge*. There is no negotiation here. No legal means of taking her out. There is this, or there is outright war. The humans—"

"Humans didn't do this, Chan! Terian did this. One of yours!"

"They are letting it happen!" she burst out. "They are *enjoying* this, Jon! You saw that bitch on the news! They are treating her like an animal. Terian's probably loaning her out to every worm with a hard on. Or did you think she got those bruises playing chess with the boy?"

Jon pressed his lips together.

For a moment, he had no response.

It occurred to him then, that the words she'd just spoken didn't feel like they came from Chandre alone. In fact, he couldn't remember ever hearing Chandre use the word "bitch" before. Once he got that much, another understanding reached him.

He glanced up and around them reflexively, as if it might help him see the construct with his physical eyes. Being human, he forgot what it was like for seers, with their minds often entwined like a single organism.

"You can hear him," he said. "Revik."

She gave him a flat look. "Lay off him, Jon. He's holding it together reasonably well under the circumstances."

"Sure he is."

"He's fine, Jon."

"He wakes up crying every night! He's fucking *drunk*, Chan... or haven't you been paying attention?"

She waved this off dismissively. "You don't understand."

"What?" Jon felt his anger rise. "Let me guess, because I'm *human?*"

"He'll get us inside! His plan is *good*, Jon! Better than what any of us came up with when we ran scenarios on the plane. It may even work without this turning into a war."

"And if he goes back to how he was?" Jon asked in a fierce whisper. "You know... when he was a *Rook*. Do you think Allie will thank him for that? Or thank us for standing by and letting it happen?"

When Chandre turned to the map, clicking her tongue, Jon caught her arm with his good hand, forcing her to look up.

"Come on, Chan! I'm not the only one who's noticed. I've watched him threaten at least four people today alone. And I don't think he was in any way bluffing." When she clicked at him, rolling her eyes dismissively, he clutched her tighter. "He flat-out doesn't *care* how many he kills, human or seer. He's *planning* on killing people, Chan. Not as unavoidable collateral damage. As part of his strategy! Does that sound like the Revik you know? He doesn't *care* if he starts a war—"

"Code won't save us in this, Jon!" she said, her voice warning. "Weren't you at least watching the news feeds when Seertown was bombed into rubble?"

"I was there too, Chan," Jon said, genuinely angry. "Don't fucking go there with me, all right? I was right in the middle of that with you."

"Fine. Well, how many deaths do you suppose they worked into the game plan for *that* little operation?" Her jaw hardened. She gestured shortly with one hand, flipping her braids back with a jerk of her head.

"He had her dressed up like a fucking whore. *His* whore. Terian is laughing at us, Jon! He deserves whatever he gets from Dehgoies and I'll do whatever I can to see to it that he receives it."

Jerking her arm out of his grasp, she closed up the map, giving him another hard look before walking back towards the staging room.

Jon just looked after her.

There was no point chasing her down. She couldn't hear him.

Chandre was like the rest of them now.

The longer they stayed with this group of tattooed seers from the mountains, the more angry and anti-human they all got. Jon glanced around at faces, wondering if that came from Revik, too. It hadn't escaped his notice that his friend had a streak of racism a mile wide at times. Allie grumbled about it. Even Yerin mentioned it once.

Lately, it had been worse.

There was something wrong.

Jon knew it had something to do with the Rebel seers and their creepy leader, Salinse.

Revik seemed to know it, too. He just didn't care.

There was something deeply unnerving about this whole army of strangers just handing over operations to Revik, no questions asked. No matter who his wife was, or what had happened to her, it just felt off to Jon. All of them, even that monster, Wreg, who seemed to hate Revik less the more he turned into a complete bastard, did whatever Revik told them.

Sitting down on one of the plush chairs that probably had stains all over it if anyone ever shone a black light on it, Jon closed his eyes, trying to calm the worry twisting his gut.

Something about the look on Revik's face…

Whatever Chan said, Revik wasn't handling this well at all.

Jon hadn't given himself much time to think about what Allie might be going through. He just couldn't go there, not yet.

He knew Revik probably wouldn't be able to block those thoughts out, not totally. He'd be making connections to everything he, Jon, and Cass experienced under Terian. He'd be imagining things with the boy. He was clearly off-balance from the whole sex-marriage thing he and Allie were in the middle of.

So yeah, Jon got why he might be losing his mind on some level.

Still, it scared him, seeing Revik like this.

Part of him thought if he couldn't do anything for his sister, he could at least keep her husband from imploding while he tried to save her life. He'd even considered trying to contact Vash—or maybe Balidor—but Revik made it pretty clear he didn't want to talk to either of them, not until this thing was finished.

He wished like hell Cass was there.

Cass had an odd knack of getting under Revik's defenses.

Revik would listen to her. He might yell at her, too, but he'd hear her out at least.

Jon had no idea where Cass was, though.

Anyway, she'd been acting pretty damned weird the last time he saw her, too.

BALIDOR PAUSED ON THE ROCKY TRAIL, HANDS ON HIS HIPS.

He gazed up the sides of the nearby cliff, to where Cass and the mountainous Wvercian edged along a hairline path hugging the striated rock. Veins of red and black twisted through the mostly gray surface, making it look like cut flesh.

Despite the altitude and the fact of her human biology, Cass seemed to be able to walk for hours without showing any sign of tiring.

Balidor was beginning to wonder how he let himself get talked into this.

When Dehgoies refused his help, he should have joined his Adhipan brothers and sisters, escorting refugees back to the Pamir and to Vash.

"Cass!" he shouted up. "Are you all right?"

"Yep," she called back. "I think we're pretty close now. This looks exactly like the drawing in the book. Baguen thinks so too."

"Do you have any idea of the odds against that?" Balidor asked in some exasperation. "And anyway, that book could be a decoy, Cass, or—"

"No," Cass shouted. "This is right."

Balidor noticed the Wvercian didn't seem to care one way or the other.

But then, it was pretty clear he was following Cass like she was some kind of human prophet, maybe because of her relationship to the Bridge. Balidor still didn't know his name, although she called him "Baguen."

Balidor suspected it was a pidgin word in Wvercian she'd misheard.

They'd been hiking for days, with only the provisions the three of them carried on their backs, and the equipment Balidor had on him when he left Seertown with the Rebels, including his gun.

He'd managed to hunt on two of those days.

Water hadn't been an issue, so far at least, but he grew increasingly uncomfortable with his diminishing ammunition stores and anxious about what they were doing out here. Cass seemed determined that this was the best way to help Dehgoies and the Bridge, but his faith in her was beginning to falter, given everything.

Whatever she intended to accomplish, he couldn't get a read on it with his sight.

For him, that was more faith than his rational mind could allow.

Yet he had to admit, for the first time in several decades, if not centuries, he couldn't say there was anything directly pressing for him to be doing.

Seertown was deserted.

The Adhipan had scattered.

Those who hadn't gone after Dehgoies and the Bridge were leading caravans of refugees to the Pamir, Sikkim, Kathmandu, or Ladakh, to assemble and determine their losses. Some of those groups would be traveling for weeks, if not months.

Balidor could be helping them, of course.

But again... his presence was not strictly needed.

The seer government was in shambles, but Balidor himself couldn't do much about that. It would fall to Vash to reorganize the Council with whomever remained.

He'd heard directly from the remnants of the Seven right before he, Cass and the Wvercian left that dugout in Southwestern China. The vast majority of the news was bad. Yerin had been killed by the Americans, or possibly accidentally by the Rebellion. The Americans still denied their involvement, and the Rebels maintained they'd only appeared following the assault, but in Yerin's case, the end result remained the same.

Vash was in mourning for his son.

That would slow the government rebuilding.

Likely as a result of his absence, and that of the Bridge, the Council had effectively gone on hiatus for now. Balidor didn't yet want to think about what they would do if that hiatus ended up being permanent.

Balidor received a list of the dead.

He could keep it all in his *aleimi* because he was a seer.

He could have recited it, if such a thing were required, but it was bad enough just to know the names himself. He had known many of the dead personally.

Beyond that, the sheer number of them was devastating.

If not the end, Balidor knew he might be seeing the beginning of the end of his race.

He should have gone with Dehgoies.

He knew why Dehgoies didn't want him along. That had been clear when he made his excuses, even before he hooked into that network of Dreng filth just because it might save him a few days in recovering his mate.

Vash had warned him that Revik retained some attachment issues still.

When Balidor asked Vash what he thought about the Adhipan recruiting the ex-Rook, it had been Vash's only misgiving. Revik had spent too much of his life alone, Vash said. He retained a vulnerability in that lack, and would until his mate helped him to heal it.

So Balidor should have gone with him to America, but he didn't, and now they might have a problem greater than the Bridge being owned by a lunatic like Terian.

If Dehgoies turned again, with his relationship to the Bridge, he became a serious liability. They might even have to kill him, if they could find a way to do it without harming her. Or worse, if Dehgoies managed to recruit her, they might have to kill both of them.

The harm they could inflict together if both of them went dark far outweighed her ability to help humans in the coming Displacement.

Balidor didn't know what to do about that right then, either.

Chances were, the issue couldn't be addressed until Allie was out of Terian's custody. As much as Balidor hated to admit it, Dehgoies, light or dark, was their best chance to accomplish that without getting her killed.

She couldn't be allowed to stay with the boy, no matter what occurred.

A dark Dehgoies, daunting though that prospect was, they could handle.

It was nothing compared to a dark Syrimne-in-training with the Bridge at his side.

So Balidor continued to follow Cass and her Wvercian, all the while trying to decide how long he could continue his stalling before he walked the long road back to Dharamsala or Delhi for a plane to North America.

He was approaching his limit, he'd decided that morning.

He was still staring up at Cass, watching her feel her way along the face of the sheer rock wall, when her arm abruptly disappeared.

Balidor blinked.

Her arm continued to be gone.

It appeared to end at the elbow, the rest stuck inside rough, featureless stone. He saw a grin break out over her face, distorting the thick scar that bisected her countenance. She flipped back her dyed, black and red hair.

Then, in front of his very eyes, she vanished.

"Hey!" Balidor yelled up the cliff in Prexci. "Baguen! What happened?"

The giant grunted, looking down.

He touched the rock wall where Cass had been. Balidor saw the Wvercian's fingers disappear. Then, while he watched, the Wvercian disappeared, too.

Balidor shouted up again. "Cass! Goddamn it!"

Neither of them answered.

Frustrated, and now a little afraid, he vaulted up the path to reach the ledge.

He slid his body and feet along the narrow trail. Fumbling to keep a good grip on the wall, he made his way to the sheer drop where the two of them had been standing. He lost his footing a few times, spraying gravel with his organic-tipped boots in his haste to reach the last point he'd seen her on the path.

It was hardly a path at all, really. Instead, it looked more like a trail for goats, a narrow, pebbled ledge with only intermittent toeholds.

How Cass managed to get up here in the first place...

He paused, concentrating as he reached the place in the cliff wall where the two of them vanished. He felt over the rock with his fingers, looking for openings, any place where the sediment gave. Taking a breath, he pressed harder, focusing on the area where he could still feel the imprints of her hands.

...and suddenly, he found himself inside the mountain.

There was no warning, no transition.

If he didn't know better, Balidor would have thought he was absorbed by the rock itself. Or perhaps teleported.

Blinking to adjust his eyes, he glanced at the rock wall behind him.

He'd examine that later. He needed to find Cass.

He stretched out his *aleimic* light. He used it to examine the cave in which he now found himself. Instead of being entirely dark, phosphorescence glowed from the walls, a living paste. He touched it briefly with his gloved fingers, inhaling the wet, rotted smell before making a face and moving deeper into the cave.

"Cass?" He kept his voice low.

Using his light, he followed the traces of her *aleimi.*

Reaching what he thought had been the end, he realized it merely constituted a bend in a longer corridor. He'd barely walked ten paces when he found himself faced with another dead end. This one appeared to be made of solid volcanic glass.

It looked like a flat, black mirror.

"*D'gaos,*" he muttered. "Where is that human?"

Extending his light, he realized there was a larger space on the other side of the rock.

He reached out with a hand. He felt over the surface, until again…

…he found himself someplace else.

For a moment he could only stand there, blinking at the sharp increase in illumination. Glancing around, he focused on the dark bank of organic machines, staring at them in disbelief before Cass's voice jerked his attention to her.

"Hey, 'Dori."

Balidor found himself staring into the elfin face of Cass.

She motioned him over impatiently, her hands hovering over what appeared to be the main console for at least a portion of the organic hardware.

"Do you recognize any of these controls?" She pointed at the array of raised keys. "I can't read the language."

Approaching warily, Balidor stared down at the console, then around at the larger bank of machinery.

The row of organics slid even deeper into the rock walls than he'd first realized.

"Where the fuck is this?" he asked in English.

Cass looked up, grinning.

Her eyes shone with a light he hadn't seen in them in all the months he'd known her. There was an easy joy there, a happy triumph that reassured him somehow.

"See that?" she asked, pointing to a monitor.

Balidor followed her finger, staring at the virtual projection. His brow furrowed as he tried to make out the image on the screen, to make sense of it.

"What is it?" he asked finally.

"Space," she said, laughing. "Can you believe it?"

"Space?" He looked at her blankly. "Who is in space?"

Her grin widened, filled with so much happiness Balidor couldn't help but smile back, bewildered by the depth of emotion there.

"Feigran is," she said. "But we're going to bring him home."

CHAPTER 41
BROKEN

When the guards released me, my knees buckled. I crumpled in the corner of the cell.

I couldn't move.

My mind displayed static.

I wondered vaguely if I was broken. Permanently broken. I wondered what that would mean, what would happen to me if I never worked right again. I fingered parts of myself, but couldn't quite bring myself to look.

I knew I was punished… had been punished.

Threats blurred in my mind with memories of physical pain.

I couldn't see very well. I waited for him. I waited for…

My mind slid back into static, then returned to its slow loop.

I'd been punished. I couldn't remember precisely why. I got vague fears, no specifics. Nothing moved right. All the muscles in my body… everything felt broken. I was paralyzed. It was a blessing. I never wanted it to wear off. For the moment…

I obsessed on a single detail. I was drooling.

I fought to keep my mouth closed. I rested my chin on my knees. I turned my head sideways, but neither thing worked.

I'd been propped there, I realized, like a broken doll.

Blood covered the floor. Quietly.

The patch didn't seem bigger than it had been, but I couldn't be sure when that was. I might be dying. I couldn't feel anything, but I might be. I wanted to care. I wanted desperately to have an opinion about that, but I couldn't find one.

He'd taken me to another of those green, tile rooms.

I felt pieces of this, but blissfully absent of my light.

No hordes of human guards. Just him.

I'd done something—something to make him angry. Or scare him, maybe. I couldn't remember. I let my mind hum to a flat, empty tone, and wished more than anything I could fall asleep, just not be there for a while longer.

He liked it. He liked it a lot.

He wanted my light. He wanted…

When I heard the voice, I was sure I was dreaming.

"Hey! Bridge!"

I knew the voice, even in a loud whisper.

I dragged my head up, once more resting my chin on my knees. I was still drooling. I couldn't move my hands to wipe it off. My fingers lay splayed at my sides, palms open. I stared at the broad, Asian face.

For some reason, the tears in his eyes were what surprised me the most.

"Bridge." He knelt down, so that we were close to the same level. He held out a hand, eyes bright, tears running down his face. "Come here. Can you?"

I fought to keep my eyes open, looking at Maygar's face.

I had to be dreaming. I had to be.

"ALLIE!"

The voice pierced my awareness, jerking open my eyes.

His panic frightened me, made me cringe.

"Allie, what happened! What's wrong?"

The boy threw himself to his knees beside me. His fingers caressed my face, pushing sweat-damp hair out of my eyes. Even the lightest touch hurt, made me flinch away.

The numbness was gone.

He stepped in my blood and whimpered, crying out. His anguish made me clutch at him. Tears came to my eyes.

"It's all right," I found myself saying, my lips numb. "It's all right, baby..."

He stared at me, his irises glowing a pale green.

I realized what I'd said only after I saw tears well in his eyes.

For a moment, a bare second, I had forgotten who I was with.

He was on his feet. He paced in front of me, his eyes never leaving me. He knelt down again, touching my face.

"Allie," he murmured. He kissed me. His voice remained soft, but I heard the violence underneath. It wasn't aimed at me. "Allie... darling. Tell me. Who did this to you? You need to tell me. Now."

I shook my head, not looking at him.

His voice softened more, again sounding too old, too familiar.

"Let me see," he coaxed. "Let me see, please, love."

He held my wrist gently in his hand. After peering again at my face, maybe for permission, he pulled my arm gently away from my body so he could look at me. I knew I was naked. Somehow that bothered me more than why he wanted to look. I tried to cover myself with my other arm. I still couldn't move very well. My arms felt ripped out of their sockets. I remembered ropes, and something else...

Nenzi broke into my thoughts, whimpering again.

When I glanced up, he was looking at my face, his eyes scared.

He touched my cheek, peering from one of my eyes to the other. He kissed me, touching my hair so lightly I barely felt it. I found myself remembering the prostitute, the one he'd had before, when he was young like this.

"Allie," he said. "...gods! Please. Please, tell me what happened!"

My body hurt, enough that I closed my eyes, willing myself back into unconsciousness. I opened them then, remembering. I looked around, but Maygar was nowhere to be seen.

Nenzi's fingers tightened on my skin. The pain made me sweat, but I still couldn't move. The tension in his hand forced my eyes back to his.

"Allie." Tears filled the dark eyes. "Who did this to you?"

I fought to think. I remembered Terian's words, what he said he'd do. "I don't know," I said.

He held my hand. He pulled it off my knee again, looking at the rest of my body. I didn't follow his eyes. I didn't need to look to know it was bad.

"I'm all right," I lied.

His jaw hardened. His eyes grew brighter, turning liquid. Tears spilled down his cheeks, making rivulets down his perfect-looking skin.

"Who did it, Allie? Was it one of the humans?" Anger thickened his voice. "Which one of them did it?"

I hesitated, a little disbelieving as I avoided his gaze.

Resting my face on my knee, I shook my head.

"Drugged," I said finally. "I don't know."

"You don't remember anything?"

I gestured negative. "No," I said.

For a long moment, he sat beside me, an arm around me in a half-hug. He placed a hand on my leg, but I didn't push it away.

More minutes passed before I realized he was doing something to me.

The leg he touched felt different, like the skin and muscles were being faintly shocked by a mild but steady pulse of electricity.

I looked up. Nenzi's eyes were concentrated, his irises glowing like the flickering pulse of a dying flashlight. The intensity of his gaze remained on the spot where his hand touched my skin.

I was still watching the light in his eyes when he moved his hand higher, to my stomach. I gave a low gasp when the tingling started there, but it didn't hurt, so I didn't move away. Eventually I realized that what-ever he was doing, it gradually lessened the pain where his hand rested.

Slowly, as he kept going, I felt my muscles starting to unclench.

I took deeper breaths when he didn't stop. My head hung between my knees as I fought oxygen into my lungs. The collar kept everything deadened of course, but I no longer felt like I was going to die. He moved his hand to my chest and I flinched, then relaxed when the warmth spread out from his fingers, vibrating my skin.

"Thank you," I managed. "Thanks, Nenzi."

His fingers tightened on me briefly.

"Will you tell me, Allie? Please? Who did this to you? Who hurt you?"

I shook my head. "I can't tell you what I don't know."

"I'll kill all of them," he growled.

"No." I laid a hand on his arm. "Please. Don't."

We were still sitting there, his hand resting on my sternum, when the door to the outside cell opened with a hollow clanking sound.

I flinched, in spite of myself, cowering behind the boy.

He stopped what he'd been doing, looking up.

I watched his eyes lose their light, melting back to dark irises in a pale face.

His gaze followed mine to the door neither of us could see. The look there made me nervous. It was fury, but restrained down to a cold focus that was somehow more frightening than anything I'd seen on him.

"Nenzi," I whispered. I touched his face until he turned. "No," I said, soft. I shook my head when he looked at me. "No. It wasn't them."

I recognized the Scandinavian's voice, and the Asian woman, Raven, before they rounded the cement wall. Nenzi's jaw hardened. He looked at the door, then back at me. His voice dropped to a near-whisper.

"You're sure, Allie? You wouldn't lie to me?"

I shook my head. "I'm not lying."

"We have to do something with her…" I heard the woman mutter.

"Really?" Terian murmured in reply. "And just what do you suggest I do, Elan, that I haven't already tried? Nenzi has refused to force her."

"What a little bastard," Raven said humorously.

"My point precisely," the Scandinavian said, his voice a smile.

The boy laid his hand back on my leg.

The gesture felt protective, and I found myself swallowing, relaxing at what I saw in his liquid gaze. He kissed me, looking at me again, his eyes holding a stillness that made me stare. There was a promise there, in his eyes.

It wouldn't happen again.

No one would ever hurt me like that again.

Lost there briefly, I found myself thinking I was seeing yet another side of him, maybe even the adult version of Syrimne. There was something there that made me think of Balidor. The look in his dark eyes belonged to someone who was used to being in charge, someone at home with it.

Touching his hand, I smiled at him.

Once I was reasonably sure I had my expression under control, I looked past his shoulder towards the door.

Once I had, I froze.

Maygar stood there, holding the bars. Behind him was Raven, the Asian seer with the black hair and the bright turquoise eyes. Maygar didn't speak. He didn't stop looking at me, barely tore his eyes off me when Raven touched his arm.

Noticing his facial expression, she frowned as she glanced at me.

"Our girl's popular," I heard her murmur. That time, there wasn't much humor in her words. "Guess we should try to keep her around. For a little while, at least."

"She knows Prexci, Raven," Terian said mildly. "So does the boy."

The woman shrugged, her bright blue eyes indifferent.

Maygar swore, loudly enough that I flinched.

Looking at him, seeing the dark look in his eyes, I receded behind the boy.

"Goddamn it." His voice was furious. "I told you she needed a *doctor!*" He gestured towards me. "I thought you were going to handle it, Rook!"

I saw the Scandinavian exchange looks with Elan, and realized Maygar's words were aimed at him. I was struggling to track this.

Maygar knew Terian? Well enough to yell at him?

Maygar glared at the Scandinavian. "What are you doing letting that little freak paw at her? Take her to a doctor! Now!"

The Scandinavian looked at me.

Instead of grinning, as I'd expected, his brows drew together in a frown.

The frown looked so sincere I found myself staring at him.

As I did, it occurred to me that he really might be erasing his own memories, to keep the boy from feeling what he'd done.

"Your boy's right," he said to Raven, stepping forward.

"You see?" Raven said scornfully. "She wants to die."

"No," Terian said, clicking at her in worry and irritation. "I don't think so." He raised his voice. "Nenzi?" He sounded deeply concerned.

"What happened to Alyson? Is she all right? It looks like she's bleeding."

Nenzi put up his arm, shielding me from the three of them.

"Did you do this?" Nenzi demanded. "Did you?"

"My friend! Of course not! What happened to her?"

"Tell me the truth!"

"I did not harm her, Nenz! I promise you!"

Nenzi looked at me. Biting my lip, I shook my head.

"I don't think it was him, Nenzi."

The boy was still looking at me when Terian reached for the cell door. I flinched back, unable to help myself, clutching Nenzi's arm. Looking at me, then back at Terian, the smaller seer's voice turned into a snarl.

"Stay out! Don't come near her!"

Terian hesitated, his hand on the door. He looked at me, then at the boy.

"I swear to you, Nenzi! I did not do this! Did she tell you I did?"

"If she had, you'd already be dead," Nenzi said.

Raven turned on Terian too, her voice furious. "Well, perhaps if you hadn't *shot* him, left him chained in the middle of nowhere to die!" She clicked at Terian sharply. "No food, no water, just lying naked in the sun! The bombing in Seertown may have delayed his rescue by days! He's probably *dead*, Terry. She's probably dying because he is already dead. You know that, don't you?"

Terian sighed, hands on his hips. "Raven, look at her! She's not starving to death. She's been beaten! Are you blind?"

But I barely heard his words.

I felt my chest clench.

Pain filled me, so physical I was sure I was having a heart attack. I clutched my chest, fighting to breathe, sure I couldn't breathe.

"*Du relante d'gaos...* you've done it now," Raven said. "Look at her. She's going to have a heart attack."

"*I've* done it?" Terian said, incredulous. "Who was just ranting about the death of her mate?"

"She needs a fucking doctor," Maygar snarled.

He slammed a hand against the bars of the cage, rattling the metal.

That, and the emotion in his voice brought me briefly back.

I looked up, wanting any distraction, anything to keep me from the thought of Revik lying naked on that plateau, crows eating whatever was left after he slowly died of exposure and dehydration.

I couldn't get my head around it or away from it. It was like a sickness eating at me from the inside out, as soon as the image solidified. I couldn't get rid of it. I couldn't get close to it without feeling like I was going to start screaming.

Terian told me Revik and I hadn't completed the bond.

He said it would hurt like hell if Revik died, but it shouldn't kill me.

He told the boy it would kill me because he had his own reasons for wanting Revik alive, and it was pretty clear Nenzi would kill Revik without a strong incentive.

When Terian told me all this, it felt true.

The idea that I might live through this only made everything hurt that much worse.

If I didn't die, this would never end. Never.

For all I knew, Vash and Balidor were dead, too… and Jon, and Cass.

I started to cry. Everything hurt. Even without my light, I wanted to die.

Maygar was staring at me, disbelief in his eyes, mixed with a fear that threw me, that was hard to look at. I remembered what Revik said, his certainty that Maygar had feelings for me, but I couldn't quite believe that, either. How was he even here, with these people?

The last I knew, he was in some kind of coma.

Had he worked for Terian all along?

"Traitor," I muttered, wiping my eyes, staring at him. "Fucking traitor."

He blinked in surprise, but his predominant expression remained shock.

Terian made a conciliatory gesture towards Maygar with one hand.

"Well? If you insist on being the strapping young buck. Take care of it." He raised his voice. "Nenzi, this young male is right. We need to take Alyson to the medical facilities. Will you permit him to pass?"

Nenzi looked at me. When I nodded, reluctantly, he frowned.

He looked at Maygar. The look in his eyes narrowed, appraising.

"All right," he said finally.

Maygar's jaw clenched.

He looked at the boy, hearing the same warning and threat in his voice that I did. Nenzi's arm remained in front of me. His hand clutched my leg protectively—or maybe possessively. I didn't know anymore, or care. He hadn't hurt me.

Nenzi hadn't hurt me, not directly.

The rest of these people had.

As if hearing me, Maygar looked from the boy back to me. He stared at the small hand on my thigh, and for an instant, disgust tainted his expression. I felt my jaw harden, but I only looked away, resting my chin on my knee. Nenzi looked at me. He caressed my face with his fingers, stroking my hair.

Maygar opened the door. He entered the cage.

Nenzi gripped my leg as he approached us.

"Don't hurt her," he said. "Please. I'll kill you if you do… but please, don't."

Maygar didn't bother to answer.

He crossed the depth of the cage. Reaching the two of us, he moved the boy out of the way, his hands not particularly gentle. Nenzi took it from him, maybe because he could feel Maygar's intentions, or maybe for some other reason.

Crouching next to me, Maygar dragged the thin blanket off the cot behind us. Carefully, he wrapped it around my back, covering me.

Somehow, the simple gesture brought tears to my eyes.

"Allie?" He touched my face, brushing hair over my shoulder. "Allie, I'm going to pick you up, okay?"

I looked at him. For an instant, he was my friend again, the person I joked around with and drank with and tried to fix up with Cass on the train ride to Russia. Behind my eyes, I glimpsed the look on his face the last time I'd seen him, that hard, hunter's look, the sweat on his upper lip.

I wanted to ask him why he'd done it.

Instead, hearing his question again in my mind, I nodded.

I didn't move as he slid his arms under my knees and upper back… and lifted. Briefly, I felt something close to relief as he brought me up in a curl against his chest. I felt his heart beat loudly under my ear. He felt real, like a real person.

Not like one of Terian's animated corpses, or the woman with those cold, lifeless eyes, or the boy who should have been dead a hundred years ago.

His hands were shaking a little.

Holding me tightly against his chest, he carried me out of the cell.

I caught another glimpse of Terian staring at me, his amber eyes concentrated, as if I was a puzzle he needed to solve.

Then Maygar's shoulder cut off my view.

When I looked down, I saw Nenzi trailing along beside us.

CHAPTER 42
UNWILLING

"Look up." The flashlight shone in Revik's face. "Right." He turned his head. "Left." He turned it again.

He felt the scanner with his light, knew it was tracking the shape of his bones inside his flesh, tracking his teeth against dental records, both in local law enforcement and SCARB. He knew the organics in the body skin he wore should be able to provide a false map to the machine, based on the young unwilling's outline, as should the detailed prosthetics he wore, also embedded with organics.

He shouldn't be worried.

Yet he knew if he hadn't been in the suit, his jacked-up heart rate likely would have set off the scanner's warning light already.

He'd done this kind of thing before.

Normally, he could keep all of his basic body functions under control; it was entry-level infiltrator training, not even an advanced skill.

But he could feel himself getting closer to her.

He could feel it in every part of his body, enough to know he'd broken out in a sweat.

He hadn't factored that in.

He shoved it from his mind. It was too late.

His light had been tougher to disguise than his body and face. He had a number of seers holding pieces of it from the Barrier, but to get past security, he was relying on Wreg's team to generate a temporary field mimicking the light of the unwilling whose identity he borrowed. It involved a superimposition of key *aleimic* markers and structural configurations to fool the seers working the front gate.

It was Barrier technology he'd only heard postulated while working for the Seven.

Wreg and his team seemed confident they could pull it off, at least long enough to get him inside. It was akin to creating a mobile construct around Revik's person.

Revik hadn't asked too many questions about the mechanics of how such a thing might be done, but he wasn't stupid.

Normally, in order to function properly, a construct had to be anchored in significant physical mass. Land. A building. A ship, if large enough. A mountain, or any large deposit of dense stone. Even a body of water might work, under certain circumstances.

For a mobile construct to work, it would need to be anchored in the Barrier.

Given that the vast majority of Barrier beings didn't operate directly on Earth, that left the Dreng, the same beings that once provided stability for the Rooks' Pyramid.

Revik didn't ask.

And since no one offered him a different explanation, he left it alone.

The guard's scanner clicked off.

The human spoke nonverbally into his headset, then looked down at their driver, Wreg. Using his fingers, the guard motioned for him to take the car through the gate.

Revik felt his heartbeat quicken.

One barrier down.

They reached the East Wing entrance, where they'd been instructed to enter, both by the client and by the unwilling Revik was now impersonating. Checking out the security markers he could see with his eyes alone, it occurred to him that he'd never actually been inside this building before, not even as a tourist.

He glanced over the façade and to either side of the East Wing entrance.

He'd barely taken in the walls and a glimpse of the garden and trees when the car came to a full stop. He couldn't see the more famous porticos of the north and south entrances or the garden on the south side, not with the building in the way, but the impact of the structure and what it represented still hit him harder than he expected.

It was strange to think Galaith had lived here.

Revik would have been here often, if he'd made a different choice earlier in his life.

He likely would have been on Galaith's staff.

Possibly in his cabinet.

A guard approached, peered inside, then stepped out of the way of the car's door, motioning for them to exit the vehicle.

Revik snapped the door's latch and slid over on the seat.

He stepped his full weight onto his good leg, then rose in a single motion. They'd padded his shoes to change his gait; it was the limp he had to watch. He hit his hurt leg hard as he stepped forward with the other, distributing his weight evenly. Sliding between the other three infiltrators as they left the car behind him, he exuded boredom with his light, winking at the guard when the man seemed to be looking at him too closely.

Frowning, the human averted his gaze.

Like Revik, the other three infiltrators' records were made to match the bone structure, light markers and facial features of three specific seers from the same house.

Unlike him, they'd done all of this by falsifying records, and without wearing prosthetics. It minimized their chances of being caught if fewer of them were relying on organics to fool the scanning equipment. Besides, there was no reason any of the other three would be sought out by security.

Still, there was some risk.

Terian might be aware of his contacts in the States.

But the plan was always to delay discovery, not prevent it entirely.

All four of them wore expensive suits. Their sight-restraint collars were the thin, lightweight variety, easy to miss in a casual glance, especially from a human.

Revik kept his light focused on the imprint of the unwilling he was mimicking.

Their clothes, hair and general appearance kept most of the humans they passed in the corridors from looking at them too closely.

At least two Revik saw noticed the collars, but they didn't react apart from a slight double-take. One glanced at a colleague, raising an eyebrow. Apparently, at least a few among the staff were well aware of the tastes of some of the higher-ups.

The women got looks, of course.

The most nerve-wracking part was psychological rather than due to any specific threat. Walking past the visitor's entrance on the east side of the main building, Revik found it difficult not to stare around at various parts of the interior as they entered the center hall, passing by some of the more famous of the ground floor rooms.

The foot traffic immediately increased as well.

Revik noticed the addition of at least three more humans watching them from the sides, unobtrusively of course, but clearly Secret Service, and armed.

Revik kept his eyes down.

He focused on the man leading them, like the guards instructed them at the gate.

Even so, he noticed things.

A door here, a set of windows there, a passageway he tied to one segment of the map or another in his head. He hadn't been well versed in the layout of the building before he started this op, but he recognized paintings, glimpses of carpet runners and stair landings, the placement of windows and walkways.

He had to rely on his physical eyes and ears alone, of course.

He wore a mock-up of a collar that exuded Barrier interference rather than a true block of his sight, but even a casual scan wouldn't go unnoticed in here. He could feel the construct shields in random touches of his light, and they were dense, multi-layered.

The team outside should still be able to feel him.

They reached the other side of the center hall, past the two porticos, and he felt himself relax slightly. He could smell the kitchen, so he knew they were getting close to the elevator, which the unwilling told him was the only way he'd ever reached their destination on the second floor.

It was time to throw up a flare—a small one, anyway.

Give them something by which to gauge the passage of time on his end.

He entered the elevator with the other two seers and folded his hands at the small of his back, whistling softly.

Raspberries, he thought clearly, letting a whisper of hunger join the word.

He let his mind wander, sliding back into the boredom of the unwilling, thinking about what he would do afterwards, if he and his friends would get high and watch old movies while they came down from the stims the client would want him to do to jack up their reactions to one another.

He let himself think about the client as well, what kind of mood he might be in, how many others might be there.

As he let the thought form, he glanced at Tobias, one of Wreg's men posing as another unwilling. He was the only one of Wreg's team able to mimic the light markers of a pro, at least to the appropriate degree.

They'd sold him as a newbie to the client, which of course intrigued him.

Revik shrugged subtly with one hand.

"Ten dollars it's four," he said.

"Twenty," Tobias countered. "And dinner."

The guard glanced at them, allowing a faint smile.

"He knows something," Revik said. "How many?"

The guard shrugged, human fashion, but the smile remained on his face. "I don't know how you icebloods do it. Honestly."

"Come on." Kat smiled from his other side. She touched the guard's arm, letting a tendril of her light snake out, wrapping around his leg. "Come with us," she murmured. "I'll show you, since you're so curious."

The guard glanced down, letting his eyes travel deliberately over her body. She, like Ullysa, wore a form-fitting, tailored suit. He raised an eyebrow.

"Not in the slightest," he said flatly.

Even so, Revik felt the man reacting to her.

He had to fight not to step away from where they stood. Keeping it off his face, he looked the human over, giving Tobias a sideways smile.

"You work for them year-round," Revik joked to the guard. "We're here a few hours. Who's the crazy one?"

"Don't tease him, Lewellyn," Ullysa said, touching Revik's arm.

Tobias laughed, but the guard's mouth tightened. He smiled at the joke, but stepped deliberately away from Kat, giving Ullysa a look that lasted a little longer.

He didn't talk to them again.

The elevator reached the top floor, then stopped for a security scan.

That one took longer.

As he waited, Revik felt his light contract sharply around his form.

He was reacting to her again.

It could be in his head. He couldn't feel her exactly, but he could feel *something*, like catching a scent that was faint, wholly dependent on wind. It was maddening. He realized he was sweating.

He forced his light deeper into the mobile construct, seeking the cold stability of the silver light. He was having a physical reaction, too.

He realized suddenly that the other seers were focused on him, in more ways than one.

Christ. She was here. He knew it suddenly, in his whole body. She was in this building somewhere. Thinking about it sent another ripple through his light, strong enough that Ullysa laid a hand on his arm.

"Llewellyn," she said softly. She waited for him to turn his head. "Honey, did you take anything?"

Hesitating, he shuffled his feet, folding his hands.

Following her cue, he muttered a low response. "Not much."

"*D'gaos*, Llewe," she said in her soft voice. "What were you thinking?"

He didn't answer, but let a flavor of annoyance flare his light.

"He won't mind."

"We'll see if Jo says the same," she murmured.

His hunter cloak wavered, then kicked back in.

He squeezed Ullysa's fingers in a silent thanks. He kept the forward part of his mind off Allie, but a second train whispered in the background, hopefully too quiet for the construct to pick up.

They wouldn't have her up here.

She'd be in the basement somewhere, if on the grounds at all.

The plan hadn't changed.

This was still the best way to get the boy to bring her to him.

The doors let out a soft ping, and slid open.

Standing on the other side was a human in his late sixties, with a head of thick, white hair. He grinned when he saw Revik, then glanced at the other three.

Revik bowed, formal seer fashion, as he might do to Vash, or any in the Council of Seven. The human loved the ceremony, mannerisms and turns of phrase of formal seer culture, despite his ignorance of their correct context.

The bow Revik had just performed belonged in a monastery, not a government building, but the man had no clue as to the significance of any of it.

The real Llewelyn had simply experimented with fragments of seer culture until he figured out what was suitably dramatic for the old man's tastes.

"Hello, Mr. Vice President," Revik said. "You are looking fine this evening."

"Come here, my boy!" the human said, holding out his arms.

Revik walked into them without hesitation. He gave the old human a hug.

The man immediately looked down, and his grin widened.

"You missed me, Lou?" he asked.

"Of course, sir," Revik said, smirking.

"Well, then... bring your friends! Come inside!"

Revik barely spared the others a glance before following the old human, his hands folded formally in front of his body.

He wouldn't have to fuck the old man.

Travers was a voyeur, and impotent.

If he knew more, he'd probably be dangerous, but as it was, he was a relatively benign form of the sub-category who got off watching seers being together. There were others of this variety who knew enough about separation pain and the bonds of mates to be full-blown sadists in their kink.

Travers didn't fit that mold, at least not yet.

Clearly the old man felt safe indulging here, due to the layers of security from outside eyes and a discreet nod from Terian. From a seer's perspective, the human had an odd idea of "safe," however. Due to the requirements of the military-grade construct, every seer in the building could see and hear everything that went on during Travers' "parties."

Terian obviously wanted the insurance, in case Travers ever stepped out of line.

He certainly had that by now.

They entered the room.

Revik took in the five humans who waited for them.

Dressed as if for a cocktail party, they sat on chairs not far from a white marble fireplace. A fire burned high in the grate, on the opposite side of a low coffee table covered with a tray of glasses, along with several bottles of hard alcohol and two ice buckets.

They stared at the four seers in open curiosity.

Revik nodded politely, bowing as he'd been told.

Then, avoiding eyes, he glanced around the room itself, taking in furniture that looked more than a century old. Love seats with gold embroidered fabric and dark cherrywood matched a king-sized bed with an elaborate headboard of the same. The headboard climbed up the wall, ending in a set of snow-white drapes hanging in arcs by giant pillows.

The room wasn't particularly big by modern standards.

It wasn't small, either.

The sitting area stretched from the double doors to two large windows with heavy gold drapes that someone had drawn. A cherry-wood desk stood in one corner, a dressing table with a matching chair sat against the opposite wall. The lamps were on low settings, but the fire in the grate provided most of the room's lighting.

Revik felt his nerves rise.

Keeping it off his face, he glanced at Ullysa, then back at the old human, watching as the latter arranged himself on one of the elaborately carved love seats before the fire. Travers positioned himself directly across from the human audience in fancy clothing.

Revik felt more than saw the door close.

He heard the outer locks slide into place, felt the security team outside the door. Nothing out of synch so far. It was all pretty much exactly as Llewelyn told him it would be. Even so, he didn't move for a few seconds, watching as the old human fixed himself a drink and exchanged pleasantries with several of the humans.

Finally, the Vice President looked at him.

"Are you coming?"

Revik barely hesitated. "Of course, sir." He adopted the formal tone and posture. "I was waiting to be invited."

The man smiled. "You're tense tonight, Lou… relax." He patted the space next to him on the couch. "Have a seat."

After the barest pause, Revik walked over and sat beside him.

He nodded to the humans who seemed to want to engage him, but didn't quite meet any one gaze. He was trying to focus again, to get his head back in the game. He found himself thinking about Allie anyway, trying not to wonder if she could see anything inside the construct, or if she was reacting to him being there as much as he was to her.

He lost himself in those thoughts for long enough to miss a few seconds of speech from the human.

"…a little under the weather tonight?"

Revik glanced over, bringing the cloak he'd woven of Llewelyn's *aleimi* more tightly over his. "I'm fine, sir."

"Would you like a drink, Lou?"

Llewelyn had instructed him on this, too. "No… thank you, sir."

The human smiled. "Have one, anyway."

"Yes, sir." Following their little ritual, he accepted the glass and took a cautious sip, feeling his nerves rise as the human motioned over Kat. Pretending to misunderstand, Ullysa stepped forward, but the old man insisted.

"No. The blond one. You."

Ullysa stepped back, folding her hands formally in front of her body.

Revik felt a sharp spike of nausea.

He tried to kill it with more swallows of the drink, but all he could think of was Allie, and what this would do to him if their positions were reversed.

He would lose his fucking mind.

Maybe she wouldn't see anything. Maybe she would only get a glimpse, and then it would be over and he could explain to her how he'd done it to get in. How it was the least risky way. How he couldn't afford to wait when he had no idea how long Terian would keep her here, if he'd move her somewhere else, somewhere he couldn't find her…

Kat knelt in front of him.

Revik averted his eyes as she unfastened his pants, feeling the nausea worsen. He finished the drink, but didn't put it down. It wasn't the nausea he felt around Allie, which was as much nerves and adrenaline and desire as anything else.

Revulsion hit him instead, a feeling that made him actually, really sick… but that didn't seem to harm his physical reaction any.

He'd sworn to her he would never do this.

He'd told her she'd never have to worry about him, that he'd never do it to her again, not for any reason.

He'd meant it. He could feel she didn't trust him, that it might be years before she fully trusted him—years where he'd be more than happy to prove to her that she *could* trust him.

Gods. What if he was wrong? What if the boy didn't come? What if the plans were wrong, if Terian or Travers had some kind of imaging device in here, or found some way to show her through the Barrier?

What if this all ended up being for nothing?

Kat started touching him, and his mind blanked out briefly.

He was back in the cabin, remembering waking up with Allie's hands on him. A sharp ribbon of desire mixed with the sickness of having another seer in his light, making the separation pain worse… so bad, he wondered if he'd be able to hold it together at all without ranting at all of them.

Or worse, trying to kill them.

He looked at the other seers, looking for help maybe.

But he could feel it already, in their light. He saw it in their faces as they looked at him. He was affecting them. They wouldn't be able to help themselves.

He looked at the old human.

But Travers was already motioning over Ullysa. He patted the back of the love seat to indicate where he wanted her.

Ullysa walked up behind where Revik sat.

She laid her hands on his shoulders, exuding calm, and he reached up, clasping her arms. He closed his eyes, and she lowered her mouth to his. They were kissing before he knew he intended to, and instead of distracting him from what Kat was doing to him, it made it worse, until he was clasping at Ullysa's hair, half holding her against him.

When he ended the kiss, she lowered her mouth to his ear.

She spoke Prexci, so the humans wouldn't understand. She made it sound like lover's talk, like she was urging him on, but he felt the sympathy behind it.

"Revi', listen to me. You can do this… you're all right…"

He fought back another thick surge of pain.

He felt Ullysa react to it, even as Tobias walked up behind her.

Looking up at the male, panic hit Revik, a reaction so physical he felt his breath stop, making him light-headed.

"You can do this," Ullysa repeated, soft, a near purr. "You can. She loves you. She'll understand. She'll know why you did this…"

He gripped her tighter, crying out as Kat took him deeper.

Then he was holding Kat's hair too, fighting another urge to let his reactions turn violent. Since none of the seers wore real collars, none of their perceptions were muted, either. There was no way for Revik to block or even dial-down the others without calling attention to himself.

Besides, the boy had to feel it.

The boy needed to feel *him* here.

He had to recognize his light.

Revik forced his eyes up, looking for distraction, anything to pull his mind back from where it wanted to go.

He tried remembering Allie at the cabin, but his pain spiked so sharply, he heard Tobias gasp. His eyes refocused on the chairs across from him. The humans sat there, nearly motionless. More than half of them held drinks they seemed to have forgotten. They were reacting to the display already.

A pretty brunette in her thirties seemed riveted to Revik's face, her eyes drifting down to where Kat had her mouth on him.

They would feel it too, the separation.

They wouldn't know what it was, but they would feel it. He caught a whisper of the brunette's thoughts as she swallowed, staring back at his face.

She'd already decided she wanted to fuck him.

He averted his eyes, holding Ullysa's arm tighter.

"Revi'," Ullysa murmured. "Revi'… calm. Remember why we're here."

He heard her, enough to fight it.

She was right. He couldn't blow this, not now. Closing his eyes, he tried to cooperate, to focus. He slid deeper into the silver strands, but couldn't find any stability there, either.

He reminded himself he was playing a part. If he broke down, really lost it, they'd probably think he was dangerous and call for help. It was a thin line for humans, between exotic difference and terrifying other.

Fighting to turn his panic into at least the outer trappings of arousal, he arched towards Kat, but the reaction in her light nearly locked his muscles, right before she dug her fingers into his hurt leg.

Then Tobias had his hand in his shirt and he felt sick all over again, trying to incorporate another seer's light as the male massaged his chest, kissing his throat.

Ullysa's voice remained in the foreground, the only anchor he had.

"She'll understand," Ullysa murmured. "She'll understand…"

He shook his head. "No," he managed. "She won't."

"She loves you, Revi'… she loves you…"

She had, he thought. She really had before this.

He'd felt it. A part of him had tried to hold onto doubt, to protect himself maybe, give himself some latitude in case something happened, or she changed her mind before they finished the bond. Even as recently as Sikkim, he'd convinced himself she might not know what she was doing, what she was really saying to him.

He'd told himself she was just young, inexperienced.

He told himself the separation was fucking with her head.

But he hadn't really believed those things, either.

She'd loved him. In spite of everything he'd done to her, everything he'd been.

But he wondered if she loved him enough.

CHAPTER 43
RESCUE

I jerked awake.

I felt sick. I tasted bile in my throat, realized I was sweating.

I didn't know what was wrong with me.

Whatever it was, it was bad.

I rolled to my side... and found that I could.

My wrists were chained together, but not to anything else. Even curled in a fetal position—fighting not to panic from how badly every square inch of my skin hurt—it occurred to me that I was in a real bed.

The mattress was thin. The blankets smelled like baby powder.

I let out a low gasp when the pain returned, then a moan when it only got worse. Cursing, I rolled to my back, but it didn't help. Whatever was wrong, it felt separate from the pain of my legs, hips, and arms.

It lived so far under my skin, I couldn't pinpoint a source.

It felt like I was dying.

Or like something was trying to rip my heart out of my chest.

"Fuck," I gasped. I stared up at the white ceiling, holding my belly with one arm. I squeezed it down, pressing it into my back. I felt sick to my stomach. It was more than that, though, like something vile was being forced down my throat.

I wondered if Terian poisoned me.

Then I wondered if Revik had died.

I screamed, losing all sense of myself, then choked when the pain worsened, now trying to crush my chest. I was still sweating, only now I wanted to throw up. My body convulsed, wracked with pain, but I couldn't make myself expel anything real.

Curling up into a tight ball on my side, I closed my eyes, groaning.

Somewhere in all that, the door must have opened.

"Allie?" A voice broke through the sickness. "Allie, what's wrong?"

I glanced up, holding my stomach, fighting to breathe.

Maygar.

Everything came flooding back.

I remembered where I was, how I got here. I'd been brought to some kind of medical area, part of the same underground series of rooms. I was pretty sure I was on a different floor now, at least one above my cell.

I was still looking at Maygar when the lights flickered overhead.

He looked up when I did, frowning. His hand rested on the head-board of my bed.

Both of us watched the electricity cut in and out.

"What's going on?" My voice was hoarse.

"I don't know," he muttered.

"Where is everyone?" It struck me that we were alone in the white room. "Where is Nenzi? Terian? That woman?"

"They left. Terian took the boy." Looking down at my naked body, he seemed to realize what he was doing and forced his eyes back to mine.

"Allie," he said. "He did this to you, didn't he? Terian."

"Can you get me out of here?" I asked.

Maygar looked at the door, then back at me. He didn't quite meet my gaze.

"It's complicated."

"Complicated? What the *fuck* does that mean?" Angry, I reached for him. I missed and ended up clutching the bedside table, squeezing it as hard as I could. Pain whited out my vision, making my voice harsh.

"You *owe* me, Maygar. You fucking *owe* me—"

"It's not that easy, Allie." Maygar frowned, shaking his head. "We wouldn't get far. The security is intense, and my mother—"

"Your what?"

He looked at the door, then back at me. He lowered his voice.

"Elan Raven. She's the seer with Terian. With the blue eyes."

"That's your mother?" I fought to think past his words.

I clutched my stomach harder when another wave of sickness ran through me. For a blank period of time, I couldn't move, couldn't think.

Behind my eyes, I saw the slim, athletic woman with the shocking turquoise eyes. I forgot sometimes, that seers weren't the ages they looked in human years.

She could be Maygar's mother. Of course she could.

"Okay." I nodded, gasping back pain. "Okay. So you don't want to leave her. Your mother—"

"It's not that," Maygar said. "Honestly, Allie, I'm a risk to you. Wherever I am, she can feel me. I can't get you out without leading her right to you."

I fought back another ripple of pain, that one through my spine.

I closed my eyes, gasping thickly. "Gods, what the *fuck* did they give me?"

"Nothing." He pressed his lips together, looking worried. "Morphine for the pain, but that was hours ago. Are you sure it's not just wearing off?"

"This isn't... pain. Not like... not like before..." I fought back another wave, then struggled to sit up with my cuffed wrists. Hunched in an awkward pile at the edge of the mattress, I looked down at myself.

"Can you at least get me some fucking clothes?" I snapped. "And get rid of these?" I held out the cuffs. "If you can get me out of the collar, too, I can do the rest."

"Allie." Maygar reached out to touch my face. He withdrew his hand when he saw the look I gave him. "Allie, they'll kill you before they let you go." He hesitated. "I think the only reason Terian hasn't killed you already is that he's worried what the boy will do. That, and he wants your husband for something."

I let out a gasping kind of laugh. "Yeah. So what else is new?"

"Allie." Maygar sighed, looking at me. "I can't believe I'm saying this, but have you thought about..." He took a breath, gesturing with one hand. "You know. With the boy. Just to buy yourself time. Get them to back off."

I turned my head, staring at him.

Maygar's lips pursed. "I know," he said, his voice frustrated. "But the kid can't be any worse than Terian, right? He seems to care for you. The boy."

My stare grew colder, even under the thread of disbelief.

But I understood now. It all clicked into place.

I'd just been too distracted to notice.

This wasn't Maygar.

I stared at his face, my jaw hard.

"Too far, huh?" Maygar's face smiled, winking at me.

I swallowed another rush of bile. "Terian."

He sighed, his voice altering, turning more melodious.

"I knew that last bit was probably over the line. But I just *had* to try."

The outline of Maygar phased.

A thin line of static tore it in two.

I was alone. I'd been alone the whole time. It was the reason "Maygar" never actually touched me. He'd been some kind of virtual reality puppet show.

I blinked, still holding my stomach. I looked at where my ankles were cuffed together, and realized I wasn't going anywhere.

"Gods. I'm an *idiot!*" I snapped.

The image of the Scandinavian popped into existence. He smiled at me.

"You can't blame a guy," he said. "Can you?"

Then, all at once, the lights went out—completely out.

I got thrown into utter dark.

I groped around in that impenetrable blackness, long enough to feel myself still sitting on the edge of a bed, to realize my hands and ankles were still cuffed, and the rest of my body hurt like hell.

I listened to myself breathe in the dark.

I could barely think past the sickness in my gut.

I was still sitting there, trying to decide what to do, when an orange light flared in the dark. From a corner of the room, it rotated within a metal cage, like one of those emergency lights that come on when a generator kicks in.

I found myself in a cement-walled cell next to what looked like a heart monitor machine and two I.V. bags hanging from metal roll stands.

I looked for a way out.

The door was located in a different wall than the VR version of the room.

Also, in this version, cabinets covered most of one wall.

On the counter below those, I saw glass jars filled with cotton balls, tongue depressors, long Q-tips, what looked like gauze. A rolling table sat in that same corner, draped in cloth and covered with metal instruments. Everything was stained orange in the rotating light that hung over an organic-component door.

I slid off the bed. I shuffled in the ankle shackles to the table.

I fumbled over rows of neatly laid out instruments. I looked for anything that might saw through the organic cuffs. I finally located cutters of some kind, thick enough and sharp enough to give me some hope.

I sat on the floor, drawing in my feet so I could reach the chain on my ankles. I worked the blades into and around one of the metal links. When I finally got it in deep enough, I turned the handles sideways so I could brace one end on the floor. Using my full weight, I pushed as hard as I could on the handle pointing up.

It slipped the first time I tried.

The second time, I felt the metal give.

I bent down to peer at the link up close, bringing my ankles up to my body so I sat in cobbler's pose. A tear had formed in the metal.

Wedging the blades deeper, I threw my weight on the handles again. After two more tries, I managed to get all the way through.

The ankle chain was the easy one, though.

After trying and failing to find an angle where I could do the same with my wrists, I crawled under the hospital bed. Using my shoulder, I propped up one corner of the frame. After wedging the cutter's blade in a link of the chain tying my wrists, I set up the handles so that they would be directly under the bed's foot.

Luckily the bed had a lot of organics in it.

It was heavy.

Sweat dripped off my forehead as I set it up, holding the metal frame with my shoulder until it dug into my back. I was gritting my teeth at the end, but after what crippled me before, it was a welcome distraction.

I was starting to panic. Too much time had passed.

Someone would come looking for me soon.

The first time I lowered the bedframe, the handles slipped and went skittering across the floor.

Letting the bed fall, I crawled around in the orange, semi-dark until I found them. Wedging them back into the same link in the chain, which now had a tiny crack, I took a breath, then used my back to lift the frame a second time.

That time, I forced myself to concentrate, holding my breath and ignoring the nausea as I held the handles in place tightly with my hands.

Slowly, I lowered the bed.

The weight of the frame closed the handles smoothly, cutting the metal clean through. I let out a startled laugh, staring down at my separated hands in something like disbelief.

Immediately, I put my hands to the collar, feeling it with my fingers.

I ran to the mirror, shoving the heart monitor out of the way while I looked at the organic ring.

There was no way.

I tried to wedge the cutters around the metal anyway. I only succeeded in cutting my neck so that it bled in a thin trickle.

Dropping the instrument on the counter, I went through the drawers next, pulling out anything I could find and holding it up to the orange light. I went through the cabinets after the drawers. I found pills. Instruments. Nothing I could use.

Then I found clothes.

Blue medical scrubs, they looked orange in the rotating light.

I threw them on, pulling the long shirt over my head and yanking on the pants. I cinched the drawstring and knotted it, then rolled the cuffs to my ankles before running for the door, feeling all over it for some kind of lock, or even a handle.

There was nothing.

I wondered if I should bang on it.

I looked for a panel next, but after several minutes of searching, I was forced to concede that the controls must be outside.

I was going through drawers again when the door jerked open behind me.

For the briefest second, my heart lifted.

I turned, holding a small saw in my hand, and the only scalpel I found in the whole room. It was as dark outside the room as it was in, with more rotating orange lights.

Nenzi stood there. His eyes glowed bright green.

"Allie?"

"What the *hell* is going on?" I snapped.

My voice came out a snarl.

The sickness was worse.

Holding my gut and chest with the arm whose hand still clutched the saw, I held out the scalpel with the other like a weapon.

If the boy reacted, it didn't show.

I fought the desperation that rose in me, the feeling of despair to see the kid there, when I was so close to being free—closer than I'd been since I got here. I was trying to decide what to say, when he held out a hand.

"Come here, Allie," he said.

His voice was older again, the adult's voice.

"Why?" I snapped. "Why should I?" I sounded like the child.

Tears came to my eyes, partly from pain, and partly because I couldn't believe it wasn't over. Without realizing it, I'd been waiting for Revik to open that door. I'd been so sure it would be him, that the orange lights meant he was alive, that he'd come for me.

The boy's voice grew cold, almost like he'd heard me.

"We're leaving." He held out his hand, insistent. "Now, Allie."

WE WERE RUNNING DOWN CORRIDORS THEN, TWISTING PAST DARK DOORWAYS and side passages that didn't have emergency lighting.

I stumbled after Nenzi, still clutching the scalpel and the saw, barefoot and jogging to keep up with his fast pace.

I hated how blind I was. I had only my eyes. I squinted at any area illuminated with a swath of rust-colored light. I sought out every line and surface I could see until the light disappeared and the contrast threw me into blindness again.

Nenzi got us to the elevator.

A pair of guards stood there.

I grabbed his arm, about to warn him, when both humans crumpled, like puppets with cut strings. I looked at Nenzi, then stepped over the guards, looking for the panel to open the elevator doors. I found it, but it was DNA coded and required a retinal scan.

"Leave the knives here, Allie."

Glancing at my hands, I hesitated, then tossed them, my eyes still on the panel's security system.

"Nenzi," I said. "We might have a problem."

He walked up to stand next to me.

I watched as he laid his hand on the external controls.

As his eyes glowed brighter, I glanced down at the human guards. I realized in some bewilderment that he hadn't just knocked them out. He'd killed them.

"Nenzi. Jesus," I said. "You didn't have to—"

"We'll talk about it later," he said.

I opened my mouth to argue, then closed it.

Fuck this. He was right.

I forgot the guards entirely when the panel lit up under the kid's fingers.

I watched the retinal scanner click on.

It sent a narrow beam of red light down over his forehead, eyes, and face, seemingly untouched by the orange generator lights. Reaching the base of his neck, it clicked off just as abruptly, leaving us in relative darkness.

The doors to the elevator slid open, letting out a low tone.

My chest clenched. Relieved, sick, scared, totally confused… I didn't know if I was happy to be leaving with him or not.

He started to enter the elevator when I grabbed his arm.

"Terian," I managed. "We're not going somewhere with him, are we, Nenz? We're not just meeting him upstairs? Him *or* Wellington?"

Nenzi gestured negative. "No."

"What about Maygar?" I asked. At his puzzled look I used my hands to indicate the male seer's rough height. "The seer who carried me. With the tattoos."

Nenzi frowned, shaking his head. "No."

I hesitated for another half-second.

Nenzi grabbed my arm, tugging on it without forcing me inside. "Come on, Allie!" he said. "We have to hurry!"

I nodded. Taking a breath, I stepped into the elevator.

I watched him hit a button, but my mind was somewhere else.

It was so strange riding in the elevator with him—the quiet whisper of the rails, the elaborate wallpaper that belonged more in the upstairs part of the building than the downstairs, the whisper and click of passing floors.

I suddenly realized we'd passed too many floors.

"Nenzi." I grasped his arm. "Nenzi! Where are we going?" I heard the edge of panic in my voice. "You said we weren't going to Terian! You said we weren't going to him or Wellington!"

"Wellington *is* Terian." He gave me a puzzled look, like he couldn't believe I didn't know. "And we're not going to him. Calm down, Allie."

"Then why didn't we get off on the main floor? Why are we—"

"We have to make a stop first," he said.

His eyes looked determined, just the slightest bit triumphant.

Seeing the expression there, I fell silent, unable to make sense of it, or how it could possibly fit with what was going on here.

Receding deeper into the wall by the brass handrail, I felt the car slow, then come to a gliding stop. For a number of seconds the elevator car remained where it was with the doors closed, going through the security protocols of scanning us, checking us against where we were supposed to be according to security.

Whatever Nenzi told the living machine must have been fairly all-encompassing.

The organic intelligence now thought it was perfectly okay for both of us to be on the second floor of the aboveground structure.

I felt my breath come short as the doors opened.

I crept out after Nenzi, half-wishing I still had the scalpel and saw, even knowing they wouldn't do me much good if we were confronted by security, who had guns at minimum, and more realistically, a bevy of organic toys a lot scarier than guns.

Still, it was oddly comforting just wearing clothes.

I followed Nenzi down the hallway, treading lightly.

The entire floor seemed to be deserted.

It hit me then. The lights were on upstairs.

Whatever was happening down below, it didn't appear to be happening here.

The rich furnishings swam into focus, and I realized again where I was, the sheer craziness of being here, wearing doctor's scrubs three sizes too big, clutching the hand of a seer kid who looked about twelve years old.

"What are we doing here, Nenzi?" I whispered.

He motioned for me to be quiet.

We rounded a corner, and I froze.

Two guards sat in chairs outside a set of closed doors.

I saw both of them slump in the same instant. One didn't even fall out of his chair. I assumed Nenzi had killed them, too, but when we got closer, I saw their chests moving.

"Thanks," I whispered.

He smiled at me. That odd look remained in his eyes. He walked to the double doors, laying his hands on the ornate handles.

"Nenzi!" I whispered urgently. "There are people in there! Thus the guards. Get it?"

"I know." His smile crept wider. "That's why we're here, Allie." Seeing my panicked look, he gestured negative. "It's not Terian. Or that woman with the sky-colored eyes."

I stared at him. "Then what? Who is it?"

"Come here." He motioned me over.

Cautiously, I stepped barefoot over the rug. I had a twinge of guilt when I saw my foot bleeding and realized I was tracking blood on the White House carpet.

Somehow, that wasn't something I thought I'd ever do.

When I was near enough, Nenzi took my hand.

"Don't be mad at me, Allie," he said, soft. "You needed to know. You needed to see what he really is."

Then, without another word, he opened the two doors.

CHAPTER 44

REUNITED

I stood by the edge of the right-side door, peering in without exposing most of my face. I was sharply aware of the daylight-bright light at our backs, the fact that it made our silhouettes stand out like cardboard cutouts from the dimly lit room.

A fire burned in the grate.

A few lamps stood on side tables, but turned down to their lowest settings.

The furnishings told me nothing. It looked like a bedroom.

My eyes focused on the people.

A woman lay sprawled on the bed, naked. A man was having sex with her, his face contorted as he neared orgasm. I stared at the man's body. I didn't know his face, which was a young, boyish kind of pretty that never really appealed to me. Blond hair hung past his shoulders, most of it sweated to his back.

At each thrust into the woman below him, she whimpered.

I stared at the muscles in his arms, the length of his back.

I watched him fuck the woman, and realized there were others in the room, in my peripheral vision. I knew they were all either watching or doing similar things, but I couldn't tear my eyes off the man who'd first pulled my attention.

Then, I knew. Somehow, I knew.

In that instant, his hand rose from where he'd been clutching the sheets beside the woman's body. His body twisted, moving so quickly I didn't have time to flinch.

I saw the gun in his hand.

Two shots fired, expelling small flames.

They went off so near my head I thought for sure I was dead.

I thought he'd been aiming for me.

They were quiet, though, like a toy's pop. The gun was organic, not metal, so small it seemed almost to be a part of his hand.

I stood there, paralyzed, as Nenzi dropped.

No, not dropped.

Despite the size of the gun and how quiet it was, the shots threw his child's body backwards, tearing his cold fingers from mine. I watched him jerk and twist in the air. I saw his spider-thin arms flail as he crashed to the floor.

I stared at his crumpled form, at his chest rising and falling too fast, the blood swiftly darkening the beige carpet I'd been so worried about staining.

The blood spread out from under him in a rapidly widening pool.

I watched as his breaths gradually slowed.

I could only look down at him, paralyzed as his eyes glazed, losing light.

The other man stood beside me before I realized he'd moved.

He stood over Nenzi, the gun pointed down at him. He was breathing hard, his eyes still glazed with sex, his cock fully hard, and I couldn't stop looking at it, or at the body it was attached to. A thin organic cast circled one thigh, and I stared at a blue and black inked pattern on his skin, just below his navel, in the shape of…

My knees buckled.

He grabbed me around the shoulders and I stared up at his face, but I didn't know it and I couldn't feel anything with my light.

The sickness was back, so bad I thought it would kill me. I closed my eyes, leaning against the door jamb, unable to breath… breathing too much…

He let go of me.

"Allie."

I knew his voice. The room swam.

I hadn't thought once about what I'd seen.

It didn't want to be in my head, so I let my eyes drift past him, into the room. They settled on a face I knew, a body I even knew, though I'd never seen it entirely naked until now. I stared at Kat's face, sure I was hallucinating.

Then I realized she'd been the woman sprawled on the bed.

My knees gave out again. That time, he didn't catch me.

I crumpled beside the door.

I knelt there for a moment, barely aware of him even though he was kneeling beside me, his arms around me, his hands shaking.

"Allie… darling… Allie…" He was having trouble talking. I stared at his face, and I didn't know it. "Allie… we don't have much time…"

The others were getting dressed.

I watched them snap back, click into infiltrator mode.

Even Kat seemed to be business-only. She pulled on a white blouse, buttoning up the front. She fit a black organic vest over it, then shouldered on a dark red jacket that looked like it belonged to a business suit.

The humans were all passed out.

Somewhere in that moment where I couldn't breathe, the seers had sent all of them into a deep sleep.

A handsome male seer I didn't know drew his own organic vest over a dress shirt, throwing another to a female with red hair. I stared at her face, lost in another sinkhole of disbelief.

"Ullysa," I breathed.

I couldn't look at him, although I was aware of him next to me, watching my face. He smelled like sex. He stank of it. I couldn't feel him, couldn't feel his light, and I'd never been so glad of anything in my whole life. I just wanted him to get away from me, to put on clothes and get the fuck away from me, and not take off the makeup or prosthetic or whatever else was on his face.

He was doing something to me though. I felt his fingers at the collar around my neck, realized he was holding some kind of tool—

"No," I managed.

It was too late. He gripped whatever it was in his hand and squeezed, hard.

The collar cracked.

I felt it break in two.

I felt the creature inside the device writhe on my spine as the connection severed. It hadn't fully occurred to me it was alive, not until animal wrapped around my throat like a parasite died on my neck.

Then Revik was pulling the tendrils out of the holes in the back of my neck, gently, his fingers shaking so badly he struggled a few times before he managed to get it off.

The difference wasn't dramatic, like I expected.

My light crawled back around my body, like someone turning the sound up on an old radio very slowly. I was staring at a man with Revik's body, feeling the careful brush of Revik's fingers, smelling him even, when his light erupted around mine, sliding into me without warning.

Feeling his heart react, I cried out, pushing him away from me.

His arms encircled me though, too strong for me to get away.

I couldn't breathe, couldn't take a breath, but he only crushed me tighter in his arms, caressing my hair back from my face, pulling me into his lap. I noticed, as if from far away, that the tattoo on his arm didn't show. They'd covered it somehow, just like the scars, just like the upper part of his chest—just like his face.

He was slick with sweat, and now that I could feel his light, it was entwined with everyone else's in the room.

I could feel Ullysa on him, the male seer I didn't know, some human, *Kat*—

"Allie." His voice was thick, full of tears. "Allie, honey… please. Please. Baby, please…" His words broke apart. They grew incoherent, jumbled, like they had been in that cabin in the mountains.

But I couldn't think about that, either.

"…only way… the only way I could think of…" His hands tightened on me painfully. "I knew he had you… had to get to him… not get you killed…"

He caressed the hair out of my face, kissing me, sliding his light tentatively into mine.

I could tell he wanted to do more.

He wanted to, but he didn't.

He was afraid.

He wasn't only afraid of what I thought of him, or that I might leave him.

He was afraid of *me*.

He kissed my cheek, holding me so tightly I couldn't move.

"Honey, please… please, *gaos*… I love you so much…"

I couldn't look at him.

It wasn't his words, or the face that wasn't his.

It was me. I couldn't stand the thought of him seeing *me*, of him looking through my eyes to the person there. I remembered this. Like on the ship, like in Seattle, only a million times worse, so bad I couldn't pretend at all. I knew he would see all of it.

I'd made a mistake. I'd made a horrible mistake.

I stared blindly into the dimly lit room, watching the three seers gear up, checking guns and ammunition clips, going through the humans' pockets, looking for organics, listening devices, weapons, money, tech, ID.

I could hear them now.

Their voices crackled through the Barrier, and I realized they weren't alone.

They were communicating with someone else, a whole lot of someones.

This was an operation. This was an op.

I tried to make it mean something in my head.

Revik was pulling on my arms, bringing me gently to my feet.

I let him, but kept my eyes away from his.

He leaned me against the doorframe, and I stood there, watching as he reentered the room. He didn't look at me as Ullysa handed him a pile of his clothes. He pulled them on, and I couldn't help but notice he was still hard, or that the other seers' lights still reacted to his, more than they reacted to one another's.

I told myself it was an op.

I repeated that it was an op.

The words meant absolutely nothing to me.

They were all dressed now, all heading towards me, but more specifically, towards the door. I watched, unable to look away as Revik pulled on a belt, then his shoes, before donning a vest like the others.

Ullysa paused at the door to touch my face.

Her eyes bright, she kissed me on the cheek, squeezing my arm.

Kat gave me a wide berth, but I felt Revik watch her do it, his light holding an open threat. I watched him stare at her, and it somehow mixed with what I'd seen on his face when Nenzi opened those doors.

I forced my eyes off both of them.

The other male, who I didn't know, bowed deeply to me, gesturing in respect.

He handed me an organic vest, bullet proof, then helped me put it on when my fingers fumbled with the catches, unable to work them. He tugged it around me snugly and coiled the organic fasteners around my waist and ribs, patting it to make sure it was tight. Once he had the vest where he wanted it, he reached into his coat, extracting a gun.

He held it out to me, handle-first.

I stared at it, then met his gaze.

He smiled, indicating for me to take it.

But it was Ullysa whose fingers closed over the organic casing, pulling it away from my eyes. When she did, I felt an odd surge of relief.

"Not right now," she murmured, glancing into the room, at Revik. "Maybe in a little while. All right, Esteemed Bridge?"

I couldn't bring myself to speak, but I nodded.

I didn't look over to where I felt Kat staring at me.

Revik approached me then. He'd pulled off most of the prosthetics.

He was peeling a final layer off one cheek. He'd already removed the contacts. His narrower face grew visible below, harder than the face he'd been wearing, and more tired than I'd ever seen it. His eyes looked deadened, and I realized I could feel other things in his light, flavors I recognized, but not from him.

He yanked the wig off his head, exposing his darker, shorter hair sweated to his head. He tossed the wig into the room without looking where it fell, running his fingers through his black hair, and I noticed he was wearing my father's ring.

For some reason, it was that one detail that stabbed into my heart.

It was he who avoided my eyes now, so I could stare at his face, force myself to take it in.

He was alive.

For a second, I managed to see past what I'd walked in on, long enough to replay what he'd said, to hear his words.

…had to get to him… not get you killed…

He took hold of my arm.

I felt the caution in his fingers, but also his worry, his wanting to get me out of there. In that, I felt a desperate protectiveness, a terror for me that completely threw me after everything else. I could feel a commotion in the Barrier, getting louder the more I listened to something besides him, the more I tore my attention off the room and the other seers.

The others began walking down the hall.

Revik pulled me to follow, and I stumbled to keep up.

I remembered the boy and turned my head, staring back at the broken body.

But it wasn't entirely broken. Not entirely.

The glazed eyes stared back at me.

They stared at me and at Revik, and I saw his lips moving, his thin chest fighting for breath. As it did, his dark eyes sparked, like a dying wire. The spark flickered brighter. Abruptly, the black irises ignited.

They flared in the dim space by the door, turning a sharp gold-green.

Revik must have felt it through me.

He turned, and the gun was back in his hand.

I hesitated. Barely an instant, but still too long.

"Wait!" I yelled.

I said it right as the gun went off.

The bullet hit the small head between the eyes. At that close of range, no one could have missed, much less Revik. I saw the boy's head break apart, then slump.

I felt him die as much as I saw it.

The end was abrupt, and as soon as it happened...

I felt Revik stumble.

I grabbed his arm.

A surge of panic hit me; it quickly overshadowed everything else.

His knees buckled. I tried to catch him, but he was too big for me. All I could do was grab hold of his shirt and his waist, fighting to hold him up. I went down with him instead. I ended up on the carpet next to where he lay on his side, gasping for breath.

I yelled for the others, bending over him.

"Revik!" I gripped his hair, looking into his face. "Revik, no. No, no, no, no..."

His eyes muddied, grew opaque.

I watched it happen. I could only kneel there, helpless as he changed in front of me. He fought to breathe, looking up at me, but it was too late. I felt it in his light. I felt it reconfiguring, pooling around him, slamming into him.

I knew. I'd known, even before I knew—maybe even in Tarsi's cave.

"No, baby. No." I whispered it, caressing his face. "No… please. Please…"

"What the fuck happened?" Kat demanded, standing over us. "What the fuck did you do? Did you stab him, Bridge?"

"No," I said.

"He did it to save you! He did it for *you*, Bridge, you ungrateful bitch—"

"Shut up, Kat." Ullysa knelt on Revik's other side.

When she reached for him, fury blazed in my light. I shoved her away, harder than I probably should have.

"Don't fucking *touch him!*" I snarled.

She stared at me, her eyes nervous.

When I struggled to breathe, I realized my eyes were glowing. I could see them reflected in Ullysa's violet irises, tainting her face the palest shade of green.

It had been so long, it shocked me.

Looking away from her, I focused back on him.

I gripped his shirt, fighting to control myself, staring into his face. His eyes were glowing, too. He stared up at me, and for an instant, I saw the boy in his eyes.

"Allie," he said. "What happened?"

I stroked his hair back from his forehead, caressing his face. "You're all right, baby. We have to get you out of here." I fought to speak, to get past the lump in my throat. "Can you walk?"

I felt it, though, snaking around him, and around me.

He stared at me, and the light in his eyes dimmed, then flashed brighter.

"Allie." I heard fear in his voice, but it was Revik again. "Allie… what happened? What happened…" He turned his head, staring at the broken body of the boy on the carpet. The small corpse didn't look real to me now.

I realized it never had been.

It hadn't been anything but a vessel—a broken doll.

I saw Revik begin to understand, and somehow that was worse. It was worse than anything I'd ever seen in anyone's face in my life.

"It's all right," I said, helpless. "It's all right."

"Allie…" Terror eclipsed his expression. "Allie…"

"Later. We'll talk about it later." I fought my voice steady, tugging on his hand. "Revik. Please, baby. We have to go. Now."

His expression broke, then seemed to… fragment.

I watched him try to incorporate what he felt, then to push it away. It was like watching two people—more, maybe—vying for the same space.

"What the hell is going on?" Kat muttered.

She sounded afraid now, though. When I looked up, still clutching his shirt, she was staring at Revik. I could tell she was looking at him with her light. She was in the Barrier, and her eyes and face held nothing but shock.

"What the *fuck* is wrong with him?" she asked.

I stammered, trying to speak, but couldn't seem to form the words.

"It's him," a different voice said.

I turned. Ullysa had spoken that time. She was so pale I didn't recognize her. Her skin was almost gray. She gripped my arm.

"It's Revi'… the boy. He was Revi'. He was split. Like Terian."

"Yes," I managed. "Yes… please, don't touch him."

"I won't." She took a breath, but her color didn't come back. "Allie!" Ullysa gripped my arm again, so tightly it hurt. *"D'gaos! What do we do?"*

"What does this mean?" Tobias asked, speaking Prexci now. "What is this?" His voice was angry, but I could hear the fear behind it, too. He was staring at Revik's glowing eyes. "Explain this!" he demanded.

Ullysa still stared at me. She looked at me like I was a lifeline.

Like I could save them all. Or maybe just save Revik.

"Is he…" She swallowed. "Who is he, Alyson?"

I debated not answering, then realized it was no use.

"You already know," I said, clenching my hand in his shirt.

Miserably, I looked at her.

Seeing the horror in her eyes, I hardened my jaw against a rush of protectiveness that hit me like a physical force.

I was still gripping his shirt in one hand when he sat up. He stared at my face, and I could feel it suddenly; I could feel his light. I still felt him within it, but it was totally different—so different it blanked out my mind. I felt him reading me and my heart pounded in my chest, making it difficult to breathe.

There was just so… *much* of it.

It was like he'd expanded to three times his size.

The confusion in him remained, but it was changing again. Turning.

"Terian." His expression contorted in rage. "He did it. You fucking *lied* to me, Allie. He's the one who hurt you." His jaw hardened, pushing out his cheek. "Goddamn it. Why did you *lie* to me?"

"Revik." I reached out with my light, trying to calm him, but he pushed me back angrily. "Revik, it's all right. You've had a shock, you need to calm down—"

"How many times? How many, Allie?"

I flinched. "Jesus. That's hardly the—"

"Where the *fuck* is he?"

I felt my jaw harden.

"I don't know. I really don't."

His face changed again. His eyes grew cold, fathomless. They looked like a snake's eyes.

No, I thought. They looked like the boy's.

"Maygar's here," he said.

I looked to Ullysa for help, then at Tobias, then realized this information meant nothing to either of them. I looked back at Revik, saw him studying my light, his expression cold, wary, angry with distrust, anguish, suspicion. I realized what I felt on him was desire, but so twisted and dark it no longer felt like anything I'd ever felt on him before, or on any other seer. I couldn't even be sure it was aimed at me.

I wondered if that was how the boy felt, too. I wondered if this was what I saw in his eyes all those nights in that cage.

Other things were wrong with his light, too, I realized.

I recognized the flavor I'd felt on him before. It was the Rooks. He had the silver light of the Dreng seething through parts of his *aleimic* structure like a bad smell.

I remembered the look on the boy's face, him insisting I wanted him, that we belonged together and suddenly I was fighting tears.

"I repulsed you," he said.

"No!"

"Bullshit. You'd rather let Terian *rape* you than let me touch you."

"Revik... Christ. I didn't know—"

"That's not my name. And you know it." His eyes hardened to glass. "Did he get you to like it, Allie? Is that the real reason you lied to me?"

I couldn't find words. For the first time since I'd known him, I was afraid of him.

I looked between his eyes, the same clear eyes I'd looked at in that cabin in the Himalayas... and I didn't know him.

He pushed me out of his way, dragging himself abruptly to his feet.

I watched as he walked away.

I knew, somewhere in the background, that I was in shock.

After what must have been some passage of time, I heard Tobias mutter the same.

They tried to get me to stand on my own, using words. After a few minutes, Ullysa and Tobias gave up trying to talk to me and pulled me physically to my feet. They headed down the corridor, now moving at a military jog, bringing me along between them.

By the time the four of us made it to the elevator, Revik was gone.

CHAPTER 45
FAILSAFE

Balidor watched Cass follow the three-dimensional display with her eyes.

She paused only to glance at the giant Wvercian, patting one of his thick hands absently with her delicate fingers.

The giant was awake now, at least.

Balidor honestly couldn't be sure whether he was grateful or not. The Wvercian spent the past five hours napping on the floor of the cave, where he'd irritated Balidor to no end with his unbroken snoring like a diesel engine.

The Wvercian hung close to Cass now, staring down at the same screen with a puzzled expression on his broad face. Balidor couldn't help but wonder if he had any idea why they were even there.

He frowned when the giant began stroking Cass's back.

He averted his gaze when Cass glanced at him.

When she saw Balidor squinting at the same set of readouts, she smiled.

"Well?" Balidor asked. "Did it work?"

"I think so." She pointed at the arc of light on the display, then sighed, blowing up her bangs. "Honestly, I have no idea."

"So what? Do we stay in this godforsaken cave until we are mystically enlightened as to how this machine actually works?"

Cass nudged him with a shoulder.

"Cranky, cranky," she chided softly.

Balidor *was* feeling more than a little cranky. Watching the Wvercian paw at her, a female he had liked, when it had been more than a few months since he'd felt anything but separation pain himself, definitely wasn't helping.

He exhaled, letting a sharp clicking sound come out with his breath.

"We don't even know what it will *do*, Cass! Why are we messing with this?"

"Just a little longer," she said, exuding more of that cheery confidence.

He rolled his eyes, seer-fashion, but didn't bother to argue.

They'd been in the cave for days, it felt like, doing everything but reprogramming every machine in the place while Cass tried to figure out how to bring "Feigran" down from his cocoon in space. It took Balidor using his sight on the organics, and a lot of trial and error working with Cass, to even get the machine to talk to them.

She'd figured out some kind of key in the margins of Galaith's book.

Once he got the machine talking, she and Balidor together used that key to decipher the encryption sequence to get into the mainframe.

All the while, she'd hammered him with questions about Terian and his bodies. She seemed to want to know every detail of what they'd discerned about the Rook over the years the Adhipan had been studying him.

As if reading his mind, she started up again.

"So the bodies don't age?" she asked him again. "Why not?"

She continued poring over the console. Her eyes showed her to be reading the small lines of symbols as she waited for his response.

When he didn't answer right away, she looked at him.

"Hey. The ageless thing. How does it work?"

Balidor gestured vaguely with one hand. "They are essentially dead, Cass. They are reanimated corpses. The only way Terian could take over a body so thoroughly is to kill the body's original host. He then readies the physical vehicle through some kind of reanimation process. He only holds onto a small portion of their *aleimi* to tie himself to the host body. In essence, it is like a puppet, Cass."

"A meat puppet," she said, grinning.

Balidor shook his head, clicking softly. "Yes," he said, with exaggerated disapproval. "If you are a depraved human, with no regard for the living light of others... it is exactly that. A meat puppet. With posable limbs."

She snorted a laugh and Balidor smiled, in spite of himself.

His irritation returned when the Wvercian's light coiled around her once more, even as the thick fingers caressed her arm.

Goddamn it. Was he really going to try to seduce her in front of him?

"So how does he control all of them?" she asked. "Terian."

Balidor exhaled out some of his annoyance. He shook off as much of the other feeling as he could as well, pulling on his shirt to straighten it.

"In that, we have only theories," he said. "We thought we knew, before the downfall of the Pyramid... but it is more complicated than we had imagined."

When her hand prompted him to continue, he clicked again, mildly.

"Within the Pyramid, Cassandra, Terian held all of his different personalities together through the use of a construct... a construct within the larger construct of the Pyramid itself. He used the Dreng to de-localize that construct so the bodies could travel anywhere in the physical world without losing their connection to the host."

Thinking aloud, he folded his arms, his voice musing.

"Come to think of it, we never tried collaring one of the bodies. That might have been interesting. Theoretically, it is possible they might have lost their connection to the host body and thus died. Although I don't know of any collar that lets *nothing* through."

He watched her hit a new sequence of keys on the board, her eyes concentrated.

Clearly, the idea didn't hold as much intrigue for her.

He added, "We have evidence that each of Terian's bodies could, at the time of the Pyramid, all speak to one another, no matter what the distance. As long as he wasn't cut off from the Pyramid's structure, Terian remained relatively intact as a single entity, no matter how 'compartmentalized' he was."

"And after the Pyramid died?" she prompted.

"After it came apart," he amended politely. "Terian managed to keep all of his remaining bodies... all of those Galaith had not killed. We do not know *how*, precisely. We had assumed they would all die without the unifying structure of the Pyramid. For the same reason, we have been forced to amend our theory."

"And?" She continued to stare at the console. "What did you come up with?"

"More theories," he said, grunting.

At her raised eyebrow, he shrugged.

"It could be that he kept his bodies merely because he was the new Head of the Rooks' network, and thus their direct connection to the Dreng. It is possible that the Dreng aided him in this, or that we were wrong in our original suppositions about how he maintained the integrity of his overall *aleimic* body under the Dreng."

He glanced down the row of organic machines, in part to avoid looking at where the Wvercian rubbed his thick hand over her back.

"We did discover that, since the Pyramid's demise, he is cut off from ongoing communication between the different bodies," Balidor offered.

He cleared his throat, focusing harder on the darkest part of the cave.

"His bodies no longer operate as part of a single, fluid mind. They behave much more like individual persons... like miniature or partial personalities occupying different physical vessels. They communicate by speaking, or through machines, just as you and I do. Or through the Barrier when they are able, like any infiltrator or regular seer."

Still thinking, Balidor shrugged with one hand.

"Of course, being so close to one another energetically, and originating from the same source, it must be assumed that they can find one another in the Barrier very easily. The principles of resonance dictate that it be so. Like a mate with their partner, a parent with a child... only more so. Do you see, Cassandra?"

She nodded, her eyes still running over symbols.

Balidor wondered how much of what he'd said she'd even heard.

He'd noticed she seemed to get quite a bit in theory, but the whole concept of *aleimi* and its different functionalities remained mostly a mystery to her.

"So explain the Feigran thing to me again," Cass said, glancing up from the glowing console. "Why is the original body different?"

Balidor stretched his back.

His whole body was increasingly sore from too many hours hung over the same blurry monitor. Rubbing his eyes from fatigue, he glanced at the sweaty face of the female human, marveling that she still looked wide awake—more awake than he felt. His eyes drifted to Baguen with reluctance, then away when he saw the giant's eyes on her body along with his light, which now coiled around her more intimately.

He could feel the male wanting him to leave.

Balidor was damned if he was going to go outside and wait while the monster tried to coerce her into rutting with him in the cave.

Biting back what he would have liked to have said, he looked at Cass. He couldn't help wondering how much the giant's light was affecting hers.

He remained unwilling to scan her to find out.

"The original body is the anchor, Cassie," he explained. "If you kill the original, then all the bodies die. There is no longer any tie to the physical world."

Seeing the puzzled look return to her eyes, he clicked at her impatiently.

"Just trust me on this. We've studied Terian and his bodies for years now. The principle is simple enough, although the process is fairly complicated. Like I told you, it becomes much simpler if you can grasp that seer consciousness does not exist in our physical bodies at all, but in our *aleimic* bodies, instead. Seers use their physical brains like a radio. It is the device that plays the signal, but it does not generate the signal. Understand?"

Cass made the "more or less" gesture with her hand. Her eyes seemed to reflect the "less" part of that in greater quantity than the "more."

"I get that," she said. "I know you guys live half here and half in the Barrier, right? That's what Allie says."

Balidor gestured affirmative. "Yes, the Bridge is right. But our *aleimi* is tied to a particular physical body. It is coded to it, you could say. Kill the body, and we return to the Barrier. The body dies... and so forth."

"Okay." Her eyes remained puzzled. "So explain the Feigran thing again."

Balidor exhaled, rubbing his temples. He glanced at the giant, who was listening to the exchange without comprehension in his eyes.

Balidor focused back on Cass.

"Terian splits his *aleimi*," he said. "Originally, Feigran alone contained

534 • JC ANDRIJESKI

everything that is now spread across all those other bodies. He did not create anything new to house in those personalities. He simply divided himself."

Seeing understanding spark in her eyes, he went on.

"Inside the Barrier, we seers are made of many different parts. These fragments each consist of their own structures, traits, abilities. Even memories. Terian has found a way to crystallize the different pieces of himself into partial personalities. He breaks his *aleimic* body, then artificially ties these pieces to other *aleimic* bodies… that are anchored in different *physical* bodies. This is where the reanimation process gets complicated. He can only use freshly dead bodies, in part because he needs to retain some of the *aleimic* structure of the original host."

Seeing from her eyes that he was losing her again, he changed course.

"But the original… the true, *living* body of Terian… still, of necessity, forms his only real anchor to the physical world. The most complicated part of the process is how he keeps those other bodies alive."

"Yeah." She waved this part off. "Don't go into the genetics thing again. It gives me a headache." She paused, looking up. "But you're really sure we can kill *all* of him? If we kill Feigran, I mean?"

"If this Feigran is the original body, then yes. Absolutely."

"So that explains the putting it in space thing."

"Yes," he conceded. "It is the thing that gives me hope for this crazy plan of yours." Balidor bent over the console once more, reading the symbols. "But we have no way of knowing what this sequence actually *does*, Cass."

"What do you *think* it does?"

He shook his head, clicking softly. "I cannot read this text any more than you can. Based on these symbols, though…" He pointed to a sequence of pictographs. "…I think it actually brings him back to Earth."

He scanned more of the text, trying to puzzle it out.

"It is this second part I cannot comprehend," he confessed. "It looks like some kind of failsafe. As best as I can make out, it is saying this will do something to the other Terian bodies if Feigran were ever to return to Earth. There is no way to tell what."

Clicking again, he sighed, throwing up his hands.

"For all we know, it will tell them to return to the host body to protect it. We do not even know whether it was Terian who put all of this here, much less the motive behind it."

"Galaith." Cass looked over, her eyes reflecting a harder focus. "You think it was *Galaith* who built this? Not Terian?"

"I don't *think* it was anyone," Balidor grumbled.

His voice turned grudging.

"But it *is* his diary. This could have been built on his instruction."

"But didn't Galaith already try to kill Terian once?"

"Yes," Balidor conceded with a gesture. "But perhaps he hadn't quite made up his mind to annihilate *all* of him, Cassandra."

His eyes scanned pictographs while she appeared to be thinking about this.

After another silence, he clicked to himself in consternation.

"Cassandra… this is all theory. We cannot read it." He touched the screen again, but the new sequence didn't illuminate anything. "In any case, it is too risky to tamper with this. It could be some kind of weapon, or—"

"Weapon?" She frowned. "You're kidding, right?"

"We do not know what contingencies Terian himself might have in place."

"Bullshit!" Cass's voice grew suddenly sharp. "He has *Allie*, Dori'! Revik could die, going after her. So could Jon. Hundreds of seers are already dead from those bombs. I *promised* I'd try to help them. This felt right. It felt *right* to me. I don't see why I would be sent here if it was just some kind of bomb."

Balidor blinked. "Sent here?"

She waved off his words in annoyance. "Figuratively."

Looking at her, Balidor hesitated.

He had to admit, her words resonated. Somehow.

It made him less likely to believe someone or something dark might have manipulated her here, something like the Rooks or even Terian himself.

"It is possible," he said, cautious. "Only *possible*, mind you… that the mechanism for keeping his *aleimi* in discrete pieces has something to do with the container for the original body in space. If that were the case, this could be a warning that if we brought Feigran down, the other bodies will die."

Balidor shrugged, keeping his voice casual.

"Dehgoies told me once that Galaith kept a close eye on Terian. He knew how unstable Terian was. It could be, if Galaith did this, he created the failsafe as a way to bring him down quickly, to wipe him out all at once. In the event he needed to."

He caught Cass's eye.

When the human burst out with a wide smile, he couldn't help but join her.

"All right," he admitted. "The prospect is intriguing."

"You want to do it?" she asked, squeezing his arm. "Or should I?"

Balidor chuckled, in spite of himself.

"Now?"

"Why wait?" she grinned.

Smiling at her in return, he touched her cheek with the back of his fingers.

He didn't think about what he was doing until he felt the Wvercian's light react in a burst of possessive irritation. Glancing up at the frowning seer, Balidor removed his fingers, clearing his throat.

He looked directly at Cass, folding his arms.

"I think it is yours to do, Cassandra," he said.

He watched her lean back over the console, reading the symbols. If she'd noticed the male posturing, on either side, she didn't let it show. He smiled faintly at the concentration on her face as she fingered in the sequence they'd uncovered.

Once she had, another set of instructions flashed on the screen.

"What do you suppose this means?" she asked.

Balidor leaned over her shoulder, looking at the line of flashing text. Reaching out with his sight, he did his best to work through the symbols, using his seer's photographic memory to compare them to others he'd seen in the book. As he did, he felt something deep in his chest begin to relax. Reading the whole thing a second time, he glanced down at Cass, smiling in spite of himself.

"Well, my friend," he said. "I believe this could be what you were looking for."

"What does it say?" she asked. "Can you read it?"

With her face only a few inches away, he found himself looking at her again, re-discovering the fact that she really was an exceptionally attractive human.

Seeing her returning grin, he realized he hadn't been quite as subtle as he'd intended.

Clearing his throat, he turned, tapping the screen.

"It is asking us if we wish to 'consolidate Feigran'."

"Consolidate?" She frowned, following his finger to the screen.

When he only smiled, understanding reached her coffee-colored eyes.

Slowly, a dim hope flashed across her face.

"Could it really be that easy?"

He grinned. "I don't know. Shall we experiment?"

Laughing, she clasped his hand. Balidor once more felt a swell of irritation from the watching Wvercian.

That time, he didn't care.

CHAPTER 46
RETURN

I stood in a small thicket of trees. We huddled there, hidden outside the long corridor on the south side of the East Wing of the White House.

I didn't let myself think too clearly about where I was, or the surreal quality of seeing it empty of people, but for the occasional uniformed figure I glimpsed darting from one lit segment of corridor to another. I saw another man's lips moving as he communicated through a headset, then he was gone, too.

He'd been clutching some kind of automatic weapon.

I tried not to think about that, either.

We hadn't been able to find him.

The others wanted to leave, and I could hardly blame them.

The East Wing was ablaze in lights. I heard the sporadic sound of automatic gunfire in several parts of the lawn-covered grounds to the south. People moved in erratic formations across the grass, some running in SWAT-like military uniforms, probably everything from SCARB to the FBI to Secret Service.

Most of them had been human so far.

Which made them easy to side-step, at least.

Even so, I was growing increasingly nervous at what I could hear on the streets outside the White House gates.

If it wasn't a shooting war yet, it would be soon.

Even as I thought it, Tobias handed me his headset, signaling for me to listen.

Once I had it situated around my ear, sound rose, hammering me with a confusion of information. Images rose next, text in numerous screens, faces, real-time video. Too much came at me to think past at first. I could barely make out the words.

Then one voice grew louder.

"...is now confirmed. A terrorist attack is taking place inside the White House as we speak... repeat, a terrorist attack is now underway at the seat of U.S. power..."

Visuals eclipsed my view of the darkened grounds, forcing me into the sharply lit newsroom of the feed broadcasters. I glimpsed the gold hair of the newscaster, Donna, who I'd met in the Oval Office. Next to her sat an African-American man wearing a grim expression under furrowed brows.

I only got the barest glimpse of their faces before the sound of firing rose in the headset.

In the foreground, an image arose of military personnel covering the mall area of the city. A shootout was taking place between dark-clad figures and what looked like Metro Police in another corner of the same screen. A third image showed soldiers wearing the black uniform of the military branch of Seer Containment. They ran alongside an equal number of human Marines as they breached the White House grounds.

They wore so many weapons and organic arms, I couldn't quite see them as real.

The male newscaster's voice once more shocked my ears.

"They haven't yet determined the exact source or motive for the attacks, but there is no doubt renegade seers are involved. Four unregistered, foreign seers were caught in the course of the initial fighting. At least ten more non-humans have been documented shooting out of the first floor of the White House, and now a third group are rumored to be holding the Vice President hostage upstairs."

The man's brown eyes seemed to meet mine through the VR space.

I wondered what he looked like in real life.

"Thankfully, it was reported that President Wellington was removed from his residence by Secret Service. We are told they brought him to a safe location along with most of his cabinet and senior advisors. He will be making a statement to the media once the situation at the White House is secure. At this time, he had only one message to us. It was one of resolve. He said, and I quote, 'Tell them, we will do whatever is necessary to ensure that the culprits do not succeed in their aims to destabilize our great nation...'"

A dramatic pause.

"Donna? You have an update?"

The blond reporter smiled, her digitally altered voice holding a false outrage that barely concealed the thread of excitement underneath.

"We just now received news that the terrorist, Alyson May Taylor, appears to have *escaped custody* as a part of this attack by the seers. Using their powers of mind-control, her accomplices managed to thwart Secret Service, as well as the expert, interspecies anti-terrorism team from the Pentagon *specially assigned* to watch over her while she was being debriefed. A new and highly dangerous terrorist cell of seers appears to have broken into the underground bunker where she was being kept, underneath the White House itself. It now appears that her release may have been the purpose of this attack—"

I focused on an image of my face, which reared up in VR.

"Called 'the Bridge' by seer religious fanatics, Taylor has done little but murder humans, commit acts of terrorism with her own hands, and incite violence and other forms of dangerous fanaticism in the seer community since her true race was discovered last year. Planted in the human city of San Francisco as a sleeper agent for decades, she managed to disguise her race with the help of her adoptive human parents and brother, as well as a number of her human 'friends,' now believed to be sympathizers to the seer cause or possibly puppets under the control of Taylor herself..."

Donna put on her serious face.

The cameras zoomed in on her enhanced avatar.

I noticed it shaved a good fifteen years off her real age, as well as giving her a nose job and fuller lips than the woman I'd met in real life.

"The question everyone is asking is this: is Alyson Taylor truly telekinetic? Is that the *real* reason these terrorists are protecting her? Do they intend to use her as a weapon against all of us? To destroy human civilization, once and for all? The answer to that question is sure to force some tough decisions among our military leaders tonight, and especially among President Wellington and his advisors. Given the history of the last known telekinetic seer to appear on Earth, the stakes could not be higher. This really *could* be the day our President decides the fate of the human race as a whole..."

Hearing the heavy blades of helicopters, I looked up once I realized the sound wasn't coming from the broadcast.

Tearing the headset off my ears, I watched a formation of military helicopters skim the grounds, passing from the north to the south side of the complex in a diagonal line.

Ducking out of sight in the shadows, I turned to Ullysa, hesitating before looking back at the White House itself.

I thought about the feeds, the number of marines and SCARB agents headed our way.

They might have visually enhanced the number to put on a good show, but somehow, I doubted the reality would be far behind.

I handed the headset back to Tobias.

It wouldn't help me, not anymore.

"You three go ahead." I kept my voice low, looking between Ullysa and Tobias. "I'll find him. I know the layout. It'll be faster if I go alone."

"Allie, no!" Ullysa protested. "That is crazy!"

"I can't leave him here!" I clenched my jaw. "Do you understand? I can't do it! So either shut up, or *help me*, goddamn it!"

The three of them just looked at me.

Then Tobias gestured in affirmative, glancing at the other two.

"All right," he said. "We'll come."

I looked at Kat. Briefly, I thought about protesting her inclusion. She jutted her chin, and I could see on her face that she fully expected me to leave her behind.

But fuck it. Maybe she'd go down in the firefight.

She surprised me, grinning. "That's the spirit, Bridge."

"You'd better stay out of my line of sight," I warned.

I expected this to piss her off, but instead she surprised me again, grinning wider.

"You sound just like him. You know that?" she asked.

I pretended to ignore that, too, but it made my heart hurt anyway.

We made our way back through the garden, heading for the rounded portico of the South entrance. We crouched in the shadow of the line of trees, outside the ring of illumination created by the lights ablaze on the lower floors.

We were about to get up, to make our way to the nearest of the ground level doors, when the planes came roaring back.

Before I could let out a sound, Tobias grabbed me around the middle.

He yanked me back, dragging me in the direction of the gardens.

The whole while, he sheltered me with his body.

I struggled, fighting his hold. Fear slid to the forward part of my light.

I knew what was coming. I could feel it, just like Tobias.

"They're going to bomb it!" he said in my ear.

The scream of the falling bombs slowly built in sound until I couldn't hear anything else, not even my own anguished yell. Tobias was right.

They weren't just going to hit the grounds, or even the surrounding areas.

Wellington had decided to go all-in.

The unreality of what was happening got overshadowed by my terror about what it meant for me.

They were bombing the White House.

And he was inside.

CHAPTER 47
REINTEGRATION

Terian felt it again. Something in his light seemed to phase out.

It came back seconds later, as if on its own.

He stared up at the low ceiling, frowning as he strained his gaze.

Another part of him listened.

It was as if some part of his collective person believed, if he tried hard enough, he might determine what was wrong with the construct by using his physical senses alone.

Even as he thought it, the sound came again.

Impact concussion.

Some kind of explosion, a bomb possibly, and it sounded like it came from directly overhead. The lights flickered, going from the white lights of the conference room to the rotating orange of the emergency lights... then back again.

The flicker of lights continued, mirroring the strange phasing occurring in his *aleimi*.

After a few more seconds, however, the white lights rose slowly, until the room appeared ordinary once more.

Terian blinked, adjusting his eyes to the sudden brightness.

He wasn't really worried about the walls caving in, not down here.

It had been the easiest thing in the world to turn the power off downstairs, then to convince the humans they were under attack, that they needed to evacuate the capital buildings at once due to the threat of terrorist seers.

Who knew he'd actually be right?

Revi' really hadn't been screwing around, in his attempt to get Alyson back. Blinded by emotion or not, he'd coordinated this jailbreak more like a military operation than his usual one-man frontal.

Terian could only suppose he'd had help, and help on a significant, possibly even grand scale. He should have remembered his old partner wouldn't be the only seer deeply motivated to liberate their precious Bridge.

Even so, from all appearances, Revi' might be holding more of a grudge than usual.

The entire cabinet, along with Wellington himself and Xarethe, had been disappeared almost two hours ago, along with a handful of aides. Everyone else had been sent home, some with police escorts or even SCARB agents. Once the perimeter breach was confirmed, the entire grounds were evacuated of staff.

Thanks to Terian also, Vice President Travers and his little entourage hadn't been able to be found. He had their vehicles moved as well, to avoid suspicion.

Now they were listed officially as "hostages" of the seer terrorists.

Terian had been looking to replace Travers almost from the moment he'd taken the official oath. He'd let that little charade of his go on for months, knowing it might come in handy one of these days, to get the little toad to resign, if nothing else.

It certainly proved useful tonight.

Wellington's team went out through the upper basement, taking a set of bulletproof SUV limousines to a safe location on the other side of town. The bunker-like facility, housed under another fifteen feet of solid concrete, reinforced steel, the gaze of a few dozen of their best seers—and, of course, a small nuclear arsenal at their immediate disposal—remained virtually impregnable.

He didn't have long to wait now.

He could feel it.

Whatever else, he knew a few bombs wouldn't dissuade his old friend from paying him a visit, not if he was feeling motivated… which Terian had no doubt he was by now.

He heard the beep through his implants when the elevator hit the bottom floor.

He smiled when he saw the stats of the car's occupant.

Lighting a *hiri*, he leaned back in his chair, propping his feet on the old-growth redwood table and crossing his ankles.

Ashing on the White House floor, even in the technically nonexistent underground compartments, gave him a perverse sort of thrill, even now.

He waited until he felt the other seer leave the elevator car.

Then he sent out a ping with his light, letting him know exactly where he was.

He was still leaning back in the chair, drink in hand, when Dehgoies walked into the room, an organic-component gun held out in front of him.

He entered slowly, checking the corners, moving from a combat crouch.

He still limped, of course. His leg couldn't be fully healed from the gunshot wound a week or so back, but his essential grace remained intact. His face appeared focused, emotionless, but Terian found himself smiling anyway.

He held out his arms, half in surrender, half in affection.

He knew the look in those eyes again.

For the first time in over fifty years, he could see his friend.

"You killed the boy?" he asked.

He heard the triumph in his own voice.

Dehgoies didn't answer.

Terian grinned anyway, holding his arms wider. "Don't shoot, pardner," he said. "I surrender."

Revik shifted the aim of the gun.

He fired before Terian could blink.

The force of the shot caught Terian off-guard, particularly from such a small gun. It knocked his leg off the table, making him question the wisdom of propping his leg up there in the first place. It nearly threw him out of the high-backed chair.

He gasped, gripping his thigh, staring at the blood squeezing between his fingers. The Elaerian had hit him in the leg. It was the same leg and roughly the same place Terian ordered his men to shoot Dehgoies out at that hovel in the Himalayas.

Despite the force of the shot, the bullet remained in his flesh.

"You want to fuck with me right now?" Revik said. "Really? That seems like a good idea to you?"

"Wait!" Terian held up his other hand. "Dehgoies... my friend. Calm yourself, please. I can explain!"

"You can explain." The light eyes turned predatory, threaded with a violence that stood on the surface. "You can explain stealing my wife. Beating her... *raping* her. Explain that to me, Terry. I dare you."

"I knew who you were," the Scandinavian said. He spoke quickly, before the Elaerian could shoot again. "Don't you see? I knew. I was trying to *help* you, Dehgoies. I knew you wouldn't get there on your own."

Revik pointed the gun at his face.

"Gee," he said. "Thanks, Terry."

"I suspected the truth. Not long after I found the boy." Terian held his hand higher, a plea for peace. "It was subtle at first. But there was just too much of *you* in him... too many freakish, Dehgoies-like similarities to count. I found a mapped blood sample of the original Syrimne, which helped..."

Seeing that the other seer was listening to him at least, he lowered his hand, long enough to take another fast drink of scotch.

"Then I realized why *I* knew him so well," he said. "And what had happened to the Revi' I once knew." He pursed his lips. "You know... my best friend? The one those fucking Seven assholes murdered to 'save his soul?'"

When Revik didn't react, Terian spoke louder, still watching the other's eyes.

"When Galaith and Vash made their little pact... hell, they already *had* the boy. They'd created him and locked him in that mountain. They'd buried fucking *Syrimne* in that dungeon, a being who did nothing but fight for our people. What kind of gratitude is that?"

"What the hell are you talking about?" Revik asked.

But Terian saw it in his face.

He was listening. At least some of this was sinking in.

Terian shrugged with his free hand, feeling his anger return as he thought about the truth behind his own words.

"So they had the boy already," he repeated. "I guess they figured, why not use him to bury my friend, Revi' the Rook, as well? So they put *you* there, too. They left *you* there, in that little rat-boy body… to rot, I guess."

Revik rearranged his hand on the gun. "A little far-fetched, Terry."

"Is it? Do you know it's impossible to truly destroy a memory, Revi'? That there is no way to wipe a mind of its past? Oh, you can do it *temporarily.* Through trauma, drugs, even suggestion. But you can't *really* get rid of it." He took another drink of alcohol. "The only way to be sure, Revi'… the only way to be *really really sure,* is to cut the offending part of the *aleimi* out. To put it somewhere else."

He paused, watching Dehgoies think about his words.

"Do you really think Galaith would have let you go, if there was *any chance* you could retrieve the memories he and the Seven had stolen from you?"

Revik's jaw hardened, but Terian saw him thinking still.

"You remember now, don't you, Revi'?"

The other seer's eyes grew opaque, but Terian saw enough there to know he'd been right.

His smile widened.

"You do. I can see that you do. That is good, Revi'. That is most excellent—"

"You're still full of shit, Terry," Revik growled. "You always were. I don't know what game you're playing, but—"

"Game? This is no game, I assure you. I am deadly serious, my friend. Are you not listening to me? You are *whole* once more!"

Revik stared at him, his pale eyes lamp-like under the white lights.

"You still don't believe me?" Terian said. "Then why don't you explain to me how that little shit knew so much about your *wife,* Revi'… given that he'd been collared and buried underground since *before she was born?* Explain to me how she was able to do telekinesis with no training, simply from being your mate. Do you know the first time she displayed this 'random' talent of hers, Revi'? Well? Do you?"

"Yes," Revik said.

"And nothing about the timing of that struck you as interesting,

Revi'?" He paused, watching the other seer's face. "Well, here's a hint. She was seven years old. What else happened when she turned seven, Revi'?"

Revik's jaw hardened. "I was assigned to her."

"Yes. You were. And now explain to me how the boy was able to find *you*, no matter where you were, no matter how tightly shielded you were by the Adhipan or whoever else? I was thrilled when he seemed to be able to pick you out so easily, but after a while, I confess I started to wonder why that was."

Revik glanced behind him, still holding the gun on Terian.

His colorless eyes looked harder, though.

Looking at him, Terian could see it.

There was understanding there, anger, recognition, but also a refusal to believe. He was struggling with the integration, having trouble keeping his thoughts linear. He likely also couldn't fully see the newer elements as his own, not yet. Such a thing would take time, and a fair bit of power struggling between the various parts of himself.

It was a process with which Terian had some measure of familiarity.

Revik motioned at Terian with the gun.

"Keep talking."

"Surely you must have guessed by now!" Terian said. He gripped his leg to slow the flow of blood, even as he continued to study Dehgoies' light.

"Guessed what?"

"You are *Syrimne*, my friend!"

There was a pause.

Then Revik let out a harsh laugh.

"Jesus. This is pathetic even for you, Terry. You *planted* that crap! You want me to believe it." His jaw hardened, even as grief plumed off his light. "You want Allie to believe it."

Terian smiled though, seeing something else in his friend's light.

"Ah, you *do* know. That is reassuring. I had worried with the number of times they've ripped out parts of your mind and filled the holes with talk of virtue and singing choirs of angels there'd be nothing of your mind left."

"Fuck you." Revik gripped the gun tighter. "I should kill you right now."

"I don't blame you for the latter sentiment. And," he smiled. "I'd be willing to entertain the former, certainly... from what I saw, you put on quite a show up there. Are you sure you're up for it, though, after all that?"

He lifted an eyebrow, smiling wanly.

"...Are you sure *she* is? It was pretty touch and go there for a minute, wasn't it? Very exciting. I almost thought she *would* kill you."

Seeing the doubt cross Revik's face, mixed with a tighter expression, Terian chuckled.

"Put the gun down, Dehgoies. You know I am telling you the truth. You are Syrimne. You always were... and I have far too much to tell you about yourself for you to want to kill me now."

Revik hesitated. Anger remained prominent in his eyes. Anger and that thread of disbelief mixed with something that edged closer to understanding, even a whisper of relief.

Terian found himself smiling at that, too.

"It's comforting, knowing who we really are," Terian said, his voice soft. "Isn't it, my friend? It explains so much."

Revik stared at him.

For a moment, he seemed like he wanted to answer, then didn't. Lowering the gun to his side, he didn't put it down.

"Are you working with Salinse?" he asked.

"Salinse? That kook in the mountains? Heavens no."

"He told me to kill the boy," Revik said. "He was pretty clear about it. Made it the price of getting access to his people."

"Ahh." Terian smiled. "Yes, that makes sense. I imagine you will have your pick of offers now, Revi'. Permit me to caution you to choose wisely, my friend."

Terian poured himself another glass of scotch, hoping it would dull the pain in his leg. Pouring a second glass for Dehgoies, he slid it expertly across the table. The glass stopped within a few feet of where Revik's hand hung by his side.

The Elaerian only stared at it, then back at Terian, his gaze flat, despite the whispers of conflict Terian could see.

He let out a short, humorless laugh.

"*Di'lanlente a' guete.* You think I'm going to *drink* with you? You really are monumentally crazy, Terry. You stole my *wife*. You nearly killed her. What part of that isn't getting through to you?"

"I think you'll want to hear what I have to say."

"You're thinking wrong." Revik raised the gun, pointing it at Terian's head. "Anything you think you can tell me, I'm sure Salinse knows more. And he didn't *rape* my wife… or chain her to a fucking floor so some messed up kid could feel her up every night." Swallowing, he clicked the trigger to activate the gun. "Salinse even held up his end of the bargain. Strictly speaking."

Terian raised his hand higher.

"Don't assume he's got your best interests at heart, Revi'! Don't assume that for a second! Who the hell do you think bombed Seertown?" He waited for that much to sink in, for the Elaerian to be listening. "Salinse has his own agenda. And I can pretty much guarantee it's a more radical one than mine…"

"I don't care," Revik said, still holding up the gun.

"Yes, you do," Terian said. "We could work together, Revi'."

"Little late for that."

"*Come on*, Revi'! Think about it! You don't remember it all yet, but you will. That bastard Menlim treated you like shit. Whatever else may have happened, you and I… we were friends once. I would never have done that to a friend! Not unless I was trying to help him! And I did *help* you, Revi'! The boy would have killed you for sure, if I hadn't intervened!"

Revik shot him in the other leg.

Terian gasped, sliding deeper in his chair.

Blood turned his other pant leg swiftly dark.

That couldn't be good, how fast that happened.

The patch began to spread. He stared at the widening stain, then up at the other seer.

Revik shrugged. "You shouldn't have fucked my wife."

"You know full well why I did it!"

Revik shot him in the arm, just above the elbow. The force of that blast ripped the muscles apart, shattering bone. Terian slumped in the chair. He looked for the scotch, but his glass was now on the floor. Scotch and water soaked into the carpet.

Terian watched, strangely disappointed.

"I don't much care why, Terry," Revik said.

"Revi'! Wait! Don't kill me yet, I—"

But before Revik could shoot him again, before Terian could tell him what he wanted him to wait for... everything went dark.

There was no warning.

He didn't even get a last breath.

All he did was exhale the one before it, his eyes locked open as he stared at the ceiling. His *aleimi* vacated the corpse of the Scandinavian seer he'd purchased for almost a million Euros from that sucker slave trader in Estonia, raping him shortly after and killing him dead for the use of his corpse.

As he left, Terian found himself observing the room from the Barrier.

Dehgoies lowered the gun, a puzzled expression on his face as he stared at the blond corpse. He walked forward, prodding the inanimate vessel with one hand, checking the pulse with his fingers.

Terian saw him look up.

Shortly after, he found he could hear a shrill sound.

The noise wound higher in even circles, like an air raid siren.

Terian realized that's exactly what it was: an air raid siren.

But it didn't matter to him anymore.

He was gone... back to the mainframe for downloading in another body, in another part of the world, or perhaps in the bunker where Xarethe and Wellington crouched right now, playing backgammon as they watched news reports about seers attacking the White House and the military being mobilized.

Or so he thought.

Turns out, he was wrong about that.

CHAPTER 48
SYRIMNE

He stood inside the elevator, watching the numbered lights ping as he rose slowly through over ten stories of basement floors under the White House's main structure.

His mind was blank.

No, not blank.

He could feel her again, but he was afraid of her still, afraid of what he would find if he sought out her light.

She would hate him now.

He stared through walls, reading organics, using his recall of the structure's blueprints, matching it against what the living machines told him as he listened with his light. He remembered this, too. He remembered speaking to the creatures that lived in the walls, knowing their language well enough that it scarcely felt like hacking.

The machines spoke to him eagerly, without restraint.

They showed him all of Terian's little back doors and rat holes.

Most of those were irrelevant now.

Impact concussions trembled the elevator car as it rose. He surfed those, hands held at his sides, his mind clicking in and out of different parts of the construct.

He felt emotion there.

He knew it as his.

Allie's face as she stared at his body, the deadened look in her eyes as she took it all in, right before her knees buckled.

He'd felt her heart close.

Hate wasn't the right word.

He hadn't earned hate. Truthfully, he'd discerned not a ripple of true emotion in her light. No feeling of anger. Nor any hurt or grief.

It was just over.

It was over for her. He'd ceased to exist.

Those moments she hadn't looked at him...

He saw a cement and organic cage, her bare back and legs, the tangle of her dark hair, her green eyes shining in the half-dark. He'd wanted her. He'd even considered forcing her, more than once. He'd been so sure she would like it once he had.

It seemed so unfair, to be judged as unfit when he wanted her so badly... when he'd asked her so many times... when he'd exercised so much restraint.

Even the collar turned him on, but he also wanted it off. He wanted it off badly enough, he had to remind himself she wouldn't stay with him if he freed her, not yet.

Maybe not ever, now that that bastard had his hooks in her.

Confusion rippled his mind, but the other resurfaced, stronger than the rest. It was maddening, having her so near but not being able to feel her.

She was like a blank doll, staring without seeing him.

Pain wracked his light. This was *Allie* he was thinking about. Allie he'd seen chained... Allie he'd considered raping.

She'd tried to trick him. Lied to him. She didn't want him.

She wanted that son of a bitch who locked him up, instead...

Confusion filled his light.

She'd refused the boy, knowing Terian would rape her for her refusal. Why had she let that happen? Had she liked it? Was it possible?

No. Terry had beaten her. He had to beat her to get what he wanted.

He nearly killed her.

Gaos. He remembered her in that cage. He'd been terrified she might die, even with his attempts to heal her. She'd bled too much. That deadened look in her eyes. He thought he'd found her too late. He remembered her crying.

Pain wracked his light.

Terry said he'd done it for a reason, but not a single reason came to Revik's mind that made sense to him, not even in terms of Terry.

His friend, Terry. He'd stolen his wife... raped her.

He gripped the elevator wall.

He couldn't believe how bad everything hurt. He'd never had separation pain like this, not even as a kid, not even in that mountain prison. He could feel that his body had had sex, a lot of it, and recently.

It didn't help.

He'd waited for her. For goddamned years, he'd waited.

They'd promised him that he wouldn't have to be alone.

They promised him, over and over, taught him all the ancient texts. They showed him how they said all the same things, that he wouldn't be alone, not once she came. They said she would recognize him, too.

They said she belonged to him.

He had to find her. He couldn't let her go.

She was raised human, she wouldn't understand. He would have to help her. But he had to get out of here first. She wouldn't have waited.

Salinse's people wouldn't have let her. They'd want her safe.

And anyway, why would she wait for him now?

The humans would be waiting, though.

Terian's people, too.

Revik's *aleimi* sought out opportunities, weapons. That part of him felt comfortable... working in that space, doing what it had always done, better than he'd ever done anything else.

Hunting was easy, uncomplicated.

Combustible gases, broken piping, liquid fuel, wooden pieces of wall and curtains like tinder already burning, residual powder, exposed wiring. He'd seen fireplaces in the plan. There'd been gas somewhere, too—maybe the kitchen.

He'd heard the bombs.

That meant planes. Fuel.

The two sides worked together, but separate... on separate rails.

The know-how, so familiar despite its years of absence, mixed with the military side of him, the part that planned the op to get inside. His fractured mind worked best with concrete goals. It only really derailed when he thought about—

Pain tried to take over his light.

He had to find her. He had to convince her… make her listen.

The doors of the elevator slid open.

He found himself facing the ground floor.

He stood there, a heartbeat too long, and the doors started to close. A guard saw him when he stuck out his arm, stopping them before they could meet. As the organic panels reopened, the black-clad human raised an automatic rifle.

Revik concentrated, briefly…

…and the gun broke apart in the man's hands.

The shell exploded backwards into his face.

The SCARB agent yelled as metal burnt flesh, but not for long because Revik broke his neck before he finished exhaling on his first scream.

He didn't have time to feel this.

He felt another gun go up and scanned.

He broke the firing mechanism before he snapped the owner's spine, causing another of the armor-plated soldiers to crumple. He stood there, panting, staring at the two men lying on the wide, red carpet runner, their bodies motionless, like broken toys.

For a second, he hesitated, filled with doubt.

Then a kind of wonder came over him as he looked from one man to the other. He gave a startled laugh, and it sounded loud in the hollow hall.

Something new pinged his light, and his focus returned again, sharper.

He stepped the rest of the way out of the elevator, reaching up high into parts of his *aleimi* that felt so much like him his chest actually hurt.

He remembered this!

Terian was right.

He remembered…

EPILOGUE
PAMIR

I sat next to Vash, cross-legged. We were alone inside an enormous cave, next to a fire that burned high and hot.

Of course, we weren't alone, not really.

This cave lay inside a vast network of other caves that wound deep into the Pamir range and beyond, between Tajikistan and China.

Since the bombing of Seertown, those caves had slowly filled with refugees from northern India. After D.C., more refugees came, the new ones hailing from the human world. The political climate for seers shifted a lot in the wake of the terrorist attack on the White House. Refugees continued to trickle in from Europe and the Americas, and even Africa and parts of Asia, joining us in what was fast becoming the new (old) seer stronghold in Asia.

The circle really was spinning back to where it started.

The monks who lived here before all this, more or less entirely on their own and in self-imposed religious seclusion, were kind enough to welcome us into their home. I knew we'd pretty much decimated the peace of their previously silent enclave.

Luckily, the caves were massive.

Even so, none of us was ever really alone here.

The whole place was one giant construct.

As in old times, that construct was now being actively maintained by the Adhipan. They'd taken on even more of their traditional duties in the wake of "the incident," as most of us referred to it now, or simply "the thing in D.C."

Fire illuminated the cave walls, flickering over a massive painting.

I stared up at it, remembering the first time I'd seen it.

A turtle sat under the world, next to a king and a queen, a knight and a rook, none of whom came from the human chessboard. My eyes traced a dragon that swam through stars, a bird that flew over the ocean. The Bridge stood with lightning in her hands, next to a laughing boy holding a blue-white sun.

His eyes were filled with joy.

I tore my eyes off the boy's face, taking a sip of my chai.

The cave was warm, surprisingly so, given how damp and dead-seeming the maze of tunnels had been just a few weeks earlier. Already, power was available in over half the occupied caves. The rest remained in some stage of progress as the techs scrambled to keep up with the influx of new residents.

Of course, it was easy to live here now. We were rolling into the hottest months of summer. From what I'd been told, most of us younger seers were in for a shock when we hit our first real storm in the later months of that year.

Most of us in the Seven were settling in to stay, just like seers had for millennia before us.

Tarsi even lived with us now.

Well, more accurately, she lived with Vash.

They shared one of the cave rooms, which surprised me, I guess—as did Cass's decision to bunk down with a giant Wvercian she'd met somewhere while I'd been held in captivity.

Actually, the Cass thing surprised me less, although I could tell there was still some serious tension with her and Chandre.

Even Jon seemed to be getting on better in the world of the seers.

He and Dorje played chess every night in the largest of the now-occupied common spaces, and I'd seen him in the sparring ring a few times, too, learning *mulei* from Tenzi and Garensche and some of the others.

He was certainly doing better than me.

It was quiet here, living in the mountains, but it wouldn't be for long.

It wasn't particularly quiet in the world outside.

I still had access to feeds, thanks to Balidor's people and a number of pretty high-tech satellite dishes arrayed further up in the mountains.

The United States was in full-fledged lockdown.

Martial law had been declared in most major cities.

Riots raged, primarily in seer-related districts and businesses, but also against the Chinese, who were blamed for colluding with seer terrorists, thanks to Terian's war-mongering of the previous year. The United States borders were closed to all seers and a large percentage of human foreigners. They'd installed mandatory DNA tests for entry into all government buildings, as well as major banks, anything to do with Wall Street, and a lot of other critical businesses.

Those seers still living in the United States—meaning those unable to leave in time, or to disguise themselves adequately—were already being rounded up.

We didn't have a lot of intelligence on the details yet, but we knew it was bad, even just from glimpses in the Barrier.

Washington D.C. remained a quasi-militarized zone.

No one in the Adhipan had managed to find Feigran, either.

His capsule splashed down somewhere in the Atlantic Ocean, but Balidor hadn't been able to direct any of his people to the coordinates in time. The heavy organics in the machinery made the location difficult to pinpoint, even apart from the logistical difficulties, given everything else going on.

By the time ships were sent, the organic container had either sunk, or it was no longer there.

While the fate of Feigran himself remained under debate by infiltrators in the Adhipan and the Seven, one thing appeared indisputable—all the other Terian bodies were dead.

Wellington was found dead in his bunker along with the Secretary of Defense, Andrea Jarvesch. The young girl the Wellingtons adopted a year earlier, Melissa Wellington, died mysteriously, too.

Their unexplained deaths hadn't stopped reverberating throughout the human world. Nor had the fact that I apparently "disappeared" out from under some of the heaviest security ever deployed to guard a single seer.

Everyone from the Chinese to homegrown insurgents to seer terrorists from the Middle East and Asia had been blamed for the attacks. The

Americans dropped a second set of bombs on the White House after Tobias drugged me and carried me off the grounds. Apparently that second bombing had been done in response to the deaths of Wellington and Jarvesch, in a desperate attempt to destroy the last of the terrorist cell.

It hadn't.

By then, no one had been left inside, apart from corpses and the odd straggler from Secret Service. The Scandinavian Terian was found later, his body dragged out of the underground levels with at least three bullet holes in his limbs.

The usual talk of conspiracies and cover-ups made the rounds of lesser-known feeds.

Elan Raven hadn't resurfaced yet. Nor had Maygar.

But I didn't much care about any of that.

"No one's heard from him?" I asked, unnecessarily.

"Since yesterday?" Vash clicked gently. "No, Alyson."

"And you're sure he got out of the United States before they closed the borders?"

"Quite certain, yes," Vash said.

He looked at me, and I saw concern in those dark eyes, a denser worry.

"Now that he is whole," Vash added. "...and uncollared, of course... he cannot hide his light so easily behind the Barrier, Alyson. He is a beacon now. Much more visible than even he probably knows." Vash shrugged with one hand. "He will learn to compensate for this, I am sure. Until then, we can monitor him, at least. Attempt to discern the progress of his reintegration, and its possible effects."

I nodded, only half hearing him.

I wasn't up to asking again, why no one had told me—or told Revik—who he really was. I could hear their reasons a hundred million times, and they still wouldn't make any sense to me.

Nor would they change anything.

"It is dangerous," Vash said softly. "What you are doing."

I didn't bother to ask him what he meant.

"I haven't done anything yet," I said.

"You must be firm in your mind, Alyson. You cannot compromise on this. You cannot. You must see how dangerous such a fiction is."

I nodded to that, too.

But I didn't feel it.

Sometimes I think the whole of human and seer thought is nothing but a story we tell ourselves, usually about things we would have done anyway.

"Alyson," Vash said softly. "The man you knew as Dehgoies Revik—he is dead. You must accept this. You must feel it as true."

He paused, likely waiting for me to look over.

I didn't.

"The other two personality configurations were always dominant. At least since he was a child, since Menlim broke his mind."

When I didn't look over that time, Vash sighed, clicking in consternation.

Sadness whispered from his light, more of that worry that felt so different from how I normally perceived him. I felt guilt there, too, I realized. I closed my light in response, squeezing my knees against my body.

Vash clicked again, softly.

"We are running out of time, Alyson," he said. "Once he integrates the different sides of himself more fully, he will become even more dangerous." He paused, again waiting for me to turn. "There will be aspects of him that remind you of your mate, but he will not *be* your mate. He never will be again, Alyson. Never. You need to understand this."

He sounded almost afraid now.

"Sooner would be good," he added. "Tarsi said she told you. She warned you in the cave. You may have to kill him, Allie. It may be necessary."

"It would be suicide," I said, feeling my jaw harden.

He laid a hand on my knee.

I don't think he'd ever been so gentle with me.

"Perhaps not," he said. "You did not fall in love with the other personalities, Alyson. I do not think his death means yours anymore... if it ever did. You married someone else. Someone who no longer exists."

Sliding my fingers into my hair, I held my head in both hands, staring at the fire, trying not to think about his words.

He let the silence stretch.

Longer than I could.

"I don't want to talk about this." I shook my head between my hands. "I can't, Vash. Not now. And it doesn't matter, anyway. He hasn't come near me."

"You cannot afford to wait," he warned. "You have seen how dangerous he is. You must know, having seen who he was then… and from your time spent with the boy. He will only grow more dangerous, Allie. He is not a child anymore, but his mind still operates as one, in many ways. It may always, given what he was forced to endure."

I let my eyes scale the wall, taking in the high mural of images.

I focused on the painting of the boy, and my eyes blurred. The depictions looked exactly as they had in my dreams, only the paint had faded.

There was probably some kind of metaphor in there somewhere, but I didn't want to think about what it was.

Instead, I climbed to my feet.

One thing about seers, you don't have to make up a reason to leave.

You can just go.

I walked down a narrow passage that twisted out of Vash's cave.

Reaching a fork in the tunnels, I veered right, taking the one that led to my room, or whatever you call a cave with a bed, wall-to-wall carpet, a desk, a comfy chair, power. The section of cave I'd chosen for myself was closer to the outside entrance than any of my friends, a fact that drove Balidor crazy for security reasons.

And yet, the decision hadn't been carelessness on my part.

Vash was right. I was being stupid.

Anyway, he would be crazy to come here.

The constructs inside these caves were thousands of years old. They made what I'd felt in the White House seem like children's toys. I'd nowhere-near figured out all the complexities residing within it, either in functionality or even access to information; the construct contained more rooms and realities than the cave structures themselves. It housed places and memories that stretched back to the time of Elaerian.

My people, or so Tarsi claimed.

Our people, I supposed.

The thought made my chest hurt.

I'd already been warned that my current room might get cold in winter, if I didn't find a way to shield it from the wind that tunneled through the mountain walls. Winters in the Pamir, I'd been told over the past few weeks, put a whole new spin to the concept of "seasons." Everything died outside the caves.

But that wouldn't matter for me.

I'd already made up my mind.

I couldn't stay here.

I couldn't just hole up in the mountains with the other seers, waiting for Armageddon. I would go to the Chinese seers first, see if they would talk to me. If not, then I would try the humans, maybe in Europe, or even in America.

I'd have to leave quietly, of course; Balidor would pitch a fit if he knew I was even contemplating leaving the Pamir.

But that was a detail, really.

I was still mulling this over in my mind, nearing my segment of the caves, when I pulled up short.

Stopping dead, I listened.

Feeling my heart tighten in my chest, I stared through the darkness, sure suddenly I wasn't alone. I looked back from where I'd come, towards the torches lighting the mouth of the cave. Nerves rippled my light, but I couldn't pinpoint their source.

"Cass?" I said. "Hey, this isn't funny."

No one answered.

Most of the other seers were asleep by now, and not many lived on this side of the settlement anyway. Generally, my only visitors were Cass and Jon, and occasionally Balidor, and even they didn't come around all that often.

I missed my friends, but I understood.

I wasn't much fun to be around these days.

The truth was, I'd mostly been alone since we got back from Salinse's stronghold, which is probably why Vash asked to see me.

I took another step.

Holding my breath, I listened.

Before I could resume breathing, pain slid through my light.

It was so insanely, heart-stoppingly strong, I couldn't move, couldn't breathe.

Maybe it was for all the reasons everyone told me it would get worse—the phase we'd left things, the fact that we'd both been alone for far too long, the fact that I still felt him sometimes, watching me, wondering about me.

I stood there, my hand on the wall, paralyzed, fighting to breathe, gasping through emotion so strong it blinded me…

When he appeared beside me.

Shock flooded my light.

Before I could make a sound, he laid a hand over my mouth, pressing into me, holding me against the wall of stone.

I didn't fight him.

"Shhh," he murmured. "Come with me." His pain worsened, turning so raw I closed my eyes, gasping against his hand. "Come with me… please, Allie."

I stared at his face, fighting to think past it, to see him as real.

"Don't scream." He pressed into me again. His eyes closed. His pain turned liquid, blindingly hot, making me grip his hands. "Promise you won't?"

I barely hesitated before I nodded.

He took his hand away.

"Come with me. Please, Allie… please."

Pain flooded his light in another surge, so much of it, I could barely see him. I felt him pulling on me. My knees buckled when he pulled harder, winding into me, much the way I had him, at the cabin.

For a long moment, I couldn't breathe.

"Forgive me," he murmured. Tears filled his eyes, right before he kissed my face. "Gods, Allie. Forgive me, please. I love you. I'll do anything."

Images tried to rise in my mind, fragments of what I'd walked in on that night in the White House. I closed my eyes, forcing them away.

"Where?" I managed. "Where could we even go?"

He pressed against me again, kissing my face. "Please, love… just come. Let me make everything up to you. Come with me."

I felt the boy in him—and the other, the one who frightened me.

I stared up at his face, though, and I saw Revik, too. He felt me wavering. He maybe even felt my decision, or maybe, like me, knew what it would be before I made it.

"Come with me." He kissed me again, his voice low, cajoling. "Gaos. Please, love. Please… I'll do anything you want. Anything. I'll be your slave."

"I can't."

"Yes… you can. You're my wife. You'll always be my wife, Allie."

Pain hit my heart, made it impossible to speak.

But he knew. He knew like I knew.

I'd never be able to say no. Not to him.

"I won't be able to stay," I said.

He smiled. It was the smile that broke my heart the first time I saw it on the boy. I couldn't look at it now, not on that face.

"You will," he promised, kissing my mouth. "You will stay, Allie. One day. I'll wait. I'll wait for you. However long it takes. You'll love me again. You'll see, Allie."

I felt my throat close. "I *do* love you. More than anything."

He smiled sadly, touching my cheek.

"No," he said. "But you will."

Tugging on my fingers, he put my hand between his legs and kissed me, harder when I returned it, sliding his other hand under the loose shirt I wore, caressing my skin until I was gasping against his mouth. His light turned invasive, pulling on mine until I felt my limbs lose all resistance, until I started massaging his cock.

He let out a low groan, kissing me again.

He was controlling it now.

He was kissing me the way I remembered. Pain and light suffused his tongue and lips. He started to push the shirt up my body but I stopped him, clutching his hand, looking around as I fought to pull my light back from his, to think.

I stared at his face, unable to look away. The light in my eyes turned his face a pale green, and I felt my chest clench.

"We can't," I said, still fighting for resolve. "Not here. They'll bring you in, Revik. They won't listen to me, not about this."

"Then come with me," he said, soft. "Please."

"Where?"

He smiled. I saw the pictures perfectly in his head.

I stood there with him again, watching a yellowing field turn red in dying sunlight. Clouds turned gold on the horizon over jagged mountains in the distance. I patted a horse with a white face while he pointed towards a house nestled in a valley under the mountains, food rotting in a small refrigerator powered by wind and solar, horses huddled against the night under the trees, broken glass and food and towels molding on the floor.

Pain slid through me, so intense that he clutched at me, kissing my throat, then my mouth, letting out a low sound, caressing my face.

I missed him so badly I wrapped my arms around him, as tight as I could, trying to pull him closer to me, as if to breathe him in under the rest.

"Shhhh," he murmured. "It's all right," he said. "We'll fix it up, Allie. I can get us food. I'll call ahead. I have people helping me now."

But that was too much reality.

The picture broke apart.

I nodded against his chest, forcing myself to smile.

"What about the horses?" I said, wiping my eyes. I smiled at him again.

"We'll bring them inside," he said, smiling back. "They'll keep us warm, Allie. We can ride them to the bathroom."

I looked up at him, helpless. "Revik—"

"Come with me," he begged. "Please. Love… please."

Looking at him, I knew I couldn't refuse him.

But I also knew Vash was right.

Whoever he was, the man in front of me wasn't really Revik.

Even as I thought it, the alarm went off inside the construct.

I felt it as Revik looked up. I saw the predatory glint return to his eyes. The darker pieces of him shifted over his head, and the fingers on me grew tight.

"I'll be back for you, Allie," he said. He kissed me, and I felt the promise behind his mouth. "I'll be back."

Pausing for the barest breath, he looked at me, and the softness returned to his face.

He caressed my cheek, tears in his eyes.

"I love you, wife," he murmured. He kissed me again. "I adore you. I positively adore you. Wait for me, Allie… please."

Before I could form words, he was gone.

I still stood there, my mind numb, in pieces, when Balidor ran up to where I stood. I stared at the gun in his hand without seeing it—then, without comprehending what it was. His steel-gray eyes looked angry, foreboding, until he looked directly into mine.

He clutched my arm.

"Alyson." He shook me gently. "Allie. Are you all right? Did he hurt you?"

I couldn't answer.

I stood there, leaning against the wall, fighting to breathe as Balidor stared into my face.

Only one thought repeated in my head, on a loop I couldn't stop, couldn't even make sense of.

Vash had been right. He'd been right all along.

My husband was dead.

Revik really was dead.

WANT MORE REVIK & ALLIE?
Grab the FREE bonus epilogue!

Link: http://bit.ly/BS02-Epilogue

WANT TO READ MORE?
Check out the next book in the series:

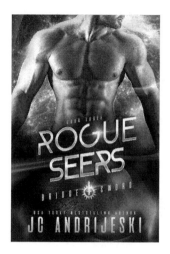

ROGUE SEERS
(Bridge and Sword: Book Three)

Link: https://bit.ly/Rogue-Seers-BS03

"I was now, officially, a real terrorist..."

After losing her husband, Allie fights to prevent the human and seer worlds from exploding into all-out war.

But her husband, Revik, isn't really gone.

Instead he's transformed into someone she barely knows.

Now they're on opposites sides of a racial war—a war he wants to see play out, a war he's ready for, and worse, one he's already fighting.

Compromise with him might be impossible, but it also might be the only way she can save him from himself.

It might also be the only way to keep him from killing everyone she loves.

*

Psychic suspense. Apocalyptic. The third chapter in an epic, soul-crushing, world-spanning romance that can get dark, dark, dark... but also contains a lot of light.

Slow burn. Fated Mates. Enemies to lovers. Forced marriage. Rejected mates.

Every book ends on a completed arc.

**NOTE: A different version of this novel was previously titled "Sword" (same series name)

FREE DOWNLOAD!

Grab a copy of KIREV'S DOOR, the exciting backstory of the main character from my "Quentin Black" series, when he's still a young slave on "his" version of Earth. Plus seven other stories, many of which you can't get anywhere else!!

⭐⭐⭐⭐⭐

This box set is TOTALLY EXCLUSIVE to those who sign up for my VIP mailing list, "The Light Brigade!"

For your FREE COPY go to:

https://www.jcandrijeski.com/mailing-list

REVIEWS ARE AWESOME

Now that you've finished reading my book,
PLEASE CONSIDER LEAVING A REVIEW!
A short review is fine and so very appreciated.
Word of mouth is truly essential for any author to succeed!

Leave a Review Here: https://bit.ly/Mated-Seers-BS02

THANK YOU NOTE

I just wanted to take a moment here to thank some of my amazing readers and supporters. Huge appreciation, long distance hugs and light-filled thanks to the following people:

Shannon Tusler
Robert Tusler
Amelia Johnson
Joy Killi
Sarah Hall
Elizabeth Meadows
Rebekkah Brainerd

I can't tell you how much I appreciate you!

JC Andrijeski

JC Andrijeski is a *USA Today* and *Wall Street Journal* bestselling author of science fiction romance, paranormal mysteries and romance, and apocalyptic science fiction, often with a sexy and metaphysical bent.

JC's background comes from journalism, history and politics. She also has a tendency to traipse around the globe, eat odd foods, and read whatever she can get her hands on. She grew up in the Bay Area of California, but has lived abroad in Europe, Australia and Asia, and from coast to coast in the continental United States.

She currently lives and writes full time in Los Angeles.

For more information, go to: https://jcandrijeski.com

patreon.com/jcandrijeski
amazon.com/JC-Andrijeski/e/B004MFTAP0
bookbub.com/authors/jc-andrijeski
tiktok.com/@jcandrijeski
facebook.com/JCAndrijeski
instagram.com/jcandrijeski
twitter.com/jcandrijeski